The golden CIRCLE

MARVIN ALBERT

BEACH BOOKS

National Press, Inc.
7508 Wiconsin Avenue
Bethesda, Maryland 20814

(301) 657-1616

Jacket design by Barry Moyer.

Library of Congress Cataloging-in-Publication Data

Albert, Marvin H.
  The Golden Circle.

  (Beach books)
  I. Title. PS351.L26G6 1987   813'.54   87-5597 ISBN
0-915765-41-1

A Beach Book

Part I

She was a Phantom of delight
When first she gleamed upon my sight;
A lovely Apparition, sent
To be a moment's ornament;
Her eyes as stars of Twilight fair;
Like Twilight's, too, her dusky hair;
But all things else about her drawn
From May-time and the cheerful Dawn;
A dancing Shape, an Image gay,
To haunt, to startle, and way-lay.

—William Wordsworth

Chapter One

Lady Victoria Alexandre, 1967

Snow was falling outside the barred windows, disturbed by brief gusts of mountain wind. Inside, a thin haze of steam hovered above the surface of the sanatorium's heated swimming pool.

Victoria swam the length of the pool for a full hour, holding to a steady, mid-speed pace. When she climbed out of the water, her nerves had relaxed to a tolerable level, and she was sufficiently under control to get through another day of her purgatory here. On her way to the stall showers, she paused at the big wall mirror and studied herself clinically and unsparingly.

There were no mirrors in her own room—nor anything else she might conceivably use to do herself serious damage. That rule had not changed, though the staff at Bellecroix—including its director and chief psychiatrist, Dr. Huber—knew she was long past any tendency toward self-destruction. If such a tendency had ever truly lurked within her.

The mirror showed her strong, supple figure in a simple, one-piece swimsuit. The healthy, vibrant firmness was still there. But her face had become thin, almost gaunt, accentuating too much the prominent cheekbones and large, dark eyes—eyes that seemed to her to have a clouded, haunted look.

But perhaps this was merely because she knew what was behind those eyes.

Her thick auburn hair, cropped too short by the barber who visited Bellecroix twice each month, had lost much of its luster and acquired some grey—but freedom and a good hairdresser would eliminate both of those problems easily enough. Victoria moved closer to the mirror to study the little wrinkles that had deepened under her eyes and at the corners of her mouth. Would those be as easy to eliminate once she got out of here?

If she ever did get out.

Victoria fought down the clutch of claustrophobia that was always latent, waiting to demolish her hard-won calm, by concentrating again, briefly, on the sum total of her reflection. Other than the duly noted flaws, she concluded that she looked better at thirty-five than she had when four years younger. Not that that was saying much. At thirty-one she had still been considered one of the reigning beauties of international society; but then, very few people had seen what she looked like the day she'd been committed to this private sanatorium, buried in the heart of the French Alps.

It was becoming difficult for Victoria to ignore something else reflected in the mirror. The hefty female attendant sitting lumpishly on a pool side bench, not realizing that she was being observed in turn, was eyeing Victoria with an undisguised scowl of hostile impatience.

Most of the staff at Bellecroix were as helpful and considerate as Victoria's special situation would allow. Out of affection as well as respect, they had dubbed her "the American Lady," a tribute to her manner more than her actual title. But Agnes, the attendant assigned to watch over Victoria's daily stint in the pool, was an exception. Her dislike was never revealed by more than a brief look or sharp word, but it was there.

Victoria understood quite well the reason for it. Agnes believed that life had gifted Victoria with everything that she herself lacked. And Victoria had stupidly fumbled all of those advantages so unfairly lavished on her. Victoria could even sympathize with her attendant's envy. She, too, often felt jealous now—of people who were free, outside, while she remained confined in this clinic. But her envy was filled with longing, not hatred.

Victoria walked to the showers, conscious of the woman's scowl following her. None of the stalls had a door she could shut for privacy. Victoria kept her back to Agnes as she stripped off the swimsuit and showered, certain that Agnes was continuing to watch her.

This didn't worry her, but it was not pleasant. Victoria had become accustomed to being looked at: at times with admiration and desire, at others with resentment. By the time she'd turned seventeen, she had come to accept both, with a certain amount of humor, as a homage to her lucky genes. The same inheritance, she thought, had at one time made her Georgetown University's youngest and most promising student. That, however, had been in the free world, when she was outside of Bellecroix. In here, where she could not decide for herself what she wanted or didn't want to do, life was horribly different.

Realistically, Victoria knew that the attendant at the pool would be too frightened to actually mistreat her in any way. That was the comforting side of Sir Solomon Alexandre's double-edged power: it protected his wife even while it kept her prisoner.

Everybody was afraid of Solomon. Victoria, too, had

finally acquired fear of her husband—fear mixed with rage that had at times spilled over into uncontrolled fury, but which she had by now tamed into something cold and small and hard inside her, under tight, purposeful control.

Victoria towelled herself dry and put on the thick, terry cloth robe, closing it around herself before she turned to face Agnes: "All right, you can convoy me back to my room now."

* * *

Dressed in corduroy slacks, a wool turtleneck and padded moccasins, Victoria brushed her hair as best she could without a mirror. Her room had a single, large window which framed part of a mountain slope now covered with deep snow. The snow was still falling, flakes pasting to the outer pane of the window's temperature-sealed double glass and turning into jewelled crystals in the cold sunlight.

The bars between the windowpanes were of wrought iron, fashioned to look ornamental. But they were still solid, set close together to prevent escape. Other than that her room was as pleasant as one would expect, considering the prices charged for each patient at Bellecroix.

But Victoria knew she was no longer a patient and hadn't been one for at least three years. She was simply a prisoner, kept by her husband.

She acknowledged that she had been in bad shape when he'd had her committed. But not bad enough to justify this. And whatever *had* been wrong with her, she'd been cured long ago: whether Bellecroix had helped or she'd accomplished it herself she did not know. The way she had survived the *worst* event that had ever happened in her lifetime —her son's death eight months ago—was final proof of her stability.

Solomon hadn't come here to see her even then. He'd left Dr. Huber to tell her, had left her to deal with her grief utterly alone. He hadn't even permitted her to attend her son's funeral. And because she had not seen Alan's body, had not seen him buried, a part of her still refused to believe her son dead.

But another part knew that it was true, and this part could not always be entirely controlled. Sometimes, still, she woke at night, screaming with the never-ending agony of his death. No one ever came when she screamed. No one ever heard her. The scream was *inside* her, where she had learned, in Bellecroix, to keep everything—including this intense and unceasing pain—while she showed her keepers only the façade she had so carefully constructed for them: calm, docile, malleable.

She was cured. But they wouldn't let her go.

More accurately: Solomon wouldn't let them let her go.

She was ready to do anything that would get her out of this place. She would have sold her soul for a few hours of freedom—just long enough to reach an international airport and board a jet for America. Once there she could use her own family connections to fight back. There, even Solomon Alexandre couldn't imprison her.

In Europe, he'd even been able, with the reluctant connivance of Dr. Huber, to prevent anyone from visiting her, even once during these four long years.

France had a terrifying history of similar cases, Victoria knew. The most infamous was that of sculptress Camille Claudel, whose family, disapproving of her way of life, had committed her to an asylum and thereafter refused to sign release papers. Though her closest friends had included such influential personages as Rodin and Debussy, though she'd written dozens of perfectly lucid letters begging to be set free, in spite of even her doctors' urging that she be released, Claudel had remained in that asylum until her death thirty years later.

Thirty years. . . . Victoria's blood ran cold whenever she allowed herself to remember that case.

There was a knock at her door. A male nurse unlocked it. "Pardon me for disturbing you, Lady Alexandre, but you are wanted in Dr. Huber's office."

That surprised her. Vincent Huber had been avoiding her lately, embarrassed in her presence. It was more than guilt over his own part in the conspiracy. In her readiness to do anything to escape, Victoria had, over the last couple years, mounted a carefully calculated campaign to seduce him. His inability to meet her eyes indicated how close she was to succeeding. He was at least half in love with her, of that Victoria was certain. But his terror of Sir Solomon Alexandre remained stronger.

Solomon had once told Victoria that he never trusted a man until he'd broken his backbone. At the time, she'd thought it was a joke. Later she understood that it was not. It had taken her longer to realize that the same applied to the few women he had ever allowed to enter the outskirts of his private life.

Dr. Huber was nowhere in sight when Victoria entered his office, and his secretary quietly closed the door behind her. The man waiting for her was Thomas Haggard, Solomon's personal attorney. Politely, he rose to his feet behind Huber's wide desk: a plump, ruddy-faced Canadian with kindly eyes, who over the years had manipulated the legal destruction of many lives and rival businesses for his employer.

"You look good, Victoria."

"Thank you, Tom. How are your wife and Gerald?"

"Marjorie's in good health, thanks. My son . . ." Haggard

sighed. "... Got himself in a spot of trouble a few months ago in Florida. Hanging around with a bad crowd involved in marijuana smuggling. I had a difficult time getting him out of that one."

"I'm sorry to hear it."

"Kids these days." Haggard gestured to a chair facing the desk. "Please sit down."

She did so, sitting very straight and folding her hands together on her lap like an obedient schoolgirl. Her face was a mask of patient docility.

Tom Haggard continued to stand for a bit, studying his employer's wife. She did look good. Remarkable, considering. He was one of the few who'd seen her the day she'd been brought here, because he was the one who'd had to work out the commitment papers with Huber. Haggard hadn't seen her since then. Almost four years. And there she was, looking almost like the young woman he'd first known.

From the start, when she'd become Sir Solomon's bride, Haggard had seen Victoria as an example of the very best kind of southern breeding: uncommonly good looking, and at the same time extremely intelligent. She had underplayed that acquisitive intelligence in a way he had found charmingly feminine, quietly observing and absorbing everything going on in the male world around her without intruding herself. Haggard was oddly touched by the resilience of her beauty, a beauty accented rather than flawed by the small but very definite break across the bridge of her nose, a souvenir from a hardball game back in her tomboy adolescence in Virginia.

But if her loveliness was still there, other qualities he remembered were gone: her humor, the vivid liveliness, her eager interest in everything—none of these were any longer visible in her face or manner. One had to expect that sort of damage, of course.

Haggard could not remember any semblance of what he would have considered a real relationship between Victoria and Sir Solomon despite their marriage. Certainly there was none after Victoria had gotten past the first heady excitement of being married, so very young, to one of the world's most powerful men. That thrill had been inevitable, considering the sort of man Solomon Alexandre was. At eighteen, the girl had thought she was marrying a god, and found herself with an iceberg.

But if Victoria hadn't gotten what she'd expected, neither had Sir Solomon. He had wanted a decorative, well-bred woman to act as a womb—not a wife in the modern western sense, but in the old oriental tradition—devoted to the single function of providing him with legal heirs to carry on his name and business empire. So very many women would have been happy to fill that role for him and would have asked nothing else of life. Instead, he'd found himself married to a girl with drives and talents of her own: talents that demanded to be used as she grew older, drives that became increasingly difficult to quell. And in addition, after Alan was born, the doctors had pronounced that she could not have any more children.

The marriage had been a mistake for both of them. It was a mistake that Solomon Alexandre had already shrugged off, but one which Haggard suspected Victoria would never recover from.

He was sorry about that. He had always liked her, been physically stirred by her, and sympathized with her. But he had his job to do.

"I felt very bad about Alan," he told her, sincerely. "I wanted to come, but—. It must have been a terrible shock for you."

"I'm not quite sure," Victoria said with careful lack of expression. "They put me back on lithium carbonate before telling me. I was kept heavily sedated for two weeks after, too. I'm sure any normal reactions I might have had were diluted by the drugs."

She still looked somewhat listless to Haggard, though he knew they'd stopped dosing her with lithium carbonate months ago. Just as he knew about the electroconvulsive treatments used when she was violently rebellious during her early days at Bellecroix. Well, she was no longer that way. He received regular, detailed reports from Dr. Huber.

Seating himself behind Huber's desk, Haggard placed his chubby hands on the manila folder he'd brought with him. "I have what I believe will be good news for you, Victoria."

"I could use some."

Haggard studied her again, briefly. He could detect neither irony nor defiance. She was just speaking the truth. Sir Solomon was right, as usual: Victoria wouldn't be a source of trouble, now or in the future. Her spirit had been too thoroughly crushed for that. Almost four years of being locked away like a lunatic—for no real reason except for her husband's cold irritation at not being able to totally control her in any other way. These hellish years were bound to have traumatized her even more deeply than she showed. It was a wonder that they hadn't driven her into genuine madness.

"You can leave here tomorrow," he told her. "I have with me an agreement to that effect, signed by Dr. Huber."

Victoria caught her breath. Her eyes narrowed. Otherwise she betrayed nothing.

"Contingent," Haggard added after a moment, "on your signing a second document I have with me."

"What is it?"

"Your agreement to an uncontested divorce." The attorney

hesitated fractionally. "Based on numerous adulterous alliances by you with various men. Their names and the circumstances need not be specified. Not if you sign the admission that these alliances did in fact occur."

Victoria was silent for a long moment. "A divorce," she said finally, flatly. "Now that Alan is dead, Solomon needs another son and heir. For which he needs another wife—and a certain amount of luck, at his age."

Haggard was not overly surprised by either her wit or her grasp of the situation. Victoria had always been quick of mind and obviously was so once more. The truth was that Solomon Alexandre had, since Alan's death, ceased taking or allowing precautions with his various mistresses. One of the women was now pregnant, and Sir Solomon wanted to be free to marry immediately.

But he did not tell Victoria any of this. What he did say was, "I have no idea about Sir Solomon's future personal plans. I do know that while Alan was alive Sir Solomon saw no reason to possibly antagonize him by divorcing you. At the same time, he did not want you to be able to influence Alan's thinking—and, I have to say, his morals. But now that—" Haggard hesitated fractionally and rephrased his thoughts: "Now there is no reason for him to be reluctant about a divorce. And no reason for you to remain here at Bellecroix—after you've signed this agreement."

"I don't need persuading, Tom. Nor implied threats. I only want to get out of here. As you well know. If I can have that, Solomon can have his divorce, and his new wife and heir, and anything else he cares for. I want *my* life. I want us to be quits."

"I didn't intend what I said as a threat, Victoria."

"Then I apologize for thinking so."

Although he was accustomed to conducting painful confrontations without emotion, Haggard found himself unaccountably embarrassed for a moment. But he did not permit it to be reflected in his voice or manner. "According to the terms of this agreement, Victoria, the divorce is to be accompanied by *no* publicity. Absolutely no statements or explanations of any kind to the news media. Now or in the future. You will also be legally binding yourself never to reveal anything whatsoever to anyone about Sir Solomon's personal or business affairs."

"That," Victoria said quietly, "is impossible to police or enforce."

Haggard nodded. "In purely private conversations, that is so. But should anything attributable to you become public knowledge—"

"For God's sake, Tom," Victoria interrupted, "I have no intention of creating that sort of problem for Solomon. Nor for myself. I said I want us to be quits. And that's all I want. May I read it?"

"Of course." Haggard opened the folder. "But perhaps you'd like to have an attorney of your own choosing go over the terms with you?"

"I don't need a lawyer to explain a simple agreement to me."

Her tone had gotten a touch hard. Again Haggard looked at Victoria and saw no harbinger of future trouble in her expression. Once more, she was merely stating the truth. Victoria's university studies had been aimed toward a career in international business law before Sir Solomon had taken her away to England and married her. According to Haggard's Washington contacts, she would have been practically assured of a brilliant future in that field had she continued with it. In the few practical conversations he'd had with her in the past, Haggard had discovered her to be exceptionally sharp about fine legal or economic points. He removed the agreement from the folder and handed it across the desk.

For the next ten minutes she read through it in silence. Finally, she went back two pages. "This alimony clause—"

"Is quite generous, in my opinion."

"I want it changed, Tom. No alimony. Not a penny."

Haggard frowned. "You're being foolish."

"Quits means *quits*. I don't want anything from him but my freedom. No future ties. No alimony."

He considered. The alimony clause had been his own idea, not his employer's. An extra precaution. Regular payments by Sir Solomon to Victoria, if she came to depend on them, could be one way of exercising some control over her in the future, should that become necessary. It was not, however, a vital consideration. Sir Solomon had shrugged it off as superfluous, and Haggard's diagnosis of Victoria's present state of mind now inclined him to agree.

"Very well, we can change that."

"Thank you." Victoria reread a few other clauses and then pushed the agreement back across the desk. "I don't object to anything else. I can't even object to that business about my various acts of adultery."

"That will never be made public," Haggard assured her.

"I hope not. But in any case, since it's true . . ." Victoria seemed to become lost in her thoughts for a moment, then snapped out of it. "You may remember my cousin, Lee Nicolson. A Washington attorney."

Haggard nodded. Nicolson had a growing reputation in political circles. "He's done quite well for himself these past few years."

"I'd like to have Lee present to witness this agreement when I sign it."

Bright of her, Haggard thought. She didn't need a lawyer

to explain the terms to her, but the presence of one would insure against the release agreement being "mislaid" after she signed the divorce papers. *If* that were her husband's intention. It was not. At this point, Sir Solomon was solely interested in being shed of his present wife and free to re-marry quickly.

"We can fly your cousin over," Haggard agreed, "but it will delay your release for several more days, you realize."

Victoria rose from her chair. "I've waited this long, a few more days will give me time to adjust."

Haggard got to his feet and held out a hand. "I wish you luck and happiness. Sincerely."

"I appreciate that," Victoria said, and let him shake her hand.

As she turned away to leave the office, something flared in her eyes that might have made Thomas Haggard rethink the whole thing.

But he didn't see it.

Even if he had, he might not have understood what it meant.

Chapter Two

The Memoirs of Garson Bishop

I'm not sure I would have understood what was in Victoria's eyes either, if I had been there that day at Bellecroix. In spite of the fact that I knew her more intimately than Haggard—or Solomon Alexandre, for that matter.

You do get certain intuitive feelings about someone you are in love with over a long period of time. But not enough, with Victoria, to fathom her deepest thoughts or predict what she really intended.

Any illusion I might have had to the contrary was dispelled, rather devastatingly, by what our relationship finally led to.

* * *

When we found each other again, over six years after she left Bellecroix and a more than full decade after I'd last seen her, the age difference between us no longer meant much. At least not to me. When we'd first met, the gulf had seemed impossible to negotiate. I had just turned sixteen then, and she was thirty. But even then, it failed to provide any defense against what happened when she smiled at me.

What the French call the *coup de foudre* translates literally as being struck by a thunderbolt, and more poetically as love at first sight. You don't believe it until it happens.

I was a heavy reader back in those days. From the first, Victoria reminded me of Wordsworth's line about "a Phantom of delight . . . a lovely Apparition." Before long I learned that my "lovely Apparition" was troubled, but this only intensified my feelings. Naturally. A princess is supposed to be in distress: it gives the young hero something to do for her.

I may be portraying myself as though I were an impressionable, naive kid. I was a long way from being either, in regards to women, by the time I reached sixteen. You get an early and varied education along the beaches of Los Angeles. That was where I'd spent most of my time after age twelve—the year my mother died under the knife of a Philadelphia surgeon who had assured her that an operation to remove half her stomach was nothing to worry about. Before that I'd been raised around Army camps. My father, Lou Bishop, was a career officer whose field of expertise was weaponry engineering. He worked at it too steadily to take care of a kid all by himself. So when my mother died, I got farmed out to his sister and her husband.

My aunt and uncle ran a health food store in Santa Monica. They were a laid-back, freethinking couple who didn't interfere with me much beyond making sure that I ate some balanced meals, went to school regularly, and didn't let all the books I took out of the local library keep me from getting a decent amount of sleep. Their store was always on the verge of bankruptcy. Most of what money my father could send for my keep had to go into keeping the place afloat. So I looked around and found a way to earn some spending money of my own.

The Golden Circle

My father had begun teaching me about weaponry from the time I was old enough to understand. Since I looked up to him and expected to follow in his footsteps, I had been an eager pupil. I found a Santa Monica gunsmith who got a lot of customers from the area's target practice ranges. Most people who use guns for fun are like the majority of car drivers: they know zilch about the innards of the machinery they use. Often the problems our customers brought us could be rectified by simply stripping down a rifle, cleaning and oiling its components, and reassembling it. Before long, the gunsmith trusted those jobs to me, along with some of the simpler repair jobs. In addition, I helped him with more intricate ones when his workload got too heavy. Since I was a kid, he didn't have to pay me much. But it put cash in my pocket and still left me plenty of free time.

During the bulk of that free time I hung out on the beach —mostly with the surfers, but sometimes with the bodybuilders. Both had their contingents of groupies, who ranged from girls of twelve to women in their fifties. I was gregarious, biologically sound, and big and strong for my age. By fourteen, I could pass for eighteen and was sampling my share of the groupies, while they took turns sampling me. By fifteen, I was expanding my education with show business divorcées who prowled the Sunset Strip, girls I met roller-skating in Venice, and rock groups who liked to spice their Malibu and Topanga Canyon orgies with young beach bums.

So there I was by sixteen: Garson Bishop, your prototype West Coast teenager. I had a lot of surface experience and practical cynicism, uniting to trigger an automatic distrust of first impressions and strong emotions. Except that somewhere in the back of my head—or wherever such booby traps lurk, waiting to play tricks on you—hid a small but persistent streak of the romantic. I still have it, which will

surprise people who know what I've done with most of my
adult life. It probably came from too much early reading.
However it originated, it was one factor at work when I met
Victoria.

The other factor was the unfamiliar terrain. Any military
officer knows that if you train a man in one type of country and then toss him into a place that is utterly different, it
knocks his habitual reactions out of whack.

I didn't meet Victoria in Los Angeles; it happened in
France.

My father held the rank of major when he quit the Army
and went to work for Solomon Alexandre. The goad that
drove him out of the Army was getting passed over for promotion twice in succession in favor of other officers with
better political and family connections. The lures that made
him switch to the British arms tycoon were triple his Army
pay and the possibility of being able to spend more time on
a weaponry invention he'd been tinkering on.

Sir Solomon Alexandre had for decades been the most
important private arms merchant in the world. By the year
my father entered his service, a few relative newcomers
were contending with Alexandre for that title. A seesaw
rivalry developed: up one war, down the next.

But up or down, Solomon Alexandre remained part of
what some in the trade call "the Golden Circle" of international arms dealing, along with Adnan Khashoggi and
Sam Cummings, Hiroshi Yukada and Ahmed al-Zadar, and
the interrelated Quandt-Flick-Mertins groups of Germany.
Among younger dealers, Alexandre was known as the Old
Wolf. Some he'd trampled over called him the Devil.

His business empire was far-flung and multi-faceted. The
operation for which he hired my father had long been one
of his most solid: the buying, reconditioning and resale of
surplus small arms and ammunition.

Left over in huge quantities after every big or small war and every successful or failed revolution, surplus small arms and ammunition can be bought cheaply—by those who know how—because they are (however temporarily) no longer needed. Once restored to prime condition, they can be sold at high profit for new wars and revolutions. Sometimes they are even sold back to the same country a dealer bought them from. Alexandre had been one of the pioneers of this aspect of the business. Never in history was resale of small arms more profitable than from the 1960s into the mid-1980s.

With today's accelerated development of modern weaponry, much of such surplus soon becomes, in theory, relatively old-fashioned. In fact, these are the kinds of weapons with which most battles continue to be fought: rifles, machine guns and grenades, with the addition of one-man rocket launchers. Small arms. Planes can fly over enemy positions and tanks can crash through defense lines, but it requires infantry to actually take a place and hold it. And most infantries still do their fighting with the same standard arms —for which they need replacements, spare parts, ammunition quickly and in quantity when shove comes to war.

Among the stocks in Alexandre's warehouses in France, my father discovered weapons that the Old Wolf had sold, bought back, and resold a dozen times over the years.

By the year my father joined the organization, Alexandre's chief competitor for this part of the arms trade, the much younger, U.S.-born Sam Cummings, had acquired a virtual lock on resale of converted surplus to American buyers of souvenirs and sporting weapons. But Alexandre continued to hold an edge in the surplus markets of much of Africa and Latin America. The heart of his surplus operation was in the Perigord region of southwestern France.

The Perigord is a peaceful, sparsely populated country of farms and lovely wooded hills and valleys, with a sprinkling of majestic old châteaux. There is also a great deal of unused land, going cheaply because the region has little industry and is far from the big cities. Sir Solomon Alexandre had bought up a considerable chunk of this real estate and built the warehouses and repair plant for his surplus weaponry in the middle of it. Big trucks brought the stuff in from the port of Bordeaux, three hours away, and later hauled it back there for shipment to new buyers. Among the surplus that arrived at Alexandre's Perigord plant, were weapons ranging from slightly used to defective, which had to be restored to decent shape before they could be profitably resold.

That was the operation my father was hired to run. Part of his job also involved travelling around the world to assess the condition of surplus stocks that Alexandre considered purchasing. But most of his time was spent at the Perigord plant, supervising the work of its staff of highly skilled gunsmiths. I was fifteen when my father took charge of this set-up. By the following summer, he had enough money in the bank to fly me over to spend my two and a half months of school vacation with him.

We celebrated my sixteenth birthday an hour's drive from the Alexandre complex: in Perigueux, the nearest town big enough to have some good restaurants. I had already grown as tall as he was, and nobody who saw us together had difficulty pegging us as father and son. The resemblance was obvious, though it would take me time to measure up to Lou Bishop in other ways.

He was strongly built, with sandy hair and wide grey eyes set in a blunt-featured face of the type that winds up attractive by just missing being ugly. And he had this slow, no-strain smile that gave him a down-home, old farm boy look—the sort of bright but not-too-bright look that can be useful in dealing with people who don't see beneath the surface.

One thing I admired about the man was his ability to be equally at ease in a tough bar simmering with liquor violence or at a dressy gathering thick with social nuance. Another thing I admired was his professional know-how.

That summer in Perigord, he resumed teaching me about weaponry. By day, he let me do apprentice work for his gunsmiths. Evenings and weekends, he taught me more—I helped him work on his own private project.

It was a design for a new type of compact, shoulder-fired rocket launcher. My father's variation would be more durable, accurate and versatile than the Soviet RPG-7, the Swedish Miniman, and other one-man antitank and antihelicopter weapons currently under development.

Like a lot of other inventors who tinkered with small arms modifications, he was probably at least partly inspired by the success of Mikhail Timofeevitch Kalashnikov, the Soviet Army sergeant who invented the automatic assault rifle named after him. Manufactured in huge quantities by Russia and other Soviet bloc nations, the Avtomat Kalashnikov (commonly known at the AK-47) was outselling all competing weapons in the international arms markets. And Kalashnikov was named a Hero of Socialist labor and upped to the dizzying heights of Supreme Soviet.

I doubt that my father anticipated that level of success for himself. But he did have high hopes. So did I—and I worked alongside him on his rocket launcher with a sense of excitement all that summer. I did it again the following summer, in addition to taking on increasingly responsible jobs as apprentice to his specialist staff. When those two summers in France were finished, I knew more than most about how to fix and fire the world's diversity of small arms, from revolvers to one-man ground-to-air missiles.

I could have learned more. But after Solomon Alexandre's wife entered my life, my time was no longer entirely at my father's disposal. Nor my own, for that matter.

* * *

I knew what she looked like before I met her in person, from a framed photograph in my father's office. He'd hung it there as a diplomatic gesture, for the benefit of visiting underlings from Alexandre's managerial organization. The picture was of Solomon Alexandre and his wife standing with the Queen of England at a Buckingham Palace garden party.

Alexandre had presented it to my father after hiring him. He'd done so without a trace of embarrassment, like an ancient king bestowing a personal relic on a knight he'd just accepted into his service. Since my father was accustomed to the manners of U.S. Army generals, he didn't find the grandiose egotism of the man too startling.

In the photograph, the Queen looked like a good-natured housewife, and Sir Solomon Alexandre looked like old-time nobility: tall, handsome, coldly dignified, with sleek black hair going grey and a hint of potential menace in his eyes. His wife looked lovely and far too young for him, I thought, but I got no premonitory tingle from her picture.

My father had met her, briefly, when Alexandre had interviewed him for the job in London. He'd found her immensely likeable, and much more than lovely, and agreed that she was too young for her husband. It was not just the matter of years, though Alexandre had been in his forties and Victoria had been only eighteen when they'd married. Solomon Alexandre seemed to my father the type of person who was born old, while his wife was the sort likely to retain her basic youthfulness.

Their wedding had been the high event of the social season in London, and it was in England that she'd spent most of her married life, presiding over their Belgravia mansion and the Alexandre estate in Surrey. But some years back Solomon Alexandre had shifted his chief business offices from London to Paris and Monaco to avoid British taxes. The year before my first trip to France, he had purchased a château not far from the Perigord plant, apparently intending to turn it into his new home base. He'd given it a new roof and a swimming pool, and the year I joined my father in Perigord, Alexandre installed his wife at the château to supervise the rest of the restoration work.

At least that was his stated reason for sending her there. In newspapers that doted on jet-set scandals there had been occasional mentions of Victoria Alexandre joining some of the wilder upper-crust parties in London, Paris and the Riviera. There was nothing like that going on in Perigord: just simple country living, far from the fleshpots favored by international society. If this life was a hardship for her, however, her distaste for it wasn't evident when she phoned my father shortly before my arrival. She sounded fully involved in seeing to all the renovations needed at the château, though she promised to visit him when the pressure eased up. Her ten-year-old son, who attended an exclusive Swiss boarding school, would be staying with her during summer holidays. She thought it might be interesting for him to see one of his father's more comprehensible enterprises in action.

But she didn't show up until a couple of weeks after my birthday outing that first summer. I still hadn't laid eyes on her husband and wouldn't until the summer had almost ended. Like most arms brokers, Solomon Alexandre knew everything about the merchandise value of weapons but very little about how any of them worked. He had technicians like my father for that, and he had sharp, young business aides who dropped by regularly to check on the management of the Perigord plant. As long as their reports were satisfactory, Alexandre had no reason to come himself. But his presence was always felt, through the pressures of his distant wheeling and dealing on the operation of the plant.

The afternoon Victoria came to visit, we were coping with the pressure of a rush order he had dumped on us without much warning. I was crossing the compound to select useable spare parts from the junk-weaponry sheds when I saw this brand new Rolls Royce sedan parked outside my father's office. A stocky man in a chauffeur's uniform leaned against the back of the Rolls, gazing at a distant hill. When I stopped and looked his way, he turned his head to give me a searching stare that didn't go with the uniform. Later I discovered that he also served as bodyguard to Victoria and, in addition, spied on her for her husband.

At that moment, my father came out of his office with Victoria and motioned for me to join them. I walked over and he introduced us.

"Lady Alexandre, my son Gar."

She studied me gravely as we shook hands. "Gar—that's a predatory fish they have down along the Louisiana coast. Like a small alligator with big, sharp teeth."

"I'm not that dangerous," I told her. "Gar's short for Garson. I was named after a grand-granduncle who got killed at Gettysburg."

"One of mine did, too," Victoria said, her expression still grave and her dark eyes searching for something in me —maybe for the real me. "That almost makes us family, doesn't it?"

Then she smiled at me.

I've explained that I wasn't an over-impressionable kid. This was a very good-looking woman, but when you've grown up around Los Angeles, you've seen your fill of the very best that God can do in the way of beautiful faces and good figures. It's like hanging around a nude beach too long: after awhile you get so accustomed to bodies that you start looking at faces instead; and after too many of those, you start looking for something unusual in character to excite you. Victoria definitely had that.

She had, for one thing, a patrician elegance about her that was the genuine article: not worn like a coat, but bred in the bone. And it was leavened by warmth, wit, passion, and just a touch of sadness, even that early. I won't swear I identified all those ingredients right off. Obviously I unconsciously added some of what I came to know of her later to my memory of that first impression. But I could *feel* the vibrations of whatever she radiated. And what I felt stirred parts of me that had not been stirred before.

I suppose by then I was staring at her with some kind of fool's expression on my face. She didn't have much trouble recognizing it for what it was. Her smile changed a little, got something tender in it. She was human; she liked being liked. Hell, even having a stray dog come over to lick your hand turns most people on.

My father had begun to fidget, having waited until he was sure that she and I got along all right. "I've got a ton of work that needs doing fast, Lady Alexandre. If you won't mind, Gar can show you and your boy around the place." He glanced around. "I guess Alan's exploring on his own . . ."

I didn't object that I had work to do, too. My father's job was more important. Somebody had to give the boss's family some polite attention, and I didn't mind being near Victoria awhile longer.

She didn't object either. "What I do mind," she told him, "is your not calling me Victoria. If you don't like that, you can call me Torie or Vi—or just Hey You. Just not Lady Alexandre. It doesn't feel right from a fellow American."

My father laughed and nodded. "Okay. Victoria." He pointed an admonishing finger at me. "Take good care of our little American lady, you hear?"

Victoria turned back to me as he went inside. "If I'd known Lou had his son staying here this summer I would have visited earlier. My son's spending his school vacation here too. I'm afraid he's tired of having nothing but boring adults to talk to. Of course, he's much younger than you, but still—"

It didn't offend me that she thought I was still a kid, or anyway, not quite an adult yet. I was too busy reading her. I liked the fact that in spite of more than a decade in England, she still wanted to get on a first-name basis with people right off. And she hadn't acquired any British accent. There was still a touch of American South in her speech, but not too far south. Her voice was a pleasure.

"We only live a few miles away," she was saying.

"I know," I told her. "I passed by your place last week on my motorbike. It looks beautiful—from out on the road, anyway."

"It is, but it still needs so much work. It's fun for me, but not so much for Alan. . . ." Victoria nodded toward the warehouse. "Let's go find him."

We found him coming out of the ammo warehouse. He was a dark, handsome kid of ten, his looks spoiled by a cold, indifferent expression. He walked toward us with his hands sunk in his pockets and his feet scuffing up dust. When his mother introduced us, he managed a stiff politeness, barely looking at me.

Well, I reminded myself of other kids I'd known who had acted like that, and had just turned out to be horribly shy. And I decided to make the effort. Not out of altruism—I hadn't been born that soft in the head. But I had enough experience to know that the surest way to most mothers' hearts is through their kids.

"Have you seen anything interesting?" Victoria asked him. He shrugged. "Not really." This kid was working hard at being a zombie; he was going to be a pain in the ass to handle. I made a mental note not to ask him if he'd like to do something because the response was sure to be negative. He'd have to be led, gently but firmly, as if he were a horse I had to tame.

I jerked a thumb at the building he'd come out of. "Not much in there but cases of ammo. Come on, I'll show you more interesting stuff."

"I don't know," he said to his mother rather than me. "It's awful hot, I'm getting tired."

Perigord summers do tend to bake the juices out of you. Victoria's face was beaded with perspiration, which made me feel less self-conscious about the fact that I was sweating like a hog. But the boy didn't look hot; he looked cool, inside and out—something like his father, in the picture.

Victoria put a hand on his head and stroked it. "We might as well see something while we're here, Alan. It won't be any cooler back at the château."

He surprised me by not pulling away from her hand. His expression even acquired a little human warmth when he looked up at her. I gave Alan Alexandre a couple of small points: at least he was fond of his mother. But with a mother like that, who wouldn't be?

"This way," I said, and started off across the compound. I didn't look back. After a moment, I heard them following.

I knew better than to take them where any of the men were handling the rush order. There was no way they would have maintained their work pace with a woman as spectacular as Victoria Alexandre around. I took them into a warehouse that contained, among other weaponry, machine guns that ranged from a couple of pre-World War I Maxims to a stockpile of recently issued Red Army Degtyarevs and rows of tripod-mounted HK21s fresh from the factory in Germany. Keeping it simple, I guided them through the stages of weaponry development represented there, lightening my talk with an occasional anecdote.

At times I caught Alan sneaking a look at me, but he always dropped his eyes when they met mine. I'd been right about him: he was one of those afflicted by the bitter, solitary pride of the shy, erecting a defensive ice barrier and praying somebody else would do the work of breaking through it to him.

I played him coolly, not smiling or trying to be friendly, keeping it relaxed and matter-of-fact. Victoria didn't say much, mostly paying polite attention to my conducted tour while she watched her son warily begin to come to life. Occasionally *I* snuck a look at her. Finally Victoria caught me at it. She gave me a kind look, with a sudden flash of puckish humor in it. I grinned back. It was as though we had established an intimate little collusion between us, as it always is when strangers meet and discover it's easy to like each other.

The most venerable machine gun was displayed separately from the rest. It was a museum piece: an original 1864 multi-barrelled Gatling. Alan was fascinated in spite of himself as I told the story of Dr. Gatling's problems in making and marketing it. He couldn't resist reaching out to touch it.

"But doesn't it make you sick sometimes," he asked with

one of those half-glances at me, "working with things like this? That kill people?"

I gave him the standard answer: "Automobiles kill people, too—thousands every year." I couldn't have said anything more prophetic to the poor kid.

Alan gave it a little thought. "Yes, but automobiles aren't made for the *purpose* of killing."

Whatever was wrong with the kid, he wasn't dumb. I wasn't about to go any further into that old debate with him. "Have you ever done any shooting?"

"No . . ."

"Well, here's as good a place as any to give her a try. Let's go find you a rifle."

Alan began to tighten up again. "Why . . .?"

"Come on," I told him, "I'll show you." I headed out of the warehouse.

After a moment Alan hurried up alongside me. He was still reluctant, but I was an older boy paying serious attention to him and that's hard for any kid to resist.

Victoria caught up to us, frowning uncertainly. "Perhaps Alan is a little young for—"

"No, he's not. I was five when I started. It's easier when you're younger, fewer wrong habits to break." I took them to our smallest test-firing range. The target posts, backed by a high, dirt embankment, were set at different distances from the firing line. Going into the shed, I brought out a .22 rifle and some ammo, along with binoculars and a bull's-eye sheet torn from a book of targets. I tacked the target to a moderate-distance post and loaded the rifle as I walked back to Victoria and Alan. This rifle was pinpoint accurate, I knew, having tried it out a few days earlier.

He was very uptight when I put the rifle in his hands. "I'm not good with things. . . ."

"A rifle's not like anything else. Just don't expect too much right off. Most men don't start hitting the target before four, five practice sessions." That was not strictly true, but I wanted to ease him out of his fear of failing in front of us.

I made it easy for him: a ground pad to sit on and rests for his elbows and the rifle barrel so he wouldn't have trouble holding it steady. Kneeling in the dirt beside him, I put my hand between his shoulder-blades while I instructed him on sighting, breathing and trigger-squeeze.

Alan squeezed off his first shot and squinted at the target. "Did I hit it?"

I looked through the binoculars. "Show me four more. Take your time and make sure your sights are lined up with the bull's-eye before each one."

After he'd fired four more, I lowered the binoculars and gave him a surprised frown. "I thought you said you never did this before."

"I haven't."

"Wait here." On my way to the target, I snuck a ballpoint pen from my pocket. He'd hit the outside edges of the target twice. His other three shots had missed and been swallowed into the dirt of the embankment. With my back hiding what I was doing, I used the pen to poke two holes in the bull's-eye when I detached the target from its post. It's an old trick to give a beginner confidence in his ability. Relaxed confidence is the first step to acquiring ability.

I slipped the pen back in my pocket before turning and taking the target over to them. "For a beginner," I told Alan as I gave it to him, "that is one damn good start."

He blushed. Then he showed the target to Victoria, so proud of himself that she laughed with pleasure. "You see," she told him, "you never know until you try something." And then she flashed me a look of gratitude that I felt clear down to the soles of my feet. I was almost certain she knew what I'd done to the bull's-eye.

Next I brought out a SIG53 automatic carbine fitted with a thirty-round box magazine. Showing Alan how to swing it in a short arc while pulling down to control its recoil, I fired a four-round burst that made them clap their hands over their ears. "Yeah, it's noisy," I agreed, "which is not good in combat situations where you don't want to give away your position. That's what this is for." I screwed on the sound-suppressor and fired another short burst into the embankment, startling them with how quiet the weapon had become. "It also reduces muzzle flash," I explained. "Gives you that much more concealment in a night fight."

What the suppressor also did was reduce the weapon's recoil, which would make it easier for Alan to use at short range. I put a big tin can on top of a post and gave him the carbine. He had enough confidence in me by then, and was gaining enough in himself, to handle it exactly as I instructed. His third short burst knocked the can high into the air, ripped almost in half. When he lowered the carbine with a delighted laugh, I knew I had him hooked.

I took the carbine from him and offered it to Victoria. "Want to try it?"

She shook her head. "I don't like guns."

The response was so easy I couldn't hold it back: "Then you married the wrong man."

She looked away abruptly, so I couldn't see her expression. Then her head turned further away and I saw she was looking at something between two of the storage buildings. It was the chauffeur, just standing there and observing us. I thought it peculiar and wondered how long he'd been there, but he wasn't the one who concerned me at that moment. "I'm sorry," I said to the back of Victoria's head. "It was supposed to be a joke. I didn't mean to offend you."

She turned to me. Her mouth had thinned and her eyes

were brooding. She studied me—that same grave look she'd given me when we met. "I'm not offended, Gar. I—I was thinking of something else." She glanced at her watch. "We'd better leave now, Alan. The mason is coming about that wall, and I have to check on how the gardeners are coming along with the new flower beds."

Alan nodded, but he was disappointed. "Maybe I can come back on my own sometime."

I said, "My pleasure," and looked at Victoria.

She was smiling again. She probably hadn't seen him get that enthusiastic very often. "We'll arrange it."

I looked again toward the chauffeur, but he was no longer there.

Chapter Three

Garson

I watched the Rolls pull away and thought about her reaction to my joke. And I wondered about the man she'd married.

What I knew of his background, at the time, was pretty much confined to what anyone could have read in the press: the spectacular success story of a young Russian aristocrat who had escaped the Revolution and arrived in England as a penniless immigrant. His social rise from acquiring British citizenship to achieving his knighthood. His business climb from salesman for weapon manufacturers to controller of his own global arms empire.

More interesting to me were the old bits of gossip my father had picked up from one of his Army buddies at the Pentagon. The stories were concerned with Victoria as much her husband.

She'd been one of the most popular young women around Washington when she'd met Sir Solomon Alexandre. Her family name meant something in Washington society, and she'd been regularly invited to high-level gatherings. It was at one of these that they'd met: a spirited beauty of eighteen and a man more than twenty years older with a dangerous reputation with women.

Word was that Alexandre kept several mistresses scattered about and changed them often enough to avoid emotional attachment to any of them. He'd never married, it was said, because marriage might interfere with pouring all his time and energy into his business activities. So what happened after he met Victoria surprised everyone.

The best guess among the Washington rumor-mongers was that their meeting coincided with Alexandre's realization that he was into middle age without anyone to inherit the empire he'd built. Victoria must have struck him as a perfect choice to give him an heir. Any future son of theirs would be guaranteed looks, brains and social standing from both parents.

Victoria came from an old Virginia family named Nicolson. Though they had lost their wealth and land after the Civil War, the Nicolsons retained their social status and added a growing intellectual reputation. Both of Victoria Nicolson's parents had become university professors, an uncle was a famous biologist, and another was with a prestigious Capitol Hill law firm. Victoria herself had skipped two grades to graduate from high school at sixteen, entering Washington's Georgetown University the same year. She'd established herself as one of its top students by the time she met Sir Solomon Alexandre two years later.

According to my father's friend at the Pentagon, eighteen-year-old Victoria Nicolson's prospects for a distinguished career had already seemed certain; and she'd had no shortage of other, younger suitors from Washington's highest-level bachelors. But nobody who knew Alexandre's ability to conquer any obstacles between him and anything he wanted was overly surprised when he managed to brush aside the competition and persuade Victoria to give up her career plans—or perhaps merely to postpone them. Within a month, he'd taken her back to England and made her his wife. And a year later he had his son and heir.

None of this explained why she'd reacted so oddly to my joke that she'd married the wrong man.

* * *

I didn't entirely stop thinking about Victoria when I went back to work inside the plant. But I didn't let her keep me from contributing my share towards getting the rush order ready on time.

This one was for twelve thousand Browning H.P. automatic pistols, plus thousands of crates of 9mm ammunition for them. Solomon Alexandre had bought the Brownings from Morocco, which had phased them out in favor of new Colt .45s. He'd immediately resold them to the Argentine police force with a considerable markup in price.

Now it might occur to you that Morocco could have sold the pistols directly to Argentina. That way neither country would have had to pay anything to Alexandre for acting fundamentally as a broker between them. But such a straight government-to-government contract would have created one problem. It would have made it difficult for politicians and generals, in both countries, to get *their* percentage from the deal—via the privately paid "consultant fees" that are sometimes unkindly referred to as kickbacks or bribes. I'll explain more about how that works later. It is one main reason private arms dealing has become such a flourishing trade.

On the scale of Alexandre's normal operations, this order was small potatoes. But he intended it as an opening wedge for bigger schemes he had cooking with Argentina. So this batch had to be delivered in prime condition.

The ammunition was no problem. It was still grease-packed in the original cases from Belgium's Fabrique Nationale factory near Liege. Indonesia had bought the ammo from FN, expecting to buy the Brownings it fitted. Then an Iron Curtain arms salesman bribed Indonesian leaders to buy Bulgarian pistols instead. Result: Indonesia no longer needed the ammunition. Alexandre got it all for a pittance—plus side payments to wives and nephews of Indonesian officials.

But while the ammo was still in mint condition, the Browning automatics were not. They'd been through a lot of misuse and careless storage. Most needed some renovation. Some had defective components which had to be replaced by cannibalizing parts from our stocks of junked weaponry.

I spent the rest of that afternoon in the junk-weaponry stocks, taking apart scrapped pistols in search of useable parts, cleaning the ones I found, and hauling them over to workshops to be integrated with the Brownings from Morocco. By quitting time we were far enough along to figure on meeting the shipping deadline. I took a long, hot and cold shower, and was climbing back into my work jeans when my father came to my room.

"Put on your nice summer things," he told me. "Alexandre's wife just phoned. You're invited to dinner at the château."

I was more excited than startled. "Both of us?"

"She asked me, but I've got too much work ahead tonight. And I don't think it'd be a good idea for me to get too friendly with her."

"Why not?"

"Her husband might not like the idea." His tone put a damper on further discussion of that subject. "Anyway, she didn't insist. It's you she wants. Big brother for her kid, I reckon."

I felt I should put up a token reluctance. "Hell, I expected to work with you tonight."

"Watch the profanity, son." When Major Lou Bishop said things like that, the corners of his mouth became deep gouges and his eyes narrowed and his voice got hard as a knife.

I said, "I'm sorry, Sir."

"Just watch it." He softened his tone and expression: "She's the boss's wife, and the kid's the boss's son. Look at it as a political necessity."

"You hate politicians."

"If I'd spent more time learning to be one, instead of hating them, I'd be more than a retired major. Give that some serious thought."

Victoria had offered to send the chauffeured Rolls for me, but he'd told her no. He didn't want me to get too much of a taste of the rich life that early. I used the motorbike that had been his birthday present to me, and reached the château with no time to spare.

* * *

Victoria executed a perfect jackknife off the diving board, straightened at the last instant, and cut into the water so cleanly that there were only a few very small ripples left on the surface to mark the spot where she'd gone under. She didn't come up until she reached the other end of the pool. Her speed and breath control surprised me. It was a long underwater haul. Solomon Alexandre had not stinted when he'd ordered that pool built.

She swam back the length of the pool in a neat surface crawl. Alan and I were treading water in the center of the pool. She went past us with the swift ease of a mermaid. Alan said proudly, "I'm a pretty good swimmer, but I can't go that fast. Can you?"

"I've done a lot of swimming," I told him, and watched Victoria swing herself up out of the end of the pool onto the brick patio. She did it in one smoothly coordinated movement, pulling off her swimming cap and shaking out her thick, shoulder length hair. Dusk was closing in, but I could see the trickles of water running down her lithe, tanned figure.

She picked up the wristwatch she'd left on one of the patio tables, looked at it and waved to us. "Time to get dressed. Dinner in fifteen minutes." She went into the pool house as Alan and I swam to the edge and climbed out.

I had arrived almost an hour earlier, well before the summer sunset. The air hadn't cooled and it was getting heavier, weighed down by a low, thickening blanket of cloud. I cruised the motorbike into the estate via a long gravel drive that cut straight through a small forest. Huge, ancient trees overhung the drive, providing a tunnel of cool shade.

The majestic, three-storey château blocked the sky at the other end of this shade tunnel. Its walls were constructed of massive stone blocks, and it was flanked by round defense towers. It had been built as the main residence of some bygone baron's castle-farm, back when such places had to stand ready to beat off attacks.

The lower part of one tower had been converted into a garage, but thus far the garage had no doors. The Rolls was inside with a Mercedes, and a small pickup truck was parked outside. I left my bike next to the truck and climbed a wide, graceful flight of weather-pocked stone entrance steps. Victoria had been alerted by the bike's noisy approach. She was waiting for me on the terrace at the top, between a couple ancient columns.

"Dinner won't be for another hour. Alan's gone swimming and I think we should join him. I've just sent the last of the workmen home and I'm sticky from rushing back and forth between them in this incredible weather."

"You must be paying stiff overtime to get people around here to work this late."

"Stiff," she agreed. "But necessary. Come, I'll give you a fast, guided tour on the way to the pool."

Victoria took me through the ground floor of the main building. As we went along, she showed me what she'd done so far and explained what still needed doing. "I'm trying to modernize enough to make it livable, without losing its sense of history. There's no point in buying a place this old, after all, unless you like the feeling of the past."

She pointed out how she was handling various restoration problems with the pleasure of someone born to get things done: to construct, fix, create. There were areas fully restored, others partway done, some not touched yet. One of the latter was an immense room with high walls full of cracks and stains, and a crumbling fireplace big enough for six people to have sat down to a meal inside it.

"I'm leaving this wreck for last," Victoria told me. "The walls alone——. The roof wasn't repaired for a couple decades and over the years so much rainwater seeped down inside, it'll take months of work."

Two of the rooms she'd finished first were a large dining room and the kitchen adjoining it. In both she had achieved what she'd wanted: a comfortable mix of up-to-date practicality and old-fashioned charm. In the kitchen Victoria chatted briefly in fluent French with the cook and a maid helping to prepare dinner. Both were local peasant women. Their fondness for their new mistress was obvious.

Going out a rear door, we entered a park of oak trees and newly laid flower beds, which separated the main residence from the disused farm complex. The amount of ground clearance and tree trimming so far accomplished was evidenced by huge piles of branches, weeds and underbrush. The only way to get rid of the stuff was to burn it. In this country, it was illegal to do any outside burning except after a rain, and it hadn't rained for over three weeks. Glancing up at the thickening cloud cover, I figured it wouldn't have to wait much longer.

Running through the park was a waterway of marble-contained lily ponds, connected by narrow stone channels. We took a path between the gurgling water and the flower beds, under the shading trees. As we walked side by side, Victoria's arm brushed mine, and I found it difficult to make casual conversation. She gave me an oblique smile that seemed, to me, a reminder of the secret understanding established between us earlier, that day at the plant.

The lovely waterway disappeared underground when we neared the farm courtyard. None of the buildings around the yard had been touched and most were in an advanced stage of decay. Our path skirted a stable whose roof had collapsed inside its stone walls. On the other side awaited the surprise splendor of the blue-tiled swimming pool, surrounded by its brick patio bordered with neatly trimmed hedges and fruit trees. Alan was floating in the water. He waved when he saw us crossing the patio.

"Come on in! It's the coolest place in France!"

"I didn't bring any swimming trunks," I called back.

"That's all right," Victoria said. "There's a pair in the pool house."

What she called the pool house was a squat building with walls of rough stone and a new, tiled roof. It might once have been a small grange for sheep. But inside it was entirely renovated. The walls were panelled, the tile flooring covered with woven straw carpets. There were gracefully made wicker furniture, colorful cushions, a small fireplace of dark marble. Doorways led to a bathroom, a small bedroom, even a little kitchen.

"I want it to serve as an extra guest house," Victoria explained as she opened the lower drawer of a bureau painted in rustic designs, "in case we're ever too crowded at the main house."

Considering the size of the main house, I thought it unlikely. But then, people as wealthy as the Alexandres might be accustomed to throwing *very* big weekend parties.

Victoria straightened, tossed me a pair of swimming trunks, and went into the bedroom. I changed in the bathroom. Whoever the trunks belonged to, it was a struggle tugging them over my hips.

She was already waiting for me when I came out. She'd put on a dark green bikini. I had never understood why the general public had gone for that fashion in swimwear, because one thing bikinis are not is figure flattering. Victoria was among the very few adult women I'd ever seen who made one look good.

I was careful not to look her over too blatantly. But Victoria had no timidity about bodies. She looked me up and down, deliberately and critically, and said, "You'd make a perfect advertisement for the superior healthiness of California living. How did you get so healthy, so young?"

I laughed. "Surfing, swimming. A little weightlifting."

"Go easy on the weightlifting," she advised me seriously. "I see so many men who build up too much muscle when they are young, and then have it all turn to fat when they're in their thirties with sedentary jobs."

"I feel too fat right now," I told her. "Either that or the guy these trunks belong to is extra lean."

Victoria nodded. "They're my husband's. I bought them for him to use when he comes here." She was speaking lightly, but with a moody edge she didn't quite conceal. "*If* he ever manages to get around to it before the summer's over."

I kept my voice matter-of-fact. "From the workloads we've been getting at the plant, I guess he's been pretty occupied this summer, businesswise."

"Yes," Victoria said, and led the way out to the pool.

* * *

The dinner that night tasted as delicious as it smelled. It had been a while since I'd had a real home-cooked meal. My father and I usually ate sandwiches for lunch and out of cans at dinner. Alan was still shy, but he kept forcing himself to respond when I prodded him. He didn't even seem to mind too much when his mother and I talked to each other, as long as it didn't go on too long. Most shy people can't tolerate being part of a three-person group because they feel left out when some of the attention isn't directed to them. But he loved his mother and he liked me, and as long as we gave him a lot of our attention, he was okay.

The night air stayed hot and heavy, and the storm broke before we finished dinner. It was one humdinger of a storm. Great sheets of lightning, thunder that rattled the windows and dishes, a downpour of raindrops that sounded as hard as pebbles when they hit. It was continuing without letup when we got up from the table.

"I found something you'll want to see," Alan told me. "Up in the attic. I'll get it." He went off for whatever it was, and Victoria took me into a small living room she'd fixed up. Through the large window-doors she'd installed, we could see the rain changing to hail. I sat on a sofa that faced the window. Victoria took a cushion and dropped it on the carpet beside my feet. She settled down on it, curling her legs under her skirt and leaning back against the sofa.

If having a woman as glamorous as Victoria sit at your feet doesn't grab you, you've got no soul.

She'd brought a glass of wine with her from the dining room. It was the last bottle she'd opened when we sat down to dinner, and neither Alan nor I had any of it. She sipped the wine and stared at the hailstones bouncing off the terrace outside the window. "I hope the new roof tiles survive this."

There was a good chance some of them wouldn't. The hailstones were coming down in all sizes, and some of them looked as big as tennis balls.

Alan came in with his treasure from the attic. He plumped himself down on the sofa and silently showed it to me. And grinned at the reverence with which I took it from him. It was an old Colt .38 military issue automatic: the 1900 model, with rounded hammer, lanyard ring, and the name COLT embossed on its checkered wooden grips along with a rearing horse carved inside a circle. It was choked with dirt, the hammer and slide were stuck from rust, and one of the grips was cracked, but it was still a collector's item.

"The only other one of these I ever saw," I told Alan, "was in a military museum."

"Will it work?"

"We'll have to strip it and clean it first, and then see. I'll bring a tool kit along, next time I come."

I already knew there'd be next times.

* * *

The hail changed back to rain. It was still raining when it was time for me to leave. Victoria wouldn't hear of me going back to the plant on my bike in that rain. She had finished the wine in her glass, the last of her evening's bottle, but it didn't affect her voice or manner. The only change in her that I could detect was an undercurrent of somber moodiness—and I couldn't be sure the wine had anything to do with that. She moved with the same easy grace when she got up and went to summon the chauffeur for me.

So I got my chauffeur-driven ride that night, after all. But not in the Rolls Royce. Sebastiani—that was the name of their chauffeur—wasn't about to risk scratching its paint by tying on my bike. He drove me in the pickup truck, with the bike stuck in back.

His English was fluent, though the French accent was strong, and he eased into pumping me as he turned out of the estate, driving cautiously on the rain-slick road. "You have made a friend of young Alan, it seems. And his mother."

"I like them, too."

"That is easier with the mother. Lady Alexandre is a most attractive woman. Didn't you find her so?"

"Sure."

"But the boy—not so easy. In school he has no friends. He says everybody there is stupid. It is surprising, the way he let you teach him to shoot. He has always refused to show any interest in anything connected with his father's business. Perhaps he spoke to you of his father?"

"No." I decided to pump him in turn: "Where'd you learn your English?"

"First, when I was a boy, from the American troops who entered Toulon at the end of the war." He was not reluctant to talk about himself, and though I figured it was his way of relaxing me for further pumping, I began finding it hard to dislike Sebastiani. "I'm Corsican," he told me, "but born in Toulon. I liked your soldiers. They inspired me to join the French Army later."

"How long were you in the Army?"

"Almost ten years. I fought in Indo-China. I rose to sergeant in the Algerian fighting. Then DeGaulle gave Algeria away and I quit in disgust. I got into some trouble for a time. But finally I found the civilian profession which suits me. As chauffeur and bodyguard."

"I didn't know you were a bodyguard, too."

"Oh, yes. Rich people like the Alexandres, they need protection these days. Sometimes even from themselves. Lady Alexandre, she is not always cautious enough with other people she meets. And sometimes she drinks too much. You noticed?"

"No."

"How did you find her? Her mood, I mean. Does she seem to you content here, so far from the more exciting life she is used to?"

"I didn't notice," I said stiffly.

Sebastiani laughed. "You are more observant than that, kid. But you don't like to gossip. That's good."

"My name's Garson," I told him. "Not kid."

He gave me a short grin. "I can call you Mr. Bishop, if you want me to be formal. I'm supposed to with friends of the Alexandres. Or I can call you Sir, as I would address Major Bishop."

"Cut the comedy. My first name'll do fine."

"Okay. Gar-son." He laughed again.

He drove into the plant complex and helped me get the bike and put it under a shed overhang, out of the rain. "Do not think badly of me for the questions I asked about the Alexandres. The more I know about people, the easier it is to protect them." He stuck out a hand and I shook it. He drove off and I went into one of the workshops where light still showed through the windows.

My father was working at a lathe, trying to smooth out a

problem we'd run into with the design of his one-man tank killer: the rocket's stabilizing fins were too susceptible to damage coming out of the launcher.

"How'd it go?" he asked without looking up.

"Fine. You missed a great dinner."

He grunted and got on with his work. I changed into my work clothes and went back in to help him.

Chapter Four

Garson

After that I was a frequent guest at the château. Twice Victoria drove Alan and me off in the Mercedes for a day's outing, once in the mountains and another time all the way out to the Atlantic coast. We didn't return from that one until late at night. She phoned my father, and I slept that night in a guest room Victoria had fixed up between Alan's room and her master bedroom. After that I stayed overnight at the château each weekend for the rest of the summer.

I let Alan help me take his 1900 Colt automatic apart and clean and repair it. Then I brought over some .38 cartridges and we tried it out, using a gully that ran down to a stream some distance from the swimming pool. The old Colt proved accurate at short range. Alan got to be a fair shot with it. When not in use, we kept it in the back of a closet in the pool house, with a couple boxes of cartridges. He swore never to use it when I wasn't present, and by that time I knew I could trust his word.

At first Victoria was uneasy about her son's growing fondness for guns. I told her about kids who'd never been taught to treat weapons with respect, as potentially deadly tools, and who'd gotten killed or hurt somebody else when they treated one they came across as if it were a toy. Victoria accepted that this made sense. She was never happy about it, but she couldn't bring herself to put a stop to Alan's first real enthusiasm in life.

Sometimes Alan had Sebastiani drive him to the plant so I could give him further lessons with the .22 rifle. He always checked first to make certain that he wasn't intruding too much on my work. I made the time for him with my father's approval. Looking ahead, my father saw that it might be handy to have Solomon Alexandre's wife and son as friends when his compact antitank weapon was ready for marketing. Part of the practical politics he'd talked to me about.

My alliance with Solomon Alexandre's family was something more than that for me. Not only because of Victoria. I was growing fond of her kid. It's hard not to respond to somebody who worships you. I reckoned that Victoria responded to me for pretty much the same reason.

Whenever I was out at the château I enjoyed watching the spirit she put into getting all that restoration work done. But now and then I'd see that somber, withdrawn look come over her again. Once, when I was giving Alan some target practice, he suddenly said, "It's a relief to be here with you for awhile. My mother had a fight with my father on the phone. She's in a bad mood."

"Married people have fights all the time," I told him. "My mother used to yell at my father a lot when I was a kid. Doesn't mean much. Just letting off steam."

Alan was silent for a time, and then went on with it: "He hurts her by never coming to see us. Not even when she had her thirtieth birthday last month. That really upset her. I heard her tell him on the phone. She said a woman ought to have her husband there to help her say goodbye to her twenties. But he didn't come."

"He was probably just too busy to get there at the time. Flying all over the world the way he does, to work out those deals . . ."

"He's *always* too busy." Alan shrugged. One of his old shrugs. "He didn't come because he doesn't care about making her happy. He doesn't care about making anybody happy. Like the way he makes me go to that school in Switzerland. Mother tried to talk him into letting me go to school near here, so I could be with her all the time—not just during school holidays. He said no." Alan's voice became bitter: "I guess he just can't stand my being with her that much. Because I love her and she loves me. He knows I don't even *like* him!"

I wondered if Alexandre realized just how *much* his son hated him. But there were more puzzling questions on my mind at that point. What kind of man would ignore a wife like Victoria? Why would someone like her put up with it? If things were that bad between them, why did they remain married to each other?

* * *

It was a few days later that I met the man named Peel for the first time. He found me in Excideuil, a village a few miles from the plant. I'd ridden there on the bike to have a big dish of ice cream at a shaded sidewalk table outside a bistro just under the old fortress ruins that towered above the village. It wasn't great ice cream, but it was cold and, on an evening so stifling, it was better than nothing. A flashy, red Porsche pulled up at the curb and a tall, broad-shouldered man climbed out. His dark sunglasses looked like a mask across his long, freckled face, and, though he didn't look that old, he was entirely bald. He came over and said, "Hello, Gar."

I was working my memory, which is usually pretty good

with faces, when he smiled and said, "Don't try. We haven't met before. I only know you from your pictures."

He spoke with a flat twang of New England. I asked him, "What pictures?"

He sat down across the table from me and called into the bistro for a glass of milk with ice cubes in it. His French was fast and easy. Then he went back to the New England twang: "There's the one in Alan's room."

Victoria had shot a camera roll of Alan and me together. He'd asked her to have one of the photographs enlarged and had hung it on his bedroom wall, next to one of him with his mother. There were no others of him with anybody else.

I said, "You're a friend of the Alexandres."

"Employee. Like your father." He took off the dark glasses and used a handkerchief to mop sweat from his sunburned head and face. His eyes were soft brown, friendly, like his smile. "My name's Stuart Peel. I'm in charge of security for Sir Solomon and his organization."

"Is there a security problem at the plant?"

"I didn't come here about the plant. I came about you." At that point the bistro owner's daughter came out with his iced milk. His eyes followed her buttocks as she walked back inside. Then he took a sip of milk and made a face. "These Frogs never will learn to refrigerate the milk they serve. Always have to wait until the ice cubes do their job."

"What do you mean, you came about me?"

"First of all, I can tell you Sir Solomon's mighty pleased the way his son's started taking an interest in at least one aspect of his business. And we know that's all your doing. You score a big point for that." Peel grinned suddenly. "Speaking of scoring, that was one neat trick you pulled off with that pen of yours, to turn the kid on. Poking holes in the target's bull's-eye."

Sebastiani had to be an awfully sharp observer to have

spotted that from where he'd stood. I'd already figured out that his watchdog duties included spying on Alexandre's wife and son. Now I knew the man Sebastiani reported to.

"The second big point for you is that Alan likes you, even looks up to you." Peel took another sip of milk, found it had cooled off sufficiently, and drank down half of it before continuing. "You know how standoffish that kid is, never made any friends before. Not a single, solitary one until you. If you can hold onto that, and push Alan's interest in arms further from time to time—and if you keep your own nose clean—you could wind up with a good job."

"What kind of job?"

"Being Alan's friend, full-time."

"That's a *job*?"

"Could be the best one you'll ever get a chance at, boy. That kid'll inherit everything Sir Solomon has one day. Help him to like the idea, and you could wind right up there with him."

"Being somebody's friend isn't my idea of a job."

"Don't kid yourself. From kings to presidents and corporation heads, it's always been that way. For the man at the top, a real friend's even harder to come by than a reliable security specialist or weaponry expert. And the friend-job pays one helluva lot more than I'll ever earn, or your Daddy."

Peel had another sip of cooled milk and gave me the friendly smile. "Only, as I started to tell you, you've got to learn to keep your nose clean. Better than you've managed so far. On your past record, you're no fit companion for Sir Solomon's kid. You've got a very bad reputation."

I felt my face go hot in a way that had nothing to do with the summer weather. "No I don't. What are you talking about?"

"I'm talking about your associating with all those no-job

weirdos back in the States, that's what I'm talking about."
Peel's voice and expression stayed friendly. "I'm talking
about you screwing half the whores in L.A."

"I never paid a whore in my life!"

"Those California broads are all whores in their hearts. We
both know that, right? They've got absolutely no morals.
Not the kind of society we'd want you introducing Alan to,
as he gets older. Or giving him a yen for with filthy talk."

I got a grip on my temper. I wanted to slug him. But I
knew it wouldn't be smart, and probably not too safe, either.
I was strong enough. But strength is one thing and acquired
skill is another. Peel had a relaxed physical assurance about
him that said he could most likely put me down and out
without half trying. "You went all the way over to California to check on my morals?"

"No need to. I used to be with the FBI—fairly high level
before Sir Solomon took me on. Like your Daddy. You get
to know police and other security people all over the place.
An old-boy network. Every profession has them. Your
Daddy must have something like it in the military. I just put
in a couple of phone calls to some people I know in California."

"And they nosed around and sent you all the dirt they
could come up with."

"Just the facts, son, like that cop on TV used to say. And
the facts about your last few years out there are not appealing. So I came here to give you a friendly warning. Be *very*
careful never to get Alan involved in that kind of filth—by
what you say or what you do when you're with him. If you
do, I'll know about it. And I'll break your connection with
him. I do mean *break*. And you'll lose the greatest opportunity you'll ever get in this life."

Stuart Peel finished off his milk, put a few coins on the

table beside his glass and stood up. He smiled down at me, his friendliness unchanged. "You get the same look as your Daddy when you're mad. Don't be, I'm only giving you some good advice. We don't want Alan corrupted. The kid's got enough character faults as it is. One day maybe I'll be working for him. Could be you who decides that for him. You've got it made. Just don't louse it up."

He got back into his red Porsche and drove away.

* * *

The next weekend that I got invited to stay overnight at the château, I found Victoria had another weekend guest.

I'd seen his picture in the sports pages. He was a Grand Prix racing driver, a South African named Pete Bruno, somewhere in his thirties with a husky build and sharp, clean-cut features. He'd gotten heavy press coverage after a bad crash in his last race, at Le Mans. Another driver had been killed, and Bruno had been dragged out of the wreckage with multiple fractures and serious burns. I suppose he was still recuperating that weekend at the château because he didn't race again until the following winter. He walked with a limp and there was a vicious burn scar across his right cheekbone and ear. But it didn't detract from his looks —just added a romantic touch that went with his cheerfully reckless expression.

It became apparent that Victoria and Bruno had been occasional companions for some years standing. Their conversation at dinner was largely about fun parties he'd escorted her to in the past—the fun part clearly somewhat censored because Alan and I were at the table with them. They'd had some hard drinks before dinner, and they'd killed a couple bottles of wine between them by the dinner's end. She looked younger than I'd ever seen her. And somehow defiant.

Alan had met the racing driver before, in London, and openly resented his presence. That didn't say anything about Bruno, of course. You could count the people Alan liked on two fingers.

After dinner Victoria and Bruno closeted themselves in the living room with a bottle of brandy. Alan and I went for a long walk in the country. Neither of us was in a very happy mood.

Alan finally blurted it out: "That's the kind of man I *hate* to see around my mother. She's a thousand times too good for people like him! If my father didn't leave her alone all the time, she wouldn't *need* friends like that."

I kept my mouth shut. My thoughts were pretty much the same. But I didn't have any relationship with Victoria that gave me a right to express them.

Returning from our night hike, I took Alan for a swim in the pool to cool both of us off. It was around midnight when we went up to our bedrooms. Victoria and Bruno were still in the living room, with the door closed.

A long, wide hallway ran the entire length of the second floor. The rooms were all on one side of it, and there were big windows on the other side that looked down on the miniature forest between the château and the main road. My room was near the east end of the hallway, sandwiched between Alan's room and the master bedroom suite. It was small and the furniture was old stuff that had been in the house when they'd bought it. Someday, Victoria planned to convert the room into a bathroom connecting to Alan's room, after she finished restoring the rest of the guest rooms. Her master suite had its own bathroom, but none of the other rooms along the second floor did as yet. Alan and I used a guest bathroom recently completed at our end of the hallway.

I let Alan use it first. He had already gone to bed when I took my turn. I soaked awhile in a warm tub and then poured in a lot of cold water and soaked some more. With that Perigord summer heat I didn't have to dry myself much after I climbed out of the tub. Just patted a little with a towel and let the night air do the rest. When I left the bathroom, I looked toward the far end of the hallway, to the partly finished guest room Victoria had given Pete Bruno. His door was ajar and there was no light inside it, so I guessed they were still downstairs.

Inside my bedroom, I shut the door and didn't turn on any lights. Nights at the château with Victoria so close, I sometimes had difficulty sleeping. This was going to be one of those nights. I had taken to observing a big, old owl that lived under the broken roof of the tower at that end of the château. I'd actually seen him only once, very briefly, flying out of the tower one evening just before full dark to do his night's hunting. One morning I'd found the torn remains of a field rat outside the base of the tower. I'd guessed the owl had sampled it, hadn't liked the taste and tossed it out.

That weekend I'd brought along infrared night binoculars, so I could get a close-up view of him, study his night habits, find out if he was a solitary or had a family up there. I pulled a chair over to my open window and settled down to wait. Alan was already asleep and Victoria hadn't come up to her room. I could tell that from where I sat. When lamps were on in any of our rooms, the light shined through the windows on the curved stone of the tower wall. The owl didn't like that. Whenever he returned from a night's hunting and any of our lights were on, he did a couple minutes of furious screeching.

I'd been watching through the binoculars for about half an hour when a lamp went on in Victoria's bedroom. I lowered the binoculars to my lap, looking at the light cast on the tower. Some nights I'd watched her shadow moving on that rough stone wall when she walked between a light and her windows.

This time, after a couple minutes, I saw two shadows projected against the tower's curved wall.

My hands tightened around the binoculars on my lap. I watched the movements of the shadows. No question: Victoria had someone in the master bedroom with her. I continued to watch. The shadows and the light from her windows vanished at the same time.

I wasn't thinking about the owl anymore, if I ever really had been. I wasn't thinking about anything but Victoria and that man. I waited about five minutes, then got up and went to my door, opened it quietly. Stepping out, I looked down the long hallway. The door to Pete Bruno's room was still open, and there was still no light inside it. I stepped back into my room, shut my door.

There was a deep recess in my side of the wall that separated Victoria's room from mine. Shelves had been set into it to hold books and knickknacks. It had probably once been part of some connection between the rooms. But the opening had been boarded over long ago; the wallpaper on the back of the recess was faded with age. I stood as close to it as I could and listened.

The murmur of voices came through. Not distinctly enough for me to identify any words. Whatever they were saying to each other, they were keeping their voices down. The murmuring ceased. I waited there, and after a time I heard what sounded like laughter, harsh and broken. Then silence again. And then, suddenly, a muffled scream. It could have come from a woman in pain. But of course Victoria wasn't in pain.

There were no further sounds after that. I finally moved

away from the wall recess, but I didn't return to my owl watch. Nor did I go to sleep for another couple hours. I sat on the edge of my bed and stared at the dark wall between my room and hers.

I knew that a person as smart as Victoria had to be aware that one of Sebastiani's functions was to report everything that went on here. And she had to be aware that he was good at it. Either she'd gotten too drunk to think straight or she no longer gave a damn if her husband found out. Or she wanted him to know.

Whatever her reasoning, the jealousy I was experiencing was murderous.

* * *

Late the next morning, the four of us—Alan and I, Victoria and Bruno—got into our bathing suits and went out to the pool to have brunch together. Pete Bruno's torso was bared, revealing the full extent of his scarring. The burns disfigured large areas of his right side and arms. He wasn't self-conscious about it, but in my state of mind, I thought it was ugly as hell. Victoria obviously did not find it so.

We were finishing the brunch when the phone inside the pool house rang. The various phones around the château were hooked up so that when someone called from outside, only the phone in the servant quarters would ring. All calls were screened before being put through to Victoria. She picked up the pool house phone and, after a few minutes, came back out with a slightly puzzled look on her face.

"It's for you," she told Bruno.

It was a few minutes before Bruno came out. His look of reckless humor was gone, replaced by nervous anger.

"I'm sorry," he told Victoria in a rigidly controlled tone,

"something's come up and I'll have to leave."

She rose to her feet slowly, her own expression tightening. "Who was that, Pete? His voice sounded familiar."

He hesitated, but finally told her. "An employee of your husband. Said his name is Peel."

Whatever Stuart Peel had said to him, Bruno was on his way to the Perigueux train station an hour later; and he never returned.

Solomon Alexandre came the following weekend.

Chapter Five

Garson

Making eye contact with Solomon Alexandre did not give you a feeling of having established a form of human communication. He looked at you as though he were a jeweler searching for flaws in a gem he might buy—or a locksmith appraising a new brand of safe he might one day have to crack.

He arrived at the château Saturday evening, picked up by Sebastiani at the little airport down near Bergerac. The photo in my father's office showed him with pitch black hair, starting to go grey. He wasn't much older now, somewhere in his early fifties, but his hair had gone almost entirely white. It didn't age him. It framed his handsome head like a sleek, silver helmet, with touches of shiny black.

Two other men climbed out of the Rolls with him. One was his chief business manager, a Frenchman named Pierre Golz. The other was head of Alexandre's legal staff, a Canadian, Thomas Haggard. Both hurried up the entrance steps to greet Victoria, Golz with deep respect and Haggard with what seemed to be genuine affection. Solomon Alexandre took his time mounting the steps, and scrutinized his wife without a smile, making no move to kiss her or touch her.

He was taller than I, taller than the two flunkies he'd brought with him: a lean man, impeccably tailored, with a cold dignity and imperious eyes. "Victoria, will you show Haggard and Golz where the phones are? They have calls to make." Those were his first words to her.

She turned to the two men: "I'll show you the guest room while we're at it. I'm afraid you'll have to share. I wasn't warned you were coming, and it's the only one I've gotten into decent shape so far."

"That will do fine," Alexandre answered for them. "We're only staying the one night. I'm due at a conference in Monte Carlo tomorrow afternoon."

Victoria started to lead Golz and Haggard inside, then stopped and turned back to her husband. She managed a crooked smile. "By the way, welcome to your home."

"You don't look well," he told her, his voice stern and clinical. "I see you've been drinking again."

Her smile was gone. She met Alexandre's impersonal scrutiny with a flat stare of her own. "You see? Or you were told?"

His eyes remained locked with hers a moment longer. It was she who turned away. As she took the other two men inside, Alexandre looked down at his son.

"You do look well, Alan. I'm pleased to see it." As with his wife, there was no kiss, no touch.

Alan ducked his head and mumbled, "Thank you, Father." He introduced me.

Nobody subjected to Solomon Alexandre's glowering stare ever forgets its piercing impact. I wasn't subjected to it often that weekend. He looked me over briefly, then nodded slightly, more to himself than to me, confirming with his own eyes what had already been reported to him. He turned away without a word, not offering to shake my hand. Afterwards he ignored my presence. I think to him I was merely another type of lower servant—like Sebastiani, or the cook or the maids—a companion for his son and heir.

He didn't pay much attention to his son, either, for the rest of that evening. Alan, in turn, sank back into his old self in his father's presence: a sullen and withdrawn figure. Alexandre didn't seem to mind. He may not have noticed. His own self-absorption was close to total. When we were all seated around the dining table that night, the few words he directed to Alan or Victoria were formal, brief, and utterly lacked emotional content.

Which did not mean that it was a silent dinner. Alexandre had myriad points to discuss with Golz and Haggard: business schemes, economic possibilities, political problems. The arms king was not inhibited by the three outsiders at the table, overhearing. Alan was his heir, and it would do him no harm to begin getting a smell of the realities of the business. Victoria had certainly heard other secret conversations in the past, and had never leaked anything from them, whatever her other sins. After all, the heir to the business was her son, too.

As for me, I was probably beneath Alexandre's worry, like the two maids coming in and out of the room, serving and removing dishes. I was still just a kid in Alexandre's eyes, and most of what the three men discussed was obviously over my head. But some of it wasn't. What I did grasp was fascinating, a window into new worlds.

Haggard's phone calls had been to the States, to a U.S. senator named Reed and a Pentagon general named Brady. Between them, the senator and the general were in a position to nudge the federal government into using the taxpayers' money to subsidize a California firm's development of new assault helicopters. Alexandre was thinking about gaining a controlling interest in that firm.

"I expressed your concerns *carefully,* of course," Haggard told his employer, "without being specific about—"

"But not so carefully," Alexandre interrupted impatiently, "as to prevent them from understanding the *quid pro quo.* "Their responses, I take it, were favorable."

His attorney smiled. *"Eager.* As you anticipated, Senator Reed needs a *substantial* contribution to his campaign funds. And General Brady *is* getting nervous about his prospects for gainful employment after retirement. The news that you'll be taking over another American company and will be in need of a good man to run it perked him up considerably."

"When do you meet with them?"

"Brady, tomorrow night. The senator, the following morning."

Solomon Alexandre told him firmly: "I want both of them sewed up before you return from Washington."

Haggard nodded. "Will do."

Alexandre turned to his business manager. Most of their discussion was beyond me: too many legal and financial technicalities in a French too rapid for that stage of my linguistic education. What I could follow seemed to concern a dummy company, untraceable to Alexandre, that Golz was creating in Switzerland to channel campaign money to Reed and other U.S. politicians—including both Republican and Democratic candidates for president.

I did my best to keep my attempts at eavesdropping from being obvious. From time to time I made low-voiced, abortive tries at casual conversation with Victoria and her son. Alan kept his head down and his answers short. Victoria's responses were pleasant enough, but her attention was on Alexandre and the other two men. She was listening shrewdly to every word. While I didn't understand all of what was being said, it was obvious that *she* did.

The final part of the discussion was fairly clear even to me. Alexandre would be meeting the next day with one of his biggest competitors: an Arab weaponry broker whose name I didn't catch. What I did get was that he and the Arab were considering joining to milk big profits from some dicey scheme.

"What worries me," Golz said nervously, "is the possibility he may learn the names of some generals we control. If he were to leak that information—."

"Don't be stupid," Alexandre snapped. "He is a shark, yes. But too intelligent and rapacious a shark to lose his share from this arrangement merely to deprive me of mine."

And with that, Alexandre brought his conference to an end. "It is time to go to bed," he announced, and got up from his chair.

Golz and Haggard stood up immediately, like marionettes whose strings the boss had pulled. They said good night to Victoria and retreated to their shared guest room.

Alexandre remained behind. "In the future, Victoria, you will please schedule your dinners here earlier than this." His tone was quiet, the words clipped. "A boy Alan's age needs more sleep than he has been getting."

Victoria's chin rose, her jaw line hardening. She gave him a polite smile and no answer.

After a moment, Alexandre transferred his attention to their son. "All right, Alan. Bedtime."

With no word of response, Alan got up and went to kiss Victoria. "Good night, Mother."

She clung to him for a moment, then released him and said tenderly, "Sleep well, darling."

He touched my shoulder with his hand in passing, and went upstairs to his room without a glance at his father.

Alexandre looked at Victoria again. Her polite smile was firmly back in place when she met his stare. He turned on his heel and stalked out.

Some of the tension left Victoria's face. Suddenly she seemed weary. "Let's go for a good night swim, Gar."

* * *

When we were in the pool, I challenged her to a race, hoping it would divert her mood. I swam all out, but she managed to keep up with me for three lengths. Then, suddenly, she climbed out onto the patio, pulling off her swimming cap.

"I'm just too exhausted," she said, and sounded it. I watched her go into the pool house and come out belting her white terry cloth robe around her. She waved a hand without looking in my direction again, and walked off toward the rear of the château.

I didn't stay in the pool much longer. When I'd changed back into my clothes, I stood on the patio and looked around. There was a wide path that started nearby and twisted its way between overgrown bushes to another point on the main road. It had once been a separate access route between the road and the farm area of the estate. I thought about going off for a very long night walk. But finally all I did was stand there by the pool a bit longer, looking up at the stars and taking deep breaths of uncontaminated and uncomplicated air.

When I was back up inside my own room, I went to the window without switching on the light. But there were no other lights shining on the tower wall: not from Alan's windows, and not from the master bedroom. Victoria and her husband had either gone to sleep or had drawn the shutters. I couldn't believe they were already asleep. They had to have more to say to each other than had been said so far since Alexandre's arrival. I put my ear to the recess in the wall.

I could hear them. Not distinctly—they weren't speaking loudly enough for me to make out the words. Not at first. Then Solomon Alexandre's voice got stronger, controlled but piercing.

"Bringing that man *here*—are you insane? Do what you wish, but with some discretion. Not for public consumption! And not before my son!"

Victoria's reply was too low for me to hear. But *his* next words came through clearly: "If it happens again, you won't enjoy the punishment I devise!"

Her voice strengthened to match Alexandre's: "Then why do you drive me to it? Solomon, be reasonable. *You* don't want me. You don't need me, for anything. *Why* won't you just let go?"

"You are still the mother of my son. I won't have his feelings torn between the two of us by a divorce."

Victoria's laugh was shaky. "Alan's *feelings*? If you really cared, you'd realize that nothing could make him feel worse about you than the present situation. If *you* have any feelings *for him*, you might try showing them."

"He is my son. And you, unfortunately for all of us, happen to be his mother. There will be no divorce."

"You can't stop me."

"You know I can." Alexandre's voice had acquired a cold ferocity that made my skin crawl. "Do you really want to provoke me into proving it? Are you *that* reckless?"

A moment passed before she answered. Her voice was lower, barely audible—and frightened. "You *are* what they call you. A devil. It took me too long to see it. I was too young, to stupidly romantic to understand. All that charm, that passion were mere tactics—that you dropped once you had what you were after."

"Go to bed," Alexandre ordered. "I'm going to take my bath now."

I heard the sound of the bathroom door slamming shut. I remained there at the wall recess for a long time after that, listening for more. But there was no more.

Finally, I went to bed.

* * *

When I came down to breakfast the next morning, Solomon Alexandre had already gone, taking the other two men with him.

There were still eight days left of my summer vacation, but the pleasure had gone out of visits to the château. Victoria had become too subdued, too thoughtful.

I became pretty thoughtful myself. The mystery of the relationship between Victoria and her husband had acquired viciously unpleasant undertones that I couldn't grasp. I had thought I had known her. But I surely did not comprehend how a man like that could keep her from leaving him. Even more surely, I didn't understand what Solomon Alexandre was all about.

Naturally I sometimes talked to my father about his boss. But what he knew of the man's history didn't go much beyond the biography handed out by Alexandre's public relations department. This small pamphlet went something like this:

> Sir Solomon Alexandre, founder of the Alexandre arms empire, was born in Russia of a noble family. His first name—extremely rare

for a Russian aristocrat—was selected by his grandmother, who had been a French Huguenot. Sir Solomon was the only member of his family to escape the Russian Revolution with his life. He reached London a few years after the war and later acquired British citizenship.

With his intelligence and cultured background, he soon became an established fixture at social gatherings of England's ruling class. These connections helped to introduce him to the country's biggest arms makers. But it was his business genius and his flare for politics and languages that earned him a fortune through his own weapons enterprises.

His knighthood was bestowed on him for prodigious services to the British War Department during World War II, and he has remained one of England's most distinguished and influential patriots.

Much of which was an amalgam of partial truths and outright lies, neatly covered by a judicious layer of horseshit.

It took years of digging, starting with some prior inside knowledge, to dredge up pieces of Solomon Alexandre's real story. The pieces came from employees he had broken, competitors he had ruined, officials he had corrupted and then discarded, and from expensive, hired investigators and old policemen with long memories. Much of it was gathered by Victoria, and some of it by me.

Nowhere is the warning "know your enemy" more vital than in the world of weapons—whether your involvement concerns buying and selling, or shooting and being shot at.

Chapter Six

Sir Solomon Alexandre, Part I

He was twelve years old. He lay on hard ground under cold stars, near the dying embers of a fire. His left ankle was tied to the right ankle of a burly, Kurdish mountaineer, who snored beside him. The man had sodomized him before falling asleep. The boy's anus still burned with the pain of it.

His mother was sprawled a few yards away. She had been repeatedly raped. At least ten of the wild Kurd tribesmen had taken turns at her. The last of them, angry at her failure to excite him with either response or resistance, had drawn his hunting knife and slit her open from groin to rib cage.

The boy cuddled closer to the man who had raped him, putting his scrawny arms around the bear-like body, imitating soft sounds he'd heard his mother use when snuggling up to his father. The Kurd stopped snoring and opened one eye.

"I'm cold," the boy whimpered.

The man chuckled, wrapped a big arm around him, and went back to sleep. Carefully, the boy raised his head and looked around the temporary night camp—at other corpses sprawled like his mother, at the still figures of surviving captives, sunk in exhausted sleep like most of their captors, at the few Kurds still moving about.

He remembered his father's words at the emergency meeting in their village: "In a savage state, people are prepared to protect themselves. A civilized people depends on its government and army to defend them. But our government and army are the ones to blame for this. We must become savages again to survive."

The meeting, however, had been too late; the emergency had become a disaster too swiftly. His father was three weeks dead, along with every other adult male of their once numerous family.

He watched the Kurdish mountaineers who were still awake begin to settle down, one by one. He waited. Occasionally he moved a little against the one to whom he was tied. Carefully—he wanted the man to become accustomed to his small movements. He didn't want him to awaken when the time came for the final, desperate, crucial move.

He was twelve years old, and his name was Solomon Azrealian. His family of Armenian peasants had lived for generations in the same, poor village in eastern Turkey. But this was 1921, and the latest in a series of officially approved massacres of Christians swept the country. In Moslem Turkey, most Christians were Greeks or Armenians. There were no Greeks in their village, but many Armenians. When soldiers sent to "round up" Armenians reached the village, the Moslem inhabitants gleefully helped them.

All the Armenian men were bound together in groups, doused with kerosene, and set on fire. Those who didn't die quickly enough were clubbed and stabbed. Twelve-year-old Solomon Azrealian watched them die.

Those women and children who survived the slaughter were force-marched south with survivors from other villages of the area. Mounted soldiers drove them relentlessly across harsh mountains, through barren deserts. Years later, a member of the Turkish government admitted to the Western press that it was intended to be "a march to nowhere."

That it became for most of the women and children: they died of exhaustion, exposure, hunger, thirst—and from assault. The guards made no attempt to defend them against the wild, mountain tribesmen who rode down on the straggling columns, carrying off the choicest survivors to become slaves in remote villages.

Now the last of the men who had carried off Solomon and his mother had fallen asleep. The smoldering embers of the campfire had gone out. Scattered along the dark ground, the still figures of the captors were indistinguishable from those of the captives and corpses.

Solomon moved again, this time towards his goal. Used to the movements of the child, the big Kurd to whom Solomon's ankle was bound went on snoring, his sleep undisturbed. Solomon's fingers found the hilt of the hunting knife on the Kurd's other hip.

He drew the knife out of its sheath and twisted upward on the man's body. He executed his final move swiftly, without hesitation. Gathering his strength, he clamped his free hand over the man's mouth, drove the knife deep into the man's throat, and sliced it sideways.

A fountain of blood gushed from the gaping wound. The man's head wrenched away from Solomon's hand. His mouth had opened wide but only a bubbling sound came out. The knife had left him nothing to yell with. But his body heaved, his arms beat the ground, his legs jerked and kicked. Even without a voice, he was making too much noise. Solomon threw himself on top of the dying man, trying to hold him still. His weight was not sufficient, and he was flung about like a doll. But he did not let go of the knife.

Across the campsite, beyond the body of his mother, a man began to curse sleepily.

Another laughed: "Who is having a nightmare?"

Solomon managed to get all of his weight across the leg to which he was bound, holding it down long enough to reach the rawhide thong connecting their ankles. He cut himself free with the dying man's bloody knife.

A figure was rising from the ground on the other side of the fire's ashes, but Solomon decided to make his break. Staying low, he scuttled away on all fours like a frightened crab. He had planned his escape route earlier, when the light of the campfire had been high. He was out of the camp and down inside a gully when a man somewhere behind him shouted. With the gully's sides concealing him, he leaped to his feet and ran as fast as he could.

He didn't throw the knife away. It was his now, won in combat, still dripping the blood of the man who had raped him. Through the rest of that night he ran, and when dawn came he found a hiding place. He waited out the day. Sometimes he slept. But he never let go of his weapon, ready, if cornered, to use it again.

* * *

Three days later, he was alone under the sun in the middle of a stony, treeless, waterless wasteland, dying of thirst and heat. He crept across the burning rocks to a thin patch of shade beside a boulder. There he curled up, the last of his strength gone, and waited for his death.

How long he waited for it he could not know. Fingers prying his mouth open brought him back to consciousness. Lips pressed down on his. Water trickled between his teeth. Solomon swallowed it, made a croaking noise. More water ran into his mouth and he swallowed again.

The fingers let go of his mouth. The lips were gone from his. Solomon forced his eyes open. Through a blur he made out a thin, bearded face, looking down at him with concerned eyes. The man picked up a goatskin water bag, filled his mouth from it. Then he bent down again and let more water run into the boy's mouth. Solomon drank, then began coughing. Struggling to sit up against the boulder, he fumbled at his waist.

"It is still there," the bearded man said quietly.

Solomon's hand found the hilt of the knife he'd thrust through his belt, its wicked blade still stained with dried blood. He relaxed, reassured by its feel and the man's voice. The man was Armenian.

Solomon reached for the water bag. The man gave it to him. He watched the boy gulp from it for a few seconds before taking it away. "More later," he said, corking the bag.

For several hours the man carried the little boy southward. Once he stopped to rest, letting Solomon drink again and sharing with him from his small bag of dried meat. That night they ate and drank again, and while the boy lay half asleep beside him, the man talked about himself.

His name was Osadour, and he'd been a shoemaker in a Turkish village similar to Solomon Azrealian's. But when soldiers tried to round up Armenians there, Osadour had escaped to the hills and hidden there, waiting and watching. He was the only adult Armenian man of that village to survive the day of slaughter. The next day, when the soldiers had begun the death march of Armenian women and children, Osadour had started trailing them. His own wife and twin daughters were among them.

For over a week he had followed, spying on the straggling column when he could, waiting for a night when he could sneak close enough to get his wife and children away. The opportunity never came. At one point he was forced to detour to a nearby village and wait until late at night to steal food. After that, it had taken him two days to catch up with the death marchers. His wife and twins were no longer among them. He'd backtracked and found their bodies.

Since then Osadour hated himself for not dying with them. And he cursed God for it. But no more: now he glimpsed the truth. He had been kept alive so that he might find and save little Solomon. God's ways were peculiar, but there it was. Solomon was given to him as his new child; he was now the boy's father.

The next day Solomon was strong enough to walk. They hiked south together, and that night the boy told Osadour his own story. Two days later they were out of food and water and had to sneak into a town at night to steal. Osadour carried a club ready, in case they were discovered. Solomon had his knife. But Osadour was learning to be a cunning thief, and they were not detected. They slipped out of the town with a quantity of salted mutton, their water bag refilled. Then they continued south, dodging troops and police and marauding tribesmen.

It took them almost two months to reach the coast of the eastern Mediterranean, another week to get to the nearest seaport. Osadour reconnoitered for three successive nights until he discovered a way to smuggle them aboard a freighter.

Its destination was Lebanon.

* * *

Beirut, as the capital of Lebanon, was always a crowded, bustling city, and its citizens always preferred being out in the streets to staying inside. Twenty-one-year-old Solomon Azrealian heard the sounds of his city as he sat on a hard stool indoors, his wrists handcuffed behind him, his eyes

76

fixed on a cop sitting behind a scarred desk.

The cop had an opened dossier on the desk in front of him, but he seldom had to consult it. "You've had an interesting career for a young man." He flicked the open dossier with a manicured and tinted fingernail. "Beginning at the age of fourteen, pimping for your mother."

"She wasn't my real mother." Solomon spoke perfect Arabic and French, and had begun picking up some English and German. An international business center like Beirut was educational, if you wanted to learn. "She was just an Armenian woman who lost her real family in Turkey. It made her feel good, having a kid to take care of again. So I moved in with her."

"Along with your father." The cop raised his hand to stop Solomon from speaking. "I know, Osadour was not your real father. No matter. The woman was a whore, and you were her pimp."

"It was the only way she could make a living. There were no jobs when she got here. Beirut was overcrowded—"

"With Armenian refugees," the cop pointed out. "Not all of whom found it necessary to become whores like your mo— your foster mother."

"You should have some respect for the dead. Especially you, a cop. It's been four years since one of her clients killed her. Four years. If the police ever caught the man, I haven't heard about it."

"We are not one hundred percent efficient. No police force can be."

The cop who killed Osadour was very efficient," Solomon said. "He shot him four times to make sure."

"That was his duty. Osadour was breaking into a shop."

"But not carrying a gun. He never did."

The cop frowned a little, glanced at Solomon's dossier, idly turned a few pages. "Our record is not the point. Yours is. You've been arrested quite often, haven't you? A somewhat strange history. Pimping for other prostitutes after your mother's death. Working with the gang of thieves your father joined. Running your own gang of teenage thieves and pimps after Osadour died. You even became part owner of an illegal brothel. It surprises me you were able to amass the kind of money required to buy into so prosperous an establishment. Nine arrests in all. And you were let go each time. It is not clear why from these records."

Solomon began to feel better. The cop knew why. This supposed interrogation was edging towards a game they both knew how to play. In the Middle East the approach to giving or taking bribes is seldom blatant. It doesn't have to be. Any approach at all is quickly understood.

The cop closed the dossier. "Well, I'm afraid your career in crime is about to come to its abrupt end." He touched a finger to the knife lying on his desk beside the dossier. It was the one Solomon had taken from the Kurd years ago. Now you've murdered a boy your own age. You'll find this charge less easy to slip out of than the previous ones."

"You don't have enough proof."

"I have the information. Proof will follow. Within a few days at most, or I'm very mistaken."

Solomon looked at the large, golden cross hanging on the cop's chest, inside his unbuttoned shirt. "You're a Christian."

"Yes. So?"

"I'm a Christian, too. The one you claim I killed, he was the leader of a Moslem gang. They tried to take our territory away from us. We fought. If he got killed in the fight, I don't know about it, but it wasn't murder. It would be self-defense."

"I am a Christian," the cop said flatly, "but I am also a police officer. And I believe that you're guilty of murder."

"Police officers are notoriously underpaid. I'm sure you are sorry you cannot afford to make a large contribution to your church. It would be a godly act."

The cop smiled, just a little. "You speak, I think, of forgiveness for sins, in the case of persons who give assistance to the Church. It has been done, certainly, for centuries. How large a contribution do you mean?"

"I have some money saved. All converted into American dollars."

"How many dollars?"

"Six hundred."

An hour later Solomon Azrealian got a metal box out of its hiding place in the basement of the building where he lived and handed it to the cop. It contained exactly six hundred dollars.

"You have two days to get out of Beirut," said the cop, after confirming that the amount was correct. "Don't come back."

"Can I have my knife?"

"No. I will keep it. Evidence, should you fail to go away."

Solomon shrugged. He'd had that knife a long time, but any sentimentality that had existed in his original soul had long since been scrubbed out.

After parting from the cop, he went to the basement of another building and removed another metal box he'd hidden. This one contained well over two thousand American dollars. That night he used a little of it to buy a passage to Germany from the captain of a cargo vessel in the Beirut harbor. Then he went to one of the forgers who worked in small rooms close to the port area and bought a German visa.

The ship left early the next morning. Destination: Hamburg. Standing out on the open deck as the freighter cleared the breakwater, Solomon watched the dawn and decided that when he reached Hamburg he would buy himself a full set of new identity papers. The time had come, he felt, to make a clean break with his past. It wouldn't be the last time.

* * *

Entering the Berlin railroad station, Solomon purchased tickets entitling him to a first class sleeper compartment on the night train to Vienna. He paid with a check, showing his passport to confirm his signature. According to the passport, his name was Samuel Anzer, born in Hungary but now a naturalized citizen of Germany. Occupation: salesman.

He was twenty-six, had lived in Berlin for more than three years, and spoke German like a native. But the suit he wore when he boarded the night train was British, tailored for him by Saville Row's John & Pegg. He had made several trips to London over the past year to improve his grasp of the English language, test the business waters, and acquire potentially useful friends. In England he was known by another name, as a Russian refugee with a distinguished family background calculated to make him a fit companion for members of the British upper classes. Naturally, Solomon had an alternate set of papers to support this identity.

So far he had used those papers only on his visits to England, in establishing a Swiss convenience address and bank account, and for several business deals he'd concluded outside Germany. When not in use, they were kept hidden in an attic wall of the elegant, discreet little nightclub and brothel Solomon owned in Berlin.

A sleeper attendant entered his compartment to make up the bed. Solomon ordered a large bottle of mineral water and told the man to wake him half an hour before they arrived in Vienna. As the train left Berlin behind, he settled back to review, once again, what he planned to accomplish in the Austrian capital.

His trip had two unrelated purposes. One was business. The other was personal: he intended to kill a man he had never met.

The business in Vienna concerned a sideline that had grown out of his smuggling operation and now seemed likely to outgrow it. The new economic policy of the Nazi government embraced economic independence and had radically curtailed the import of many goods. Thus, smuggling on a major scale had served Solomon well. But now he was considering giving up this business entirely to concentrate on the sideline. Arms dealing had an even higher profit margin than smuggling, and it involved less risk.

But if he did get out of the black market, he decided, he would keep his nightclub and brothel. Conveniently located in the same building, they would prove as useful in the new business as they had in the old. The nightclub and brothel provided the perfect place to spot the weaknesses of government functionaries, military officers and visiting businessmen. Solomon had developed his talent for encouraging other men's flaws to surface. As an aid to exploiting their weaknesses, he had installed some two-way mirrors in the brothel and retained a skillful photographer.

During trips for his black market enterprise, Solomon became aware that great quantities of arms and ammunition, left over from World War I, were rusting away in warehouses all over Europe. For the most part, no European country intended to use these supplies again. They were just taking up valuable storage space. To acquire this unwanted surplus cheaply only required bribing or coercing the right government ministers and generals. Solomon's purchases had increased as he discovered how much he could get for the surplus—from rebel movements in Africa, the Middle East,

Latin America.

Rebel groups, he had discovered, were the best possible kind of customers. Often unable to obtain arms through normal channels, they would pay the highest price for anything they could get—including obsolete materiel nobody else wanted. But gunrunning to rebels was only the first part of a three-stage operation which Solomon pioneered and which other dealers have copied since.

When a group of rebels ran out of funds to buy any more arms, he would inform the government they intended to overthrow of what he had sold them. Alarmed by how heavily armed the rebels had become, this government would buy more of his weapons and ammunition to launch an anti-guerrilla campaign. Sometimes this resulted in a full-scale civil war. When the carnage was over—and either the government had fallen or the rebel army had been wiped out—the victor was left with surplus arms of its own. Solomon then bought these weapons back, cheaply, and began the same process over again, elsewhere.

Some miles outside Vienna, he had learned recently, were eleven government warehouses crammed with World War I surplus ranging from old tanks to bayonets. Solomon believed he knew just the man to see about this opportunity, an officer in the Austrian War Ministry.

The train sped south across a night-shrouded Germany. Solomon changed into his pajamas and stretched out on the bed. But before switching off the compartment lights, he devoted a few minutes to the details of his personal reason for this trip to Vienna.

It had cropped up unexpectedly. But that it had cropped up in Berlin was not surprising. Berlin was no longer the capital of sin that it had been when Solomon had first arrived, which had made it a perfect place for him to find his feet in Europe. But it was still a major center for political intrigue.

One minor rebel group with Berlin headquarters was made up of Armenian hotheads secretly dedicated to vengeance against the Turks. Since their most famous attack, the assassination of a former Turkish government leader on the streets of Berlin, Nazis had forced the group further underground. The new Nazi government was anxious for international recognition and could not—yet—afford diplomatic entanglements. Solomon sometimes helped this Armenian band with small sums of cash, never letting them know that he, too, was Armenian. He explained that his contributions came out of a certain humane sympathy with their cause. But this contact also had its practical side. It helped Solomon to keep in touch with what was going on in Germany's political underworld.

Yesterday it had brought him a different kind of information. He learned from the group that a former Turkish army officer—one of those who had directed the "march to nowhere"—had recently joined the Turkish embassy in Vienna.

It had become Solomon's custom in Berlin, because of the dangerous milieu in which he moved, to wear a small pistol concealed under his jacket. In addition, he usually carried an elegant, silver-headed cane which was heavier than it looked: it was filled with lead. Both came with him on the night train to Vienna.

* * *

Two mornings later Solomon boarded a train which would carry him back to Berlin. He settled into his compartment and opened a newspaper he had bought in the Vienna railroad station. It contained no mention at all of the arms purchase he had concluded with the government, not even on the financial pages. Solomon hadn't expected it would.

The front page headline story concerned the brutal murder of a Turkish diplomat early the previous night. He had been last seen alive when leaving a Viennese coffee house where it had become his habit to relax every evening before going to dinner. His body had been discovered two hours later in an alley half a block away. The diplomat had been beaten to death with repeated blows administered with some heavy instrument. Since his wallet, rings and watch were missing, it was assumed that he had been attacked by a particularly vicious robber. Police were investigating among the lower criminals of Vienna.

Solomon folded the paper, put it aside, and rested a hand on the elegant, silver handle of his lead-weighted cane.

* * *

The suburbs of Vienna streamed backward past his compartment windows. He stared through the windows without seeing, planning the details of his next moves. The time for another complete break with the past was approaching faster than he'd anticipated.

This had become clear to him after concluding the Austrian deal yesterday afternoon. He had used his alternate identity, as he had for previous arms deals. This one was his biggest so far and would certainly lead to others even bigger. For legitimate operations on a large scale, he was going to need a more permanent business base than a Swiss bank and convenience address.

He would have to avoid Berlin for the next few years, giving his present identity there time to die. And Nazi Germany was no longer a suitable place for an arms dealer of allegedly Hungarian extraction and a Jewish sounding name. London was the logical choice for his new base. England had a solid economy and government, and he had never used his Samuel Anzer identity there. In London he was known only as Solomon Alexandre.

One month later, he dropped his Samuel Anzer identity into the English Channel as he made the crossing. The identity had served him well, like the German black market and the knife he'd taken from the Kurdish tribesman. But a new line of business called for new weapons.

He didn't laugh at his choice of words in forming that thought.

He never laughed.

Chapter Seven

Sir Solomon Alexandre, Part II

"You told me that Berlin house was *safe*," Lord Henry Dausse reminded him. He kept his voice low, but it was charged with anxiety and indignation. "Safe and discreet, you said."

"I've always had every reason to think it was," Solomon Alexandre replied.

"Well you were wrong! And I'm the one getting hurt by your mistake!" When Lord Henry's blood pressure mounted, his plump cheeks, normally pink, became bright red. He was several years younger than Solomon Alexandre. His wealth and title were inherited, but he'd built his reputation as a loveable, dissolute rake by himself. He'd first met Alexandre while on one of his pleasure-seeking tours of the continent. The chance acquaintance had ripened as Lord Henry found the man an enjoyable companion and a knowledgeable guide to some of the more excitingly kinky private establishments.

"The amount of money the blackmailer is demanding," he told Alexandre, "is simply ridiculous. And suppose he holds on to some of the pictures? Goes on blackmailing me forever?"

"Don't pay him," Alexandre advised flatly.

"Don't *pay*? Easy enough for you to say. My God, man, just look at these pictures." Lord Henry took a brown envelope from his pocket, then hesitated and looked anxiously around the clubroom. It was called the Green Room, for some reason. Its walls and carpet were dingy brown, as were most of the solid old armchairs and sofas. One of the oldest gentlemen's clubs in London, it was Lord Henry's favorite. He had proposed Solomon Alexandre for membership just two days before.

The only other member in the room at this time was asleep in a wing chair near the fire at the other end. The waiter who had brought their brandies had left. Reassured, Lord Henry handed over the brown envelope.

Solomon opened it. There were eight photographs: the ones he had chosen from a selection of twenty his photographer had shot. The first showed Lord Henry grovelling under the boots of a buxom young prostitute. He was naked and she wore nothing but the boots. In the remaining photos, they were doing sundry things to each other, none of which most people would consider normal. Lord Henry's face was clearly identifiable in each picture. Solomon slid the photographs back into the envelope.

"Most embarrassing," he said.

"Embarrassing? Is that all you have to say?" Lord Henry's gaze was hurt and accusing. "You do have some responsibility in this, you know. After all, it *was* you who steered me to that filthy place."

Solomon Alexandre nodded. "And I accept that responsibility. You can stop worrying, Henry. I know certain extremely unpleasant gentlemen in Berlin. I'll see to it they get every picture that was taken of you. Including the negatives."

"But—how can we be sure the blackmailer doesn't keep

substitutes of some negatives?"

"I told you—these gentlemen I know can be unpleasant. The blackmailer will withhold nothing. *All* of the photographs and negatives will be in your hands within the week."

Lord Henry's cheeks began to regain their normal color. "That's—awfully decent of you, Solly. Ummm . . . how much do you reckon your unpleasant friends will charge me for—ah—their services."

"They are not friends," Solomon said stiffly. "Merely useful contacts."

"I'm sorry, I didn't mean to imply—"

"They will charge you nothing. I will pay them."

"But—that's completely unnecessary, Solly. I do have sufficient funds, after all."

Solomon Alexandre detested being called Solly. But it was too early in his rise to show it to someone of Lord Henry's unearned but formidable eminence. His expression remained that of a concerned friend in need: "You did point out my responsibility in this matter. I have accepted that responsibility and I will pay whatever is required to discharge it. Between gentlemen, Henry, I think that enough has been said on the subject. I will take care of everything."

He fashioned a modest smile and lightened his tone: "And now, I do believe it's time for us to order more brandy."

Lord Henry's eyes became damp, but he managed to stop himself short of actually crying. "I will be forever obliged to you, Solly."

Solomon Alexandre was certain he would be. He intended to see to it. Several of the juiciest photographs he'd had taken of Lord Henry in Berlin would remain in his Swiss bank vault, just in case the stupid young rake ever considered forgetting his obligation any time in the future.

Lord Henry's gratitude would be of a practical nature. Not in cash, but in social and business advances. Lord Henry had the ear of several members of the royal family. His inherited holdings included choice areas of London real estate and a sizeable amount of stock in a number of international companies, including—though probably the fool didn't know it—the British arms firm Solomon Alexandre represented abroad.

Alexandre represented a number of arms firms in other countries as well. Some years ago the nations of Europe, smelling another war approaching, had begun gearing up for it with new weaponry. This left them with a surplus of old weaponry. Solomon Alexandre bought all the old stock he could get. His success in selling it to what are now called Third World nations had caught the interest of the big arms manufacturers: giants like Krupp of Germany, Vickers of Great Britain, Bethlehem Steel of America, Schneider of France. They began making him offers to act as their salesman abroad. He accepted the best offers and now sold their new arms while continuing with his own surplus dealings.

He consistently beat out rival salesmen. One reason was that they hadn't yet caught on to something he'd learned long ago as a teenager. Bribery was considered a crime in Europe and North America. But for the rest of the world it was an accepted part of life.

The other reason was that in every country he visited, Solomon Alexandre hired police detectives to moonlight for him. These men formed a private spy network, which he referred to as his security department. Its function was to find out which officials could most influence what their countries purchased—and then the extent of each man's need and greed, plus any special vulnerability which could be exploited. Armed with this intelligence, Solomon Alexandre charmed and bribed, and blackmailed where necessary.

The arms makers he represented were doing very well through him. And he was doing very well through them: via the flat representation fee he charged each, plus percentage bonuses on sales he concluded. He also now owned shares in each of these firms.

At times he considered making a concentrated effort to gain control of one of them. But he was holding off on that. First of all, he was convinced that in the future the biggest profits in arms would go, not to their manufacturers, but to those who acted as middlemen between makers and buyers. Secondly, a manufacturing company could be ruined in a disaster to its country, such as defeat in war. A middleman need not be hurt by such a disaster unless he'd been foolish enough to invest his own money in anything that did not bring a very quick return.

The sole incentive to acquiring control of a manufacturing company would be that it would increase his profit from deals he worked out for it. But Solomon Alexandre had decided to wait on that until after the new global war was brewing. In the meantime, he would continue to grow stronger through his present methods of operation. He had the arms makers coming to him hat in hand now. Along with a number of governments.

Solomon Alexandre was becoming a rich and powerful man. His wealth did not come only from his considerable above-the-table income in fees, bonuses and shares. There was also the double contract system he had developed. It worked like this:

If an arms firm he represented sold machine guns for three hundred dollars apiece, Solomon Alexandre informed the company that bribes amounting to twenty dollars per gun would have to be paid to certain officials of the purchasing government to close the sale. The company added this extra twenty dollars per item to its contract, listed as a legitimate expense for "consultation fees." Solomon slipped half of the extra twenty dollars to the officials and pocketed the other half.

The second contract was the one the corrupted officials turned over to their government. It listed the price of each machine gun as four hundred dollars. Half of the extra eighty dollars paid by their government was kept by these officials; the other half they turned over to Solomon Alexandre. In this way he got a secret rake-off from both ends of every deal.

In time, almost every arms go-between would be using his system of double contracts. The sharpest of them were to become billionaires after the end of World War II.

Lord Henry, smiling happily, raised his glass of brandy and offered a toast before gulping it down. "Here's to you, Solly."

Solomon Alexandre took a small sip from his own glass and smiled back.

* * *

In June of 1962, Solomon Alexandre sat down at the conference table of a soundproofed room inside the Pentagon. There were only two other men present, seated across the table from him. One was General Brady, a military attorney specializing in contract negotiations for the Defense Department. The other was a close friend of the President of the United States, and one of his key advisors on foreign affairs.

"Sir Solomon," General Brady said, "before we get down to the matter at hand, I'd just like to say I'm real pleased to finally meet you in person."

"The pleasure is mutual, General." Solomon Alexandre

reflected that his knighthood was worth everything it cost him.

It had cost him plenty. He'd had to squeeze every last drop of Lord Henry's obligation to him—and also gain the obligation of other men who could apply discreet pressure at the highest level, the same men who had helped to get him a position with good political leverage in the British War Department during World War II. He also had to bribe members of the British press, as well as buy a newspaper of his own, to insure frequent mention of his valuable contributions to the war effort.

But it had been worth every penny. The knighthood gained him an extra prestige, the kind of prestige that could be translated into increased profits. It enhanced his effectiveness in dealing with other nations as well as in Great Britain. The supposedly classless Americans were more impressed than most by titles.

"By the way," the President's advisor said, "tomorrow evening the President is having a small gathering at the White House. The British ambassador will be attending. The President would be happy if you could, too."

The invitation did not surprise Sir Solomon Alexandre. Heads of state had to deal respectfully with the head of a global arms empire that was growing at the accelerative rate his had achieved. The world climate had become conducive to such gigantic growth since the end of the war for two chief reasons.

First of all, in order to cope with the Cold War, the governments of North America, Europe, and the Soviet bloc were doing everything possible to stimulate their arms industries. Sales of arms abroad aided this stimulation, as well as provided an increasing source of revenue from abroad, and a means for exerting political leverage in foreign countries.

Secondly, there were all those emerging Third World countries, many with tremendous funds from oil, eager to buy endless quantities of expensive modern weapons with which they could insure their independence, prove their manhood, fight each other, and crush any new internal freedom movements.

In some cases both the Soviet Union and the United States were prepared to give certain of these Third World nations what they wanted, as a gift, in return for political cooperation. The United States had recently attempted to make one such deal without using a private middleman and the results were embarrassing. Solomon Alexandre had come to the Pentagon on this warm June afternoon to teach the United States the facts of life.

"Please tell the President," he said, "that I would be honored to attend, if I am still in Washington tomorrow. That will depend on the result of this meeting."

"In that case—" the President's advisor said.

"Let me summarize the situation briefly," Alexandre interrupted smoothly. "Malaya wants more modern tanks. It is also sliding rapidly into the communist sphere of influence. To stop this slide, you one month ago offered to supply the tanks at a cut rate. With payment over two decades, which in practical terms means never. They turned you down.

"I still don't understand why," General Brady growled. "Those crazy gook governments ..."

Alexandre knew why. A straight government-to-government deal meant no private kickbacks to relatives, friends and advisors of the Paramount Ruler. But he didn't say that. What he said was:

"Malaya is afraid that if it gets the tanks directly from you it will offend the communists. One week ago I was invited to Kuala Lumpur to discuss the problem with Malayan military leaders in an advisory capacity. The results are positive for you, I believe. If you sell the tanks to *me*, Malaya will buy them from me. That way the communists won't be able to charge the Malayan government with making some secret political arrangement with America.

"Of course," he added, "the tanks would still be American, which would inevitably establish certain mutual interests between you and Malaya. I believe you would prefer this small compromise to letting Malaya get the tanks from Russia."

General Brady scowled over it, and turned to the President's advisor. "It's crazy, but if it's the only way to do the deal with the Malayans, and if the President really wants the deal that bad . . ."

"I'm sure he must," Alexandre put in blandly, "considering that Malaya is the world's largest source of natural rubber."

The general smiled crookedly: "In addition to being the world's biggest exporter of condoms—which God knows we can't get along without."

Alexandre made a mental note to have his intelligence department bring its dossier on General Brady up to date with more detailed information on his finances and personal life. Brady had a touch of irreverence in his approach to serious matters that could indicate that, if approached carefully concerning his private needs, he might prove susceptible to discreet manipulation at some future stage.

"Before we can begin to consider your proposition," the President's advisor was saying solemnly, "we would have to be positive that you could really pull it off."

"I can have my authorization from the Malayan government on your desk within the hour."

"Thank you, Sir Solomon. You do realize I will have to

confer with the President before we go much deeper into this discussion."

"Certainly. But have your talk with him before tomorrow morning. If he accepts my proposal, I would stay a couple more days to work out the details. But if my arrangement is a problem for you, I'll have to try elsewhere. And immediately. Germany has expressed interest in supplying Malaya with Krauss Maffei's new Leopard—which is on par with your Chrysler-made tank."

The President's advisor gave him an awkward smile. "And which would leave us out in the cold."

"Yes."

General Brady made an exasperated noise. "It's still insane. We offer to practically *give* the Malayans the tanks, but they'd rather pay big money for them. Out of curiosity, Sir Solomon, you sure they've got enough ready cash to pay you for them?"

Alexandre looked at the President's advisor. "The Malayan government hopes," he said pointedly, "that the United States will help them out with a loan. Quietly."

"This may be getting too complicated, Sir Solomon."

He shrugged. "That is between you and the President to decide. Between you and myself there is still the uncomplicated matter of the price I can pay for your tanks."

"Those babies," General Brady told him darkly, "retail for a million and a half bucks apiece."

"I can pay you one million each."

"Hell, that wouldn't even reimburse what we had to pay Chrysler to develop those tanks!"

Alexandre knew that. He'd had a talk with the general manager of Chrysler's Defense Division the previous evening. "You were ready to give the tanks away," he reminded Brady. "You would have had to pay the company *all* of it out of your taxpayers' pockets. This way you only have to come up with one third the cost. I contribute the other two thirds. A considerable saving, in the end, for your taxpayers."

Solomon Alexandre's agreement with Malaya was that it would pay him the full million and a half for each tank. The order was for two hundred tanks: a total profit of one hundred million dollars for the entire order.

The President's advisor prepared to stand up. "I'll call you as soon as I've discussed it with the President."

"There is one other small condition," Alexandre informed him. "Chrysler is not acceptable to me as the company supplying the tanks."

General Brady eyed him with weary cynicism: "I guess you have another firm in mind?"

"Yes." Alexandre named the company. It was in California, one of the American firms in which he'd been quietly buying up controlling interest.

"That company," the general objected, "hasn't even finished tooling up to produce a tank of that quality. Could be years before it's turning them out in quantity."

"Perhaps," Solomon Alexandre suggested, "your government will consider giving it financial assistance to do so more quickly."

He was back in his suite at Washington's Hay-Adams Hotel, having dinner with two of his chief aides, when the President's advisor phoned:

"Okay, Sir Solomon, you've got a deal."

"I thought I might."

* * *

Two of his strongest competitors were Arab arms dealers: Adnan Khashoggi of Saudi Arabia and Ahmed al-Zadar from the emirates along the southwest coast of the Persian Gulf. But sometimes rivals cooperated when it was to their mutual advantage. By that time Alexandre was no longer merely a powerful man: he was emperor of a multinational conglomerate, with control over a large combination of companies that were each powerful in their own right. But al-Zadar was an equal power, and Alexandre scheduled a meeting with him in Monte Carlo.

The discussion between them bore some resemblance to people playing a game of Monopoly: "I'll trade you Park Place and fifty million for Boardwalk." In this case the pieces in the game were Greece, Turkey and four North African countries—the real ones, not Monopoly fabrications. Al-Zadar had a virtual lock on arms deals with the North Africans. Alexandre had Greece pretty much sewed up. They both dealt with Turkey. Alexandre had no lingering dislike of doing business with the Turks; he had discharged his last vestige of vengeful anger with the murder in Vienna long ago.

Greece and Turkey were both NATO members. They were also ancient enemies. Their enmity sometimes got too hot for other NATO countries, which would then feel forced by public opinion to stop sending them more arms for awhile. Each time this happened, the Soviet bloc offered to supply whatever Greece and Turkey wanted—with strings. To counter this, Western nations then took the only practical option left. They sold the arms to Alexandre and al-Zadar— with the condition that none of them be resold to a list of countries which included Greece and Turkey. Of course, the two dealers then sold the arms to Greece and Turkey, and the countries who were the original suppliers looked the other way.

That is the final reason for the meteoric rise of private

arms dealers since World War II. Private dealers help respectable governments to do what they want to do without getting caught at it.

Solomon Alexandre had three Greek generals ready to secretly sell off a large part of their country's most up-to-date NATO-supplied arms—a bit at a time over the coming years, so the loss would not be noticed before they became rich. Payment to them was to be put into numbered accounts they'd set up for themselves in Switzerland. The price they asked was ridiculously small considering the quantity and quality of arms involved. But each general would have millions of dollars waiting for him outside Greece when the time came for him to leave.

Ahmed al-Zadar's North African countries were ready to buy Greek arms without questioning the source. Al-Zadar agreed to share equally in the payment to the generals and also share equally with Alexandre the profits from the North African sales.

That was the first stage of the game. The second would begin when Alexandre informed Greece that Turkish officials had learned it was critically short of modern arms. That would frighten the Greeks into replenishing their stocks. The Turks, not knowing the reason for these big, new purchases, would be alarmed into matching them with new purchases of their own. Then the new Greek arms could be once again siphoned off to North Africa. The process could be repeated regularly.

The discussion between Alexandre and al-Zadar ended in complete agreement. Each went off to carry out his part in getting the scheme under way. It was to work without a hitch for twelve years—until it resulted in the Cyprus War, an eventuality unforeseen by most and devastating for the people of Cyprus, but not unwelcome to the arms dealing fraternity.

* * *

That, then, was the story of Solomon Alexandre's career, in itself a pocket history of the arms business and a glimpse into how our world got into its present, fragile state.

Chapter Eight

Garson

In California after that first summer in France, I returned to the same school and the same beaches, but not to quite the same old Garson Bishop.

At school the change was a minor one. I figured I was going to wind up working for my father; he was in France and so was Victoria, so I switched my compulsory foreign language course from Spanish to French. As it turned out, I needn't have bothered.

As for the change in my free-time activities, Stuart Peel, with his distaste for California morals, would have considered it an improvement. I wasn't sure I did. No shortage in the female population had occurred in my absence, and I hadn't turned into a monk. But I became more selective. It proved to be a surly discipline and the results were frustrating. I knew I'd never find anyone like Victoria, even a younger version with the potential. But at least I wanted something with more emotional content than eating a good pizza.

I didn't find it; and the next summer I was back to France, my father, and the arms plant. And Victoria. But things had changed there, too—and this time the change was not inside me.

Garson

* * *

I got out my motorbike and went over to the château my first day back. Sebastiani was still there as watchdog, but it turned out that Victoria wasn't using him as a chauffeur much. Most of the time she drove herself wherever she wanted to go, in the Mercedes. He was the first one I met, climbing off my bike, and he shook my hand as though he was genuinely pleased to see me again. I wasn't irritated by the way he watched me go up the steps to Victoria. He wasn't a bad guy, just somebody earning his living, doing what he was hired to do.

Alan wasn't due to come down from his Swiss school for another two weeks, so I had Victoria to myself that afternoon. She didn't seem different from the Victoria of the previous summer, before her husband had spoiled it. She looked me over and echoed my thought:

"Well, you're the same young man I remember. Thank goodness."

"I'm a year older."

She laughed. "So am I. Does it show?"

"Not that I can see."

"And you still look and act much older than you are. It's disconcerting at times." She hugged and kissed me, and I was happy I was back.

She seemed her old self when she showed me around the place, enthusiastically pointing out all the restoration work she'd accomplished between summers, both inside the château and then out on the grounds surrounding it. I noticed one difference in Victoria. She carried a large glass of iced vodka with her, taking regular sips as we walked along. By the time we completed our inspection tour, her glass was empty. She went back inside and refilled it: a little ice, a lot of vodka.

But she'd been drinking the previous summer, too. It still didn't seem to affect her. She remained vibrantly alive, full of warm humor, superbly attractive. So that first visit to the château the change wasn't obvious.

Changes at the plant were, however. I returned to working as an apprentice, taking up my weaponry education where I'd left off, but my father no longer did any work on his own project there. He didn't even keep any of his designs around the workshop anymore, nor in his room, either.

"I've got everything in a garage I rented in Exideuil," he told me, and since it was my first night back, we went out to a nearby restaurant to take a look at it. "After the summer, I'll go back to California and start working on it again. I'll be joining you there a couple weeks after you go back."

"How come?"

"My contract with Alexandre's up then. I'm quitting."

The news hit hard. I might never see Victoria again. "I thought this was a good job."

"I thought it was, too." Then he explained that the man he had replaced had dropped by the plant for a visit last March —a retired French Army colonel named Paul Rambert. An old school officer from a military family. He'd served in the second World War, Indo-China and then Algeria. He got torn up pretty badly by a bomb, though, and got his medical discharge. "Rambert's maybe the best weaponry specialist I've ever met," my father said.

"I still don't get why you're quitting here," I said, impatient for him to get to the point.

"Rambert was just like me," my father told me. "Worked on an invention of his own while he ran the plant. Then when he had it ready and tried to market it, Alexandre sued him for breach of contract." Then he explained that according to some legal fine print, all work completed during the term of the contract was for Alexandre. Rambert had interpreted this clause to mean that he wasn't allowed to work for another company at the same time. He didn't figure it applied to an independent project that he was working on for himself and on his own time. Alexandre's lawyer claimed that any work Rambert did while under contract belonged to his boss, and he won the suit. "Alexandre got the invention without having to pay Rambert a penny," said my father.

"And your contract has the same clause?"

My father nodded. "Only I'm not going to get caught in the same trap, thanks to Rambert. I won't touch my invention again until the contract's expired. And I won't be marketing it for a long time."

He gave me the rest of the story over dinner. "Rambert's working on something new. A compact assault rifle. It's a big improvement over the American M16 and *could* outclass the Russian AK-47. I showed him what I've been working on and he's hot for it. He's coming to California with me. We're going to team up, equal partners. He's got his Army pension and has inherited some cash, too. And I've got my pension and I'm saving everything I can from this job. We'll put everything into the pot to develop both weapons. Whichever we get ready first, we go with."

He gave me a squinty little smile. "We'll need a good assistant. I told Rambert I think you're ready to handle the job. Part-time until you finish that last year of high school. Full-time after that.

I grinned and felt a little better. I was disappointed that we wouldn't be working together on the rocket launcher that summer. But I figured there was a compensation. That summer, I'd have all my evenings and weekends free to visit Victoria.

But when I called the château four days later, after waiting for an invitation and not getting one, she wasn't there. She'd taken a plane south to spend a week by herself on the Riviera.

* * *

She came back two days before her son was scheduled to arrive and one day before my seventeenth birthday, so she was able to make my birthday dinner in Perigueux a threesome. Victoria was cheerful enough during that dinner. But some of it was forced. She was distracted by something; her mind was in another sphere than our conversations. Each time she spoke, it took an effort to wrench herself out of whatever was bothering her.

"That little lady has troubles," my father said afterwards.

"She's got one trouble," I told him. "Her husband. I don't understand why she doesn't just divorce him and get it over with."

"Maybe he doesn't want a divorce."

"Could he stop her from getting one? I think she's just too scared of him to do it."

"Well, look at what he did to Paul Rambert. When Solomon Alexandre is sore at you, it's dumb not to be scared. And dumb is one thing that lady is not."

After Alan came back, the pleasant times I remembered from the year before seemed to return. I was invited all the time to the château. The three of us took our swims in the pool, played cards under the shade trees, had our dinners together. Alan came around to the plant for more target practice. Victoria drove us off in the Mercedes for picnics in the mountains. She continued to drink too much, but it still didn't show. My feelings for her kept getting stronger. Some nights at the château, I had trouble getting to sleep, thinking about her in the next room.

Then, two weeks after Alan's arrival, I was invited for the weekend and found myself spending it with Alan, alone. Victoria had flown off to the Riviera again. Which left me to keep Alan busy all weekend. I liked the kid fine, but he wasn't Victoria and I didn't want to play baby-sitter if I didn't even get to see her. But the next weekend she drove Alan and me all the way to the big harbor city of Bordeaux to see a travelling circus that was playing there.

It was a long drive, so Victoria booked the three of us into the best hotel in Bordeaux overnight. Alan and I shared a twin-bedded room. Victoria's room was on another floor. I found myself speculating why.

After we'd checked in that afternoon, the three of us went out to look over the city until evening. First we headed into the waterfront area. But it had too many sinister bars for Victoria; the rough characters hanging around outside them eyed her in a way that got too uncomfortable. We found another area to walk in until dinner time.

We were finishing the dinner when Victoria announced that she was getting a bad headache. "I hope you don't mind too much, going to the circus without me."

"You bought three tickets," Alan said. "What'll we do with yours?"

"Give it to someone. I'm sorry, Alan, I just don't feel up to going."

We went without her, and the circus was okay. A friendly old man ended up in her seat next to us, pleased to have gotten in without paying. At first we'd tried to give the ticket to a good looking girl in her teens. But a very tough character who turned out to be her pimp snarled at us to let her go on with her work. Bordeaux seemed to have a lot like him.

When we got back to the hotel, there was a note for us

from Victoria: "Have taken some pills and gone to bed. Hope you had fun, see you in the morning. Not too early."

The next morning I woke up early and decided I wanted a pre-breakfast coffee and croissant more than another hour's sleep. Alan was still sleeping when I went down to the lobby. The hotel dining room wasn't open yet, so I crossed the street to a small bar. I was finishing a second croissant when I saw Victoria come out of the hotel.

A man was with her: about Victoria's age, blond, athletically built, beautifully dressed, carrying an overnight bag. He signalled for a taxi and turned to give her a light kiss on the mouth. Victoria put her arms around him and kissed him back, fiercely. Then, still holding on to him, she looked up into his face. I couldn't see her expression.

He grinned and said something, and got into the taxi. Victoria watched it pull away. Then she turned and went back inside.

I waited five minutes and then returned to the hotel. Alan was up and getting dressed when I came into our room. "Mother just called. She's ordering breakfast for us in her room. Where were you?"

"Taking a walk."

Victoria asked me the same thing when we joined her. I gave her the same answer. She regarded me for a moment, gave me a probing look, and then let it drop. Whatever went on between her and the man I'd seen hadn't left her looking happy.

* * *

The next two weekends in a row, she flew off to the Riviera without warning me ahead of time, and once again I found myself alone with her son. I was beginning to get sore about it. But when I came to the château during the week, she would always be there. Well, she was there, but not there —showing the symptoms of some strain she could no longer manage to shake off. Her steady drinking began to take its toll on the way she looked.

When she had drunk too much, her mood went down very low. When she controlled the drinking, her mood was higher, but sometimes too high. I started to suspect that she might be taking coke, but I never spotted any of the usual accessories around the château or in her car. Once I even snuck a look through her handbag, but I didn't find anything there, either.

The next time she phoned me with an invitation for the weekend, I told her I couldn't make it.

Victoria was silent for a beat. Then she said, "Please come, Gar." She added, after a pause, "I'll be here."

The tug was too strong. I went.

That was the beginning of the week in which everything finally went completely bad.

Chapter Nine

Victoria

The final scene between them in Jack's beachfront apartment in Cannes—which she had paid the rent on for almost a year—kept running unpleasantly through her mind. She loathed herself for her part in it—for having tolerated the situation in which it could occur.

Jack was standing there, his strong figure as beautifully dressed as always, every blond hair in place. His face, which had never been handsome, was somehow appealing when he smiled at her blandly. "Victoria, these arrangements never last forever. You know that, darling."

"Who are you leaving me for?"

"I wouldn't exactly call it leaving you. After all, we haven't been together that much lately."

"I came here every time I could last winter. I thought you liked having some free time to yourself."

"Of course, but you've given me too much free time. I saw you maybe three weekends all summer, Victoria. And that nervous little side-rendezvous in unlovely Bordeaux. Even when I see you, your mood spoils everything. This is not my notion of a satisfying relationship."

"My son is home from school. You know that I want to

spend *some* time with him. I see too little of Alan as it is."

"I understand the problem, Victoria. You love the kid and you miss him. Okay. But it's not *my* problem. And it's not the only reason I'm going. I'm a bird of passage. I get bored if I stay in one place too long. Can't help it, that's my nature."

Victoria forced a grin that just managed to keep from being a grimace of pain. "Just a gigolo, everywhere you go?"

"Everywhere I go. 'Go' being the operative word. I like to move around, see new faces."

"It's Naomi Thayer you're going with."

"I see no point in—"

"Yes, she's the one. I've seen the way she always looks at you. Hungry cat and juicy bird. And of course she's perfect for you. As rich as me—and much younger. You always did prefer them as young as possible."

"Naomi's not that much younger than you. She's at least twenty-five."

"And I'm thirty-one now. Where is she taking you off to?"

He shrugged. "We were thinking of Switzerland, first. Maybe London in the fall. Don't be upset, Victoria. It's not—"

"Do I look upset? It must be something I drank."

He grinned at that, relieved, and she laughed. Her laugh was throaty: low but strong, betraying no self-pity.

He took her shoulders lightly in his strong hands and kissed her closed lips. "We've had some fun, haven't we? And we probably will again someday."

"Not too probably, Jack." She said it lightly, trying to keep the anger, the hurt, the disgust with herself out of her tone. "But everything's possible."

This time he was the one who laughed. "You're a good girl, Victoria."

She gave him a steady look. "Do you think so?"

In the taxi on her way back to the Côte d'Azur Airport, the self-hatred began with a vengeance. She detested herself for having started the relationship in the first place. But she'd needed to be desired and used as a woman. And Jack knew how to fulfill that need extremely well.

She detested herself more for the sharp ache of loss she was experiencing now that he had left her, now that she was once more alone.

* * *

Whenever she remembered her first impressions of Sir Solomon Alexandre all those years ago in Washington, it was with bitter anger at her failure to read the warning signs. They had been there, obvious to anyone with enough experience to read them properly. But she hadn't had that kind of experience yet. At eighteen she had been advanced beyond her years in some ways, but excellence in the classroom and at cocktail party conversations could not help her fathom the depths of a man like Solomon.

He reminded her, when they first met, of James Mason in *The Seventh Veil*—direct and dominating with a hint of cruelty that she found irresistibly erotic. Frightening but fascinating, he'd seemed to her an emotional volcano under almost superhuman control. Until she learned better, she interpreted that smoldering force within him as passion.

And he was so very *alien*. That was especially important. The other men who courted her were too familiar, too predictable. They could make her laugh, but could never trigger the scary thrill she experienced with this foreigner whose dark armor she could not pierce, whose thoughts she could not fathom, whose desires were at once so direct and so confusing.

He came after her with the same relentless drive he used in business, overwhelming her with the strength of his personality and purpose. His aura of success and power, and the glamor of his knighthood—those had certainly been factors, too.

That he was so much older was another factor in his favor, during that period of her life. She was eighteen and her parents had drowned in a yachting accident the previous year. Even today Victoria could remember vividly the aching void caused by their deaths, the deep sense of loss, of needing and missing them. And then this exotic, famous man had appeared, a man their age, a man of enormous strength and sureness, who seemed, for a time, to take their place. Oh, yes, Victoria told herself bitterly, she *had* been stupid. So horribly stupid.

She had not even objected to quitting the university to go with him to England. Her thought had been that she would soon resume her studies there; her dream had been of later becoming a part of Solomon's business empire, someone he would trust and need and depend on. He did not exactly refuse to allow her to continue her education once they were married. Instead, he handed her a role as hostess to the most famous names in international politics and finance—a role so exciting, so glamorous that it seemed ridiculous to go back to being a schoolgirl.

In time that role had palled—but by then it was too late. She was pregnant, and Solomon had begun making it quite clear that he would not tolerate her doing anything other than fulfilling the functions for which he'd married her: mother to his children, hostess to his business contacts.

Her youth and inexperience had made it an unequal contest of wills. Gradually, she'd found herself unable to assert her independence against the crushing force of Solomon Alexandre's domineering character. Gradually, she was pressed into what he wanted her to be.

Victoria grimaced as she acknowledged the truth. She simply hadn't been strong enough, at the time, to just break through his opposition and go after what *she* wanted.

Then she'd had Alan. It was a difficult birth, leaving her ill for almost a year. The doctors warned that she must never risk another pregnancy. After that, Solomon was seldom around; he returned to full-time globe trotting. Whenever he did come home, it was as if a storm had descended on her life. And then he would be gone again, leaving her dazed and shaken—and with a growing sense of being cast aside, worthless.

The long period of recuperation after Alan was born seemed to turn off the last vestige of Solomon's desire for her. Since he had his son and heir, and Victoria could bear him no more children, he had no further *need* for her in that way. He had always had a plenitude of beautiful women to satisfy his fierce but brief sexual requirements—and he did once more. He never made love to her again.

Even as a mother, Victoria found her role increasingly restricted, much of it taken over by servants, and later by Alan's boarding schools. Left with no outlets for the energies pent up inside her, alternately overwhelmed and ignored by Solomon Alexandre, a self-destructive form of defiance began to gather strength within her.

Sir Solomon's intelligence network kept him as well-informed of what was going on "at home" as it did on business matters. He was not pleased about the drinking parties she began frequenting, the various men with whom she spent her time. Though no longer interested in her physically, he had no intention of allowing her to drag his name into the scandal tabloids.

Victoria

Victoria remembered with burning embarrassment the occasion on which he'd coldly delivered his first warning to her. It was a terrifying one, and in his presence she'd found herself still incapable of resistance. But once he was gone, she had rebelled again, knowing while she did so that her rebellion was generated by contradictory impulses: a child trying to force a father's attention back to her, an adult demanding a full life.

Finally Solomon had bought the château in Perigord and installed her there. He bought it as a refuge far from "temptations," as he put it—and as a toy for her. The idea was that it would be something into which she could pour her drive and intelligence harmlessly. For a time it had almost worked. Then her need to break free of his restraint had again become too strong for her to contain.

So far, Victoria knew all too well, her efforts had been irrational and demeaning, more a stubborn striking out than a genuine declaration of independence. But Solomon's ultimatum left her little choice.

Solomon had delivered his final warning the previous summer, that weekend when he'd descended upon her at the château, after she'd had Pete Bruno as her house guest.

The threat hanging over her was always the same, whether she failed to be more "discreet" or attempted to divorce Solomon. In either case, he intended to take Alan away from her and make sure she never saw her son again as long as she lived.

* * *

"Can he do that?" she asked the two attorneys.

One was her uncle, George Nicolson. The other was his son, Lee. Victoria had made the flight to Washington to consult with them. Uncle George was senior partner in one of the best Washington law firms. Her cousin Lee had been brought into the firm to eventually take over his father's position. But Lee was too restless for that; he'd stayed only long enough to garner useful contacts, and was about to quit to start his own firm and lobby on the side.

"Legally," her uncle told her, "it's unlikely that your husband could take Alan away from you. You're the boy's mother, Victoria. It would be extremely difficult for Sir Solomon to gain custody of Alan in a divorce suit. Even if he should somehow manage to win custody, he probably couldn't stop you from seeing your own son. You ought to at least get visitation rights. Legally, that is."

George Nicolson gave his niece a worried frown. "However, from what you've told me and inquiries I've made on my own, I gather that legal niceties are not always important to your husband. He is not above using illegal means. And he is not a man to be tampered with lightly."

"I already know that, Uncle George." Victoria was aware of Lee regarding her shrewdly. Her cousin was a clever young man, only three years her senior, though already afflicted with his father's baldness and corpulence.

"Torie," Lee said carefully, "he can even take your son away from you *legally* if he can prove you're not a fit mother. For instance, if he could come up with evidence that your morals are questionable, that you've been indulging in extramarital affairs. . . . Could he have that kind of evidence, Torie?"

She was quite certain Solomon would have no trouble producing that kind of evidence. With it or without it, she could imagine a variety of ways in which he could retaliate against her—"punish" her, as he put it—and the possibilities were chilling.

She said tensely, "I don't need to be told what Solomon can do, legally or illegally. I knew that when I came here. What I want you to do is find a way that I can defend myself against whatever he does."

Her Uncle George and Lee came up with a few suggestions, but none of them, Victoria was sure, would be sufficient against an enemy like Solomon, if she ever dared to push him into open retaliation.

* * *

According to the road sign, she was approaching Bordeaux. Victoria wondered what she was doing there, so far from home.

She had started out for a morning drive and just kept going, too deep in brooding to register miles, hours, direction. It was lucky she hadn't smashed up the car.

Victoria glanced at her watch. It was past lunch time and she hadn't eaten a thing with her breakfast coffee before taking out the Mercedes. At this point Bordeaux was only ten minutes away. She might as well have lunch there before starting back. She was hungry, and in need of a drink as well. Not too many drinks, though: it would be a long ride back. She'd made Gar Bishop a definite promise that she'd be there for dinner when she'd phoned to invite him for the weekend.

Funny kid. No, that wasn't right—not funny, and not at all a kid. She'd only been one year older than Gar, Victoria reminded herself, when she had married, and she had not considered herself a kid at that time. Any error in her choice of husband stemmed less from her age than from an ignorance of the man she'd married. In a way, Victoria realized, she knew more about Gar Bishop—who countless evenings had sat up with her and her son, keeping them company, being their friend—than she knew about Solomon, both when she'd married him and even now.

Gar was so much like his father. But Lou Bishop was afraid of her; his son was not. It was flattering, certainly, the strength of his feeling for her: admiration, friendship, sympathy—and a desire so strong she didn't have to look at him to feel it. Whenever he was there, it was there too. Should it be discouraged? Victoria grimaced and put the question out of her mind, and Gar with it. Her problem was not Gar Bishop: it was Solomon Alexandre.

She thought of what she had been before she met Solomon, and of what she was becoming now. It infuriated her to be so *afraid* of the man—afraid to fight him, afraid to leave him. Fear, resentment, frustration, fury—all compounded in a pervasive depression which kept becoming harder for her to break out of.

Since Jack had broken with her, Victoria had found herself sinking ever deeper into that depression, her feelings of rejection and uselessness at their worst. The arrangement with Jack had not been morally uplifting, but at least it had provided her with periods of forgetfulness, companionship, sexual release. Now she found she was beginning to think of herself as prematurely old.

It was ridiculous, of course, but she couldn't shake off the image: a woman heading toward middle-age without either a real husband or any kind of purposeful job, unable to discover a motivation for her continued existence. Nor could she find any reason to believe the future held anything better.

Entering Bordeaux, Victoria found herself driving through the waterfront area. She remembered the shudder she'd felt when the hoodlums and pimps had looked at her as she'd walked the area with Alan and Gar. She kept going, angling into another street leading to the hotel where they'd stayed.

The hotel held bitter memories of her clandestine night with Jack. But at least she knew she could count on the lunch being a good one, in the hotel's dining room. And its lounge bar served up drinks the way she liked them. She went into the bar first, ordered a dry martini.

While the bartender mixed it, Victoria became aware of three tough looking men watching her from a curved booth. The way their hard eyes stripped her made her remember the characters around the waterfront. These three were much further up the scale. They were obviously at home in this, the best hotel in town, and their suits, though flashy, were fashionably tailored of good cloth. So they weren't pimps or hoods. Probably, Victoria thought as she downed half of her martini, they were the kings of pimps and hoods; and this was their hangout, as befitted their eminence in the city's underworld. The thought made her smile as she lowered her glass.

She saw their faces reflected in the mirror behind the bar, and stopped smiling. They were still looking at her in the same way. She finished off her martini, paid for it, and left the bar without looking at them again. The lobby newsstand carried foreign papers. Victoria bought several and took them with her into the dining room.

It was late for lunch, and the maitre d' had to go search for a waiter after showing her to a table. While she waited, Victoria opened one of the British papers.

There was a picture of her husband on the third page, escorting a gorgeous, blonde starlet, who couldn't have been more than nineteen, to a movie premiere in New York.

Victoria got up and left the hotel, taking the newspaper with her. It was not until Bordeaux was half an hour behind her that she realized she had still not eaten anything that day. But her stop at the next town she came to was not for food. She bought a bottle of vodka. Returning to the car, she opened the bottle and drank from it before driving on. During the three more hours it took to reach the château, she stopped several times to have another drink. When she parked the car in the tower garage, she left the bottle hidden under its front seat. There were plenty of full bottles waiting for her inside.

She went up the entrance steps steadily enough, greeted Alan and Gar with smiles and kisses, laughed at a joke Alan had just learned from Gar, exchanged light banter without strain. She would probably, Victoria thought numbly, have made a better actress than the blonde starlet. The problem would be maintaining her role through the evening ahead.

* * *

She sat at her dressing table and looked at the article again. According to the caption beneath the picture, the girl had been seen at a number of other affairs with him—in Los Angeles as well as New York. An opened vodka bottle was on the table beside the newspaper, a filled glass on the other side of it. Victoria picked up the glass, took a sip, and continued to look at the newspaper photograph.

The dinner hadn't been a disaster. The wine had helped her get through it without coming apart at the seams. But she had excused herself shortly afterwards and retired to the master bedroom to be alone with the newspaper and her thoughts.

Victoria put down the glass and picked up her nail scissors. She cut the picture out of the page, threw the rest of the paper on the carpet. She got up, crossed to a bureau and got a small roll of Scotch tape out of a drawer. There was a small supply of cocaine hidden at the back of the drawer—bought in Cannes, used several times since, but not all gone. For several moments she considered using the last of it to try to bring her mood up out of the deep, dark pit into which it had sunk. But finally she went back to her dressing table without it.

She heard Alan and Gar, outside in the hallway, saying good night to each other before going to their rooms. Taking another drink, she began taping the news photo to the oval mirror above her dressing table. When it was done, she squinted for a time at the picture of the young starlet, then looked at her own reflection in the glass.

She saw the puffiness under her eyes, the lines of weariness that hadn't been there before. But those, she knew, only meant she needed more sleep and less liquor. She recognized something more significant in her face: the last of her youth was leaving it.

Not a tragedy, Victoria told herself. Part of a normal progression for everybody, from one stage of life to another. Each stage normally contained its own problems and pleasures. No, aging was not a tragedy—not unless you had failed to build anything to substitute for your passing youth.

Victoria looked at the picture of her husband. He was more than two decades older than she, and aging was no tragedy for him—not even an inconvenience.

She looked at the young girl clinging to Solomon's arm in the picture, smiling into the camera.

Then she looked again at her own reflection.

Chapter Ten

Garson

It was about one o'clock in the morning and I was taking a late, lazy swim in the pool when I heard her voice:

"You couldn't sleep either."

I treaded water and looked up at Victoria, standing on the pool patio, wearing a summer robe of light cotton. Mostly I saw the robe because it was white; there wasn't much moonlight and her face was in shadow.

"It was too hot to sleep," I told her.

"For me, too," she said. "Too hot and I'm too tense." Her tone was casual, but there was an undercurrent of emotion that I couldn't identify. "The next thing I ought to do with the house is install air conditioning. But it's not easy with a place like this."

"Well it's cool in here, and swimming's the best unwinder I know."

"Exactly my thought." Victoria took off her robe and let it drop to the brick paving of the patio.

She wasn't wearing anything underneath.

Concealing night shadows and revealing patches of misted moonlight clothed her nudity with a clinging pattern that altered as she came to the pool's edge. She dove in and swam past me in an easy, steady crawl.

I swam after her, but slowly. I still hadn't recovered from the shock of having seen her like that. She kept ahead of me for three lengths, then climbed out of the pool. I felt the hot excitement mounting as I watched the patterns of shadow and moonlight clinging to her wet figure, changing constantly as she moved across the patio. She picked up her robe and put it on, pulled the big cushions off a lounge chair and dropped them on the patio, knelt and stretched herself out on them.

I reached her side of the pool and hauled myself out. Victoria lay on her back across the cushions, hands linked under her wet hair, staring at the night sky. I sat down on a cushion beside her.

"There's the big dipper," she said, idly, "and that's the North Star, over there. . . . Those are the only ones I really know. Do you know much about the stars?"

"I look at them a lot. I've done some reading about them."

"What's that very bright one, over there to the left of the moon?"

"Venus."

"She's only a planet. And a trouble maker. It's stars I'm searching for."

I pointed out Vega, and showed her how it formed a triangle with Deneb and Altar. But my interest wasn't up there in the sky. It was down close beside me, and my rising lust for her was becoming tyrannical. My hands moved with a will of their own, opening her robe. I sat very still, looking at her.

She said softly, still gazing at the night sky, "You see? No different from any other woman you've known."

"Yes you are." I bent to kiss her nipples, and felt them spring erect between my lips. She made a small, quivering movement. Her fingers seized my hair and raised my face from her breasts. She was looking at me now.

"No."

But my need for her had grown too fierce by then. My hands explored the glory of her, fondling what they found.

"All right then . . ." Her whisper was like a sigh. "All right . . ."

And then she startled me with an answering passion as fierce as my own.

* * *

Sleepily content, I lay sprawled on the cushions, watching her get up and put on the white robe, go into the pool house. When she came out, she was smoking a cigarette. I hadn't often seen Victoria smoke; it wasn't a habit with her. She sat down in a chair near me and put the cigarette in a stone ashtray on the marble-topped table beside her. Leaning forward she rested her elbows on her thighs and cupped her chin in her joined hands, gazing down at me. Her lips curved a bit, in what seemed to be part of a smile; but her eyes were in pockets of shadow so I couldn't make out what kind of smile.

"Feel better now?" she asked quietly.

I sat up on the cushion and kissed her knee. "Happy as hell. What about you?"

"Better. A little better." Even that close, her eyes were hidden, making it impossible to be sure of her expression. "But Gar," she added, "I don't want it to happen again."

"If you're afraid I'm too dumb to keep it between the two of us—"

"No."

"Then why stop it?" I tried to lighten my tone, get the urgency out of it.

Victoria laughed, but there wasn't much mirth in it. She sat up straighter, picked up her cigarette and took a short drag at it, watched what the weak moonlight did with the smoke. "I don't intend to add corrupting you to my other sins and failures."

This time I grinned at her. "If what just happened is what you mean by corrupting me, forget it. It's not the first time I've been there. The best, but not the first."

"I never thought you were a virgin, Gar. That's obvious, and it's not what I'm talking about." Victoria took another drag at the cigarette, then crushed it out in the stone tray. She was no longer looking at me.

"There is some part of me," she said slowly, "that is becoming sick and twisted. It's contagious. Others can get caught in it. If I'm going to infect other people, I don't want it to be someone I care about."

I got to my feet. "Listen, I don't need a lot of complicated excuses." My voice was almost shaking. "If you're worried about me bothering you, just say so. I don't push in where I'm not wanted."

Victoria stood up, too, facing me. "I've just told you I care for you. I think you know how much."

"Then there's no reason—"

"There is my reason. And it's important to me."

"Wait a minute—." I took hold of her shoulders and tried to draw her to me without being rough about it.

She gripped my wrists, gently but firmly, and stepped back out of my grasp. "Listen to me, because I don't want to have to stop seeing you. What happened between us tonight can't happen again. Ever. Please remember that, Gar."

She reached out and touched my cheek with her fingertips. Then she turned away and strode off toward the rear of the château.

I let her go because I believed she meant what she said. I

didn't follow her, and I didn't go back into the pool. I stayed where I was, looking at the darkness into which she'd disappeared.

* * *

The next morning when I joined Alan for Sunday breakfast, Victoria wasn't there.

"She went off for a drive somewhere," he told me.

I figured she wanted to avoid me for awhile. She was probably afraid we'd be uptight with each other. Well, if it worried her, I could spare her that. Excusing myself to Alan with an explanation about some work I had to do at the plant, I took off on my motorbike. I stayed away from the château for the next four evenings. She didn't phone me.

Late in the fifth afternoon, Alan came by the plant for some target practice. Sebastiani brought him over, and joined us on the range. He'd taken to giving the boy some additional instruction. I hadn't been able to come up with a weapon yet that Sebastiani couldn't handle.

"Mother took off before I got up this morning," Alan told me. "She didn't come back for lunch. I don't know what's the matter with her lately."

I shot a glance at Sebastiani, but the watchdog's expression stayed stolid, giving away nothing.

At ten that night I got a phone call from Alan. "Mother didn't come back for dinner, and she still isn't home. I'm worried."

"Did you talk to Sebastiani?"

"Yes. He drove around looking for her and he's been phoning all over, and he still hasn't found out where she is."

"She probably just got delayed somewhere. She'll show up, don't worry. If it'll make you feel better, I'll come over and wait up with you."

"Thanks."

I got the motorbike and took off for the château—not just to calm down Alan; he wasn't the only one who was worried.

The lights were on in Sebastiani's tower rooms when I parked the bike below. I went up there first. I heard him hanging up his phone before he opened the door to me. He was worried, too.

"Anything?" I asked him.

Sebastiani gestured at the phone. "That was a cop friend of mine in Bordeaux. Lady Alexandre was seen there this evening, about four hours ago. In the bar of the Sofitel Hotel. According to the bartender, she was pretty drunk, and a couple of rich cocaine dealers were making a play for her. He thinks she left with them."

"That doesn't sound good."

"Not good," Sebastiani agreed. "I hope nothing happens to her. She is a nice woman, and I am supposed to be responsible for her safety. But how can I protect her when she never lets me go with her or tells me where she is going?"

He looked so unhappy that I said, "It's not your fault."

"Tell her husband that. He is not a forgiving man."

His phone rang. He snatched it up, listened, said: "Good, call when you have anything. Anything."

"My contact in Bordeaux," Sebastiani told me. "He has three well-connected detectives combing the city for her. Working black—nothing on the record, and I pay for their time."

"Not out of your own pocket."

"No, but perhaps out of my blood."

I left him to his phone vigil and went into the château. Alan was in Victoria's library, trying to get himself interested in one of the books. He was very relieved to see me.

"You can stop worrying," I told him. "Sebastiani just found out she was in Bordeaux four hours ago, perfectly all right. So either she's on her way home, or she's decided to stay there."

"She should've let me know."

"So she got involved with some friends she met and she's late remembering to call you. Or she's on her way back here. Look, if she'd had an accident, or anything else bad had happened to her, the police would have phoned here by now." I gave Alan a grin. "So relax."

He did, a little. I was getting to know how gratifying it could be, even if you tried to be cynical about it, to have somebody respond to you like that. "Let's go for a swim," I told him. "She'll probably have phoned or be home by the time we come back."

* * *

There were two cars parked in the dark lane that ran from the back of the farm area out to the main road. One was Victoria's. The other, also a Mercedes, had Bordeaux area numbers on its license plates.

We saw the cars when we came around the old, ruined stable. When we got to the swimming pool patio, we saw that lights were on in the pool house. Alan sprinted toward it before I could stop him. I ran after him, but but before I could catch him, he'd barged through the door. He was standing frozen with shock just inside it.

Victoria was on the carpet of the main room with two upper-class hoods. She was stark naked and so were they. Their clothes were scattered all over, and there was coke paraphernalia on the table with an opened plastic bag of powder. Victoria lay on her back with one hood on top of her, the other kneeling beside her head, grinning and keeping her face turned to him with a grip on her long, disheveled hair. Her nails were clawing the shoulders of the one on top of her, but whether to pull him off or closer I couldn't tell.

Alan let out a scared scream and broke out of his shock. He charged across the room and threw himself on the kneeling hood, knocking the man off his knees and tumbling down beside him.

The scream snapped Victoria back to some semblance of reality and she began struggling to get up. The hood on top of her got both his hands around her throat and shoved her back down, his hips continuing to work without missing a beat. Alan was trying to claw the other hood's eyes when the man's big fist struck his jaw and dropped him to the floor unconscious. Then it was Victoria who was screaming, fighting to get to her son. The hood on top of her snarled and tightened his grip on her throat.

I sidestepped to the fireplace and snatched up the poker, took two fast strides and clubbed him across the ear with the solid weight of it. He toppled sideways with a soft, grunting cry, sprawled out on his back and stopped making noise. I started for the other hood, but he was already scrambling across the floor to a pair of trousers. He got to his feet with a switchblade in his fist, the blade flicking out, long and sharp.

We were circling each other, him with his knife and me with the poker, when Sebastiani came in.

Sebastiani growled something in a rapid, slangy French I couldn't understand. The hood spun away from me to face him, with the knife ready to attack. He came to an abrupt halt when he saw the black Beretta pistol pointing at him. Sebastiani growled something else. The hood cursed and let go of his knife. When it hit the floor, Sebastiani lowered his Beretta, stepped forward, and kicked the man in the balls.

Once again the hood was down on his knees, this time

doubled over, clutching himself, sobbing and throwing up on the carpet.

Victoria had reached her son and was sitting on the floor with his head in her lap, crying. I went to the bedroom and got a bathrobe for her. Sebastiani went to the phone and rang the château, telling the maids to come over fast. Then he called the doctor in Exideuil and the home of a local cop.

I guessed the other calls he'd have to make would be long-distance, put through from the privacy of his own tower apartment.

* * *

From where I sat, I could watch what was going on inside Alan's bedroom. I was perched on the windowsill of the big casement window across the hallway, with a direct view through his open door. There was enough of a crowd in the room without me: the local doctor, two maids and Victoria. The side of Alan's face was bruised and swollen where he'd been clouted, but nothing was broken. He sank into a deep sleep under the sedatives the doctor had given him for the pain.

I thought about the calls Sebastiani must be making—to Stuart Peel, I was sure, but probably none to Solomon Alexandre directly. Sebastiani must have been an efficient sergeant in the old days. He'd had two local cops on the premises by the time Victoria and Alan were brought to the château. I'd watched the police shove the two hoods into their car and get them off the estate. From the way they'd handled the pair, I didn't think those hoods would care to come to this area again. The cops did the job black: there'd be no record of what had happened here. Sebastiani would slip them enough cash to make sure of that.

The doctor gave some painkillers to the maid Sebastiani had assigned to stand watch over Alan, instructing her to use them if the kid woke up before morning. Then he took Victoria by the arm and turned her away from her son's bed. The maid Sebastiani had put in charge of Victoria took her other arm, and they led her out into the hallway.

"I'd give you sedatives, too, but God knows what you've already put in your body," the doctor said as they went past me. Victoria moved like a sleepwalker, her eyes glassy, her mouth twisted in an ugly way. She was still wearing the bathrobe I'd put on her in the pool house. She hadn't said a word inside Alan's room, just stood there staring down at her son, and she didn't say anything as the doctor and maid took her into the master bedroom.

A few minutes later, the doctor came out with the maid. I asked if Victoria had finally passed out.

The doctor nodded. "She's been through a lot. She should sleep it off," he said. He went down the front staircase with the maid, instructing her to make herbal tea in case Victoria woke before he returned in the morning. He didn't consider it likely that she would.

The door of the master bedroom was slightly ajar, so I walked over and looked in. Victoria wasn't in her bed—she wasn't anywhere in sight. I rushed inside. She wasn't in the dressing room, either, and the door to the bathroom was shut and locked. I could hear the noise of running water. I rapped on the door and called her name—but no one answered.

I didn't hesitate: I broke the lock with a hard kick and barged in. Water was gushing into the big marble tub from both faucets. Victoria sat on a raised ledge at one side of the tub. She had a small penknife in one hand, poised to slash her other wrist under the rising water.

I leaped at her. Victoria twisted around with her teeth bared in a mask of fury, slashing at me with the knife. I don't think she registered who I was in those first seconds. The cut did not sting, but I could feel the blood gush from my left cheek. She fought against me as I tried to take the knife from her, and I had to drag her halfway out of the tub before I got it.

She fell on the bathroom floor, huddling there motionless. I closed the knife and pocketed it. She put both hands against the floor and pushed herself to a sitting position. Victoria stared up at my bleeding face, her eyes growing wide, her pupils shrinking to pinpoints. She put a hand to her open mouth and bent forward, rocking a little. The sound of her broken weeping was nerve tearing.

Blood dripped into the bath water when I bent to turn off the faucets. I looked in the mirror. It wasn't a large cut, but deep enough to scar. I used facial tissues to wipe some of the blood from my face, pressed a square of it against the cut until the bleeding pasted it there. Then I got my hands under Victoria's armpits and hauled her to her feet. She was still crying weakly as I helped her stumble into the bedroom.

I dumped her on the bed and stretched her out. She was limp, uncoordinated. I pulled the sheet up over her and settled down in a chair beside the bed. Victoria turned her face away from me on the pillows. Gradually the weeping died. She passed out before the maid came back.

What was left of that night didn't net me much sleep. Twice I got up to check on Victoria and Alan. Both patients continued to sleep; both maids were where they were supposed to be, keeping watch.

The doctor came back from Exideuil the next morning and went in to see Victoria first. When he came out of her bedroom, he told me, "Don't go in there. We just got her calmed down again, and she's about to fall asleep. She needs to sleep for the rest of the day. I don't want her disturbed."

"How is she?"

He considered his answer, and when he spoke it was with an odd stiffness: "Upset. Very. In my opinion what she needs to get over it is a great deal of rest. And perhaps medication to calm her over the next week or two." He paused and shrugged. "But that's just my opinion, of course. I've heard that her husband is flying in a psychiatrist from Paris. I'm sure he's had more experience with such conditions."

He saw Alan next, and then he told me I could visit: "For a minute. I'm sure he will be well enough to get up by this evening. But for the moment, don't strain him."

Alan didn't look great to me, but other than the swollen bruise on one side of his face, most of his problem was shock. Also, the sedatives were still working in him. His head turned listlessly on the pillow and he tried to smile at me. And I tried to say cheerful things. But he slipped back into sleep before my minute was up.

Alexandre's chief of security, Stuart Peel, arrived before the doctor from Paris. He didn't bother going up to see Victoria or her son. First he had a talk with Sebastiani, then a short one with me.

"I want you off the premises, kid." Peel was friendly as ever, but he meant what he said. "Don't want anybody but family here for awhile."

"You're not family."

Peel grinned. "Right now I'm better than family, as far as Sir Solomon's concerned."

"Is he coming?"

"No reason he should. I'm here. And one of the best psychiatrists in France will be here in the next hour or so. Go home, kid. Now."

"Okay, but I'll be back to see how Alan and his mother are

doing."

"Phone first, and we'll tell you. I understand your being worried about them, kid. But right now there's only one thing you can do if you want to help them—especially Lady Alexandre. Keep your mouth shut. Don't talk about what happened here to anybody."

"I don't need your telling me," I growled at Peel. "And stop calling me kid."

"Sure. One other thing. Sebastiani tells me you were real good in there last night. My opinion, you did a better job than he did. You've got some compensation coming for that —and for keeping your mouth shut." Peel dug into his pocket. "Ever had two hundred bucks all your own before?"

"Go fuck yourself," I told him. I got my bike and rode back to the plant.

* * *

When I phoned the château that evening, it was Sebastiani who answered.

"Alan's up and seems to be recovering," he told me. "Lady Alexandre—that Parisian psychiatrist has been in to see her. I understand she is sleeping again."

"Does he think she'll be all right?"

"He doesn't speak to me. Only to Stuart Peel and Thomas Haggard."

"Alexandre's lawyer is there, too?"

"He came with the doctor."

"Look," I said, "I'm coming over there. Just for a couple of minutes—"

"No. I would just have to stop you at the door. I am sorry, but I have to obey my orders." Sebastiani did sound sorry about it. "Don't worry so much," he added. "I will call you in the morning, and tell you how she is."

He didn't say he'd tell me how Alan was—just her—so I guessed he'd understood a lot more than I'd thought.

At ten the next morning, Sebastiani still hadn't called me, so I got on my bike and rode to the château. Sebastiani was outside the tower garage, piling some suitcases and a heavy duffle bag into the back of his pickup truck.

"What's happening?" I asked him.

"It has already happened. I no longer have a job here." Sebastiani shrugged. "For the best, perhaps. I never liked it that much, and I never considered looking for a job I would enjoy. I was paid too much for that."

I started past him toward the entrance steps, but he said, "There is no one in there you want to see."

I stopped dead and turned back to him. "What does that mean?"

"Alan went off to Paris with his father's business manager. He will stay with Monsieur Golz's family until his school starts again. Lady Alexandre—the doctor says she is having a nervous breakdown. Peel and Haggard took her to some private sanatorium.

I didn't know what to say. I was stunned, confused. What did it mean to have a nervous breakdown? For all I knew, maybe Victoria did need a little time in a sanatorium.

A little guilt began creeping in when I thought about our night together beside the pool. But I didn't really believe I could be in any way responsible for what had happened to her. I knew damn well who was to blame for that.

"Her husband never came around to see her, did he? Before they took her away."

"No. He is on his way to Thailand. Important business."

"Well, I'm sorry you got fired."

Sebastiani shrugged again. "I suppose I should be grateful

Alexandre didn't have something worse done to me."

I started to ride away, but before I got to the main road, I had to stop, look back at the château. But the place didn't mean anything to me anymore. It was empty now, like I felt inside.

I turned away from the château and rode off, never to come back. As I rode, I kept thinking of Victoria, wondering if I would ever see her again.

I didn't, for over ten years.

By then it was 1974, and I'd been in and out of the war in Vietnam, my father was in prison, and I was shoving my way into the same business as Victoria's husband.

Part II

No one believes that it is possible to overcome force except by greater force. There is no 'Law', there is only power.

—George Orwell

Chapter Eleven

Garson

She was coming out of the Excelsior Hotel when I saw her again, after a lapse of more than ten years.

She was there, and then she was gone before I could reach her.

The problem was that in 1974 much of Rome's famed *dolce vita* was concentrated on that block of the Via Veneto, and the wide streets were packed with crawling, horn-blaring traffic: cars, taxis, buses bringing people of assorted celebrity status to the sidewalk tables in front of Doney's and the Café de Paris, or carting them away, or dawdling so that passengers could try to catch glimpses of famous faces.

I had an appointment at the Excelsior. My taxi was inching out of a sidestreet across from the hotel, trying to bluff its way into the intersection chaos. Then she appeared, on the other side of the traffic, beside a doorman waving to snag her a cab.

I noticed her because she was a natural attention-getter, even at that distance and on what some called the Street of the Beautiful People. I didn't recognize her at first. All I saw was this unusually attractive, stylish woman with a confident stance. She was in the deep shade of the Excelsior's short, covered horseshoe driveway. My mind was a decade removed from her, preoccupied with the upcoming appointment to finalize my first solid arms deal.

As usual, parked limousines blocked the entrance drive where she stood. When the doorman caught her a cab, it was out on the street. He opened its rear door and beckoned to her. Her loose-limbed stride as she crossed the pavement was the first thing that jogged my memory. Most women don't walk like that. But for a moment I couldn't believe it was her. Then the sunlight hit her face and that luxuriant mane of auburn hair cascading to her shoulders. It was no illusion. It was Victoria.

I jumped out of my taxi and yelled her name, but she couldn't hear it through all the street noise. I pushed my money at my driver and began dodging my way through honking vehicles, threatening to run me over or crush me between them. The only way to cross a crowded Roman street is to trust the natives to stop on time and pray none of the cars coming at you is driven by a tourist.

Victoria's cab gunned away from the gridlocked intersection and was swallowed up in the traffic before I got there. I didn't even catch its license number.

The Excelsior doorman didn't know her by name, nor where she'd gone off to. He did know she was a guest in the hotel. She'd checked in that morning. I went inside to the desk. Yes, Victoria Nicolson was registered there. No, they could not give me the number of her suite. They never did unless a guest authorized it. They couldn't tell me where she'd gone, either, or when she would return. They could take a message, and see that she got it.

I wrote the message, with the phone number of my own hotel, over near the river, off the Via Flaminia. A decent enough little hotel, though a long way down from the Excelsior. I was prepared to go back there and stay put until she called me, however long it took. I had a date for that evening with a Dutch girl named Judith, a publicist with one of Rome's movie talent agencies, but I was already planning my cancellation excuse. Judith was bright and deliciously pretty, fun to be with anywhere, delightful in bed. But she wasn't Victoria.

Before I could call Judith or wait for Victoria to get in touch with me, however, I had business to take care of: my appointment in the lounge bar with my partner and a Vatican banker, Enrico Cardina.

Cardina was a member of the select group of nonclerical financiers the Vatican called its "men of trust." He had put Church money into arms deals before. That wasn't anything out of the ordinary for the men of trust. They'd organized a diversified investment portfolio for the Vatican, spread from controlling shares in insurance and construction companies to occasional dips into porn movies. The rationale was simple: anything that made the Church richer—and thus better able to do good in the world—had God's approval.

The deal Cardina was cutting with us was as solid as the Vatican's main bank, the Institute for Religious Works. We'd lucked into a great opportunity early, before any of the other dealers had gotten wind of it. We were to act as broker in supplying Brazil with a shipment of Italian small arms and ammunition. If we pulled it off, our take would amount to almost a hundred and forty thousand bucks. That would give our fledgling firm its first real financial base. Completion of this deal would also attract other and bigger ones our way.

I'd spent most of the firm's ready cash flying back and forth several times between Italy and Brazil, working out the arrangement and its terms. It was now set to click.

But we'd run into a severe hitch. An arms dealer acting as

a broker between two countries—in a legitimate transaction —has to obtain three vital pieces of paper. One is an end-user certificate, naming the country buying the arms shipment. The second is a license from the selling country to export the shipment to the buyer. The third is a letter of credit for the amount the buyer country is paying for the shipment.

I'd gotten the end-user certificate, but I still hadn't been able to come up with the other two. The Italian government wouldn't give us an export license until we could produce a letter of credit proving the Brazilian payment had been put in a Swiss bank, to be passed on to Italy upon the shipment's arrival. And Brazil was stalling about the letter of credit.

Actually, payoffs and three weeks were holding the deal up. Three weeks was the length of time it would take to ship the arms from Italy to Brazil. We wouldn't see our profit until after the shipment arrived, but without it we didn't have enough money to bribe government officials at both ends of the deal. Until we bribed them, we wouldn't get the export license or letter of credit.

Enter Enrico Cardina, the Vatican banker. He liked our stalled deal. He was willing to invest the sum we needed to get it unstalled: a short-term loan for one month. He wanted forty percent of our profit in exchange. The terms were hard to chew down—but Cardina was our last hope.

That afternoon he was supposed to come to the Excelsior with the financial agreement he'd drawn up. I walked into the lounge bar hoping I had the nerves to read it very carefully before grabbing his money.

My partner, Christian Frosch, was sitting at a corner table, nursing a tall drink and staring off into space. A scrawny German of thirty, he was an electronic surveillance wizard, with a growing European clientele, a yen to get big-rich through investing his income in the arms business, and a happy-go-lucky attitude toward his own human folly. Almost all the capital for our little company—optimistically named "Tri-Arms International"—had so far come out of Frosch's pocket.

"Cardina's late," I said when I reached him.

Frosch looked up with a dreamy smile. "Been and gone, kiddo." His grasp of the American way with the English language was sometimes a little out of date. His tone told me the deal had fallen through.

I walked over to the bar and ordered a double scotch on the rocks. Carrying my glass back to Frosch's table, I sat down and took a drink. Then I asked him: "What happened?"

"Cardina said there's nothing for us to talk about anymore. He found out this morning from somebody in the government here. Our Brazil-Italy deal's been snatched by one of the biggies. Ahmed al-Zadar, himself. He must have heard about it at the last minute, walked in and plunked down the money."

"Last minute, hell! Al-Zadar's probably known we had the deal cooking for a long time. He sat back and let me do all the work of putting it together for him. Slipped something to people here or in Brazil, or both, to let him know when it was ripe."

"Either way," Frosch said philosophically, "he's grabbed it from us. The arms shipment and our profit. Bye-bye."

"Bastard," I growled. "A hundred and forty thousand doesn't mean a thing to al-Zadar—a man who can say twenty million dollars is peanuts and mean it. He just stole it from us for the exercise."

"Could be." Frosch took a sip of his drink. "But he didn't do anything we wouldn't have done in his place. The world of business ain't a Sunday school. You bug as many office phones as I have, you learn that. Par for the course, Captain."

Frosch usually only called me by my former Army rank when other people were around. He figured it was good for business, which was one reason he'd teamed up with me. I guessed he was more upset than he showed. I probably showed how upset I was.

"That's what I should have been doing," he added, "instead of sitting here in Rome, sure we'd get the deal. I should have been bugging al-Zadar's offices. Then we'd have had enough warning."

"His offices are a big jet and a yacht," I said. "Hard to bug those."

Frosch looked hurt. "Easy for me—if I know where they are and can get in or near them for long enough at the right time."

I wasn't interested in his dreams of what might have been. The deal's collapse had left me bitter. "Cardina came here just to drop the bomb and walk off? He could have called us. Bad news doesn't hurt worse by phone."

"He was already here when I arrived. Finishing up a discussion with a gorgeous lady. The way she acted, their talk was all business. But Cardina wasn't hiding that he fancies her."

"Keeping up his reputation as a skirt chaser."

"A *really* gorgeous lady," Frosch said. He was regarding me with an odd curiosity. "Turns out she knows you." He took a folded slip of notepaper from his pocket and handed it across our table.

"Gar," she'd written, "please try to call me here at seven this evening. Suite 501-502. I'd like dinner with you, if you can make it. My treat. —Victoria."

I looked up at Frosch. "What did she say when you told her I'm your partner?"

"I didn't tell her anything, Captain. She already knew it."

* * *

She wasn't in when I called the Excelsior at seven. But the desk had a message for me to meet her at nine in the Toscana restaurant, if I could make it. Previously I had considered refusing her offer to treat me to dinner. But the Toscana was one of Rome's most expensive. I didn't have enough cash on me to cover a meal for two there, and my credit cards were in danger of being cancelled for late payments.

The Toscana was also over-popular with the *dolce vita* people. There was always a crowd on the stairs—including some who had reservations—waiting for tables to become available. It was that way when I came in from the Via Porta Pinciana at nine that night. But the mention of Victoria's name to the owner's wife got me escorted past the waiting mob to table in a secluded alcove. The table was big enough to seat five, but had been set for two. Victoria wasn't there yet so I sat down and ordered a drink. I hadn't been waiting more than three minutes before she arrived.

I stood up and watched Victoria thread her way between the crowded tables. She was dressed with a stunning chic that had other women in the place looking at her with speculative eyes. The warm, patrician beauty was as devastating as I remembered. But I saw now that the long-legged stride was powered by a new facet in Victoria's personality, something that I had not seen before: a drive, the kind that you see in the best race horses—superbly controlled, highly motivated.

This estimation of Victoria may be hindsight on my part, but I don't think so. She had a different kind of energy in her, and I felt it, even if I couldn't identify it.

The restaurant's owner cut over and intercepted Victoria with a big smile and some fast chatter. She laughed and told him something that had him beaming as he turned and led her the rest of the way to the alcove. Obviously she was a favorite customer. When they reached the alcove, the owner studied me narrowly for an instant, judging whether I deserved to have Victoria all to myself for a whole evening. Then he stepped aside, bowed her in, and went away.

Victoria and I stood there for a moment looking at each other, neither of us smiling. It was a pregnant moment. I kissed her, but I didn't make a big thing of it. There was an entire decade that had to be put behind us before we could begin to discover how we felt about each other.

She touched a fingertip to my left cheek. "You have a scar. Is it from what I did to you that night?"

"I like it," I said, smiling. "Every time I shave I see a part of you in the mirror."

She didn't laugh at that, didn't smile. Seeing me had reminded her of that bad time. I held her chair for her, took my seat and signalled the waiter. "What are you drinking?" I asked her.

She ordered a glass of wine, got a cigarette out of a silver case with an oriental design, and lit it with a tiny amber lighter. She looked at me through the smoke. "You know about Alan, I think. . . ."

I nodded. "I was in Washington for a few days last year before I left for Europe. I had just gotten out of the Army. I heard you were working for your cousin there, so I went over to see you. Your cousin told me you'd gone to Tokyo on business—and he told me what happened to Alan."

A chauffeur had been driving the kid to his father's office in Paris when a drunk driver crashed through a red light and slammed into the side of the the car. Alan had died in a hospital five hours later.

"I'm sorry, Victoria. I liked him."

"He liked you. I think you and I were the only people in the world he ever felt good with. Poor boy ..."

I didn't see any tears in her eyes. Whatever she used to deal with the trauma of her son's death, crying wasn't part of it. Maybe it should have been.

The waiter brought her glass of wine to our table. Victoria took a last drag at her cigarette and crushed it out in the ashtray. We touched glasses and I said, "To better times."

"Better times ..."

I saw her make the effort to pull herself out of the bad memories. She gave me a smile and took a small sip from her glass. When she got another cigarette out of the silver case, I took the lighter from her: "If you're going into chain-smoking these days, at least let me show you how attentive I can be, in the right company."

Victoria's smile got wider, and she leaned forward to let me light her cigarette. The she looked at me again, differently. "The same Gar Bishop. Older ... harder, I think ... sadder, perhaps ... but the same."

"You haven't changed, either."

"Yes I have. She said it without regret. "For one thing, I'm an old girl now."

"Uh-uh. Not a grey hair."

Her laugh was soft and short, but it was a real one. "No, a lot," she told me. "I just don't care to flaunt them. I'm forty-one, Gar. Going on forty-two."

And I was going on twenty-eight. She couldn't tell herself I was a kid she might corrupt. Not anymore. We'd only been together in that alcove for about five minutes, but I already knew that I felt the same about her. Maybe my feelings were stronger—because what I wanted was no longer impossible. I didn't intend to push it too fast. There was time—time to play it like a fisherman going to the same part of a lake regularly, after the same wily fish as always. He wouldn't expect to get it the first time, maybe not for a long time. But if he kept going there and playing it patiently, he'd make the catch sooner or later.

I said, "I was hoping, before I got the bad news this afternoon, that this would be a celebration dinner tonight. And I'd be paying for it. But—I guess Enrico Cardina told you what happened to my deal."

Victoria nodded. "Don't worry. There'll be other deals you won't lose. And we'll have other dinners, which you can pay for."

That sounded encouraging. "Christian—he's the partner you met—thinks old Cardina fancies you. 'Fancies' is the way he put it."

Victoria smiled. "Your Christian Frosch is observant. But with Enrico it's more out of habit than anything else. At his age, he just wants to prove he's still Italian."

"What were you doing there with him?"

"Working." Her firm, she explained, represented big companies and organizations in Washington. Her job was to persuade key figures in Congress and various government offices to make decisions favorable to her clients. "'Lobbying,' it's called." Victoria made a deprecating smile. "'Influence peddling' is the less pleasant but quite accurate term for it. I've been trying to persuade Enrico Cardina to let us peddle some influence for Vatican holdings in the United States."

"You seem to be doing well at it."

"With Enrico? I'm not sure yet. He's more wary than he pretends."

"I meant with your company. I saw that it's named Nicolson and Nicolson. Your cousin told me that the other Nicolson is you."

Victoria nodded. "He made me his partner, finally. Lee is a topnotch attorney. But he decided he's not at ease with influence peddling."

"And you are."

"I hope so. But right now what I am is hungry." She opened the menu and suggested some dishes as the restaurant's best. After we'd ordered, she took a sip of wine and got out another cigarette.

I lit it and glanced at her glass. It was still half full. She didn't act like a person who needed to control her drinking. She took little sips as if she enjoyed the taste but did not need too much to be satisfied. If she still had any trouble with nerves, the chain-smoking was the only sign I could see of it.

I said, warily: "Your cousin told me about Alexandre keeping you in that sanatorium. That—must have been a bad time for you."

"Very bad." Then Victoria told me a little about it. She didn't let her imprisonment sound tragic, though she didn't hide the fact that those years had been nightmarish for her.

"You must hate Alexandre's guts for doing that to you."

"No," Victoria said evenly. "To go on hating him wouldn't serve any purpose except to keep reminding me of the nightmare. I put that experience behind me long ago, Gar. And it is better left there. I prefer to forget that it ever happened."

There was absolutely nothing in the way she said it to indicate that it was a straight-faced lie.

Chapter Twelve

Garson

"I hear he got married again to some young Italian countess."

Victoria nodded. "She had a baby three months later. And another since." Victoria's laugh was low and wicked. "Both of them daughters. Poor Solomon—he must be furious." And then, without humor: "Poor girl he married."

The waiter brought us the first course. As we began to eat, Victoria said, "Tell me a little about yourself, Gar."

"I guess you know about my father?"

"My cousin Lee told me."

"Your cousin was real decent to me." I explained that I had come to Washington with plans to discuss my father's case with somebody in the Justice Department, but couldn't get anyone important to talk with me. He'd made a phone call and got me an appointment with an assistant attorney general. Not a bad guy, either—but he couldn't come up with a way to get my father released before he served full term. He said the charges were too rough."

I put down my fork and looked at Victoria. "He shot a cop," I said. "And later the cop died."

"I heard."

"I saw him in prison. If he stays there, he won't live out his sentence. And nothing will get him out earlier—except money and political pull."

"You would need an enormous amount of both," Victoria said reflectively. "Especially pull. More than anyone could hope to acquire—even in my field—for years and years. If then."

"Sure. There's only one field I know of, where I'd have any chance at that kind of dough and leverage fast enough to matter."

"I thought that might be your reason for going into arms dealing."

"If it got your ex-husband enough power to keep you *behind* bars, it can give me enough to get my father *out*."

Victoria regarded me judiciously. "Solomon started a lot earlier than you, Gar. And he had less competition. To come anywhere close to matching what he has, you'll have to play some very hard catch-up."

"I know. And get lucky." I didn't pick up my fork again for awhile. Thinking of what had happened to my father had cut my appetite.

* * *

Three hours before dawn, I was pacing back and forth beside the old Chevy hidden in the middle of a group of barren hills, waiting nervously for my father to arrive at our night rendezvous. It was in a stretch of Texas desert north of the Mexican border and northwest of the point where El Paso and Ciudad Juarez sit on opposite sides of the Rio Grande. I wasn't supposed to be there. According to the plan, it was my uncle who should have been waiting with the car.

I'd made the trip with him from Los Angeles to the motel in El Paso, in case the old Chevy developed engine trouble. My uncle wasn't any good at fixing cars, and I was. The idea was for me to make sure the Chevy reached El Paso and was in fit condition to take my uncle to the rendezvous and safely away from it. Then I was supposed to hop a bus back to L.A. But half an hour before my uncle was due to head out to pick up my father, he began having heart spasms. Nobody had figured on that, though we should have. He'd had heart trouble in the past—never bad enough to hospitalize him more than a few days, but bad enough to prevent him from driving that night.

So I was the one at the rendezvous, waiting for my father to show up carrying his backpack loaded with smuggled cocaine, bought from a Mexican dealer across the frontier in Juarez. The cash he'd used to pay for it was everything he and my uncle had been able to scrape together, and most of it was borrowed from friends.

The trouble that had driven my father to this dangerous extreme was a costly lawsuit.

For a few years after he quit his job in France and moved to L.A., everything went fine. He and the retired French colonel, Paul Rambert, rented an old barn in Topanga Canyon and converted it into their weaponry workshop. After graduating from high school, I went to work for them fulltime. The technical know-how they both kept feeding me was the best education I could have gotten, considering what I intended to do with it at the time—build a career with my father and Rambert—and also what I finally did do. I liked Rambert: a tough, efficient, old-fashioned officer type with a cool sense of humor. He got to like me, too: his one weakness was young girls, and I introduced him to a few.

Then the lawsuit hit us. Haggard, Solomon Alexandre's attorney, showed up in Los Angeles with photographs of some of my father's rocket-launcher designs and early-stage prototypes he'd built. We never did find out who the spy in the Perigord plant who'd taken the pictures was.

Before a judge—who he probably had in his pocket— Haggard claimed that the designs and the launcher were the property of Alexandre, and that my father had committed an act of theft in taking them from the plant when he'd left Alexandre's employ. He demanded the return of the designs and prototypes, along with any work done on "Alexandre's" rocket launcher since.

My father was sore, but mostly at himself. In private he admitted that, under the contract terms, the weapon did belong to his ex-boss—and that in Alexandre's place he would have also tried to grab it. But that admission didn't stop him from fighting back. My uncle found a lawyer—a young one who'd only been in practice three years, but who surprised everyone with a tigerish courtroom cunning that later earned him a prestigious career. His first victory came before the trial started. He pushed for a jury trial and was very sharp about the choice of jurors.

Haggard brought his witnesses into court: employees from the Perigord plant who swore under oath that they'd seen my father working on the launcher there. Narrowly dodging Haggard's sustained objections, our lawyer managed to make the jury understand that these witnesses couldn't very well testify differently. Their jobs with Alexandre were on the line. He also pointed out that the dates on the photos could easily have been faked, and that there was no proof that they'd actually been taken inside Alexandre's plant. I enjoyed thinking that the spy who'd taken them must have been fired for that oversight.

We won the trial—mostly because the average juror, in such an obviously uneven fight, likes to see the small-time David beat the tycoon Goliath once in awhile. But the legal cost had eaten the last of my father's savings, plus everything he'd been able to borrow against his future pension payments. That left Rambert bankrolling their two-man company by himself. My father had too much pride for that. Besides, Rambert's money alone wasn't enough to keep their development of the two weapons going at the rate they'd set before the lawsuit.

My uncle, having solved one problem by coming up with the sharp, young lawyer, tried to do it again. His solution was a one-shot coke-smuggling venture. He knew an L.A. drug dealer who'd buy anything they could bring him, and who was willing to put them in contact with a supplier in Mexico. My father's profit would be enough to match Rambert's share of the development expenses for the next couple years—so he took the chance.

There were only two hours left before dawn when he emerged from the darkness around our rendezvous point. He didn't ask why I was there instead of my uncle; he was too tired from the long, fast trek across the border on foot, and this was no time or place to hold a discussion. I got the Chevy started while he shoved the backpack load of coke into the trunk. He was climbing in beside me when the big searchlights snapped on, pinning the car in their strong beams. A loudspeaker blared at us to come out with our hands held high.

They had been there, hidden in the dark hills around our rendezvous spot, longer than I had—deputies from the county sheriff's office, plus an assortment of federal and state narcs. One narc later explained to the press that they'd been tipped off by a source close to the Mexican who'd sold my father the coke. One reporter explained that professional dope traffickers often tipped the cops about deals they made with one-time amateurs like us to prevent the police from busting their regular dealers.

I gunned the Chevy into a squealing turn and headed it for a dark break between the two hills. A barrage of bullets slammed into the car. It was a miracle neither of us got hit. The motor died abruptly and one of the tires exploded at the same time. The Chevy slued around and rammed to a stop against a big rock.

My father snapped an order, and I had no choice but to follow it. I dove through one door while he went out the other. I was on my knees behind the cover of the wrecked car when he crawled around to me, drawing the revolver he'd holstered on the back of his belt, under his lumberjacket. He'd brought it along in case he ran into some of the hijackers who infested both sides of the border. Now he used it to knock out two of the searchlights.

Between shots he pointed at the darkest spot around us and growled at me: "Get going. *Keep* going."

I went. When you've been raised around the Army, the habit of obeying an order issued in that tone of command sinks in deep. You follow it automatically, without taking time to think it over or argue. That's how armies brainwash ordinary men into good soldiers.

When I scrambled away, my father began shooting again. The sound of his shots couldn't be distinguished over the continuing barrage from the hidden lawmen. I didn't get far. Five minutes later I was dragged back between two lawmen with my wrists manacled.

My father was sitting on the ground, leaning against the Chevy's side with his right leg crooked and his left arm dangling, both of them broken by bullets. A police car was parked near him and a cop was yelling into its radio for a helicopter to come in, fast. A couple of sheriff's deputies came down the slope of a dark hill, carrying a third man. They put him down very gently. He'd been shot in the gut.

My father hadn't meant to do it. And perhaps if he'd had the time to think the situation through—if he hadn't relied so much on his military instincts—the incident would have ended differently. He'd only been firing to concentrate their attention on him and give me my chance to slip away. But it had happened. The deputy didn't look good, I thought, when they lifted him carefully into the chopper—and watching the sight, my father didn't look too good either. They shoved me and my father in less gently. The chopper lifted off and headed first to the nearest hospital, and then to the jail.

They locked me into a different cell from my father, in another part of the jailhouse. For three days I waited, getting my food regularly but no information. On the fifth day I was taken to a room where an Army lawyer was waiting to have a private talk with me. Some years back, he explained, he and my father had been buddies. But there was nothing he could do for him. The charges were too serious: attempting to traffic in illegal drugs, international smuggling, obstructing police officers in the performance of their duties, and intentionally shooting one of them.

For me, however, there was one possible out. He had already talked it over with both my father and the proper authorities, and they'd agreed to it. Considering my youth, charges against me would be dropped—if I volunteered to join the Army and serve my country. As the Army lawyer reminded me, I was twenty-one and the draft would probably get me anyway, sooner or later. I thought about the war in Vietnam waiting for me and said I preferred later.

He had a guard escort me to my father's cell. My father was on his bunk, with his leg in a plaster cast and his arm in a sling.

"Take it," he told me flatly.

"They'll send me to Vietnam."

"Better than going to prison, on these charges."

"I'm not so sure of that."

"Take it," he repeated, a hard growl this time.

* * *

Four months after I'd joined, my expertise with weapons got me up to sergeant. That was the same week I was put on a troop carrier bound across the Pacific.

Paul Rambert had already left the country going in the opposite direction: back home to France. He was sensibly averse to being charged as an accessory to our crime. Such charges would have been false, of course, and maybe they wouldn't stick; but Rambert didn't intend to take the risk in a country where he had no useful connections at all. So he went where he felt safer, and took everything he and my father had been working on with him.

Despite appearances, Rambert wasn't actually deserting my father. He kept sending money for legal expenses, and those kept mounting. I'd been in Vietnam for almost two years—scrambling in and out of helicopters and trying to stay alive while being shot at and shooting back—before my father finally came to trial. He had the same sharp, young lawyer again, but that wasn't enough. The deputy he'd shot had died a year later and one of the charges had been changed to murder.

I was on an operating table in a Saigon military hospital having shell fragments removed from my stomach and hip the day my father was sentenced to twenty-eight years in prison.

By the time I had recovered sufficiently to be flown to Japan for five weeks of rest and recuperation, I had received what they call a battlefield promotion: to lieutenant. I also got a medal for "exceptional valor." I had demonstrated my so-called "valor" by becoming one of the four men in my unit to survive action that was part of a clandestine operation in Cambodia. I leaned on my new officer status, my honorable wounds and my medal, and finally got permission to spend six days in California.

The first thing I did when I got back to the States was visit my father in prison. My initial impression was that he looked quite well. He had been participating in prison athletics and had acquired a good tan. But there was something in his eyes I'd never expected to see there: he was frightened. Nevertheless, he was trying hard to maintain some hope. He told me that his young lawyer was appealing the severity of his sentence.

"Don't worry," he told me. "With my record in the service and the fact that I've never committed any kind of criminal act before in my whole life, they're bound to reduce the sentence."

"Sure," I agreed; but it still seemed to me that his service record and status as a first-time offender wouldn't be worth beans in his situation. The only appeal that would be of any use would have to come from people much higher up than anybody he or anyone around him knew. I'd already begun thinking about the only way I knew to eventually gain influence with that sort of people.

Most of that night and the next day I spent working out a long letter to the Army lawyer who'd once been buddies with my father, asking him to forward it through proper channels to higher military authorities. In it I stressed that with my exceptional background in weaponry engineering, I was being wasted as a combat soldier. My two years of combat duty, I pointed out, had already given me enough practical experience in using all kinds of small arms. This plus my pre-Army training, I hoped, qualified me for a transfer to some technical department of military intelligence. What I had in mind, I lied, was to build myself up as a career officer specializing in weapon technology.

What I actually had in mind was something quite different, and it did not involve the Army, but I knew that a couple of years specializing in weapons in an official capacity would give me more credibility to achieve this goal. I knew I couldn't expect a reply to my request before leaving the States, and probably not for a long time after. "Proper channels" are not noted for their quick response to anything. I also knew that only a fluke would get me a favorable response, whenever it came. To have any real chance, I needed what I didn't have: a high-level sponsor inside the military or government.

During the rest of my short stay in California, my father didn't talk much about his predicament. Most of the time he avoided the subject by asking me questions about combat in Vietnam. When the day came for me to fly back there, I stopped off at the prison on my way to the airport. He said goodbye with the old soldier's farewell: "Keep your head down, boy."

Those were his last words to me before the trial was over. His full sentence was affirmed on appeal: it hadn't been reduced.

* * *

There was a surprise waiting for me in Saigon. My request had been okayed by military authorities in Washington. The fluke I'd hardly dared hope for had occurred, I figured. I certainly didn't have any high-level sponsor interested in my career—not that I knew of.

I was transferred to an Army intelligence unit assigned to evaluate the effectiveness of the arms being used in the war, both by us and the Vietcong. Over the next year I analyzed and experimented with everything from rifle-propelled grenades and booby traps to helicopter gunships and heat-seeking antiaircraft missiles. It wasn't a desk job. Part of it was test-firing captured enemy weapons, taking them apart and making judgments on their good and bad points. A lot of it was done out in the field: studying weaponry under battle conditions, scavenging for Cong materiel, tape-recording my findings with the war raging around me. All in all, Vietnam was a lesson in how fast the products of arms industries get used up and have to be replaced.

Then I got another surprise. I was being transferred again, this time to a training camp the CIA had set up in the jungles of Central America. Its main purpose was to teach anti-guerrilla methods to military officers from Latin American countries friendly to the U.S. My job would be to instruct them about new weaponry Washington was supplying to their governments. I was promoted to temporary rank of captain so that I'd get more respect from the foreign officers. The promotion would become permanent, I was told, when I finished my present hitch and signed up for another.

I had no intention of doing so. Temporary or not, for my future purposes my rank of captain would still net me the additional credibility I was after for my civilian career.

They flew me from Vietnam to Manila, and then directly to Panama. The camp wasn't a joy. The wet heat was enervating and the recreation possibilities minimal. Worse, it was hard for me to stomach the specialities of some of the CIA instructors. Teaching men how to use and repair a weapon properly was one thing. Teaching them the proper way to attach electric torture instruments to the nipples and testicles of a prisoner under interrogation was something else.

One night I got into a barroom brawl with one of the CIA teachers, in a nearby town that had been stocked with liquor and women to service the men from the camp. The hookers were low-grade, nothing to tempt me up to their non-air-conditioned rooms in that heat. But the whisky was good, imported stuff. So when I felt the need, I would go into town strictly for the purpose of having a drunken night. I'd had more than a few drinks when I made the remarks that started the CIA guy swinging at me.

He was no pushover. We were both considerably battered when we finished in the dirt street outside the bar. It wasn't like some fights, where the two guys, having let off the steam, wind up back at the bar with their arms around each other's shoulders, sharing drinks. We hadn't liked each other from the start, and after the fight we went on hating each other. Some other CIA instructors carried him off, and I stumbled back inside the bar with the help of a couple Army boys.

There was this scrawny, cheerful guy who'd been sitting at one of the tables, watching the fight. I'd seen him around almost every night I'd gone into town for the last two weeks. He seemed to spend most of his time getting friendly with the Latin American officers who came through camp for their CIA and weaponry courses, buying them drinks and telling them jokes in a wild mixture of pretty good English and ragged Spanish. I had sometimes wondered why.

He came over to the bar beside me, bought a fresh bottle of scotch, paid a fortune for a tiny container of ice cubes, and grinned at me:

"Hey, Captain, how about sitting down and sharing this with me."

That's how I met Christian Frosch.

Garson

* * *

We just drank together that first night, and told each other something about ourselves. He'd been born in Berlin, father unknown, mother a prostitute who'd had to give it up when she got older and take odd, menial jobs to feed and house both of them. As soon as he'd been old enough, Christian Frosch had gone to work for a man who repaired radios and other electrical appliances. By fourteen he'd seen where the real money was in that line: electronic surveillance.

He'd started out on his own tapping phones and bugging hotel rooms for divorce lawyers. By twenty he was hopping all over Europe to either bug somebody's business quarters or to protect them from being bugged. He kept inventing new gadgetry to help him get both kinds of work done more effectively. Some of the gadgets he marketed, which made him more money from his genius. Christian wasn't modest about his talent: "genius" was his own word for it, and it was making him very well off. Over the last few years, his genius had gotten him invited to the States a number of times, and more recently to Latin America.

"So if you're doing so well," I asked him, "what are you doing in a dump like this?"

He didn't answer me that first night. Instead he said, "You're right, kiddo, this *is* a dump. There's a bigger town only two hours from here by car. And I got a car. How about going with me tomorrow night? There's a great little nightclub, and I know a couple girls there you'll like better than the ones around here."

The next night I went with Christian, and he was right: the nightclub was fun, and I did like the girls. Christian and I wound up buddies, and when he was sure it had the makings of a lifetime friendship he told me:

"I make good dough with my specialty, Captain. But I've got big ambitions, you know. Being well off, that's okay for some. Me, I want to get *filthy* rich." He grinned at me when he said that, but he meant it. "In the business I got right now, there's a limit to how rich I can get. Because I'm a one-man business. I can't teach what I know to other guys, and let them take over some of my work for me. Soon as they knew everything I do, they'd take off and go work for themselves. You see?"

"I see," I assured him, and had another drink.

"I want to get into a business where the sky's the limit. Arms dealing."

I sat up a little straighter.

"I've got a friend in Italy. Vincenzo Borelli. Old war hero, on the winning side. Partisan leader, tortured by the Gestapo, all that. It's important because now he's a lawyer, and out of what he did in the war, he's got good connections in Rome and Milan where it counts. Including a contact inside the Beretta arms company. So Borelli got me a chance to take my first swing at it—trying to sell Beretta-made small arms to Latin America."

"How've you done?"

"Lousy. I'm a good salesman. I haven't had much trouble getting to see government and military people in a couple of these countries. But then they start asking me technical stuff about sample weapons, and that's not my field. I have to keep making long-distance calls to Borelli in Rome, and he don't know the answers either. He has to ask his contact at Beretta. Pretty soon anybody can figure out I don't know enough about what I'm trying to sell."

"I still don't understand what you're doing around here," I told him. "We've got all the weapons we need in the camp, and there's nobody else to buy from you."

"Yes there is," he said. "Not now, but later. I'm dumb about guns, okay, but I can learn. Give me a few years and I can learn enough to get by. Meanwhile, you have all these young Latin American officers at your camp. A different batch every few weeks. Someday, some of those boys are gonna be generals in their countries, maybe even running their governments."

I smiled at Christian. "And you'll walk in and remind them you're their old drinking buddy from way back."

"Sure. That's the idea." He paused and looked at me. "But you'll know them a lot better."

That was not a new thought to me. I'd figured that one out my first week at camp, but I didn't mention this to Christian.

He said, "Nobody can be good at everything. I've got some useful contacts and I'm a good salesman. But I don't know much about weapons, and that's what I want to sell. *You* know all there is to know about them."

"A lot, not everything."

"Enough. We'd make a great team, you and me."

We sat there and looked at each other.

He said, "I contribute my contacts and the capital to get us started. You contribute your know-how, plus the contacts you've made here. And we see how it works out. Interested?"

I didn't have to think about it for long. In the year just ending, U.S. firms had sold over seven *billion* dollars worth of nonnuclear arms abroad. Russia had exported some five billion dollars worth. European firms had totalled foreign sales close to those figures. It seemed there was no nation, no matter how impoverished, that didn't prefer guns before butter. Even India, which couldn't feed its millions of starving citizens, had recently contracted to pay the Soviet Union one billion dollars a year for the latest weaponry.

An economist's report I'd just read put total world military spending at about two hundred and fifty billion a year. A billion was such an alien number to me that I'd had to spend a little time figuring out what that meant. One million dollars had to be multiplied by one thousand to reach that billion. Multiply that in turn by two hundred and fifty: it boggled the mind. With my background, if I couldn't snare some small piece of the action, I didn't have a brain worth the name. I wasn't greedy. I was ready to set my sights on a very tiny fraction. A mere two-hundredth would do fine: one billion dollars.

I figured I was as prepared as I would ever get to start making my try. Henry the Fifth had been exactly my age when he led England's Army into France and conquered. So had Qadhafi, when he launched his coup and took over Libya.

"I get out of the Army in six weeks," I told Christian Frosch. "Where will you be then?"

"Rome."

"Give me your phone number there. I'll call you. Six weeks."

* * *

Between leaving the Army and going to Rome, I went to see my father. He'd degenerated a lot since I'd last seen him, and it was a shock. He'd lost too much weight, he was getting old too fast, and his voice had an exhausted drag when we spoke to each other through the wire mesh that separated prisoner from visitor.

"Are you sick?" I asked him.

"No, I'm okay. Don't worry about me. Why'd you quit the army? It's a good career."

I told him what I intended to do. I didn't tell him why. He thought about it and nodded tiredly. "It's a possibility, if you're careful. You should look up Paul Rambert. I get letters from him. The rocket launcher is ready to market. I get half of whatever he makes off it, remember?"

"I'll go see him about it," I said.

My father gave me Rambert's address and I wrote it down. "You let me know where you settle for awhile," he said. "I'll send you a legal paper giving you my interest in the launcher. Nothing I can use it for, in here. Maybe you can do something with it."

"Okay."

"Remember something else, Gar. The arms business—it can get real tricky. Look what happened to me." He tried to smile. "Like I told you when you went back to Vietnam—keep your head down, boy."

But it wasn't my head I was worrying about when I left the prison and boarded the plane for Rome.

My father had that thousand yard stare I'd seen too often in combat—on soldiers who had been through more than their minds could take.

* * *

By the early 1970s Rome had become a hotbed for the weapons traffic, both open and clandestine. The continuing oil crisis had shifted the markets geographically. The wealth —and weapons—of the big powers were pouring into Third World countries which supplied the oil. Most of these countries formed a crescent around the Mediterranean, from Iran in the east, south through the Arabian countries, and then west across North Africa. Rome, then, was a strategic location for selling weaponry, as well as a center for spies and terrorists.

The biggest arms dealers had all set up branch offices

there: Khashoggi, Cummings, Merex and the Quandt group of Germany, Solomon Alexandre, al-Zadar, Hiroshi Yukada. The communist bloc was represented by arms salesmen from the factories of Czechoslovakia's Omnipol and Bulgaria's Texim. Rome had also become infested with the smaller fry. There were gunrunners and munitions manipulators of uncertain nationality—plus some catch-as-catch-can go-betweens known as bedroom brokers. These dealers couldn't afford to set up staffed offices, so they worked out of their hotel bedrooms.

It was this last, inglorious group I found myself joining at the beginning of 1974. Christian Frosch, it turned out, didn't have an office in Rome. When he was there, he operated out of the apartment of his Italian girlfriend. This burst one of my illusions. I took a cheap hotel room near the girlfriend's apartment, and we began trying to scrounge up some business.

Christian did have some prospects. For one, he had the temporary license to sell Beretta small arms to Latin America. He'd been right: with my know-how added to his contacts, we did make some sales. But we didn't have the right kind of leverage, as yet, to gouge more than a minimal profit out of each. Then there was a stock of old surplus weapons Christian had bought cheaply. I spent a few weeks putting the stuff in reasonably decent condition, and we sold it all off to guerrilla groups in Africa and Venezuela. But again our profit was very small, in this case because most of it got used up in the high costs of smuggling the shipments to the guerrillas. Christian had to go on contributing his earnings to keep us in business.

Nevertheless, the small-profit deals we'd accomplished encouraged us to form a legal partnership. We added Paul Rambert to the partnership and enlarged our activities to include trying to market the rocket-launcher he'd developed out of my father's original designs. That was when we gave our company a solid-sounding name: Tri-Arms International. But after that we found ourselves scrounging for another three months, without turning up a penny until we got a smell of a big (for us) opportunity.

That was the Brazil-Italy deal that al-Zadar stole out from under us.

* * *

"So there we are," I told Victoria, over our post-dinner coffee. "A little company with a big name and dim prospects."

She didn't commiserate with me. Instead she asked, "How good is your rocket launcher?"

I was getting odd undercurrent vibrations from her that I couldn't grasp. But I didn't mention it because I wasn't sure. "I tested it out with Rambert," I said, "near his place in France. In my opinion it's the best one-man antitank and antifortification weapon anybody's come up with yet."

"But you haven't been able to market it."

Again, that odd vibration. I shrugged. "Rambert's made four sample prototypes. The next step would be to get a big arms manufacturer interested in making a deal with us to tool up and go into mass-production with it. So far we've tried with Beretta, Rheinmetall in Dusseldorf, Belgium's Fabrique Nationale. They weren't even interested in testing it."

I paused long enough for Victoria to ask me why not. But she didn't ask. "Everybody's convinced ahead of time," I said, "that our launcher can't match the sophistication of similar weapons. Like Israel's B-300 and Sweden's Miniman. The word around is that if the launcher were worthwhile, your ex-husband would have tried for a higher court reversal after he lost the patent suit. They figure Alexandre realized it was already becoming obsolete.

"Solomon's Mr. Peel," Victoria said evenly, "is an expert at spreading that sort of rumor."

"I guess he is," I said slowly. And then: "You know, Victoria, I get the distinct impression that not much of what I've told you about myself is news to you."

She took another cigarette from her silver case, and waited until I'd lighted it before answering. "I've kept track of you from time to time," she acknowledged. "Some of the connections I've developed are in positions that made it fairly easy for me to do so."

"Tell me about your connections."

Victoria made a deprecatory gesture. "Like I said, I'm basically an influence peddler. Not a very big one, yet. But I have made progress since I started."

I was watching her closely. "Which was when you went to work for your cousin who wasn't too good at it."

"Lee isn't really *bad* at it. But he gets bored if he has to attend too many social functions in one day. And being an effective influence peddler does not depend, in most cases, on an ability to apply *pressure* on people in key positions. It depends on developing a personal friendship with them.

"Most of the top Washington lobbyists are golf and drinking buddies of men in power. I couldn't go that route, so I had to approach the power men obliquely. In many cases I've done it by first cultivating friendships with the women close to them. Their wives, for example. Or their mothers, personal secretaries, sisters—whoever is most important to them." Victoria smiled a little. "In some cases their mistresses."

I said, only half joking, "You're a sneaky critter."

"I hope I'm learning to be," Victoria told me seriously.

Then she smiled again. "The press is beginning to refer to my unofficial women's group as Victoria Nicolson's Sewing Circle."

"Tell me," I asked her, "about two and a half years ago, did you happen to have among your girlfriends a mistress of somebody high up in the U.S. Army?"

Victoria's eyes met mine. "No. But I did have—and still do have—a friend whose husband is a Pentagon admiral. Naturally, at that level, the Navy and Army do exchange small favors."

I said: "So *you* were the one who got me transferred out of combat duty and into weaponry intelligence, and then to that instruction camp in Central America."

"Yes."

Chapter Thirteen

Garson

"Why?"

"Firstly, because I was concerned for you. I didn't want you going back into combat and getting killed—or wounded worse than you already had been."

"Tell me about *secondly*."

"Secondly, your request to Army authorities indicated, I thought, that you might be considering a civilian career in the arms business. It seemed to me a good idea. It still does."

"And you've watched my progress, or lack of it, since I left the Army."

"Yes."

"Again, why? Not just out of curiosity."

"No," Victoria said, in a way that made me know we had reached the real reason for our dinner together that night. "I'd like to become a partner in your Tri-Arms company, Gar. A secret partner, at first. But a full one."

The news didn't surprise me as much as it would have earlier that evening. "I keep asking you why."

"For much the same reason you're in it. I want to become as successful in the world as my own abilities allow. I want to find out just how potent those abilities are—how far they can take me. The best and quickest way I know of is in the arms business."

"It's strictly a man's business, Victoria."

"I know that. When the toys are guns, the boys only play with other boys. They don't want girls around."

I grinned at her. "Not nice girls, anyway. Or smart girls, either."

Victoria nodded. "Only stag party girls—dumb, dirty and disposable."

"Like cans of beer," I agreed, "which you are not."

She reached across the table and rested a hand on mine. "That's why I need you, up front."

"Mr. Outside and Ms. Inside?" I shook my head. "I've got two partners already. And like me, they want to exercise control over what goes on *inside* the company, too."

"Of course. Just as I'd want some control over your outside moves. Eventually, and discreetly, I'd also want to make some of those outside moves. But inside or outside, Gar, I'd only be one partner among four. A single woman against three men, if it came to a disagreement. I couldn't do anything at all without the agreement of at least two of you."

"Come off it, Victoria. A woman like you wouldn't have much trouble persuading at least one male partner to side with her. That would be enough to stop the other two from going ahead with anything you didn't like."

"The same applies in reverse," she pointed out gently. "Any two of you could stop me and the fourth partner."

I called a brandy order to a passing waiter without asking if Victoria wanted one, too. She removed her hand from mine and we looked at each other until it came. I took a healthy sip, and then told her, "You know how shaky Tri-Arms is. Nobody takes us seriously yet, with reason. If you want into the business, it's a lousy place to start."

"No, it's perfect. For my purposes. Because you're part of it. I know you and I trust you. Also, at this moment your firm is nothing but potential. You need me. I can help you to realize that potential."

"Through your connections in Washington?"

Victoria nodded. "And here."

"Yeah, I was forgetting about Enrico Cardina."

"And some others," Victoria said evenly. She studied me. "Perhaps it would be best for me to give a little proof—to you and your partners, Frosch and Rambert—of *how* useful I can be. *Then* we can discuss whether the three of you need me."

"What sort of proof?"

Victoria picked up my half-finished glass of brandy and took a small sip from it. "Tomorrow. First I want to discuss it with someone."

"Who—and what?"

"Phone me in the morning. We'll make a date for a stroll, and I'll explain it then. Right now, I've had a long day and I'm tired." She was already getting out a credit card to pay our bill. "Will you take me back to my hotel?"

I accompanied her to the Excelsior, and up in the elevator to her floor. She stopped outside her suite, giving me a good night hug and kiss on the cheek. "Until tomorrow . . ."

I kissed her back, not on the cheek. "I guess you may have noticed by now—I still feel the same about you."

Victoria shook her head, a touch of the somber look I remembered in her eyes. "I'm sorry, Gar. . . . I'm afraid you're still too associated in my mind with Alan for me to—"

I refused to let her sink back into that old sorrow: "You always manage to come up with another excuse for saying no to me."

Her small smile was surprisingly impish. "It does seem that way, doesn't it?" Her smile faded. "But it's much too soon for me to shake that feeling. Perhaps, with time ..."

I grinned at her: "But in the meantime you won't even trust the two of us alone together in your hotel room, is that it? You didn't let me pick you up here, and now you don't invite me in for a good night drink."

There was no trace of the smile left in her expression now: "Not for the reason you think. Stuart Peel used to set up electronic surveillance on me from time to time—checking to make sure, I suppose, that I wasn't up to some mischief that might embarrass Solomon. I think they've given that up as unnecessary. But I've gotten into the habit of being careful."

* * *

Hiroshi Yukada was taller than most Japanese, and was built like a small tank. He looked fat in his conservative, French-cut business suit, but he didn't look soft. Trying to judge his age from his solid, round, unlined face was difficult. He could have been anywhere from forty to sixty. A quiet man with an unassuming manner, he had the aura of someone who knew his power but hoarded it for use when occasion demanded.

Victoria had told me about our noon appointment with him during a morning stroll in the park of the Villa Borghese. His name was enough to rivet my full attention. Everyone in the arms world knew it. Weaponry had begun as a sideline among the Asian industries and commercial enterprises Yukada controlled, but his interest in it had grown considerably over the last five years. In Japan, his influence reached all the way up to the heads of government—and, it was rumored, all the way down into his country's powerful gangster clans. When it came to buying, selling or acting as broker for anything there, Yukada generally had his fingers in it somewhere. Recently, his tentacles had begun spreading out beyond the Orient, into Europe and America.

"He was the reason I was in Tokyo that day you spoke with my cousin Lee in Washington," Victoria told me.

She had first met Hiroshi Yukada, Victoria explained, when he'd come to Washington to obtain for Japan an end-user certificate to buy one of the most sophisticated new U.S. airborne ECMs (electronic countermeasure systems). "I introduced him to administration and Pentagon contacts. They were able to get him what he was after. Since then he's kept me on a retainer, representing his interests in Washington. Officially, I'm listed as his public relations consultant."

"How far does he trust your judgment?"

Victoria shrugged. "I haven't failed him so far."

We took a taxi to the small operational base Yukada had established in Rome the previous year: a three-floor house off the Piazza Colonna. It was centuries old, and the exterior looked it. Inside, everything was new, with modern Scandinavian style furnishings. From what I saw in the ground-floor offices, Yukada's Rome branch was not too active. The only staff in sight were two young male secretaries, one Japanese and the other Italian. The Italian conducted us to Yukada and went back to his duties.

Yukada's inner office was spare to the point of being Spartan. He stood up behind a small, functional desk, bowing politely to Victoria and then to me: "I am so happy, Captain Bishop, that you could come to see me." He spoke English slowly and precisely. "Won't you please sit down?"

I took the chair he indicated, across the desk from him. Victoria chose a chair placed against a side wall. For the rest of our time in Yukada's office she stayed there, demurely, off to one side, observing us but not contributing one word.

Yukada sat down and placed his hands on the glass top of his desk. They were square, solid hands, with unusually thick fingers and short thumbs. He regarded me from behind rimless glasses for at least half a minute before he spoke again.

"Captain Bishop, I am in Rome only briefly. I came to take care of several business matters. One of these is to meet with the heads of an Italian company wishing to sell its new APCs to my country."

"APC" was the common term for armored personnel carrier, the fastest growing product in the arms trade. One single U.S. company alone had that year exported two hundred and seventy million dollars worth of its latest APCs. I wasn't surprised to learn Japan might be in the market for new ones.

Echoing my thought, Yukada asked, "Have you seen any of the APCs currently used by my country?"

I nodded. "Seen them, ridden in them, checked them out."

"In Vietnam?"

"There, and during a short stay in Japan."

"What do you think of them?"

"They're not up to the latest developments in APCs elsewhere."

"Ah." Yukada flicked a smile in Victoria's direction, then smiled at me. "And what do you think of the Russian makes? You surely came across those in the Vietnam War."

"How much do you know about APCs, Mr. Yukada?"

"I am not an expert, Captain Bishop."

"Okay—there are two schools of military thought about the APC. One holds that its purpose is to get a squad of soldiers as close as possible to where they're needed, at which point they can jump out and go the rest of the way on foot, from cover to cover.

"The other school figures an APC should be made to fight *from*, with heavy guns and ports for the men inside to fire out of. That's what the Soviet APC is made to do. Trouble is, if it gets knocked out by antitank fire, it's stranded wherever it was hit. The men are left inside, trying to get out and to some point of infantry action. Which isn't easy. The Arabs using Russian APCs learned that in their war with Israel last year. They got clobbered."

"On the other hand," Yukada interjected mildly, "the Russians do sell their APCs for less than other sources."

"Right, and that makes them a bargain—if the safety of the infantry squad inside isn't a consideration. But it should be. Because the real usefulness of an APC is to get troops as close to a point of infantry combat as it can, quickly and safely. From there, as I said, the men jump out and head for the action. The way the Soviet job is built, the exit port has to be *on top*. At the moment of climbing out, a man is completely exposed and entirely visible. If he's killed before he can jump down, there's no point in having an APC carry him that far. Just a waste of money and manpower."

Yukada glanced over at Victoria again. "Miss Nicolson, so far I am pleased with your Captain Bishop." He looked at me again. "My country is not ready to buy new APCs at this moment, but eventually it will be. The Italian manufacturer is offering its product at an attractive price, and claims it is an improved development in what you call the state of the art. A demonstration of this product has been arranged for me, tomorrow morning. My opinion of this military vehicle will have some influence on whether my government chooses to buy it when the time is ripe."

If what I had heard about Yukada was accurate, his

opinion would *clinch* Japan's choice.

"Unfortunately," he continued, "I am not sufficiently knowledgeable, technically. When I set up these offices last year, I hired a retired British officer, Colonel Thoressen, to serve as my arms advisor in Rome. Last month I discovered that he had been taking bribes to send me inflated judgments on certain weapons offered for sale. I also have reason to believe information from this office has reached my competitors. I have dismissed Colonel Thoressen—along with my entire Roman staff, as an added precaution. The two gentlemen you met outside are the beginning of a new staff."

He paused and gazed at me shrewdly. "So at the moment I am without an expert in weapons, and the APC demonstration is tomorrow. I am prepared to pay you two thousand dollars, Captain Bishop, to attend it for me and report your findings to me."

Two thousand wasn't enough to get Tri-Arms out of the hole, but it was a good piece of change for half a day's work. More importantly, I had Victoria's certainty that if Yukada was satisfied with the job I did, it would lead to others for him. For one thing, he did need a permanent arms specialist to represent him in Rome. That alone was far from the ultimate goal I had in mind. But Yukada's stamp of approval was bound to help me in going after the big deals.

"I'll be glad to do it," I told him. "But if you want the very best evaluation you can get, one of my partners is *the* best arms expert I know. Colonel Rambert. I'd like him to fly down from Paris to attend the demonstration with me."

"I would be pleased to have his advice as well as yours, Captain. But I cannot pay more than the fee I've suggested. You would have to share it between you."

"Agreed, if you'll pay his air fare."

Yukada nodded, smiling. "Agreed. I will see to it that the APC maker has you and your partner picked up at your hotel in the morning." He rose to his feet.

It was clearly a dismissal, so I stood up and said goodbye. Victoria stood up and said goodbye, too—but to me. "I've other business to talk over with Mr. Yukada," she explained. "I'll phone you later."

As soon as I got to my hotel, I put through a long-distance call to Rambert in Normandy. He never hung around Rome when he wasn't needed. Most of the time he was up there in his workshop. The rocket launcher was ready, but his own invention wasn't. Sophisticated improvements in assault rifles by other inventors had rendered his out-of-date a couple years back. He'd been working to leapfrog the others ever since.

Rambert got to Paris in time to catch the last evening jet to Rome out of Charles DeGaulle Airport. Victoria still hadn't phoned me by the time he reached my hotel late that night. I called her hotel twice, but she wasn't there.

* * *

The proprietor of my little hotel was visibly impressed by the chauffeured limousine that picked Rambert and me up the next morning at nine. The plant where the Italian company manufactured its full range of military vehicles was a complex of factories thirty miles outside Rome. High chain-mesh fences with signs warning that they were electrically charged surrounded this complex. The limousine took us through a well-guarded gateway and carried us past the factories to the company's vast testing grounds.

The four company representatives waiting for us there took Rambert for the boss and me for his assistant. I didn't disabuse them, and didn't blame them. Paul Rambert had been a commanding figure when I'd first met him and he'd become more so with age. The short-cropped white hair, the icy blue eyes, the clipped speech were unmistakably those of a traditional high career officer. His lurching walk, the result of the bomb blast that had shattered his hip, drew extra respect when put together with the *Croix de Guerre* and *Legion d'honneur* Rambert wore on the lapel of his old, somewhat shabby suit.

The APC that the company wanted to sell to Japan was a six-wheeled job with a revolving turret mounting a 90mm gun and 7.62mm machine gun, plus gunports for infantry weapons and a carrying capacity of eleven men and a driver. A crew of former sergeants from the Italian Army demonstrated its abilities in action. Then Rambert and I went over, under and through the vehicle, in detail, with the crew and company reps. Finally, the two of us shooed away both crew and reps, and tested out the APC for ourselves, driving it at top speed over the roughest terrain on the grounds and firing its turret armament at targets, bunkers and wrecked vehicles that had been put there for that purpose.

Afterwards, the reps gave us a suitcase-load of literature on their APC and invited us to lunch in the company's executive dining room. It was a good lunch, spiced with subtle offers of a substantial rake-off to us if Japan bought their product through Hiroshi Yukada. Rambert and I pretended not to understand. We were aiming for bigger things than a fast bribe, and right then Yukada was our best hope.

At four that afternoon we were in Yukada's office, delivering our findings. "It depends," I told Yukada, "on what your country wants to use the APC for. The strongest points of this one are its speed and excellent maneuverability. And the gunports are beautifully designed. A good product for riot control or other internal security uses. But for battle-field conditions it has many disadvantages. It's not tough enough to withstand modern, armor-piercing shells, first of all. And over rugged terrain, its speed and maneuverability would be reduced considerably, cutting both advantages."

"The problem of its performance on rugged terrain," Rambert explained, "arises because it is a wheeled vehicle, rather than a tracked one. A wheeled APC will get blocked where one with tracks can get through. Of course, this APC could be converted to a tracked vehicle—though that would mean giving away, in some measure, the twin advantages of speed and maneuvering ability."

Rambert began a technical explanation of how the conversion could best be accomplished, but Yukada smiled and raised both hands, palms outward: "Please, Colonel Rambert, I am only a businessman. In Japan we have military engineers who will understand such details, but I cannot. I would appreciate your dictating your findings, fully, for them to study when I return to my country."

"Fine," Rambert said.

"Thank you, Captain. And you, Colonel. You'll both find that one of my secretaries, Itokawa, is quite fluent in both English and French. After you have finished with him, I would like to have a short talk with you."

Rambert glanced at his watch. "I have an appointment in two hours with an old friend who now works in Beretta's engineering department."

Yukada nodded and smiled. "I understand. If you agree, I will tell Captain Bishop what I have in mind, and he can discuss it with you—and your other partner—later."

His Japanese secretary was as good as he'd said. He recorded what Rambert and I dictated on tape to be extra sure that he didn't miss anything. But at the same time he took it all down in an amazingly swift shorthand. Then he went into another office to begin typing it up, and Rambert took off for his appointment. I went back into Yukada's inner sanctum.

He began by presenting me with a check from a New York bank for two thousand dollars—along with his thanks for a job well done. Then he had a small question for me: "Did the Italians offer a bribe to recommend their product?"

I nodded.

"May I give you a bit of advice, based on my own experience as a young man? Always take a small bribe. One can claim later that one tried one's best, and unfortunately failed to achieve what was asked. It does no harm, and provides an additional source of income. Beware of *large* bribes—those can lead to serious trouble if you don't deliver. But a small one—it is merely one way the man offering it proves to his boss that *he* tried *his* best. And it establishes a complicity between you and the giver, which can often be turned to your advantage."

"I'll keep it in mind," I assured Yukada.

He smiled briefly. Then he got down to what was on his mind:

"I am considering, Captain Bishop, asking you—and your Tri-Arms company—to represent me here in Europe, and possibly later in America. I do not mean that you would merely become my new technical arms advisors. I am thinking of having you represent my arms interests here in every way. The terms of your employment in this capacity I would prefer to leave for a later discussion—a few days from now. First of all, you would have to consult with your partners before giving me an answer."

I knew damned well my partners would jump on the opportunity. "I'm interested, naturally," I told Yukada, "but there's a problem. How much leeway would the job leave Tri-Arms to conduct our own business activities?"

"The position would not consume all your time, Captain. And you would be free to pursue your other interests in any way you wished—as long as they did not conflict with *my* interests."

"Could we use your offices here to handle our own business as well as yours?"

"Certainly. Again, as long as your interests did not conflict with mine, I would not object. I would, though, expect Tri-Arms to pay me rent—when your own enterprises began to bring you a profit."

"That's fair enough," I said, making an effort to keep my voice steady. It was more than fair enough, it was gorgeous. Acting as Yukada's representative would give Tri-Arms a big step up in the world by itself. Operating out of his European headquarters would show everyone how much faith he placed in us.

"As I mentioned," Yukada said, "the position would not require all your time. For one thing, you would not have to sell anything for me. At least for some years. In the West, I have not so far been a major seller of arms. In the East, yes, but not here. Primarily, I have been known as a buyer, from Western countries, for resale to Japan and other Asian nations.

"Your position, as my representative, would be, first, to keep me informed of your opinion of what is offered for sale here. Second, I would be sending you my arms shopping lists. It would be your job to acquire the items needed, the best available, for the lowest prices possible.

"We could handle that for you," I assured him. I managed not to fall on my knees and tell him how much we would *love* to handle it for him. It would, in a single step, put

Tri-Arms into a power position, vis-à-vis every big arms maker and broker in the West.

Yukada had folded his thick, powerful hands together on the desk between us. "There is one other matter, Captain. As you know, I have neither been a seller nor a manufacturer of arms in the West. In my own country, however, I have begun to involve myself in the making of weaponry—in a very small way, so far. I have plans to expand in that direction." Yukada paused, briefly. "This is extremely confidential, Captain. I would not want any of my competitors to learn of my intentions."

"This room could be bugged," I warned him.

"It was. But not now. I had a very good man flown here from Japan to make certain of that."

"One of my partners is probably better at it than the man you imported. Wouldn't do any harm to have him double check."

"I will keep that in mind for the future. At this moment I am quite sure we are not being overheard."

"Then you've got nothing to worry about. Your competitors won't learn a thing from me."

"So Miss Nicolson has assured me." Yukada regarded me for a long moment through his rimless lens. "Miss Nicolson is a woman whose opinions I have come to rely on. She informs me that you own the patent on a new man-held rocket launcher which you believe to be better than any similar weapon on the market."

"It *is* better," I told him flatly.

"If we do become associated, Captain, I would be interested in obtaining the designs for this weapon—to show to a Japanese weaponry engineer I have recently hired. And I would like to show him one of your prototypes, too. If his report on it proves positive, I would have you and Colonel

Rambert flown to Japan to consult with him—and me. The next step would be for me to set up a plant to manufacture the weapon in Japan. Under an agreement with you, of course. We could determine the terms then. Is this possibility agreeable to you?"

"It is," I said. The understatement of the year. I was proud of how casually I'd said it.

"Everything I have suggested," Yukada told me smoothly, "is, as I warned you, subject to my making a final decision. I need a few more days to think it over. So do you, I am sure. When I have made up my mind, we will meet again."

He rose to his feet in what I would come to know as his end-of-discussion manner.

"I'll talk it over with my partners," I said as I stood up.

"And with Miss Nicolson also, I hope," he said blandly. "By now, I am sure you realize how much I depend upon her in forming my decisions—here in the West, where I am somewhat of a new boy, as they say."

He didn't come right out and say the whole deal he'd offered me hinged on Victoria giving it the go-ahead. He didn't have to. And I already knew Victoria's terms for giving it that go-ahead.

* * *

Rambert and Christian Frosch didn't take long to agree. Yukada was offering us a golden ladder to climb, *if* Victoria okayed it. He had faith in her, based on past performance, and no doubt he reasoned that her presence in Tri-Arms, as a full partner, would assure him of *our* performance in the future. Giving Victoria an equal share in our company was a small price for us to pay, considering that Tri-Arms wasn't worth a damn at that moment—and could become what we dreamed of with the addition of Victoria. With her, we'd have more than Yukada: her other European connections, like the Vatican banker; her American connections, like the admiral and general who'd gotten me transferred.

Christian made a call to his Italian lawyer friend, Borelli. I phoned the Excelsior Hotel. Victoria was there, waiting for my call. Because of Peel's past surveillance of her, I asked her to come over. Nobody important enough to bug had ever checked into our little hotel before.

Victoria got there a few minutes after Borelli. She gave the old lawyer a smile that had him bubbling with good will towards her.

"I represent the other three parties here," he warned her like a loving uncle. "You should have an attorney of your own present."

Victoria let him have another of those smiles. "I don't need one for this preliminary talk. When you've drawn up our contract, I'll have my cousin fly in to go over it."

Her terms remained straightforward: equal partnership. Plus, whenever Tri-Arms opened a branch in the United States—as we hoped and she expected—Victoria wanted to be officially named as its director. As she pointed out, the position would be in name only. It wouldn't alter the fact that each of the four of us would have an equal say in any decisions. Her name up front would benefit all of us because hers were the connections that could bring us success in the States—and without success there, you couldn't make it to the top in the arms business.

Until that time, her partnership in Tri-Arms International was to be kept quiet. If we did get big enough to operate in the U.S., we would be too big for her ex-husband to squash, out of any annoyance with her.

Once we were all agreed, Victoria stood up and said, "I'm

late for another appointment. Please forgive me."

I escorted her out of our hotel and over to a cab rank on the Via Flaminia. "When will you get back to the Excelsior?" I asked her.

"I'm not sure. Phone me there later." Victoria gave me a quick kiss and jumped into her cab.

When I called the Excelsior at eight that night, she was still out. So I phoned my Dutch playmate, Judith, and took her to Crazy Chess, a discotheque behind the Piazza del Popolo. It and Numero Uno were favorite night spots of rich Third World terrorists, dope smugglers and spies. The manager was a former Italian air force test pilot with whom I'd become friends. I had a short talk with him before Judith and I took to the crowded dance floor.

We were back at our tiny table, having a snack and a drink, when my ex-pilot friend brought a Japanese smuggler over to meet me and took Judith off to dance. When I left the Crazy Chess with Judith an hour later, my head was full of new information about Hiroshi Yukada. Some of it was rumor—from teenaged murders to middle-aged control of powerful, criminal clans. More was solid fact—from an early stint in prison to bank takeovers and his present position as *éminence grise* behind Japan's strongest political party. None of it made me less inclined to become associated with Yukada.

Since I was sharing my hotel room with Rambert, Judith and I wound up our night in her bed. After Judith finally settled into a sound sleep, I slipped out to her living room and phoned the Excelsior again. Victoria had not returned.

At that point I naturally began to wonder what Victoria did with her nights. Just as naturally I had some specific suspicions about it.

Chapter Fourteen

Victoria

The two layers of heavy bath towels that served as a cushion between her flesh and the hard wood of the big sauna bench were already sopping wet with her perspiration. Enveloped in the steam of the small sauna, she rolled over, yawned, and sat up on the bench, took a cup from the shelf on the wall beside it. She filled the cup with cold water from a wall faucet, gulped it down, and replaced the cup. Then she stretched out again, face-down this time, and continued to sweat the weariness of the long day out of her system.

It had been a day of promising but often irritating verbal maneuvering. Before the meeting with Gar Bishop and his partners, she'd spent lunch and most of the afternoon with the Sicilian. Enrico Cardina had introduced Victoria to the man: a rising industrialist who was also a respected Mafia don and a patron of the Church. Like most new-rich Italians, he was afraid of an eventual communist takeover, and sought safe ways to slip his profits out of the country before it happened. Most old-rich Italians had done so long ago.

She had convinced him that the best legitimate way would be to open a branch in the U.S.—and to let her choose the right influential Americans to front it for him. But he'd made her spend hours persuading him to do what he already wanted to do—giving himself those hours to try to seduce her.

Then the dinner with Enrico to thank him for the introduction—and more of the same. The Vatican banker was still stalling about letting her handle "public relations" in Washington for a group of Church holdings while he continued with his attempt to get her into his bed. Once again, as with the Sicilian, she'd managed to tell him no without saying never.

In her professional life, she had become, of necessity, adept at the game of putting men off without turning them off. Outright rejection could spell finish to a potentially profitable relationship. So she learned to turn her appeal to these men into a tool of her trade, using it, carefully, to further her business interests. It was never necessary to go to bed with any of them to serve this purpose: it was enough to keep them intrigued by the possibility. For most men, especially established men, anticipation was a stronger persuader than fulfillment. The latter could prove disappointing to them or even embarrassing. Expectation kept the juices of youth stirring in them.

There was no business advantage great enough to induce her to let a man make love to her if she did not feel powerfully drawn to him by some special personal magnetism. In the seven years since Bellecroix, she had met only one such man.

Victoria raised her head a bit and rested her chin on the drenched towels cushioning the bench. She peered through the steam at the barbells and other exercise weights in their rack against the opposite wall. But she found herself thinking, not of the man to whom they and the sauna belonged, but of Garson Bishop. Not as he was today: the Gar Bishop of long ago. The tall, infatuated boy, wearing Solomon's swimming trunks that first time at the pool and telling her how he'd achieved such a strong build so young.

It occurred to her that she had used, with the adult Gar Bishop, the same technique she so often used when making business deals with men who desired her. Not giving in to him, but holding out the future possibility. And partly for the same reason. But partly not: partly out of feelings that remained uncertain.

She had not entirely lied to him. It was true that she could not see him without remembering him as the boy Alan had come to worship. Too many images of her dead son intruded, still, for her to know her feelings about Gar Bishop as he was now. That *could* change, in time. So perhaps she hadn't lied. Perhaps . . .

Victoria let her eyes droop shut, let herself drift into a half sleep. When the sauna door opened and closed she didn't hear it. She wasn't aware of his presence until he sat down on the bench beside her and the broad, heavy hand came to rest on her bare back, between her shoulder blades. His touch was unmistakable. She came awake slowly, delaying it, drawing pleasure from the hand as it slid down her slippery-wet spine to her buttocks. The hand cupped one of her buttocks and squeezed, then moved to her other buttock. The restrained power with which it caressed her naked flesh made her curl up inside like a purring kitten.

She had responded to the inner force of the man from their first meeting Washington. He was the only man she knew who exuded this force as potently as her ex-husband. But he exploited it differently than Solomon Alexandre. And Victoria had changed a great deal since the years of her early marriage. She had acquired her own kind of strength, and could respond to such power without being overwhelmed by it. She could control what it did with her and what she did with it, could even, sometimes, toy with that power in a man.

The hand delved between her buttocks, igniting a fire in her loins that made her thighs open of their own volition. Victoria held back, deliberately, delaying the pleasure again. Rolling on her side, bringing her knees up together, she squinted at him with a taunting smile.

Without clothing, Hiroshi Yukada didn't look at all fat. He looked *solid*: as powerful physically as he was in every other way. An hour each day of working out with weights kept him so. And without clothing, Yukada was a different man in another way. All of his heavily muscled torso, front and back, was covered by tattoos of vividly colored dragons.

In Japan, the tattoos had a special meaning. There, young men submitted to this ritual tattooing on being initiated into one of the quasi-religious and highly political criminal cults. It was not only the tattoos which were indelible. Whether the man so marked eventually settled down as a petty shopkeeper or rose as high as Yukada, he would remain connected for life to this underworld milieu.

Victoria now experienced the same thrill of fascinated horror she'd felt the first time she'd seen that monstrous melange of tattoos. But they did not make the man himself horrible. Not to her. She had known a real monster too intimately to mistake Yukada for one.

When he rose to his feet, she saw how ready he was for her. He reached for her but she stopped him, seizing his organ in her hand, gripping it tightly. "Not yet," she told him firmly.

He stood still over her, his hands closing into fists with the effort it cost to restrain himself. She felt him grown hard as an iron bar in her grasp.

"You're my prisoner," she told him.

"Yes ..." It was more of a hiss than a word.

"Dry me first," she said, playing a variation on the passion game they'd evolved between them: increasing his excitement and her own through prolonged denial of his ultimate gratification.

Yukada took a towel from a wall hook and obeyed. By the time he had finished drying her body, he was trembling.

"Carry me," she told him.

He threw the towel to the floor and scooped her up effortlessly from the bench. Cradled in his massive arms, Victoria chuckled softly as she planned the next delay of his fulfillment—though not her own. She bit into the red dragon tattoo on his broad shoulder as her bore her out of the sauna, into the bedroom of the top-floor apartment above his Roman headquarters.

* * *

It was not poverty but political fanaticism that led the young Hiroshi Yukada into Japan's criminal underworld. His family was wealthy enough to send him to the Kyoto Imperial University, where he first showed his exceptional talent for practical finance and organization. It was there that he also acquired a passion for the harsh ideals of the ancient samurai warriors, with their allegiance to authoritarian rule and military conquest. By the time World War II ended, he was the leader of a group of like-minded students involved in breaking up meetings of antagonistic political bands and beating up their members.

It was Yukada's leadership at an especially violent public demonstration, protesting against Japan's surrender, that landed him in prison. His cell-mate was a waterfront gangster. The two developed a mutual respect, based at first on certain beliefs they had in common. The gangsters of Japan had long been active in politics, always on the far right. The gangster was impressed by Yukada's superior education and implacable determination. The youthful Yukada, in turn, found that the gangster code of obedience to death had a striking similarity to the samurai ideals. He decided that the underworld could provide him with a base for his political activism.

The gangster was released before Yukada, who upon his own release went to see him and asked to join his mob.

He was tested first: he had to extort protection money from dock merchants and workers, and participate in murderous battles over territory with other underworld gangs. After he had proved himself, there came the painfully prolonged, ritual tattooing, followed by initiation as a *yakuza*, as Japanese gangsters were called.

His education enabled Yukada to become the gang's business advisor. With him in charge of its finances, its income skyrocketed. At this point, he used his ability as a negotiator to combine his original gang with others that had formerly been rivals—for mutual profit. With his own profits from this criminal merger, Yukada began buying up legitimate businesses.

At the same time, he began backing political candidates of his choice—using the criminal gangs to wreck the campaigns of other candidates. These politicians, in turn, helped the growth of his businesses, both legitimate and illicit.

His wealth, government leverage and spread of business interests grew swiftly under the American occupation of Japan. Through his family and government connections he became friends with a number of occupation officials, doing them favors which they returned in kind. From these Americans, he learned how worried their chief, General MacArthur, was about a "Red Menace" inside Japan. The authorities under MacArthur were anxious to soothe his worries by finding someone capable of fighting every emergence of communist influence.

And Yukada could do this for them with his *yakuza* gangs —in return for a diversity of special privileges. It was through acting as the main contact between these obliging criminal bands and the occupation authorities that Yukada, finally, became the supreme *oyabun*: the equivalent of a Mafia boss of bosses. With both the underworld and the authorities in his pocket, the rise of his business empire and political power became unstoppable.

After the U.S. occupation ended, Japanese politicians discovered that Yukada's special position was also indestructible. They had little chance of achieving high government office without his support. By the time Yukada made his first visit to Washington, he had become the key behind-the-scenes manipulator in the strongest party in Japan, and a private financial advisor to the current Prime Minister as well.

But the livid dragons indelibly etched into his skin remained, as a reminder of Yukada's other connections, and as another facet of the man who made exquisite love to Victoria in Rome.

* * *

The soft ringing of the bedroom telephone awakened her gently. She kept her eyes closed and curled over on her side as she felt Yukada get out of bed to pick up the phone. He began speaking quietly, in rapid Japanese. Then he was silent. Victoria opened her eyes a bit. Early morning light filtered into his bedroom through the slats of the venetian blinds. Yukada stood holding the phone, frowning as he listened to whoever was at the other end.

He spoke again, briefly, and hung up the phone. Picking up his black silk robe, Yukada went into the bathroom and quietly shut the door. Victoria sat up in the wide bed, pushing the pillows to form a bolster for her back. Lolling against them, she let herself come fully awake slowly, relishing the utter physical contentment in every nerve of her body.

She had taken pleasure in him for a long time that night before allowing him to take pleasure in her. That was part of the game they both enjoyed, each in a different way.

For Victoria its excitement was in exulting, for however long the interlude lasted, in a brief period of total power over this immensely powerful man. For Yukada it was another kind of exultation: a challenging exercise of his resources of stoic control, a cruel self-testing imbedded in his samurai code.

Victoria knew that many would consider this aspect of their sexual relationship unusual and didn't care. That it was odd and unexpected, she admitted. But that applied, in some measure, to the rest of their relationship as well. Certainly their connection had grown into something neither had expected when they'd met.

First, it was incredible that a man of Yukada's background would've come to respect so totally any woman's judgment in business and politics, and come to depend so entirely on her discretion. Not until he had surprised them both by developing so much trust in her, had he let her know how much he desired her. He was not a man who ran after women. At home in Japan he had a beautiful, young wife, and she satisfied him. Victoria had met her, liked her, and never had contact with Yukada other than for business when she visited him in Japan. But in the West, he'd been a man in his prime without a woman—until Victoria.

That she did not love him didn't trouble Yukada. For him it was enough that he desired her, and knew she desired him in return—at least during his short visits to Europe and America. Both knew that her desire for him was not likely to survive a longer stay. And these brief interludes of passion never affected the other aspects of their relationship in any way.

Victoria looked at the small clock on one of the bedside tables. It was a few minutes past seven a.m. She pressed a button on the table. It would signal Yukada's Japanese man-servant to serve them a continental breakfast. Probably the servant was already preparing it. He would have been awakened by the phone call before passing it through to Yukada's bedroom.

Yukada emerged from the bathroom, belting the black robe around his thick bulk. He smiled when he saw her awake. "It is early. If you want to get more sleep, I will—"

"No, I've had enough." That was something she shared with Yukada: an ability to restore her energies with only a few hours sleep. "I'm glad to see you smiling again. You looked worried by that call."

"Not worried. A bit angry. It seems that your former husband has found himself another go-between in Japan."

Victoria knew about Solomon using Yukada several times in the past as his go-between in selling arms to Japan. She also knew he'd begun objecting to the very large fees Yukada charged for his services.

"Is it someone as effective as you?" she asked.

Yukada nodded. "General Tashiro. Have you heard of him? He has excellent family and political connections. And a distinguished military career. I'm afraid Sir Solomon will find him quite satisfactory. Never mind, I will find some way to retaliate, sooner or later."

Victoria said, questioningly: "This General Tashiro sounds like someone I would be interested in meeting."

"Perhaps, but not through me. The general and I have no love for each other. We've been on opposite sides politically too often." Yukada smiled at Victoria again. "Though I'm sure he would enjoy knowing you."

She smiled back at him. "But not as much as you enjoy it." Her tone made him fall silent, gazing at her. She saw the reawakening of desire in his eyes.

There was a gentle knock at the bedroom door. Yukada opened it and his servant entered carrying their breakfast tray. Victoria didn't bother pulling up the sheet to cover her breasts, as she would have in the early days. The man set the tray on the bedroom table and bowed on his way out. Victoria swung off the bed and walked to the table without putting on her robe.

Yukada laughed thickly, watching her sit down naked at the table. Victoria felt her own sexual appetite reviving under his stare. But she picked up one of the sugared rolls and said perversely, "Breakfast time." She bit into the roll as Yukada took his seat across from her and picked up the silver coffee pot. "You were late getting back last night," she said while he filled their cups.

"The company's chairman and president are desperately eager to sell their APCs to Japan. It was difficult to get away from them without making a commitment."

Victoria stirred cream and sugar into her coffee. "You're not going to recommend the Italian product to your government?"

He didn't give her a direct answer. "I told them to send one of their APCs to me in Japan so our people there can examine it before coming to a decision." Yukada paused and then added: "I will also be asking Captain Bishop to contact the heads of other APC manufacturers, in Europe and America, to make similar arrangements for me—after he and Colonel Rambert have made a detailed assessment of the strong and weak points of each."

Victoria had her own suspicions about Yukada's real purpose. She wondered how long it would take Gar to get a hunch along the same lines. But with her it was more than a hunch. She knew more about Yukada's preparations to become a major arms maker. If her suspicion was correct, Yukada would use the weak features in the foreign APCs to dissuade Japan from buying any of them for the next couple of years. That would be long enough for one of his own companies—which presently made trucks and construction vehicles—to develop a better APC, based on the strongest features of each foreign make.

But she sipped her coffee and said nothing. He would tell her about it when he was ready, not before.

Yukada took a sip from his own cup. "I am giving a great deal of responsibility to your young friend," he said quietly. "But I am sure he will not abuse my trust."

"You *can* be sure of it."

Yukada nodded. "I can, with you to look after my interests."

Victoria dunked the last of her sweet roll in coffee and finished it off. "Even without me, you could be certain Gar Bishop wouldn't betray you. He's aiming very high. Too high to hurt his chances by turning you against him now."

"You are quite fond of the young man."

"Yes."

"And he is more fond of you. But that will not affect your judgment."

"No." Victoria wasn't worried that Yukada might become jealous of another man in her life. Jealousy wouldn't be his style. She drank the last of her coffee and got up, strolled to a window and opened the blinds. The view was a lovely one: over red-tiled roofs to the dome of the Pantheon, gleaming with morning light.

Yukada came up behind her. "You'll scandalize the Romans, standing at an open window like this." When he put his massive arms around her she realized he'd removed his robe. His thick-fingered hands cupped the underslopes of her breasts, lifting them slightly in his palms. She felt the hard strength of him rising between her thighs.

"No one is looking," she tried to say, but there was a tremor in her voice and the words became impossible to finish. She turned in his embrace and wrapped her arms around his neck, her breasts flattening against his dragon-tattooed chest, her pelvis moving.

He picked her up and carried her back to the bed.

Chapter Fifteen

Garson

A week after Hiroshi Yukada returned to Japan, I got an object lesson, if I needed one, in what could happen to people who betrayed his trust. The body of his previous Rome arms agent, Colonel Thoresson, was fished out of the Tiber. The police verdict was death by drowning: an accident or suicide.

A month later, in July of 1974, I got a lesson in what could happen to entire nations if they let any of the big arms tycoons play games with them. Turkey invaded the Greek island of Cyprus. Since Greece's defense capability had been eroded by the secret sales of its best NATO weaponry to North Africa, Turkey won possession of half the island with startling swiftness. It was not until months later that the rumor spread about who had manipulated the sell-off of Greek arms: Solomon Alexandre and Ahmed al-Zadar. The rumor didn't hurt either of them one bit. It merely confirmed their positions in the trade's Golden Circle.

* * *

"Surprise, surprise," Stuart Peel said. "Fancy meeting you here."

"Here" was the lobby of the best hotel in Munich, the Four Seasons. I was there for meetings with the sales chief of Kruass-Maffei, one of Germany's biggest manufacturers of artillery and military vehicles. Peel, I figured, was there for the purpose of running into me by surprise.

He didn't make any serious attempt at pretending otherwise: "Got time for a drink?"

I glanced at my watch. "A quick one."

He led me into the tiny bar off the lobby. One of the four tables had a reserved sign. The bartender whipped it off when he saw Peel. We sat and ordered, and looked at each other. It was more than a decade since I'd last seen him, but he hadn't changed much. The same freckled face, bald pate, and soft brown, friendly eyes.

"Let's get something out of the way first," he said directly. "You got any hard feelings about that old lawsuit between Sir Solomon and your father?"

"Since my father won it, no."

"Good. Shame what's happened to him. But that was real dumb, getting mixed up with dope smuggling."

I took a swig of my scotch. "I agree."

Peel leaned across the table and fingered the lapel of my new suit. "Nice material. British tailor?"

"Huntsman."

Peel whistled softly. "Savile Row's best. Must've set you back a thousand pounds."

"Not that much." But he was close. It had reduced our Tri-Arms bank balance by over eight hundred pounds. With the kind of people I'd begun meeting in the five months since becoming Yukada's representative, and the kind of money I talked with them, it wasn't good business to look like a bum scrounging for handouts.

Peel took a sip from his glass, made a face, and put it down. "So you're not doing too bad with Yukada," he said tentatively.

"Not bad."

"But you could do better—judging from your bank account."

I didn't ask how he knew about my bank account. That was his profession. "Tell me how. I'm ready to learn."

"You always were a smart kid. Smart and careful." Peel gave me a flash of the old grin. "I guess you're old enough now for me to call you a kid without insulting you."

"I guess. So *how* can I do better?"

"You ought to have a talk with Sir Solomon one of these days."

"About doing better?"

"A lot better. By the way, how close would you guess Japan is to making up its mind on which APC to take?"

One of the APC firms after that contract was, I knew through Victoria, controlled by Alexandre via a series of holding companies. "Search me," I said blandly. "I'm not part of the Japanese government."

"Yukada is, practically."

"I don't see him that often, and he doesn't tell me much." I drank more of my scotch. "You used to be Alexandre's chief spy," I said with curiosity. "Have you graduated to handling business for him, too?"

"Golz doesn't really know you," Peel said, dropping any pretense of having met me by accident. "Not like I do." Another grin. "Look on me as a Dutch uncle, giving some good advice. Have a talk with Sir Solomon."

"About Yukada and Japan?"

"Among other things." Peel took two business cards from his pocket and laid them on the table. "Here's my number and that's Golz's. Call either of us whenever you're ready. We'll pass the word."

I pocketed the cards. Looking at my watch, I said, "I've got an appointment."

"Me too." Peel put money down for our drinks. "Just remember one thing, kid. A job's only as good as it pays. You could make ten times more working for Sir Solomon than you're getting out of Yukada."

"You think Alexandre would be interested in how well I do after he's sucked out everything I know about Yukada?"

Peel shrugged. "That'd be up to you. If you don't figure you've got anything else to offer, find yourself another business. But if you've got the right stuff, you could have a job for life with Sir Solomon."

"I'm not in the market for a job. I've got a company of my own, in case you haven't heard."

His smile was deprecating. "I heard. Tri-Arms International. Strictly bush league. And likely to stay that way." Peel got up, raised a hand in farewell, and strolled off.

I finished my scotch. He wasn't wrong about Tri-Arms still being a long way down from the big leagues. But the very fact that Alexandre had sent him sniffing around meant we were heading in the right direction.

* * *

At first I'd had the running of the Tri-Arms office in Rome pretty much to myself. Rambert had flown back to his workshop in France. Victoria was in Washington starting quiet preliminary work for Tri-Arms there. Christian Frosch was finishing off a job he'd previously contracted in Holland.

Before he'd left, Christian had gone over Yukada's building minutely, making certain there were no bugs or taps. Then he'd installed an anti-surveillance security system of his own invention, and employed an Italian he trusted to check us out daily when he wasn't there to handle it himself.

Not until that was accomplished did Tri-Arms move into a couple offices on the second floor of Yukada's building. Just me and a secretary, at first. She was a sharp woman in her fifties who spoke and typed flawlessly in seven languages. She had been thoroughly cleared by a detective friend of Borelli's before we'd hired her. The same detective was under contract to check on her again, from time to time, to make sure she didn't get romantically entangled with somebody trying to use her as a pipeline to us.

Before long I had to bring Christian back and turn over the running of the Rome office to him. I was off on planes too often, going to check out APCs for Yukada. Usually I dragged Rambert away from his workshop to go with me. Fortunately for our small Tri-Arms bank account, eager APC makers paid for our flights and hotel expenses, in addition to wining and dining us often enough that we didn't have to dig into our own pockets for many meals.

Twice in five weeks these trips got me to Washington. Victoria was busy as hell, and it was an education to watch her in professional action.

Her cousin, Lee Nicolson, was the only one in on the fact that she was preparing to set up her own offices devoted entirely to our arms firm. He had to know because he was already beginning to act as Tri-Arms' legal eagle in the States. But for a time Victoria planned to continue operating out of his offices, preserving the fiction for others that her only connection with Tri-Arms International was as its Washington "public relations" agent. We were supposed to be just a new client she worked for. In fact, she was already quietly shifting most of the work for her other clients to her subordinates.

Several times I got to spend my evenings with her. In order to keep Rambert pleasantly occupied those evenings, I found a young hooker who looked like a fourteen-year-old schoolgirl—exactly his taste. I'd checked her out, however, and made sure she was actually twenty. We didn't need statutory rape trouble for one of the Tri-Arms partners at that stage.

Victoria couldn't spare me too many evenings. She was too busy buttering all those upper-level connections for Tri-Arms' upwardly mobile future. I couldn't very well object to being turned down for that kind of night work. Two evenings we ate out, and one she cooked a meal for us at her house in Alexandria, across the Potomac from Washington.

She neatly managed to continue putting off my attempts at more personal closeness without giving me any reason to think she didn't care for me—or wouldn't care more, given time. I didn't press; and I didn't mention any suspicions I had about her means of manipulating Hiroshi Yukada.

On my first return visit to the States, I'd also gone to see my father. I didn't do it again. He looked so much worse that I could hardly bear to see him, and a couple weeks later I got a letter from him begging me not to come again.

"Being in here is tough enough," he wrote me. "Seeing you makes it worse. It reminds me too much that there's a world outside I probably won't ever see again."

That kind of self-pity was so unlike Lou Bishop that I knew his state of mind was even lower than I'd thought. I went back to work with redoubled determination to use the arms business as my lever for getting him out before he died in that prison. But Tri-Arms was a long way from achieving the wealth and power I needed.

Tri-Arms began making money—but in dribs and drabs. Yukada's payments to us for acting as his buying agent were on the small side. Part of the compensation, he'd pointed out, was that Tri-Arms should begin to pull in a lot more, in time, through mere association with his name. He was right, of course. Almost immediately it did attract some small deals our way—enough to keep Tri-Arms ticking. But bigger deals were slower in coming. First the big boys had to feel us out, and their interest in doing so, naturally, was to try to sell to Yukada.

But Yukada wasn't in a big buying mood at the time—not even where APCs were concerned. He continued to want our assessments of the different makes and to have sample vehicles sent to Japan, but took no action. I began to form interesting notions about his true motivations—based partly on what he was doing with our rocket launcher.

A couple weeks after Yukada had returned to Japan, he flew Rambert and me there to meet with a weaponry engineer at a small arms plant he'd set up outside Kyoto. Three days later we had a contract. Yukada's small arms plant would tool up to mass-produce our rocket launcher—secretly until he was ready to market it. Tri-Arms would get a decent royalty on all sales in the East; terms in the West were dependent on when and whether Tri-Arms found an American producer to turn out the launcher in quantity.

I saw enough of the small arms plant in those few days to observe that it had spare facilities to turn out a lot more than our launcher and the assault rifles and machine guns already on production lines. Yukada had a way to go before he could match such small arms firms as Switzerland's SIG or Italy's Beretta—but that was apparently what he was aiming for.

After that visit to Japan, I did some further checking on Yukada through a Japanese freelance journalist who was based in Rome and had a good researcher back in Tokyo. I got a list of Yukada's industries—those known to be his and those believed to be under his control. One company he controlled made farm and construction vehicles—and had recently set up a new plant for some secret project. Putting two and two together, I figured that if he was secretly preparing to produce our rocket launcher, he could be doing the same to turn out his own APC.

No reason he shouldn't, as far as we were concerned. Since we were associated with him, the bigger Yukada got in the arms business the better for Tri-Arms. Eventually we could be raking in substantial broker's commissions from sales of the rocket launcher and his APCs. But eventually was not right now. Right now Tri-Arms was still hungering for its first really large deal.

However, our association with Yukada *was* getting Tri-Arms VIP treatment from highly prestigious circles. Military attachés began inviting me to embassy functions, which introduced me into one useful circle of connections. The meetings with arms manufacturers built me another. It had to pay off sooner or later.

It did, less than two weeks after my drink with Stuart Peel in Munich. Our first big deal came from an unexpected source: from behind the Iron Curtain.

* * *

Bulgaria's Texim arms-manufacturing complex, like that of Czechoslovakia's Omnipol, had as its first task the augmentation of Soviet policy abroad. But its second task was to bring in much needed currency from outside the Soviet sphere. Yukada was a potential key to such currency from Japan. Tri-Arms was a potential key to Yukada. So Texim flew Rambert and me to Bulgaria to talk business.

First we were treated to a couple days and nights of lavish entertainment at the Vitosha Hotel. The Vitosha was already notorious as an international relaxation center for high-living Arab, Turk and German smugglers of arms and drugs to capitalist Europe. Later the hotel would gain further infamy as the possible birthplace of the plot to assassinate the Pope.

The entertainment laid on for us included a bevy of luscious girls, some young enough to indicate that Bulgaria had obtained a detailed dossier on Rambert's foibles from its agents abroad. Then we were taken out to one of Texim's proving grounds for a day of demonstrating and testing its latest APCs. We arranged to have one sent to Yukada, along with our own run-down on its strong and weak features.

Everything was routine up to that point, with no apparent opportunity that would make the finances of Tri-Arms much healthier. But then we were taken back into the Vitosha Hotel for a final night's entertainment. While Rambert was kept occupied by a pair of frisky Lolitas, a Texim sales commissar had a private talk with me about another matter.

"There is a well-financed group of Ugandan rebels," he told me, "who want to organize a coup to seize control of their country. One of their leaders has approached us to supply their needs. But of course we had to refuse."

Of course. Uganda's blood-drenched dictator, Idi Amin Dada, was supported and armed by the Soviet Union.

"However," the Texim sales commissar continued delicately, "there is no reason *somebody* shouldn't gain a profit from the needs of these Ugandan rebels. Their leader will be in Rome later this week. I can put you in touch with him. A goodwill gesture, from us to you, in the hope that you will speak well of our APC to Hiroshi Yukada."

Goodwill gesture, hell. Texim had a problem, and I was a possible solution. The Bulgarians were lusting after the rebel money, but couldn't sell directly to them without incurring wrath from Russia. Texim could, however, sell what the Ugandan rebels wanted to Tri-Arms—and later swear I had lied about the ultimate destination of their products.

"I am confident," the Bulgarian told me with a smile, "that between us, we understand each other."

"Completely," I assured him.

What was understood was that I would come to Texim to fill the rebel shopping list. Tri-Arms, of course, would get a commission—a *small* commission because Soviet bloc firms were tightfisted about the percentages they would pay capitalist middlemen. Three days later I met with the rebel leader in Rome. Two days after that I double-crossed Texim.

The Ugandan rebel group had approached Texim first because the bulk of the weapons in rebel hands were from behind the Iron Curtain, stolen from the stocks supplied to Idi Amin Dada's army by the Soviet Union. The rebels needed a lot of ammunition, plus spare parts and replacements—plus more of the same kinds of weapons and some heavier stuff. The size of their order was startling. They had set up six guerrilla camps across the border from Uganda, in Tanzania, and each camp was filled with Ugandan tribesmen who hated Amin's guts. Though it was to take four more years for them to topple their dictator, they were eager to get started; and, as Texim's man had said, they were well-financed.

Victoria flew in from Washington to discuss the possibilities, in detail, with Christian, Rambert and myself. I didn't go back to Bulgaria with the rebel shopping list. I went instead to see a recent acquaintance: Egypt's military attaché in Rome.

In the past, the Soviet bloc had liberally supplied Egypt with arms. Since then, relations between Egypt and Russia had cooled and the United States totally rearmed Egypt.

Hence, Egypt was left with huge stocks of Soviet bloc weaponry and ammunition that it no longer needed.

Two days after my preliminary talk with the attaché, I flew to Cairo for separate talks with select Egyptian military leaders. In my dealings, I used everything Victoria had told me about how the master did it. Wolf or devil, Solomon Alexandre was still the one who had pioneered the way.

Tri-Arms' slice of the rake-offs arranged with the Egyptians, plus our hiked-up charges to the Ugandan rebels, netted us close to a quarter of a million dollars. Tri-Arms was still a little fish, trying to stay alive between the big sharks, but we were a genuine company with a real financial base to operate from. We put half the profit in a Swiss bank. Victoria took the other half back with her to grease the wheels for Tri-Arms in Washington.

That was early in 1975. By the middle of that year we'd acted as broker in a number of smaller deals and won and lost on two fairly big ones.

The deal we won was snatched from the shark who had stolen our Italy-Brazil sale the previous year: Ahmed al-Zadar. Spain had seven hundred M16 assault rifles for sale, used but in good condition. On the open market M16s were going for eighty to a hundred dollars apiece. I got there just after al-Zadar's Spanish representative had bid eighty for each with black market resale in mind. I bid ninety. The rep had to check with al-Zadar by phone. While he was gone I jumped my bid to one hundred, plunking down the full price: seventy thousand bucks from our Tri-Arms account. Al-Zadar's rep returned with a higher bid too late. The Spanish government had sold the goods to me.

In the Philippines, where the insurgents were having a difficult time obtaining weapons, the black market price for an M16 had skyrocketed to one thousand dollars: nine hundred more than I'd invested. After subtracting our cost to ship them to Yukada and his cost to smuggle them into the Philippines, the profit was six hundred thousand. We split it equally with Yukada, banking half our share in Switzerland and half in Rome.

The one we lost was a lot bigger. Libya was offering ten million dollars for two thousand high-tech Star-Tron night vision scopes. The scopes were made in the U.S., which had an embargo on arms sales to Libya. So Victoria popped over to Japan to get a fake end-user certificate from Yukada. But before she returned with it, her ex-husband had grabbed the deal. Alexandre had moved in fast with a fake end-user certificate from Iran. That loss hurt.

After that I had a talk with Victoria about whether she could move faster on deals involving the U.S. if she came out in the open, now, as a Tri-Arms partner. But we finally decided it would be smarter to wait until we were ready to establish a full-fledged headquarters there.

"And there's no point in opening up in the States," I acknowledged, "until we can do it big."

Victoria nodded. "I've got some of the high-level contacts Tri-Arms will need. I'm making more. But we can't make the best use of them until we can offer them something in exchange—something they need, be it money or support against opponents or exchange of favors from equal power positions. Washington connections of that caliber are for operating on the scale of al-Zadar, Cummings and Khashoggi."

"Or Solomon Alexandre," I added.

"Yes. Of course we *could* open a Washington branch as Hiroshi Yukada's agent. But Tri-Arms would only be an appendage to his operation." Victoria gave me a deceptively mild look. "I don't think we want that. Do we?"

I certainly didn't. I wanted Tri-Arms to launch itself in the

States as a power to be reckoned with—and I doubted we'd reach that level for a long time. How we were going to reach it was far from clear.

Then, in mid September, Tri-Arms got its biggest break since tying up with Yukada.

Ahmed al-Zadar got in touch with me.

Chapter Sixteen

Garson

At first I didn't realize it was al-Zadar. The approach was oblique, to say the least.

I was in London to talk with the heads of the military vehicles division of Land Rover. My hotel was the Dorchester, and I was having breakfast in its dining room when I met Faith Warren, undoubtedly one of the most stunning girls in England.

She bumped against my table while walking to her own, upsetting my coffee. Her apology was profuse and pleasant, and my invitation to breakfast was accepted. I had to cut it short because of my morning appointment, but Faith assured me she was staying at the hotel and likely to be in that evening.

Sure enough, she was there, and amenable to having drinks in my suite. Drinks led to bed with startling ease. A generously-tipped bellhop had told me Faith was an earl's daughter. Later I affirmed this, and also discovered that she was one of the highest-priced call girls in England.

I was in bed with her, phoning room service for dinner for two in my suite, when a guy barged in claiming to be her husband and threatening to kill me. The fabrication was so transparent he didn't try to make it believable. He was prepared to be mollified. In fact, he was also willing to give me a certified bank check for ten thousand pounds, in return for information about Japan's plans to buy APCs.

I threw them both out, and less than an hour later I received a long-distance phone call from Ahmed al-Zadar— *himself*, not an intermediary. "You were a bit rough with my two friends tonight," he began pleasantly after introducing himself.

"If those two were yours," I told him thinly, "thanks for the girl but not for the guy. And it was a waste of your dough and their time."

A booming laugh came over the phone. "I don't consider it a waste. I knew a good deal about you before. But now I know you better. I like you, Captain Bishop."

"That's mighty generous, considering the way I aced you out of those Spanish M16s."

Another booming laugh. "But that is precisely one of the reasons I like you, Captain. You handled that neatly."

"Tell me about your other reasons for liking me."

"Your absolute discretion about Hiroshi Yukada. I've tested that before, though you may not have known it. Tonight was only a final try—not even that, more of a joke, perhaps. A man of talent *and* discretion is a rare jewel. Could you be my guest this weekend? I want to discuss some business with you."

I boarded one of his private jets at Gatwick the next morning for the flight down to the Mediterranean. The plane lived up to everything I'd read about in the papers: a DC-8 converted into a sumptuous flying apartment. As publicized, the living room was mahogany-panelled and the bathroom had a gold-plated bidet. The bedroom furnishings included a stunning girl: Faith Warren in a see-through, black lace nightie.

The jet had just leveled off above the clouds when I discovered her there, awaiting me. "Al-Zadar," I said, "has a funny sense of humor."

"I'm not really the same girl," she told me with a pretty smile. "Last night I was playing naughty wife in a French bedroom farce. Today—what would you call this role?"

"Arabian Nights houri?"

"Houri—I do like that. So much nicer than whore." Faith spread her white arms wide in theatrical invitation: "On the house, Captain Bishop. Or should I say on the plane?"

It was a short flight, but she did her best to deliver me to al-Zadar in a pleasant, relaxed mood.

* * *

Ahmed al-Zadar's birthplace was the barren country of Oman, at the entrance of the Persian Gulf. His father came from equally barren Kuwait, higher in the Gulf. In the old days anyone in any Persian Gulf country who was not fortunate enough to be a relative of one of the hereditary rulers had few choices in ways of making a living. You could rise just above starvation level through fishing or scratch-farming the arid earth. Or you could make a higher but dangerous income through piracy and smuggling.

Al-Zadar's grandfather had been decapitated for piracy. His father's left hand had been chopped off when he was caught in an act of smuggling.

One-handed, his father continued smuggling, establishing contacts in every little desert sheikdom along the western coast of the Persian Gulf. He made enough to support one family at the top of the Gulf and another at the bottom, so that whether his sailing ventures took him north or south there was a home awaiting him at the end of the voyage.

Then oil began to gush forth in quantity along the Persian Gulf, bringing in a flood of wealth. Most of this new wealth, naturally, went to the vast families of hereditary rulers. But there was so much wealth pouring in that some of it began leaking out to others—al-Zadar's father among them. He used his contacts, and his growing sons, to switch from full-time smuggling to a small business in legitimate transport, up and down his Gulf.

Working for his father and travelling with him as his brightest son, Ahmed al-Zadar got to know his father's increasingly important connections in each Persian Gulf country. But his father wisely saw that this was not sufficient. The oil came out of the ground of these little, desert countries—but the wealth came from Europe and America. So when Ahmed al-Zadar was old enough, he was sent off to school: first in Switzerland, where he acquired French, German and Italian, and a taste for pretty European girls; then to business college in California.

There he learned to speak and think like an American. There, too, he established contacts with fellow students who were destined to be managers of American industry and government. His father always sent him enough money to cement these contacts into friendships through lavish entertainment.

When al-Zadar had left the Persian Gulf, he'd thought his one-handed father a rich man. When he returned from America, he knew differently. His father had a nice little business, but he was not a millionaire. Al-Zadar intended to become a millionaire. In the next ten years he became more than that.

First, he travelled up and down the Gulf, reestablishing and improving the contacts obtained through his father. Each Gulf country, still barren and with an infinitesimal population, now had more wealth than it knew what to do with. From each country al-Zadar obtained a shopping list for everything the country "needed" (which translates as anything the ruler craved).

High on each sheikdom's shopping list were the tools and toys of war—from the latest rifles to the biggest tanks and fastest jet fighters. No matter that these countries had no possible use for weaponry of such sophistication and in such quantities: their sultans, emirs and sheiks *wanted* them.

By the beginning of the 1960s almost half of all arms exports—from America, Europe and the Soviet sphere—were going to the oil-rich Moslem nations. Every year an increasing part of those arms were bought by al-Zadar's section of the Persian Gulf: the United Arab Emirates. It didn't take al-Zadar long to discover that arms dealing was where the greatest profit potential lay.

He took his clients' shopping lists to Europe and America —and went shopping. To each company wishing to fill these orders, he explained Arab ways without coyness. Nobody along the Persian Gulf had ever done any kind of business without some money passing hands under the table. *Baksheesh* was more than customary: it was tradition, close to religion.

No sale could be made to any of his countries without an assortment of people being paid off to okay the deal: dozens of relatives of the rulers, ranging from spendthrift playboys to hard-working generals. No foreign company with the prospect of eventually making sales of close to a billion dollars was going to louse it up by quibbling over having to deliver a few measly million in bribes and "consultant fees." The money was given to al-Zadar and added to the final price. He gave some of it to those back home who had to be bribed and kept the rest. The Western firms made their sales and grew fatter on them. The Persian Gulf sheikdoms got their shopping lists filled and wanted more.

After a few years of this, certain very large companies—like Dassault of France and General Dynamics of the U.S.—tried going around al-Zadar and dealing in the Persian Gulf without him. They figured what the hell, they could fork out the *baksheesh* themselves, and be surer of where the money was going. Al-Zadar let them try. They came up empty: in each case the sale had gone to a rival company working through al-Zadar. Arabs just didn't feel comfortable talking business directly to foreigners. No company tried to deal in al-Zadar's part of the Persian Gulf twice without him.

Like Adnan Khashoggi of Saudi Arabia, Ahmed al-Zadar of the Persian Gulf skyrocketed in less than a decade from neophyte hustler to established billionaire. Dealing in weapons of war remained his most profitable line. The reason was simple. With other items, once the sale was made that was the end of it. With arms this was not so:

Under the pressures of the Cold War, weapon technology was developing at an unprecedented rate. Whatever missiles, planes and other weaponry the Persian Gulf rulers purchased were, within six or seven years, no longer considered the very latest and best. The rulers, trying to outdo each other in consumer lust for such toys, kept wanting nothing but the newest. They could afford it. And they got it through Ahmed al-Zadar.

Naturally, each of these rulers found himself left with a tremendous surplus of unwanted, "old fashioned" weaponry. This provided al-Zadar with his other source of income: selling off the unwanted stocks for them—to Africa, to Latin America, and (often through Hiroshi Yukada) to Asia.

All of this wheeling and dealing kept al-Zadar travelling constantly. Where his father's business travels had caused him to create two homes at either end of the Persian Gulf, Ahmed al-Zadar had acquired places he called home in every part of the world. He was resting briefly at his Monte Carlo home the weekend he flew me down to join him. By then he was part of the Golden Circle of private arms dealers, and on *Forbes* magazine's annual list of the world's wealthiest businessmen.

* * *

After the DC-8 landed at the Nice-Côte d'Azur airport, I found out that Faith would be returning with it to England in an hour.

"Ahmed thinks variety is a man's best refresher," she explained as she walked me to a waiting helicopter. "My own considerable experience inclines me to agree."

"I'll miss you."

"You won't miss me too much," Faith assured me, and gave me a friendly farewell kiss. "You'll see."

She strolled back toward the DC-8 and the helicopter lifted me over a dark blue sea to Monaco. A limousine was waiting at the heliport to carry me up the hill, to one of the modern high-rise condominiums looming above the 1870s casino complex. My driver was a lovely Chinese girl wearing a jaunty chauffeur's cap, white damask jacket and tapestry trousers. She chucked the cap in the back seat after parking in the condominium's underground garage, led me to an elevator, and accompanied me to al-Zadar's penthouse duplex.

"I'll be your guide until you feel at home," she told me. "Newcomers sometimes find it confusing."

Confusing it was: a carnival mix of men, girls, music and more girls, and an anything-goes ambience on both floors. The kind of round-the-clock party reporters drool over in their stories about al-Zadar's lifestyle. Several buffet tables were constantly replenished by scurrying waiters and bartenders. Among the male guests were a number I recognized: military officers, diplomats, industrial executives and politicians. The girls outnumbered them roughly three to one. None of the men looked unhappy about it.

Some might have been call girls. But most looked like movie starlets, neophyte models, college co-eds, Playboy bunnies, Penthouse pets and just plain fun-lovers. Each had the basic qualifications: young, pretty, uninhibited. All were drawn there by the aura of money-no-object gaiety surrounding the al-Zadar legend; by such presents as jewels and high-fashion clothes; by "cab money" which could include round-trip airfare from anywhere to everywhere.

My chauffeur-guide led me past a three-piece band playing old-fashioned swing for a group of sleepy dancers, into a luxurious bedroom with everything one expected an al-Zadar to provide: big, round bed heaped with colorful cushions, more cushions scattered about the thick Persian carpeting, small bar, walls and ceiling of antiqued mirrors, videocassette player with giant screen.

"This is your room," my guide told me, and gave me the key. I tossed my overnight bag on the bed and followed her on a guided tour of the rest of the bottom floor. We went through a movie-TV center where a group of men and girls were cuddling in the semi-darkness while watching a soft-core porn film. After that there were several doors that on testing proved to be locked, and we passed on into a game room where four men and ten girls were playing billiards and ping-pong. It took ten minutes to find al-Zadar.

He was in a small, womb-like room: carpeted floor, walls and ceiling, no furniture other than heaps of cushions. Al-Zadar lounged comfortably among the cushions, having a quiet talk with a distinguished, elderly man who looked less comfortable but not unhappy in a similar position. There were six girls in various stages of near-nudity sprawled around them, silently sipping champagne and showing no more interest than the cushions in what the two men were saying.

A couple of the girls were sleeping with their heads in the lap of the distinguished gentleman. Al-Zadar was absent-mindedly stroking the long hair of one resting against his leg, as if she were a kitten that he was giving some good-natured affection but no real attention. According to what I'd heard, he never knew the names of girls of this changing *mélange*, and seldom indulged in any of them. They were there for the same purpose as the rest of the carnival atmosphere, it was said. Male guests tended to become unusually relaxed and uninhibited in the midst of it all. That, coupled with gratitude to their host for a rare good time, sometimes caused them to commit to deals they would have studied more carefully in the sober ambience of a company conference room.

Al-Zadar stood up with a cheerful grin and came over to the doorway to pump my hand in a large, strong grasp. He was not distinguished looking: nothing like the ice cold, lordly Alexandre or the quiet, guarded Yukada. About forty-three, Ahmed al-Zadar was a big, roly-poly teddy bear of a man, with a vast gusto for life. His appearance fitted his reputation as an extravagant, fun-loving playboy. But the green eyes were very alert, and the brain inside the chubby, jolly exterior was, I knew damn well, one of the leanest and sharpest in the business.

"Man, am I pleased you could make it here this weekend," he greeted me, still pumping my hand. "I hope you don't mind, but I've gotten a little tied up with my friend the ambassador here. Why don't we get together tomorrow morning? Set your alarm for eight. Just relax and have fun till then. Okay?"

If I'd shut my eyes I would have sworn I was in Houston listening to an all-American oil man. I said, "Okay," and found myself grinning back at him. The thing was, I was sure there was nothing phony about his act. This was a man who got a genuine kick out everything he did. Being a billionaire might have its problems, but I doubted that they'd ever give al-Zadar an ulcer.

"Thanks a lot." He clapped me on the shoulder and gave my chauffeur-guide a mock-stern look. "You make sure Captain Bishop finds his way and has a good time, y'hear?"

As I followed her out, al-Zadar settled back down among the cushions and the girls. From the way it looked, he didn't distinguish much between the two.

The Chinese girl led me up a curved, open stairway with mosaic steps inlaid with alternating pieces of lapis lazuli and gold. Real gold, my guide assured me. There was another three-piece band on the top floor, on a bronze raised platform surrounded by a shiny, steel railing. This one was playing hard rock for a bunch of dedicated dancers, most of them in dripping bathing suits that left puddles and damp spots on the mahogany flooring under their bare feet.

We went through a wide hall and came out onto the marble patio of an indoor swimming pool. It was surrounded by gleaming white columns and arches, with recessed alcoves behind them. There were girls frolicking in the pool and men lounging around it, fondling the ones who were with them and watching the ones in the water.

"What about a swim?" my guide suggested.

"I didn't bring swimming trunks," I said, and remembered saying the same thing, very long ago, to another woman.

The Chinese girl took my hand and led me into one of the alcoves. She opened a large built-in closet. It was full of shelves piled with brand-new bathing suits of every kind, divided by sex and by size. I selected trunks that would fit me.

"When you're finished with them," my guide said, pointing out a small door in the wall, "just toss them down there."

"Laundry chute?"

"No, it goes down to a furnace," she told me, as though it were the most natural thing in the world to burn the swimsuits after one use. She went out leaving me to change. When I came out in my trunks she was gone. Apparently she'd decided I was feeling enough at home by then to be left to my own devices.

I dove into the water. I'd done less than the length of the pool when a girl jumped in on top of me, sinking us both to the bottom. We came up sputtering and she wrapped strong arms around my neck and screamed, "I can't swim!"

I floated her over to the side of the pool and lifted her out. It wasn't easy. She was statuesque. She was also blonde all over and nude.

Grinning down at me, she said, "Thank you for saving me. My name's Norma. I'm from Australia."

"You ought to learn to swim before you jump into deep water."

"I get impulses." She pointed toward an alcove. "I was on my way for a suntan. Join me?"

"In a minute."

"Great, see you. . . ." Norma got up and walked off to the alcove. She had some walk.

I swam four lengths but no other girls jumped on me and I began to feel lonely as well as horny. Climbing out, I went into the alcove where Norma had disappeared. She was there, stretched out under a bank of sunlamps beside a slender, raven-haired girl who turned out to be from Brazil. Like the Australian, the Brazilian didn't have a stitch that would interfere with improving her all-over tan. They both looked up at me and smiled.

Faith had not been wrong: I didn't miss her too much.

But later, sharing my bed with the blonde Australian and the dark Brazilian, I found myself missing someone else. And remembering what she'd said about the kind of girls men tolerated around their gatherings.

I didn't go along with Victoria's harsh way of putting it. The girls around al-Zadar's carnival weren't dumb and dirty: they just weren't interested in much besides fun and were without many inhibitions in having it. But they *were* definitely disposable. A certain boredom factor intruded pretty soon in romping with them.

Also, I had the nagging suspicion that the romp was probably being recorded on video tape. I looked at the ceiling and corners of my bedroom, but couldn't spot any camera lens. It didn't matter, anyway. Al-Zadar could do me little damage with it. I wouldn't *enjoy* it if Victoria saw the romp, but al-Zadar had no reason to show it to her—and he wouldn't be taping these sessions just to annoy the participants. If he showed the stuff shot at his parties too often, people would stop coming. He'd save it for blackmailing *important* guests, and even then only for very urgent reasons.

Thinking about Victoria brought to the surface a worry that always lurked somewhere in the back of my mind. I'd asked her to see if her friends in the Justice Department would do something to make my father's life in prison less of a hell for him. Rolling over to the side of the bed, I put through an overseas phone call. The two girls didn't notice. It was a large bed, and they were busy with each other.

I got the answering machine at Victoria's house, and dialed her private office number. All al-Zadar's phones were certainly tapped, but calling her was okay. I *was* supposed to be one of her clients, with a right to ask for help. I'd just have to be careful of how much we said and how it was said.

"Are you with al-Zadar?" she asked me. Her voice did the same old things to me, even across several thousand miles.

"I'm at his place, yes," I hedged. "I got to wondering if you'd heard anything about Lou."

"One of my friends had a talk yesterday with the prison psychiatrist. Lou's suffering from depression, but not because he's being treated badly. He isn't. He just can't resign himself to accepting life as a prisoner, anywhere. God knows, I understand what he's going through more than most. But there's nothing to be done about it, short of getting him out. The only way to do that remains the same."

"I'm doing my best," I said. "That's why I'm here."

"Do you know what al-Zadar has in mind?"

"He hasn't said yet. We're going to talk about it in the morning."

There was a small silence at the other end. "The sort of entertainment al-Zadar lavishes on his business guests, I imagine you're enjoying the wait."

"Sort of. But I began missing you."

"That's nice to hear. But at this moment I've got to dash off for an appointment—with the Defense Department's director for contract policy. Followed by another with the director of the Marine Corps weapons evaluation program. And then a late one with Brigadier General Russell of the Air Force. All of it ground work. So—"

"Victoria," I cut in on her, "do you ever miss *me*?"

There was another small silence. "Yes," she said softly. And then: "I have to leave now, Gar. Go back to enjoying yourself." She hung up, and after a couple seconds I did too.

I turned around on the bed and watched the Australian and the Brazilian. After awhile I joined them. I did enjoy. But I didn't stop wishing I were with Victoria.

Chapter Seventeen

Garson

Al-Zadar steered the motorboat across the calm sea, away from his yacht anchored outside the Monaco harbor. The wind was warm, the late morning sky cloudless. I looked back at the yacht. It was immense: too big to fit inside the harbor. The helicopter that had carried us out to it from the heliport was waiting for our return, resting on its pad on the main deck next to the yacht's swimming pool.

According to rumor, the skippers of the Niarchos and Khashoggi yachts were under orders to sail away if al-Zadar's showed up at any port where they were moored because his boat made theirs look like midgets. The comforts of his yacht included a discotheque, full-scale movie theater, a gymnasium and twenty-two guest suites.

"That's some ship," I said.

"It's not a *ship*," al-Zadar retorted disparagingly. "It's just a floating hotel and entertainment center. Part of my image and useful in doing business. But I love *real* ships. I'm a sailor at heart, Captain. My father was a master seaman. I sailed many times as a member of his crew when I was a boy."

When we landed on the huge yacht, at a few minutes before nine that morning, some guests were already aboard:

a French movie actor and an official of the Austrian Defense Ministry, plus the usual bevy of girls. We'd had breakfast with the two men in the yacht's vast, brass-panelled dining room. A few of the girls trickled down from the swimming pool to join us, putting on their bikini bottoms before sitting down at the table. After breakfast al-Zadar had led me down the gangplank to the waiting motorboat, to have our private talk.

When we were out pretty far, al-Zadar began steering the boat in slow, wide circles. "Okay, this should be far enough to stymie any attempt at long-distance electronic eavesdropping." He gestured toward Monaco. "From the top of one of those buildings, for example."

"The noise of this motor would prevent that, anyway."

"Maybe. But you'd be surprised at what acoustic technology can accomplish these days." He looked at me and smiled. "No, of course *you* wouldn't be surprised. Not with Christian Frosch as your partner."

"You're well informed."

"It's always best to be, don't you think? I guess you're pretty well informed about me, too."

"Not as well as I'd like to be."

Al-Zadar laughed. "I sure hope not. Okay, Captain, now the reason I invited you down here, and why what we talk about has to stay secret: I've got a large problem with Lebanon."

By that September of 1975 *everybody* had a large problem with Lebanon. A civil war had broken out there in April: the PLO and Moslem Lebanese versus the Christian Arabs of Lebanon. By September it was reaching a crescendo of unrestrained internal warfare. Russia was nosing into it. The United States was trying to make Russia back out without nosing in more than its citizens would tolerate. The rest of the world was watching with increasing nervousness, scared that Lebanon's civil war might trigger World War III.

"I have stocks of weapons and ammunition in Cyprus," al-Zadar continued, "which I'd like to unload in Lebanon."

We eyed each other. I said, "Your problem being that the profits would be bigger selling to the Christians than to the Moslems. But you're a Moslem and so are your biggest clients."

"You said it."

The PLO and its Moslem allies in Lebanon had been very heavily armed over the past years by the Soviet bloc—with weapons bought by oil-rich Libya, Saudi Arabia and the Persian Gulf countries al-Zadar represented. The eruption of the civil war had caught the Lebanese Christians short of weapons. They needed everything they could get, and fast. Since a majority of Lebanon's wealthy businessmen were Christian, they could afford to pay through the nose for it.

Most NATO nations were too worried about offending the Arab countries to supply the Christian needs. Private arms dealers had been flocking into the country, attracted by the Christians' willingness to pay more for any weapon than it would bring elsewhere.

"But you could sell to me," I said slowly, "if I lie to you, on paper, saying I intend to sell your goods in Asia—maybe through my known connection with Yukada. Nobody could prove what I sold in Lebanon was what came from you. And you'd still get your profit."

"That's it in a nutshell," al-Zadar acknowledged. "But my profit motive is secondary, in this case. Though naturally I'm not spitting on that part. The primary motive is political. My Persian Gulf clients *are* among the Moslem nations that paid for the Iron Curtain weapons that have made the PLO so strong. But now they're worried."

"I don't blame them. If the PLO takes over Lebanon, its

communist faction could become the strongest element in Lebanon—posing a threat to the hereditary rulers of your Persian Gulf clients."

Al-Zadar nodded. "They would prefer to see the Christian Lebanese armed sufficiently so the civil war there will become a stagnated standoff." He waited for me to say the rest of it, as though in spite of our distance out on the water and the noise of the boat's motor, he was reluctant to state the situation baldly himself.

"At the same time," I said, "your clients, being Moslem, don't want to be caught arming Christians to fight against other Moslems."

Khashoggi of Saudi Arabia had the same problem, which, as I understood it, he was solving by supplying the Christians through a Paris cover company. Now al-Zadar wanted to do the same, using Tri-Arms. "What's your offer?" I asked him.

"You get ten percent of everything you sell in Lebanon. At prices determined by me beforehand. But—I won't give you a contract to that effect."

"Without a contract, where's my guarantee?"

"You'll have my weapons and ammo. On paper, I sell you all my Cyprus stocks. In fact, I give them to you. After you make the sales, you send me my ninety percent, keeping your ten. Guarantee enough?"

He wasn't scared I'd sell and not pay him. Jolly he might be, but like Yukada he wouldn't let a man who did that to him go on living. For Tri-Arms, of course, it was an excellent deal—and I'd been considering going to Lebanon anyway. In addition to all the arms dealers flocking there, the civil war had attracted a concentration of the world's press: reporters, photographers, TV teams. That made Lebanon's carnage a rare opportunity to get some advance publicity for my father's rocket launcher—and a new version of Rambert's assault rifle.

"What kind of goods do you have for me to sell?" I asked al-Zadar. "And how much of it?"

He told me.

Calculating rapidly in my head, I figured that Tri-Arms could wind up with between two and three million dollars in profits if we unloaded all of it. Considering the desperate needs of the Christians, there was no reason we wouldn't— assuming I could avoid getting myself killed in the crossfire between the Christians and Moslems. The selling would have to be done piecemeal, on the spot. But if we worked it right, Tri-Arms would graduate from the cellar of the arms business to its middle class.

"You could have gotten any of the smaller dealers to handle this for you," I said. "Why Tri-Arms?"

Al-Zadar grinned at me. "You complaining?"

I grinned back. "Curious."

"Discretion is essential to me in this situation, obviously. Your discretion, Captain, is a proven quality. Also, you've handled every deal you've tackled pretty damn well."

"Not that Brazil-Italy deal, I didn't." I didn't say it bitterly. After all, he wasn't bitter about the Spanish M16s.

Al-Zadar laughed. "You can't win 'em all. But you've won enough to get Tri-Arms moving."

"A bit too slowly."

"But surely. You are already well thought of in certain Washington circles. Of course, your public relations woman there is one of the best. An extraordinary woman, in every way."

"You've met her?" I knew he had.

"Twice. First, seven months ago. I should have retained her immediately to handle my affairs in Washington. I have some holdings in the United States, as you may know."

I did know. Out in the open he'd bought control of several U.S. banks, a considerable amount of real estate, an insurance company and a movie studio. There were rumors of his secret control of a couple American arms firms, as well.

"One month ago," al-Zadar continued, "when I did ask Miss Nicolson to become my representative, she told me her client-load had become to heavy to take on more. It was smart of you, Captain, to retain her services before that happened."

"More luck than smarts," I said carelessly.

He was studying me shrewdly. "Miss Nicolson's optimistic about the future of Tri-Arms. And she has a high opinion of you, personally. I'm hoping this deal with you is only the first, Captain. Maybe you'll be handling more negotiations for me, later. In the States, for example."

And anytime he got Tri-Arms to act for him on any deal in the States, he'd be getting Victoria at the same time, to handle the Washington contacts. *That* was his real reason for wanting to tie in with us.

Victoria had given Tri-Arms its real start: Yukada. Now she'd gotten us al-Zadar, and through him another support for our eventual debut in America.

Al-Zadar had said it: she was extraordinary.

* * *

"Get down!" I shouted at Mei-lin. I had to shout to be heard over the racket of automatic weapons outside the bomb-wrecked clothing shop inside of which we'd taken temporary shelter.

"Take care of your own ass," she snarled back, "and let me take care of my own! I've been in more wars than you have, Bishop!"

228

About that, she was right. The daughter of a part Chinese mother and an American father, Mei-lin Shaw had dropped out of her Chicago high school at sixteen to cover student riots and government perfidy for underground newspapers. A strong-minded twenty-five now, she had become an established freelance reporter and photographer covering her choice of the world's newsworthy events: usually wars. Her reportage, on radio and in news journals, was brilliant. Her camera work was less expert, but she made up for that by taking her pictures as close to the heart of battle as possible.

Most of the news photographers Rambert and I had met in Lebanon didn't venture that close. Some spent most of their time in relatively safe hotel bars, buying their photos from Arab kids, Christian and Moslem, who shot them with cameras and film they'd looted from war-shattered photography shops.

At that moment Mei-lin was standing up against a corner inside the clothing shop, taking pictures through a shattered window of the fire fight in the street, while the tape recorder, hanging on a strap around her neck, picked up the noise.

Rambert snapped at her: "Get *down!*" Him she obeyed. She couldn't claim more wars than Rambert.

Sitting on a mound of fallen plaster between us, Mei-lin turned off her recorder and wiped white dust from her hair and face. The hair was red but the face was pure Asian. She'd had a harder struggle than most women to get accepted as a serious professional. Her small stature had always made her look younger than she was; her exotic look, a redhead with Oriental features, hadn't helped in that direction either. The way she was regarded accounted for her habit of acting tougher than she actually was.

Mei-lin patted Rambert's knee. "If my father had lived, he'd probably be trying to take care of me just like you. You're a lovely man."

"I'm an old pervert," he growled, "and you are too old for my tastes, so no nonsense." He pointed to a compact automatic assault rifle cradled against the chest of one of the seven young Christian Arabs hunkered down inside the store with us. With its hinged stock of lightweight metal folded, the weapon wasn't much bigger than a machine pistol. "Now *that* is lovely. Turn your recorder back on and let me tell you more about it."

It was the latest prototype of Rambert's own assault rifle. He'd dubbed it the PR-100, and it incorporated brand new features no other weapon could match at that point in time. It had an integral spring-operated bipod that folded into the forestock. In addition to its normal automatic and semiautomatic controls, it could be set to fire short bursts of exactly four shots with each trigger squeeze. Its revolutionary vented compensator eliminated muzzle flash and suppressed firing noise to a minimum, making it especially effective for night fighting. The vents reduced the barrel climb that plagued similar arms in firing bursts, which made it easier to hit targets without expending too much ammunition. Field stripping down to only five parts, Rambert's PR-100 was rugged enough to stand up to steady rough handling. A beauty of a weapon.

The other prototype we'd brought to Lebanon lay across the lap of another young Christian Arab: the rocket launcher my father had designed and Rambert had improved. We'd named it with my father's initials: the LB-75.

Rambert and I never carried either of the prototypes out where we could be seen—nor any other weapons, for that matter. The reason was simple: we didn't want to get shot at. The phony "PRESS" signs stenciled in white on our caps and jackets were our best protection in Beirut, and the press didn't carry guns.

Nobody on either side of the Lebanese civil war wanted to kill a journalist. Not even the trigger-happy "cowboys" on both sides who generally shot at anything that moved. Journalists were too valuable to their cause—and to their egos even more so. Christian or Moslem, the Arab fighters wanted their pictures and names to appear in the world's newspaper and TV coverage of their war. For that kind of personal glory, the cowboys would run risks they'd seldom take for their political and religious convictions.

That was why this group of Christian gunmen had taken us, and the two prototype weapons, along on their evening raid into the Moslem-controlled western section of their chewed-up capital. And the prototypes were why we'd gone in with them. There we still were, trapped by the battle raging outside, with it getting too dark for the fighters on either side to see our press signs before they shot at us.

* * *

It had taken Rambert and me less than three weeks to sell off al-Zadar's stocks to the Christian Arabs. For the Lebanese—with their cities collapsing in ruin—the civil war was pure hell. Most of the big companies that had brought their country wealth were gone, and their streets had been taken over by roaming bands of trigger-happy gunmen. But it was an arms seller's bonanza.

Dozens of political and religious factions, on both sides, and several private armies wanted every brand of street-fighting weapon they could get: Automatic rifles, machine guns, submachine guns, revolvers and pistols, explosives. Mortars, APCs, tanks, hand grenades, rifle-fired grenades. Antiaircraft guns that the Beirut fighters converted for urban warfare and used to smash up entire blocks where their enemies had holed up. Infantry rocket launchers and the grenade-firing rifles, both of which, in current versions, got ruined fast under regular use. And tons of ammunition for all of it.

Rambert and I waited for cloudy nights to ferry the orders over from Cyprus in fishing vessels. Usually we off-loaded at one of the two Christian-held ports north of Beirut: Jounieh or Chekka. The buyers worked fast to get it done before dawn. Some of what we delivered was taken off into the Lebanese hills. The rest was transferred to other vessels for swift runs to a section of Beirut beachfront still in Christian hands.

They paid on delivery, on the spot, sometimes in cash, but usually in certified checks from Swiss banks. Before the war Lebanon had been the banking center of the Middle East. By October, some of the Beirut banks—those that hadn't been too badly torn up and looted—had begun opening for business again a few days each month. But they'd long ago transferred the greater part of their funds out of the country.

Each time we returned to Cyprus we sent the payments to Christian Frosch. He sent al-Zadar his ninety percent. Part of our ten percent he put into our Rome bank. The rest went into the Swiss numbered account we'd established for Tri-Arms. By the time we'd sold off the last of al-Zadar's stocks, Tri-Arms International was richer by just over two and a half million dollars. Victoria immediately took half a million out of the Swiss account to push her Tri-Arms groundwork in Washington along faster. Rambert and I moved into Beirut to get on with our second purpose for being in Lebanon. We'd already gotten to know a lot of the press in Beirut, journalists seldom being averse to free drinks. Now we concentrated on using some of these contacts to publicize our two prototype weapons.

First we had to find a place to live and operate from. Many reporters and television crews stayed at the luxury hotels by the beach: the St. Georges, Martinez, Phoenicia and Holiday Inn. But the inexorable pressure of the Moslem advance through the city was almost on top of them by then. Some of the journalists were pulling out to safer quarters, and it didn't seem a wise place for us: the Moslems could have learned about what we'd sold the Christians. So we looked around in the Christian-controlled sections of East Beirut.

It was Mei-lin Shaw who found us the apartment there.

She had been among the journalists we'd met during our first visits to Beirut. Actually, I'd seen her before Beirut—in Rome, though we'd never met there. I'd seen her at the Crazy Chess with a good-looking but somewhat stiff-necked character in his forties. According to the word around the discotheque, he was her regular boyfriend whenever he was in Rome, and Mei-lin didn't have any others when he wasn't. The word around also had it that he was some kind of upper-level trouble shooter for the U.S. State Department.

Mei-lin was familiar to some of the lower and middle-bracket arms dealers in Rome because she had a special interest in the business. She'd acquired it during the various wars she had covered. The dealers she'd questioned said she was researching a full-scale series she wanted to do someday, about the part they played in those wars. She had a theory that they were partly responsible for starting some of them. But she hadn't gotten around to questioning me because at that point I'd begun travelling outside of Rome much of the time.

In Beirut, Mei-lin's interest in arms dealers was stronger than ever, heightened by the numbers of them feasting off the civil war. Her interest made her perfect for our own purpose. So I cultivated her—and then discovered myself growing unusually fond of being with her. On her part, when she wasn't lashing me with her violent loathing of what I did for a living, Mei-lin began to indicate, somewhat reluctantly, that other aspects of me added up to agreeable company.

The apartment she got for Rambert and me was on a once fashionable street of boutiques, department stores, modern office buildings and plush condominiums. Those stores which hadn't been smashed out of existence were boarded up now. The walls of buildings still standing had gaping holes where their windows had been. The smoke and smell of garbage piles being burned in adjacent streets sometimes drifted over. Entering our street required threading one's way over and around fallen walls, shattered cars and delivery trucks, the burned-out hulk of a bus, and hills of trash which nobody had been around to collect for weeks. Broken glass crunched underfoot all the way.

Most of the former inhabitants of our apartment building had fled elsewhere, which left plenty of space to choose from. The bottom two floors had been gutted by rockets, grenades and fire. There was no electricity. All that was left of the two elevators were cut cables dangling down the shafts and a couple melted globs at the bottom. It was a six-floor climb up a bullet-gouged stairway to our apartment.

Its windows were shattered and the wind blowing in from the sea and the mountains was turning cold, so we had to get the windowpanes replaced at black market prices: fifty bucks per. With or without glass, we had views—through empty spaces where neighboring apartment houses had collapsed under the impact of cannon shells, of buildings burning in other parts of the city. For light at night we had to make do with candles and battery-lamps. But the apartment was spacious, with two big, well-separated bedrooms and a bathroom where the cold water still worked. And anyway I was spending as much time at Mei-lin's apartment, just down the corridor, as I was at our own. Mei-lin had it a bit easier than we did: she'd paid a small fortune on the black market for a portable electrical generator for her darkroom equipment.

Rambert and I laid in a good supply of liquor—again, at black market prices that were staggering. We found a guy to supply us with ice at twenty dollars a bucket. With liquor and ice as our main ammunition, we invited journalists to the apartment by day and talked to them about our prototype weapons. Those who expressed interest wanted to see practical demonstrations that tied in with their coverage of the war. But we decided to give the first to Mei-lin.

Her interest was genuine. Our attempt to use the civil war to publicize new weapons gave her a new angle for the series she wanted to do on arms dealers. She took pictures of the weapons, both assembled and broken down, recording our explanations of their fine points. And she promised to do a separate news feature on them in return for a complete explanation of what and how we'd sold to the Christians. We gave her a pretty full description without mentioning al-Zadar or any other names. We also decided to give her an exclusive first demonstration of our prototypes in action —with genuine Beirut street fighters.

We were put in touch with a group of them through the Christian leaders who'd bought our shipments. It was a small group, all of them very young but veterans of months of urban battles. We showed them how to use our weapons, and explained what we wanted. When assured that there'd be a journalist along, with a camera, to record them in action, they agreed.

That was how we came to set out with them, one early evening, when they headed off to join other Christian guerrillas on their raid into the Moslem-held Kantari neighborhood of Beirut. There was no occasion to use the LB-75 rocket launcher on the way in. But Mei-lin got plenty of action pictures of Rambert's PR-100 doing its deadly work against small knots of opposition. The cowboy handling it exulted in its accuracy as our group made its way across Hamra Street to their rendezvous point.

We got that far and no farther. The Moslems had a well-entrenched ambush waiting for us at the rendezvous.

I grabbed Mei-lin's arm when gunfire from the ambushers began to rip across the street, and pulled her with me into the shelter of the gutted clothing shop. Rambert dodged in after us, followed by seven of our young guerrillas. Other groups of Christians sprinted for other shelters, leaving their dead behind in the street. The Moslem ambushers began shooting up the buildings that provided the shelters.

So there we were, stuck inside our own shelter. The crossfire in the street out front stayed intense, making it impossibly dangerous as an escape route. Night was closing in. Night, in Beirut, was the worst possible time of all to be out on any street.

* * *

A long burst from a heavy machine gun slashed through the window where Mei-lin had been standing minutes before, and slammed off the back wall. The plaster there disintegrated, showering us with more white dust. I eyed the wall behind the plaster. The building had been constructed the old way: solid walls of heavy stone blocks. If the back wall was like the front one, it was three feet thick.

Rambert was looking at the same thing. "Time to go."

I nodded. Most of the bullets that had ricocheted off the solid stone wall had plunged into the ceiling, and the few that had spun downward hadn't hit any of us. We might not come through the next burst—or the ones after that—so lucky. I told Mei-lin: "Get some before and after shots, we're gonna make a rear exit."

Another burst of automatic fire flailed over our heads. This time all of it thudded into the ceiling, bringing much of it down on us. Mei-lin didn't appear to notice. She was up on one knee, coolly snapping pictures of the back wall. Her eyes had become holes in a mask of plaster dust.

I crawled over to the guy carrying our LB-75, yelling to be heard as the thunder of weaponry out front suddenly increased. Rambert nudged Mei-lin ahead of him into one of the shop's dressing alcoves. I shifted position with my launcher carrier to a front corner of the shop, where an overturned counter and fallen ceiling timbers gave us some low cover. The rest scuttled into other alcoves.

Plugging a rocket-loaded round into the rear of the LB-75's launch tube, I took the assembled system from my carrier and balanced it on my right shoulder. It was nice and light, easy to handle. When I pressed the trigger the roar in the confines of the shop was nearly deafening. When the dust settled Mei-lin was already snapping pictures of the hole the rocket had kicked clear through the solid back wall. It was big enough for three people to jump through at the same time.

Two of our street fighters went out together, with their automatic rifles aimed in opposite directions, ready to shoot any opposition they ran into out back. There was none. Rambert and Mei-lin jumped out after them and the rest followed. I gave the LB-75 back to its carrier and slapped his back. We went through last, following the young guerrilla carrying Rambert's PR-100 prototype, into a big cobbled courtyard.

The others were running to the shelter of a wide doorway in the rear of a building on the other side of the courtyard. Bringing up the rear, I and my LB-75 carrier went after them. Bullets began spanging off the courtyard cobbles ahead of me: a sniper operating out of some high window in one of the buildings siding the courtyard.

The young fighter ahead of me stopped and twisted to fire Rambert's assault rifle up at the sniper.

"Get to *cover!*" I shouted at him as I sprinted past. A second later I was within the protection of the wide doorway, ramming into my LB-75 carrier with so much force we both spilled to the brick flooring inside the back entryway.

The fighter who'd had Rambert's weapon stumbled in after me without it, tripped over us and sat down hard, groaning as he clutched at his right arm. It hung useless. The fatigue jacket around his bullet-smashed shoulder was dark-wet with blood.

"*Merde!*" Rambert growled, looking out. His PR-100 lay on the courtyard cobbles.

The youngest of our Christian guerrilla group, a thin boy of about fourteen, nudged Mei-lin, pointed to her camera, and snapped, "Get me!"

"Wait!" I shouted, and Rambert made a grab for him. But the boy was already darting outside. Mei-lin's reaction was ingrained in her by then: snatching up her camera and switching it on automatic, she aimed for him. Newspaper readers of many countries got to see that series of shots. They were blurred with motion and murky with dusk, but riveting:

The boy sprinting into the open with slugs from the sniper chopping up stone dust from the courtyard cobbles around him.

The boy bending to snatch up the dropped weapon.

Turning to dash back, holding the assault rifle and grinning in triumph.

The grin freezing as blood spouted from the side of his thin chest.

Another bullet pulping the side of his head as he fell.

The boy sprawled on his back, gazing up at the dark sky with eyes that would never see anything again, his brains spilling out of the place where his ear had been, the PR-100 lying on the cobbles between him and us.

Mei-lin lowered the camera with its motor still clicking, staring at the dead boy. Rambert had already taken the launcher and was plugging in a rocket round.

"Middle building to the right," I said, getting ready. "Fourth or fifth floor."

"*Fifth,*" Rambert said, and leaned against the left wall of our wide doorway, just inside its protection. He got the LB-75 tilt-balanced, set to aim fast when the moment came for the final step out.

I went out on the jump, crouched and shifting direction with every other step. The sniper zeroed in on me—for one shot. The bullet ricocheted off the cobbles inches from my left leg. Then there was a roar from the LB-75 behind me, and the rocket explosion above. Broken glass and chunks of wood and cinder-block rained down into the courtyard as I picked up Rambert's prototype.

There were no further shots. Above me, a fifth floor window and part of the wall around it were gone. Knowing what the rocket did after punching through a barrier, I doubted that there was much left of the sniper behind that big hole.

Chapter Eighteen

Garson

Back in our apartment, I washed and changed. Rambert had already done this and gone down to the Café Moussin. A small restaurant at the end of our block, it had been reopened for the last six days, during a lull in fighting in our immediate vicinity, and would close its steel shutters tight again whenever that lull ended. The owner made a pretty good couscous, and sometimes procured young girls for Rambert.

Lacking electricity, the refrigerator in our kitchen didn't keep anything cold. But it remained a good place to store food where rats couldn't get at it. I took out bread, cheese and some salted lamb. That night I wasn't in the mood for a cooked meal, and I was sure Mei-lin wasn't either. I took the food and a bottle of scotch with me down the corridor to her apartment.

She didn't answer when I knocked, so I walked right in. The bathroom door was shut and I could hear the shower running. I set the bottle on her dining table and made sandwiches for us in her kitchen. I carried them out to the table, and poured scotch into two glasses. Taking a long swallow from one, I walked to a window. The night was beautiful: half-moon, bright stars, no clouds. Beneath, parts of the city were illuminated by big fires. Most were garbage fires, but some were more buildings going up in flames. The sounds of rockets and heavy guns drifted my way on the wind.

Mei-lin came out, drying herself with a huge towel she'd stolen from the Hotel St. Georges, her red hair still wet from the cold shower. I could see her photo developing and printing equipment in the bathroom. She stopped when she saw me, and tied the towel under her armpits. It covered her like a sarong, down to her knees. Her face was drawn. She looked at me with pure hatred.

"I don't want you here tonight," she told me tightly.

"Have a drink," I said. I picked up her glass and held it to her.

She slapped the glass out of my hand. It landed on one of the straw rugs, splashing scotch across rug and floor.

"All right," I said, "get it out of your system."

"God damn you! That little boy got killed for your fucking gun!"

"He got *himself* killed, Mei-lin. Because he wanted his picture in the papers, playing hero. Because he didn't wait until we could give him covering fire. Because he was afraid somebody else would grab the glory first. His own fault."

She hit me. Not a slap: she swung with her balled fist. I rolled with the punch and it skidded off my jaw. Catching her wrists, I held on while she struggled to break free. I knew all of her fury wasn't really directed at me. Some of it was guilt fury: she knew the boy wouldn't have done it if she hadn't been there with her camera.

"It's not your fault either," I told her. "If he'd given you half a chance you'd have stopped him. We *all* would have. Kids think they're immortal. That's why most soldiers are so young."

Her struggle collapsed abruptly and she fell against me, sobbing. From Mei-lin, tears were a surprise—not part of the image she projected. I held her and let her cry out the grief and guilt. Then I took her to the bed and propped her against the cushions. I refilled the glass and gave it to her. She sipped at it while I got the sandwiches and sat on the bed beside her. She chewed and swallowed absently, mechanically.

We didn't talk. And afterwards we didn't make love. Emotionally wrung out, she fell asleep in my arms, clinging. A couple times in the night she stirred fitfully, making unhappy sounds. Each time, I held her closer, and she calmed down. Outside, the Beirut night continued its jarring symphony of rocketry, mortars, machine guns and cannon fire.

When I woke in the morning, she was gone from the bed. I went into the main room and saw the bathroom door closed. On it she'd hung the "Do Not Disturb" sign she'd lifted from Holiday Inn: her warning that she was developing and printing film inside. In her kitchen, the coffee pot was missing. That meant she had made some and taken it into the improvised darkroom with her. Coffee was her only breakfast; she never got around to anything solid until lunch time.

I went along to my own apartment to have a real breakfast. Rambert's bedroom door was closed, which meant he was still asleep. I made scrambled eggs and coffee on the two-burner kerosene stove we'd bought, and downed them with cheese and three rolls, feeling ready to handle the day. When I went back to Mei-lin's apartment she was sitting in a chair with her feet up on a windowsill, gazing pensively at a column of black smoke rising toward the cloudless sky.

The bathroom door was open now. Strips of negatives and squares of contact prints hung from the clothesline inside, drying. More were clothespinned to another line she'd strung across one side of the main room. Along with the negatives and prints, there was an eight-by-ten print of the dead boy sprawled in the courtyard.

I got prepared for another of our fights, and it came.

"How can you do it?" she asked quietly, without turning her head to look at me. "Arms dealing is *such* a *filthy* business."

I'd never told her it was the only hope of getting my father out of prison alive. I'd never talked about Lou Bishop to anybody except Victoria. Instead I said, "I buy and sell a commodity the world wants. Don't blame me for the world's troubles."

"Your business *feeds* off those troubles," she replied, still facing the window, her nose pointed piously upward.

Maybe it was her oh-so-righteous attitude, maybe it was the thought of my father growing old before his time in some god-forsaken cell, maybe I *was* feeling a little guilty— I don't know. But I do have a mean streak, and it surfaced at that point. "Don't be a hypocrite," I said harshly. "Your business feeds off them, too. Why do you run from one war to the next? Why don't you cover baby contests and other nice events? Because they don't make the front pages. Because they won't make you famous, like covering wars can. And that's what you want. So cut the shit. If people didn't want wars, I'd have to sell them something else or go broke."

She dropped her feet from the windowsill and stood up, turning to face me angrily. "There's a *big* difference, Bishop. You sell people things to kill with and be killed by. I record it happening so people can know how bad it is. Hopefully, they'll finally get horrified enough to reduce the number of wars."

"Don't kid yourself, it'll never happen. A thinning out of excess population is essential to race health—of deer *and* people. It's instinctive, bred in the bone."

"Race health, that's rich." Her laugh was vicious. "If people like you finally tumble us into World War III, there won't *be* any race left to worry about its health."

"If they only fight with the kind of weapons *I* supply, humankind will survive and flourish. It's idealists like you who could trigger an atomic war—to protect your political or religious faiths." I gave her a nasty smile. "Arms dealers don't want that. There wouldn't be anybody left to do business with."

"Get out of here, Bishop. I can't take you or your faulty, egoistic logic."

"Sure. But first . . ." I strode over to where she'd left her recorder, on top of a bookcase. As I pressed the record button, she came at me, furious.

"Don't touch that!"

I shoved her and she fell across the sofa. "Stay there," I snapped. "I'll give you something for that series of yours. One arms dealer's philosophy of life and death."

She glared up at me. I glared back and picked up the recorder and began talking, too mad to give a damn what I said and not sure how much of it I really believed:

"Let's deal with what we are, okay? Not what you'd like us to be. The hand God dealt mankind is this. We're like wolves. Wolves make loving couples, devoted parents, loyal members of their pack. But they are wolves, and they fight to survive. If they didn't fight, their enemies would starve them out or wipe them out.

"Personally, I don't believe in just standing there as a defenseless target so some enemy can wipe me out. I'm not interested, either, in bending my neck under somebody's heel hoping that he won't scrunch down on it. Anybody who won't fight his enemies is deficient in survival instinct. If people lose the will to win, you can give the planet back to the ants.

"My own will to survive tells me that as long as our

enemies have weapons, we'd damn well better have them too: the best we can make."

Mei-lin clapped her hands, twice. "Great speech, Bishop. Entirely incoherent, but passionate. Now will you get the hell out, you son of a bitch. And don't come back."

"My pleasure," I assured her, and went.

But that evening I found myself knocking on her door.

"Oh, it's *you*," she said, starting to shut the door again.

"Look, Mei-lin—" I began.

"I thought I made it pretty clear what I thought of you."

"Just give me a minute. There's something I have to tell you about."

"You've got one minute then, Bishop," she said, still blocking the entrance.

"I lied," I told her, wondering if I was lying now. "Those *aren't* my reasons for being in the arms business." Then I gave it to her: "It's my father."

I paused a moment. She didn't say anything.

"He's in prison." Still she was silent, but she moved away from the door and indicated the sofa.

At first she didn't look at me much while I was telling my story. She paced a little, her brow furrowed. But when I got to the part about that night in Texas, I found that she was sitting next to me, studying my face intently.

"Oh, Garson," she said, taking my hand. "Oh, Garson. . . ."

But then she dropped it and turned her face to the blank wall. "I'm sorry about everything. But it was wrong, you know."

I couldn't tell whether she was talking about my father's history or mine. But it didn't matter: she leaned back and put her head on my shoulder. "Let's call a truce," she said.

We made up completely that night. The next morning she got out of bed ahead of me to take a shower. She was still in there when somebody knocked at her apartment door. I figured it was Rambert, so I got up and put on my undershorts and went to open the door.

The handsome, greying man waiting in the corridor was the middle-aging boyfriend I'd seen with Mei-lin in Rome: the one with the State Department.

He looked down at my underpants, and then back up at my face. His own face went from surprise to cool control in an instant, though the effort left spots of color in his lean cheeks. He was not pleased, but he hid his chagrin like the gentleman he was.

"Hello," he said politely. "I'm Arthur Richmond."

"Garson Bishop," I told him. Neither of us offered to shake hands.

He looked past me into the apartment. "Isn't Miss Shaw here?"

Before I could think of something clever, she came out of the bathroom drying herself with the big towel.

She came to an abrupt standstill when she saw Richmond there in the open doorway.

"Hello, Mei-lin," he said, stiff and formal.

"Hello, Art," she responded in much the same tone. And then: "Come in."

I stepped aside and he entered, closing the door quietly. Mei-lin was wrapping the towel around her. As she knotted it under one armpit, she looked from him to me. "I'll talk to you later, Gar." Her voice was calm, almost back to normal.

I got my clothes on in the bedroom. Back in the main room, Richmond stood looking out a window, his hands clasped together behind him, his head held very straight. Mei-lin had gone back into the bathroom and shut the door. I let myself out and went down the corridor to my apartment.

Rambert sat at the table in our dining alcove, having coffee in his bathrobe. Alone. His bedmate of the night before had left, for which I was grateful. He looked at me and said, "What hit you?"

I sat down across from him. "Mei-lin's boyfriend just showed up."

Rambert smiled. "At least you are still alive."

"Don't smile, it could happen to you one of these days. Only it won't be a boyfriend. It'll be an irate father or older brother, which is worse."

"I'm sure it will happen," Rambert agreed. "With a gun. It is my destiny to survive all battles, and to die in bed with the wrong young lady."

I got up and made myself breakfast, sat down across from him again and ate it. Richmond hadn't spoiled my appetite. I was finishing when Mei-lin came in. She walked past into the kitchen without a word. Rambert got up and went to his bedroom to get dressed, closing his door behind him. In his own way, he was at least as much a gentleman as Arthur Richmond.

Mei-lin came out of the kitchen with a cup of coffee, sat down in the chair that Rambert had vacated, took a sip, and gave me a small smile, just a bit strained.

"Where's your friend?" I asked her.

"Art has gone to the embassy for a few hours. I'll be joining him for lunch."

"Do you belong to him?"

"He thought so," she said quietly, a bit sadly. "I had to disabuse him of that. It's a bit hard for him to accept."

"Around Rome they say Arthur Richmond pays for the apartment you use there for your European base."

Mei-lin shook her head. "No, and not for my apartment in New York, either. I pay my own way, Bishop."

"They also say he's pretty solidly married."

"Yes, and I never had any desire to change that. Art and I

spent a lot of time together when I was working in Washington and whenever he was there. Now we see less of each other. Only when we happen to be in some part of the world at the same time."

Mei-lin drank more of her coffee. "Art knows I'm not promiscuous," she said carefully, not looking at me. "That's why it was a shock for him. He was on his way to India for the State Department, and he made a detour here just to spend a couple days with me. Now he's decided to leave again this evening."

"End of a beautiful relationship?"

"I hope not completely. I like him. And I'm grateful to him."

"For what?"

She looked at me for a moment. "I never told you where I'm from."

"Chicago, you said."

"But I wasn't born there. I was born in Manila. My father was a soldier stationed in the Philippines. My mother was what they call *hua ch'iao*: part Chinese living outside China. They had me, and then my father was sent to the war in Korea and died there."

"How old were you when he got killed?"

"Two. When I was five my mother found out she was dying of tuberculosis. She wrote to my father's sister in Chicago. My Aunt Alice has no children of her own, and never married. She flew to Manila and fell in love with me. She needed an expedient way to get me back to the States—but she couldn't find documented proof of my paternity. So she found someone in Manila to forge papers showing that my father and mother were married. They weren't, because my father couldn't get permission from his superiors."

"A lot of Army officers are stiff-necked about white

troops and non-Caucasian foreigners."

Mei-lin forced a smile. "Especially the wily Chinese. Dragon Ladies are the most dangerous, you know. Bear that in mind. Anyway, there I was for most of my life, an alien of questionable status in the United States."

"Until you met Richmond," I hazarded.

"Yes. When I got to trust him enough, I told him about it. You're the only other one I've ever told. He was able to clear up my citizenship."

That was all it took, I reflected, thinking about my father: the right connections at a sufficiently high level. "Could he change that back," I asked her, "if he got sore at you?"

"No, he couldn't—and he wouldn't. He's not that kind of man."

I wasn't so sure. "What does Richmond do in the State Department, exactly?"

Mei-lin shrugged. "When our government has a problem in a foreign country, he's sometimes the one who goes to see what can be done about it. Usually successfully. Art is something of a legend in the foreign service."

That was pretty vague. But if she knew more than that, it was obvious she didn't intend to tell it. I considered asking Victoria to run a check on Richmond. Then I decided against it. I didn't feel like talking to Victoria about the girl who'd gotten me interested in him.

* * *

Nine days later Rambert and I wound up our stay in Beirut. We'd gotten mentions of our two new weapons in a number of wire service stories. A TV team had filmed another street fight using our prototypes. Though it never appeared on television, we were able to buy footage later and use it as a sales tool. A paragraph about the LB-75 and another about the PR-100 ran in the multi-lingual editions of *Armies and Weapons*, the top trade journal of the arms business. Mei-lin's article about the arms demonstration and the photos accompanying it turned up in a couple European weeklies and several Sunday supplements in the States. It wasn't as much publicity as we'd hoped for, but at least we hadn't come up empty.

Rambert flew to Paris and I headed back to Rome. Mei-lin decided she'd had all she could stomach of the Lebanese civil war and went back with me. In Rome we began winding up nights together, whenever both our work schedules permitted.

Usually we ended up at my place rather than hers. She had what was essentially a crowded working studio, with a narrow couch for a bed and a shared bathroom at the other end of the hall: not an ideal space for two to relax together. I'd moved up from the little hotel to a comfortable apartment in the chic Parioli neighborhood, with its own little terrace garden. But the nights we shared in it were hard to come by. Mei-lin had her deadlines to meet and assignments to rush off to. I was snowed under by increased business that was finally coming our way.

In November the Portuguese government had given Angola independence, triggering fresh warfare in the former African colony between pro-Soviet and pro-U.S. factions. Relations between Morocco and Algeria had turned nasty over a mineral-rich chunk of desert formerly known as the Spanish Sahara. Both conflicts created escalated opportunities for arms brokers, including Tri-Arms International.

Portugal, having rid itself of its overseas colonies, had depots full of weaponry it no longer needed to control those colonies. Victoria got word of it first, over dinner with the Portuguese ambassador in Washington. I made a fast trip to

Portugal while Victoria applied pressure through the ambassador to make my reception a hospitable one. Algeria, getting set to meet a possible attack from Morocco, had gone on an arms buying spree. I wound up selling Algeria everything I got from Portugal: fifty million rounds of 7.62mm ammunition for four million dollars, thirty-five thousand G3 automatic rifles for over five million, plus an assortment of APCs, machine guns and grenades. Tri-Arms' commission, plus rake-offs from both ends, netted us just under a million dollars profit.

At the same time Morocco, preparing to fend off any invasion from Algeria, was buying brand new heavy tanks from America, and wanted to get rid of a lot of old tanks. These included fifty-two medium M-47 Patton tanks dating back to World War II. Rambert got this tip from French government friends stationed in Morocco, and Tri-Arms made a modest investment. We bought the Pattons for their scrap value: three thousand bucks apiece. Then Rambert and I, with a team of technicians, went to work making the tanks serviceable.

We had to work fast. Christian had learned from friends in Germany that Bolivian military purchasers were dickering with the Germans for new Leopard tanks. While I'd been an instructor at the camp in Central America, I'd gotten friendly with a young Bolivian student. He'd been a lieutenant then. Now he was a colonel. This type of speedy promotion wasn't odd in Latin America. He belonged to one of Bolivia's wealthiest families; his father was a general and his uncle was a power in the Bolivian finance ministry. I flew over for a conference with the young colonel, his father and his uncle—and offered them our perfectly serviceable Pattons for thirty thousand apiece.

It was a big markup for Tri-Arms, but an immense saving

for Bolivia. I pointed out that they could buy all fifty-two of our Pattons for the price of one and a half Leopards. I also pointed out that since Bolivia had already allocated the money for the purchase, an awful lot would be left over for the officials handling the deal to pocket. Bolivia wound up buying four Leopards to show off in military parades—and the rest of the tanks it purchased were ours: a profit of one and a quarter million dollars for Tri-Arms.

We were still nowhere near the heights of the Golden Circle; but we were definitely climbing the ladder.

Some of our steps up that ladder had come from unexpected sources. But none more unexpected than the next one. I was back in Rome, and Mei-lin had gone for a week of talks with publishers in Hamburg, when I got an overseas call from Argentina.

"This is Arthur Richmond," the voice at the other end said. "We met briefly in Beirut. Through a mutual friend, Miss . . ."

"I remember," I assured him.

"Good. Do you know that I work for the State Department?"

"Vaguely," I said, and tried the question on him: "Doing what, exactly?"

The question remained unanswered. "I've done some checking up on you, Bishop. And on your firm. At first for a personal reason, I have to admit. But what I've learned has caused me to take a different kind of interest in you. There is an emergency situation in which, I believe, you could render a service to our country. At the same time, I'm absolutely certain it would be excellent for Tri-Arms International. Could you meet me in Washington to discuss it?"

"When?" If Richmond swung the kind of weight Mei-lin had said, I definitely wanted to find out what he had in mind.

"I'm leaving Buenos Aires in two days. That's Tuesday. Could you be in Washington by Wednesday?"

"No, but I can be there Friday." He'd run a check on me; I wanted the extra days for one on him.

"Friday is fine," he agreed. "I'll still be in Washington then." He gave me his number at the State Department. "Call me before noon and we'll have lunch."

I hung up and then phoned Washington and asked Victoria to find out everything she could about Arthur Richmond before I got there.

Chapter Nineteen

Garson

"Arthur Richmond joined the government's foreign service immediately after leaving school," Victoria told me, glancing at a dossier she'd compiled on him. "He went up through the ranks with unusual speed. Partly because of family connections. One of his grandfathers was on the Supreme Court and one of his uncles was an admiral in the Pacific in the Second World War. His wife is top family, too. Her father has an international construction company and her mother's family owns choice real estate in Florida and California."

"Sounds like a marriage that has everything," I put in. "Government and the military wedded to money."

"It helps," Victoria agreed. "But Richmond also happens to be very good at what he does. At the moment he's one of the most effective trouble shooters the State Department has. Some would say *the* best. His admirers consider him a combination of Lawrence of Arabia and an undercover Kissinger."

"An adventurer with a realistic streak."

"Or a realist with a streak of the adventurer." She returned to the dossier. "He was in Vietnam well before you were. Disappeared into the mountains for over a year, organizing tribes against the Viet-Cong. In Indonesia he's credited with

254

having personally outmaneuvered a communist attempt to seize power. He's also one of the Americans who slipped into Iran to create the coup that brought the Shah to power. And he was in Santiago when General Pinochet's military junta killed President Allende and became Chile's new government—so he probably had a hand in that, too."

"I hope he's had *some* failures," I said sourly. "I'm not up to out-thinking a superman."

Victoria held up a slender finger: "One: Richmond was supposed to be close buddies with the Shah of Iran, after the way he helped him gain his throne. Now the Shah's going hog wild in both his internal and foreign policies, and refusing to listen to advice from America. Richmond tried his best to get him back under control. He failed and is no longer welcome in Iran."

She held up a second finger: "Two: he tried to organize a Syrian coup that would bring men favorable to Washington into power. The coup was a complete flop. Syria became more solidly tied to Russia than ever, as a result. He's made some minor mistakes, as well, but those two are the big ones." Victoria regarded me reflectively, "So Richmond *is* fallible. Reassuring, in case he doesn't have your best interests in mind—whatever it is he wants to talk to you about."

"I doubt that he's too interested in my welfare," I told her. I didn't explain why I thought that—and when she didn't ask, I wondered if she'd also been updating her dossier on me.

It was Wednesday, two days before my appointment with Arthur Richmond. I'd arrived in Washington that morning. Victoria had rented me a car and booked a motel room for me—both under fake names, as an added insurance against Richmond finding out I was already around.

Our conversation took place over lunch in the dining room

of her house in Alexandria. The room was the kind she felt happiest in: warmly old-fashioned and comfortable, with french windows looking out into a lovely enclosed garden. There were no buildings that overlooked the garden. We could talk anyplace inside the house without being worried that somebody might pick up what we said. Christian Frosch had been there for three days, installing his security system, and he'd retained an expert to check on it once each day.

From the way Christian had spoken about those three days with Victoria, I'd gathered that he'd become as smitten with her as men generally got when she cared to turn on all that magnetism. My own response to her remained as disturbing as ever, in spite of Mei-lin. But this time I had no desire to turn our get-together into something more intimate. We were both under too much pressure to solve the mystery of my appointment with Richmond, and too concerned about how we would wrest potential benefits for Tri-Arms out of the booby traps that would almost certainly be hidden in whatever proposal he had for me. I was beginning to sympathize with businessmen who neglected their wives, and even their mistresses, under the all-consuming press of negotiations and decision-making.

"You've managed to gather a lot of information since I called you from Rome," I said over our post-lunch coffees. "Did you do much of this asking around yourself?" That was important because we weren't ready to reveal, as yet, that Victoria was one of the partners in Tri-Arms.

"Most of it was handled by a man named Collins," she told me. "I've used him in the past. He's a former State Department spook who shifted into investigations for business attorneys and lobbyists. Collins worked for Richmond at one time, which makes it that much easier for him." Victoria finished her coffee and lit a cigarette. "*Some* of the information I've gathered myself, discreetly. I've had, for example, a long lunch with Richmond's wife. A group of society women are planning a charity ball for Christmas. Mrs. Richmond would like to be chairwoman for the affair. I offered to help her."

"While you pumped her about her husband."

Victoria nodded matter-of-factly. "Everything she knows. She's proud of him. He responds to that by occasionally telling her about his exploits. It was a useful lunch."

We got up from the table and she led me into her study for the rest of our discussion. It was a large, elegant room: nineteenth century French carpets, walls of old Tudor panelling, window curtains of green damask woven in Italy. Over the years, Victoria certainly hadn't lost her gift for decorating. A folding screen with panels upholstered in magenta silk partially divided the study into two sections: Victoria's office at home, and a small conference room. She'd spent eighty thousand dollars of the half million she'd taken out of the Tri-Arms Swiss account on fixing up the interior of her house. It was worth it. This was where Victoria conducted much of her work for us, including business entertaining and private meetings.

We entered the conference section of the study and settled into comfortable armchairs covered in linen tapestry. Victoria killed her cigarette in an antique, pewter ashtray as she resumed:

"On a personal level, Richmond has a contented if not exciting marriage. Three children, two already in college."

She lit another cigarette before continuing, with no change of tone and her eyes fixed on the dossier: "His sometimes mistress is an interesting newspaperwoman. Part Chinese. Mei-lin Shaw. She had a syndicated column about Washington for a time. Called it *Alice in Blunderland*. Then she grew bored with it and went back to globe trotting. So she and Richmond don't see as much of each other as they used to."

Still no particular emphasis in Victoria's voice, no questioning looks in my direction. "He saw her in Beirut," she added. "He hasn't visited her again since she returned to Rome. But he did have some inquiries made recently about her—and you. He knows you've been living with her in Rome. I doubt he's happy about it."

I said, "Nobody's secrets are safe from you anymore."

"I hope not, for the sake of Tri-Arms."

"I don't live with Mei-lin. We see each other. I like her. Sometimes she likes me. And sometimes she doesn't. That's all of it."

"How *much* do you like her?"

I laughed and said, "I wish I thought you were jealous."

Victoria smiled. "Don't be so sure I'm not. But that isn't why I asked. It's important to know because Richmond has something in mind for our company, and at the same time considers the lady his."

"She isn't. They had a relationship. Past tense."

Victoria nodded, accepting that. "But possibly to be renewed at some time. That possibility has to be kept in mind, Gar." She paused and then added quietly: "Because, for one thing, Arthur Richmond is Solomon Alexandre's man inside the State Department."

I took a moment to absorb that one. "Your informers earn their money—or whatever you trade in exchange."

"It's not something I turned up in the last few days. I like to know as much as I can about Solomon's connections. This one isn't too much of a secret, in some circles. Solomon does favors for the government, and the government does favors for him—when his interests and those of the United States coincide. Richmond is the liaison between the two."

"Interesting."

"More than interesting. You said Richmond was in Buenos Aires when he called you."

"That's right."

"Solomon was there at the same time."

I knew that I was nursing the same intriguing suspicion as Victoria. "I hope," I told Victoria, "that you'll be talking with Richmond's wife again."

She nodded. "We've agreed to meet for lunch once a week until arrangements for the ball are completed. More often if either of us wishes."

"Fine."

I left and headed for New York. That was where Alexandre had his American headquarters. When I got there I hired a business investigator of my own to dig into recent dealings between Victoria's former husband and Mei-lin's former boyfriend.

Chapter Twenty

Victoria

After Garson had left, Victoria returned to Washington to get the latest report from her former State Department spook, and to pay him to continue with his investigation of Richmond's current activities. Then she settled down in her office to read updated dossiers on a congressman who was having difficulties with his reelection campaign and a rear admiral who served as a key military science advisor to the American President. She had a dinner date with the latter that night, and one with the former on the following night. Neither appointment was directly related to the Richmond mystery. But each of these men could become a key factor in the future of Tri-Arms in the United States, according to her plans.

* * *

Rear Admiral John Carrighar's wife, Alison, was one of the charter members of the old girl network that the *Washington Post* had dubbed "Victoria Nicolson's Sewing Circle." She was six years older than Victoria, but the ravages of heavy drinking, a problem of many military wives, made her look much older than that. Their friendship had first developed because of Alison Carrighar's respect for Victoria's taste in clothes. Whenever the rear admiral's wife was in the market for new apparel, she took Victoria shopping with her.

Victoria dined with the Carrighars on Wednesday night at their suburban house in Fairfax County. After dinner Carrighar excused himself to watch one of his favorite TV programs. Alison took Victoria into the drawing room, poured her a cognac, and mixed a drink for herself. Victoria was still nursing her cognac and Alison was into her third bourbon and water when Rear Admiral Carrighar joined them, carrying a fresh can of beer.

"You having one of those secret girl talks, or can a fella listen in?"

"We've been talking *business*, Johnny," his wife informed him excitedly. "Victoria had somebody who wants to buy that land of ours down in Granville. Could solve our—"

Carrighar quickly stopped her from saying anything more: "Hold on there, Allie. If it's business you better let me do the talking." He turned to Victoria with a poker smile, but she spotted the gleam of eagerness the smile was hiding. "First of all, Vicky, who is this somebody who's interested in our land?"

"A Japanese industrialist I sometimes represent," Victoria told him. "He wants to build a plant in North Carolina, and your property's in the right location. He would be making the purchase through an American holding company he controls, so his name wouldn't enter into the negotiations. Since you bought the land in Alison's name, *yours* wouldn't have to either."

She could see how much Carrighar liked that last part. But he hid it, shaking his head dubiously. "I don't know, Vicky. We bought that land as an investment for our old age.

261

Money gets worth less all the time, and property keeps going up. I figured on holding on to it for another ten years. By then some big real estate company will be drooling to build a housing project on it."

"Hey, Johnny," Victoria said with a good-natured smile, "I'm a friend, remember? You don't have to kid me. I wouldn't recommend anything to a client without checking it out first. Right after you bought that land you discovered most of it turns to soggy marsh when it rains. I know you're trying to get rid of it. Now, my client can afford the cost to drain it just because the location's good for his plant."

Carrighar's smile was embarrassed. "I should've known better than to play it cute with you. For a girl, you're just too darn smart."

"You're my friends," Victoria told him gently. "There are other properties in the same area as yours that would suit my client as well. But as a friend, why shouldn't I give it to you, and let you benefit from it?"

Alison told her, almost tearfully, "We'll always be grateful, Vicky."

Her husband raised a hand to stop her again. "The thing is," he said to Victoria, "how much is your client ready to pay us? Remember, we invested almost ninety thousand bucks in that land. And that was back when money was worth more."

Victoria knew they'd only paid forty thousand for it, and had later failed in an attempt to sell it for half that price. But she had her own reason for not saying so. "His offer is a hundred and sixty thousand. Not a bad profit for you, considering."

"Not bad . . ." Carrighar conceded, and was unable to hold back a grin of relief.

Yukada was willing to put out the money solely because Rear Admiral Carrighar, as a military science advisor to the

President, was in a position to help put through arms deals with the U.S. government. In Victoria's opinion, President Ford would not return to office. But Carrighar's prestige and deliberate avoidance of political affiliations almost guaranteed that he would continue in the same or a similar position in subsequent administrations.

His debt to Victoria—for ridding him of a dead-loss investment for a whopping profit—guaranteed his help in putting through her deals, for Yukada as well as Tri-Arms.

* * *

"I've long considered you one of the most charming ladies in town," Congressman Shan Huxley said contentedly the very next night, as Victoria cleared her dining room table. "Now I know you're one of its most accomplished cooks, as well. Best home-cooked dinner I've had since my wife died, bless her memory."

"You're an old flatterer. But do keep it up."

"Being a flatterer's a habit a politician gets into, Miss Vicky. Being old, that's something that just jumps on you and is hard to get used to. Like a flea, only you can't just scratch it away."

"Judging by your healthy appetite," Victoria laughed, "it isn't harming you much." She brought their desserts to the table. "Coffee with or after?"

"Not at all, thank you, ma'am. I drink coffee this late and I can't sleep. And outside of sleeping, there's not much to do with my nights lately."

Victoria sat down across from him and smiled indulgently. "According to what I've heard, Congressman, that is an outrageous lie. Ever since you became a widower, half the unattached women in Washington have been acting as though you're catnip. And some attached ones, who should be paying more attention to their husbands and less to you."

"Used to be that way," Representative Huxley admitted, grinning at the memory. *"Used* to. But I got to tell you about Washington ladies. They're attracted to power. A man without power has no interest for them. And power—that's what everybody's saying I'll soon be without."

"Everybody could be wrong," Victoria said.

Huxley shook his head. "I've served in the House of Representatives for almost thirty years. But now I can't even raise enough dough for my next election campaign to pay for some television time. Why should people contribute if they figure I'm a has-been? They look at Sam Gillian and figure he's sure to beat me. Young, vigorous man. Made a sterling reputation for himself as a district attorney. A tough campaigner on his way up. For Gillian, taking my seat away from me is only one step on his way to the top. And he's got the brains and the backing to make it."

Congressman Huxley took another spoonful of his dessert, and then put down the spoon with a sigh. "And look at me. An old man. I was seventy a month ago. And midway through the year I got so sick I couldn't even show up in the House for over two months."

"Young or old," Victoria said, "anybody can get sick for awhile."

"Sure. If you're young, that's the way people see it. But if you're old and get sick, they think it means you're about to cash in your chips. Nobody wants to contribute to a campaigner who may not live long enough to show his appreciation in practical terms."

"I had a talk with your doctor," Victoria told Huxley. "He says you're entirely well now and likely to continue for many years to come."

Victoria

The congressman leaned back in his dining chair and regarded her thoughtfully. "What they say about you is true. When you want to know something, you find it out." He watched Victoria open her cigarette case. "Those are poison, honey. Why don't you have one of these instead?" He took two cigars from his breast pocket and offered her one.

Victoria smiled and said, "Thank you, but I'm used to my own brand of poison."

Huxley returned one cigar to his pocket, lit her cigarette and then his own cigar. He blew a perfect smoke ring and smiled at her through it. "Okay, honey—what's on your mind?"

"I'm considering investing a hundred thousand dollars in your campaign for reelection, Congressman."

He stared at her. Then he said, a bit dazed, "I think that offer entitles you to call me by my first name. Shan, short for Leshansky. My mother's family name."

"All right, Shan. I wouldn't contribute the whole amount in one chunk. That could be an embarrassment to you. It would reach you divided into smaller sums from different contributors. It should pay for enough TV spots to get your bandwagon rolling."

A hundred thousand would use up most of what she had left from the half million she'd withdrawn from the Tri-Arms Swiss account. But the company was continuing to make money now, and the investment was a sound one.

Huxley was nodding, beginning to look younger already. "Sure. Once people find out I've got that much backing, some of them will start contributing, too. Just to make sure they're not left out, in case I win after all."

"You *will* win."

He laughed. "I'm beginning to think I just might, and surprise everybody. Your confidence in me is infectious."

Huxley blew another smoke ring and studied Victoria some more. "You've built quite a reputation for yourself pretty quickly. Besides that sewing circle of yours, you've got a lot of influential men wrapped around your finger, the way I hear it. How come you waited until now to get around to *me*?"

"You didn't *need* me before. Now you do. I'm acting on the certainty that you won't forget I was the *first* to have faith in you when others didn't. You're on a number of committees that are important to me, including the House Armed Services Committee. When you're reelected, you'll become the chairman of some of those committees. And I'm sure you'll become a member of even more. I know you'll want to express your appreciation to me."

"You are some lady," Huxley said slowly. "That's very straight talk."

Victoria's eyes met his. "You're a man who understands straight talk."

"Yes," he said after a moment, "I do. Don't worry, I won't forget my obligation to you."

Victoria was sure of that. Huxley had a solid reputation concerning matters of that sort. No member of the House or Senate could operate effectively if he became known as a man who reneged on his campaign commitments.

After Congressman Huxley had gone, Victoria reflected on the amount she had learned from Solomon Alexandre merely by observing and listening during the early years of their marriage. But in applying what she had learned, she added variations of her own. She thought of these variations as insurance policies.

There was Huxley's reelection, for example, and the possibility that he might lose, in spite of the injection of financial vitality into his campaign. Solomon Alexandre always shrugged off such occasional losses. He played percentages, backing enough politicians so that while some lost, others won. Victoria could not afford to play it that way—not yet.

Her insurance policy in the Huxley campaign centered on his opponent, District Attorney Gillian. For some months she'd had a private detective digging into his professional and private activities. Listed among his official expenses were weekly payments to a personal secretary, a young man who had been a physical education instructor, and who, it turned out, knew nothing about typing or shorthand. The payments included rent of his apartment, which was often visited by District Attorney Gillian. Victoria's private detective had even obtained photographic proof of the love affair between the two men.

It was not until she had seen this proof that Victoria had decided to invest so much of Tri-Arms' money in Huxley. She would wait until the last week before the election and then have that proof released to the press, radio and TV. It was a conservative state, and she was fairly confident that most voters would be disgusted by the revelation. Gillian's campaign could not possibly survive it. Huxley would be reelected.

With Rear Admiral Carrighar, Victoria's insurance policy was of a different kind. Carrighar did not have Huxley's reputation, nor a reason to remember his obligation to her. But if he ever chose to forget it, she had the blackmail prepared to change his mind. His career would collapse if she exposed his sale of land known to be worthless to a foreign arms dealer, Yukada. The payment of a hundred and sixty thousand to a military officer in a position to help grease the way for arms deals in the United States couldn't be explained away as an innocent mistake. World-wise Washington would draw the natural conclusions. The threat would be enough to keep Carrighar in line, should that prove necessary.

Even in these variations, Victoria acknowledged that she learned much from her ex-husband. She had learned to be a vicious fighter, keeping her ultimate goal always in mind.

She'd never revealed that goal to anyone. Yukada was the only one who might have some understanding of what it was. He was so much like her in that: with the same ability to put an old injury in cold storage for as long as it required, while working slowly toward the time for retaliation.

Thinking about Solomon Alexandre and her goal brought Victoria's tension to an unbearable level.

She had to take a pill to put herself to sleep that night.

Chapter Twenty-one

Garson

Richmond was waiting for me that Friday in the glass enclosed terrace of a Maryland country inn.

"The food here is only so-so," he apologized ahead of time as I took my seat across the table from him. "But for keeping our talk private it's a hard place to beat."

The table was next to an artificial waterfall. Its noise mixed unpleasantly with the blare of country-western tunes over the inn's loudspeakers. I doubted that even Christian Frosch could come up with any eavesdropping contrivance that could get much through that combination.

"I have something personal to say first," Richmond told me stiffly after we'd ordered. "I don't think you're the sort of man with whom Mei-lin should be associating herself."

"Tell *her* that."

"I have. But she's too infatuated at the moment. So I'm telling you." Richmond held up a hand to stop me from replying. "I realize my feeling about this—this affair—cuts no ice at all, as long as her infatuation lasts. I merely wanted to get it off my chest."

He forced a smile. "Now we can get on with the subject of this meeting. How much do you know about Pranagua?"

"I know it's in bad shape, even compared to other Central American countries. None of them are exactly healthy right now."

"True," said Richmond. "Go on."

"Well, it's poverty-stricken—in spite of a good seaport and plenty of mineral resources. Its military dictator's a blood-thirsty, sadistic paranoid." In fact, thousands of political protesters had been tortured and killed by General Calderon's secret police, whole villages wiped out by his troops on the slightest suspicion that they'd harbored rebels. "He'll slaughter half his population if he goes on much longer."

"The press exaggerates," Richmond said blandly. "Actually Calderon has begun making some definite improvements in his attitude toward human rights. Under pressure from us."

"I should have added," I said drily, "that Calderon supports U.S. policy in Latin America—in return for some millions in military and economic aid."

"Sixty million a year," Richmond specified coolly.

"My opinion, that's lost money. With all the different rebel movements going on down there, one of them's bound to boot Calderon out before long."

Richmond nodded. "That about summarizes our problem in Pranagua. I believe you met two officers from there during your period as a weapons instructor at our Latin American camp. Only *two*—is my information correct?"

"On the button. A couple young lieutenants from rich families."

Richmond looked satisfied. "Neither of them is stationed where you might run into them down there. So we can stop worrying on that score."

"I wasn't worried about it. Why were you?"

"Because we want you to go to Pranagua. For a time."

"We?"

"You know my professional position, Bishop. That's answer enough. Our problem in Pranagua is becoming urgent. There are the various rebel groups you mentioned. Calderon can't continue to squash every one that pops up, unless he gets escalated military support. The exaggerated news coverage of his so-called atrocities has made it too uncomfortable for the American government to give him support of that scope. But if *we* don't, General Calderon threatens to switch allegiance and get it from the Soviet Union—which would just *love* to take over our role in Pranagua."

"According to what I hear," I put in, "one of the strongest underground groups opposing Calderon is communist."

"Right. Financed by Russia and military advisors from Cuba. But, of course, if Calderon ever does switch allegiance to the Soviets, that group would switch, too—allying itself with Calderon." Richmond paused, and made his point flatly: "We cannot allow that to happen."

The waiter brought our lunches. Richmond was right: it wasn't the best. We ate sparingly while he filled me in on the rest of it. As far as the American President and his Secretary of State were concerned, the shit had really hit the fan in Pranagua early the previous year. That was when students at the University of Pranagua had staged a demonstration against General Calderon's use of paramilitary death squads to eliminate anyone and everyone in the capital suspected of disloyalty to his rule. Calderon's National Guard had taken over the university, killing sixteen students in the process.

The student demonstration exploded into a protest strike that brought the capital and two other main cities to a virtual standstill. Calderon broke the strike with the bloodiest reign of terror in his ten years in power. Almost two thousand citizens were killed by his troops and secret police.

Hundreds more vanished, never to be seen again. The only protesters who survived were those who fled from the cities on time, going off to join one or another of the guerrilla groups hidden in the mountains.

It was coverage of this slaughter by American newspapers and television that made continued U.S. support of Calderon a political embarrassment for the administration.

"So you warned Calderon to ease up," I said.

"And he *has*," Richmond insisted again. "There have been far fewer killings and disappearances of dissidents in Pranagua since then."

"Naturally. There aren't many dissidents left alive anymore—not where Calderon can get his hands on them. They're up in the mountains now. And his troops haven't been able to force them out."

Richmond gave me a hard stare. "They could, if we increased our military aid program for Calderon. That's what he's asking for."

"But you can't give it to him. It would get more unpleasant publicity from the media."

"Right. At the same time there's Calderon's threat. And he means it. If we don't give him what he wants, he'll turn to the Soviet Union for it."

"You're in a bind," I agreed. "How am I supposed to help you get out of it?"

"Some of the Pranaguan dissidents who ran away from the cities joined the communist guerrillas," Richmond told me. "But most of them went to another guerrilla group, in the mountains near the southeastern border. The one led by Augustin DelMundo. Are you familiar with him? He was a general in the government Calderon knocked over ten years ago. Now he calls himself a social democrat. Which means socialist. DelMundo has more men with him than any other rebel movement. What he doesn't have is enough arms, nor the money to get what he needs."

At that point I began to understand why he was talking to me. I kept quiet and waited.

"The Reds won't help DelMundo because he's the most effective opponent of the communist rebels in attracting Pranaguan dissidents. At the same time *our* relations with him have always been distinctly frigid. DelMundo has said some extremely unpleasant things about American policies in Latin America."

"But right now he may be your only way out of your bind in Pranagua."

"Exactly. We can't bolster General Calderon's regime much longer, and we don't want the Reds to take over—either with him or without him. DelMundo is the least objectionable alternative. If he overthrew Calderon, we could be sure of one thing at least: he would not ally himself with the communists or the Soviet Union.

"However," Richmond added quietly, "*we* can't give Del-Mundo military aid. Not openly. If Calderon learned about it he'd jump into the hands of the Russians before we could draw our next breath."

"But," I said, "a smallish private arms firm—based in Europe and with no known connections with the U.S. government—*could* supply DelMundo with what his guerrillas need."

Richmond smiled at me as though I were a bright student who'd come up with the right answer. "Tri-Arms International does fit that requirement rather neatly. The money for Tri-Arms to buy weapons for DelMundo would be supplied by me—channeled through a firm with no traceable connection to the United States. And as you said, Tri-Arms also has no known relationship with our government. But if

DelMundo *does* overthrow General Calderon, *he* would know that we were behind it."

"And be properly cooperative in gratitude, you hope. How much are you prepared to bet on it?"

"Three million dollars," Richmond answered promptly. "Your percentage would come out of that. I would supply it to you in stages, as you needed it. And I would expect you to keep me informed of DelMundo's progress, every step of the way. I want that understood."

"Understood." I thought about it for a few moments. "For pulling off a successful coup, three million's not much of an investment. If you *want* it to succeed, you'll have to come up with more than that."

"You don't know that until you've talked to DelMundo," Richmond pointed out. "I can assure you it's a lot more than he's ever been able to get from any other source. In any case, it will *have* to be enough. We can't commit ourselves to DelMundo any deeper than that—at this stage, at least. Perhaps by the time he is ready to make his move, we'll have gained enough confidence in him to contribute more. But not until then."

I studied Richmond and decided the man wasn't bluffing. There was no way to talk him into raising his initial offer. I wondered why.

"For gathering the weapons and ammo," I told him, "and smuggling them in to DelMundo's guerrillas, Tri-Arms would take ten percent of the three million. That comes to three hundred thousand."

"The deal I'm authorized to offer you is sweeter than that," Richmond confided smoothly. "We'd expect you to do more than supply DelMundo with the arms. We'd want you to stay with him, to help train his men in their use. Right up to the end. That would enable you to keep me in touch with

DelMundo's plans. Every step of the way, as I told you. I would arrange the method of communication between us."

Richmond rested his elbows on the table and leaned forward a bit, looking at me confidently. "In return for that, we're prepared to offer Tri-Arms a bonus—if DelMundo does succeed in taking over the government. A bonus of an additional three hundred thousand dollars."

That did sweeten the deal. Considerably. I could be sure he'd deliver the bonus if the conditions he'd stated were fulfilled. If he didn't, the word would spread, and nobody would trust any offers he made in the future.

"Of course," Richmond went on, your firm stands to gain far more than that. Should DelMundo become the new ruler of Pranagua, he'd be grateful to you—as well as to the American government." He smiled thinly. "I'm sure you've already considered that."

I had indeed. *If* DelMundo pulled it off, Tri-Arms could wind up filling most of Pranagua's future military orders.

"Sounds nice," I admitted cautiously. "But the if-come part doesn't. DelMundo could take the arms we supply and just stay put in his mountain hideouts with it. *If* he decides he still doesn't have enough to take on Calderon's forces. No takeover. No bonus for Tri-Arms. No prospects of the other rewards you mentioned."

"As I mentioned," Richmond reminded me with practiced sincerity, "we *might* up the funds for arms eventually. But whether we do or not, we don't expect DelMundo to take on Calderon's entire army with what you supply him. He doesn't have enough men for that, even if we gave him twenty times as much. Most of Calderon's troops are stationed in various parts of Pranagua's back country, dealing with the different guerrilla movements. We would expect DelMundo to avoid direct confrontation with most of them:

to slip past them and concentrate on the capital alone. If Pranagua City falls to him, the rest of the country falls with it. And Pranagua City *is* vulnerable."

Richmond glanced around the restaurant before continuing. When he did, he kept his voice low: "I would arrange to make it even more vulnerable. When you informed me that DelMundo was ready to launch his attack, I would see to it that the commander-in-chief of Calderon's armed forces was summoned to an important conference in Washington. With him gone, the defenses of Pranagua City would become less cohesive, less motivated. I would be there in Pranagua City by then, prepared to help further. On the day before Del-Mundo attacked, I would see that our military advisors there informed the officer left in charge of Pranagua City's defenses that an attack was coming—from a different direction.

"Much of the defense force would leave the city to head off the attack—but they'd be going the wrong way. Making it that much easier for DelMundo to break into Pranagua City. And once he's inside, most of its population is certain to join his guerrillas in the final assault."

Richmond gave me a smug smile: "Do the prospects sound a bit better now?"

"Better," I admitted. If the conditions he promised were likely to be fulfilled, DelMundo was practically certain to make the try. He'd never get a better chance than that. I asked Richmond, "Do I have to find my own way to get in touch with DelMundo?"

He shook his head. "His closest aide has been here in the States for the last couple months. Trying to raise money to buy weapons for DelMundo's guerrillas. Miguel Gomez. A colonel in the army before Calderon took over. When DelMundo was a general, Gomez was his aide-de-camp.

We've let him operate here with this contingency in mind, keeping close tabs on him." Richmond smiled briefly: "We've even prevented one attempt by Calderon agents to assassinate him."

"How's this Gomez doing so far with his fund raising?"

"Badly. No more than a few thousand dollars. You can imagine how excited he'd get about the amount you'd be offering. Even after you sliced off your percentage. He'll get you to DelMundo, fast."

I asked Richmond some more questions, but mostly I was stalling while I tried to read his vibes. I might as well have tried to read the face of an old poker hustler. Richmond was no debutante.

"I'll need some time," I told him finally, "to talk it over with my partners."

"Sure, but not for too long." He was sure there was no chance of our turning it down. It *was* a sweet offer, on the surface. "I have people to answer to. They worry that the Pranagua situation could get out of our control. And— there's no shortage of other private arms dealers. Any of them would jump on this opportunity."

That was true enough. But his offering it to me meant there had to be hidden hazards. One reason for his choice was obvious. Pranagua would involve me totally for months to come. That would give him time to try to reestablish his relationship with Mei-lin. Pranagua could also get me killed, which wouldn't make him too unhappy. But I found it hard to believe that there wasn't some other danger—one that would affect Tri-Arms as well as myself—veiled in the scheme.

I thought about Victoria's revelation that Richmond was Solomon Alexandre's man in the State Department—and that they'd been together when Richmond phoned me from

Argentina. I thought, also, about what Tri-Arms must represent for Alexandre: two former employees who'd become his enemies—plus he must know that his former wife, who'd defeated his efforts to crush her, represented our interests in Washington. The temerity of the woman to compete in his own world.

So he wouldn't go along with Richmond handing Tri-Arms a plum. Unless the plum was poisoned.

* * *

The first partner I consulted was the one Richmond didn't know about. Victoria buckled down to learning everything she could, in a short time, about current Washington opinions and options regarding Pranagua. I left her to it, and flew back to Europe to fill in our other two partners.

Rambert first, in Paris. He had friends in the French foreign ministry that he could go to for intelligence about Pranagua. Then down to Rome, where Christian Frosch had been handling deals for Tri-Arms competently in my absence. He had learned a lot since I'd first met him, and no longer needed much help from Rambert or me in appraising and discussing arms. All it had required was introductory instruction and time for his technological brain to make the shift into the field of weaponry.

When I left Christian, he was making calls to his contacts in the Italian and German governments about Pranagua. It was late when I got to my apartment and phoned Mei-lin's studio. She came over and we celebrated our reunion. "Where've you been?" she asked me a bit later.

"The States," I told her. "Richmond doesn't think I'm good for you."

She stared at me, and then laughed. "I'm not sure of that,

either. But you don't mean you went just to talk about me
with him?"

"Not entirely. But the rest is classified."

Mei-lin cocked her head and regarded me. "Do *you* think
you're good for me?"

"Time will tell," I answered carelessly.

Chapter Twenty-two

Garson

"It's a trap for fools," Victoria told us.

It was eight days after my lunch with Richmond. That was as long as I judged his patience could be stretched, in spite of his personal reasons for wanting it to be me who got involved with Pranagua. He did have his superiors to answer to; and there *were* plenty of other smallish European arms dealers who'd fit the requirements.

For Victoria it had been an intensive eight days. The other three of us hadn't been idle either. We'd formed a rough outline of the true Pranagua situation by piecing together what each of us had gathered: from my New York investigator, from Rambert's friends in French Intelligence, from Christian's contacts in Italy and Germany. Then we'd flown in to meet in the conference area of Victoria's home.

Her information squared with ours and went some distance beyond it. Victoria's sources were closer to the situation than ours.

"Richmond told you the truth about the basic situation in Pranagua," she said. "Our government wants Calderon out of there before he either falls to the communists or joins them. That's the future danger. Meanwhile, he remains an embarrassment. The atrocities he committed last year did force the

President to refuse him additional military aid."

"According to French Intelligence," Rambert put in quietly, "that cut was merely for public show. Your government is giving Calderon everything he demanded—but through your ex-husband."

"*My* sources," Christian added, "figure Alexandre sold Pranagua twenty million bucks worth of U.S. weaponry over just this past year. That's a nice chunk of annual income, even in his league."

Victoria nodded. "An income he certainly wouldn't agree to give up. Especially not to Tri-Arms." She looked at me. "What Richmond didn't say is that the guerrillas led by your DelMundo are *not* the only alternative to Calderon on one hand or the communists on the other. And they are definitely not the alternative chosen by the President and Secretary of State."

One of the first people Victoria had gone to see, after I'd dropped the Pranagua mystery in her lap, had been Clark Alwin, chairman of the board of the Alwin Chemicals and Minerals Corporation. Alwin was one of the most hardheaded businessmen around, but he was also a romantic widower. They'd met before at Washington functions. He was always refreshingly frank about being "smitten by her charms"—that was his old-fashioned way of putting it.

Victoria went to see him on the pretense of asking to handle lobbying for his company. There was no chance of that. Alwin already had a man who was better connected for it than she: his friends included most of the town's important politicians. Where the President was concerned, Clark Alwin was his own best lobbyist. He had direct access. Like Solomon Alexandre, he contributed heavily to both presidential candidates, each and every election.

The hardheaded businessman gave Victoria a regretful but

definite refusal. The romantic widower invited her to dinner. She dined with him twice in that one week. There was nothing unusual in their talking about Pranagua during both dinners. Alwin's company owned most of the mineral exploitation rights in that country.

Victoria's other sources of information included an undersecretary of state for inter-American affairs and a deputy assistant secretary of defense for foreign security assistance. Plus Congressman Shan Huxley. Since he was a ranking member of both the House Armed Services Committee and its Defense Appropriations Subcommittee, it was normal for the Secretary of State and the Director of the CIA to discuss certain classified matters with him. Since Huxley was also a politician who didn't forget his obligations, and Tri-Arms was investing heavily in his reelection campaign, it was normal for him to pass on what they'd said to Victoria.

"Our government would never help DelMundo take over Pranagua. Nor will anyone else give him serious backing. He would be too difficult a man to control, once in power. On one point, everybody I talked to agreed. DelMundo has no chance at all. The people of Pranagua like him, but they're the only ones. He probably has the largest number of guerrillas of any rebel group, and they include a lot of seasoned fighters. But they don't have the quality and quantity of arms they'd need in a direct confrontation with Calderon's troops. We couldn't supply them with enough of what they need for only three million dollars. I'm almost certain that would be far too little."

"It is not even three million," Rambert reminded her, "after our ten percent. That's three hundred thousand of it off the top."

I was paying close attention to Victoria's expression. "You said DelMundo isn't the alternative Richmond's people would choose. That means they've got some other alternative in mind."

"More than in mind," Victoria said. "Their choice—approved by Solomon—has been preparing in Puerto Rico for almost a year. Several thousand Pranaguan exiles. Stiffened by a few hundred experienced anti-Castro Cuban fighters. Trained by U.S. military advisors. Their weapons are supplied by Solomon, and paid for by the United States."

"These arms," Rambert said sourly, "would naturally be the very best and latest. In sufficient quantity."

"Naturally," Victoria agreed.

"One thing's sure," Christian said, scowling over it, "if that bunch kicks out Calderon and takes over Pranagua, they'll be plenty cooperative with Richmond's people. No question."

"And," Victoria added, in a deceptively casual tone, "Solomon Alexandre would continue to sell his millions in arms to Pranagua. No question about that, either."

Christian was still scowling: "Okay, I'm dumb. They've got this other group in Puerto Rico, dependably pro-U.S. and all set to go. So why are they giving us three million to play games with DelMundo's group?"

"The people Richmond answers to believe in the group they've prepared," Victoria explained. "But there are others in the State Department, as well as in the CIA and the President's kitchen cabinet, who have grave doubts about making use of it. Richmond's faction is stronger, but they're still worried about those doubters."

"It is the same in the French government," Rambert said. "Nobody makes a decision without first covering himself so his political enemies can't destroy him if it goes wrong."

"In this case," Victoria continued, "what worries Richmond's people is twofold. Suppose the group they're backing fails, in spite of all the help it's getting from the United States. Our government would be left with nothing but egg on its face. Remember the Bay of Pigs fiasco. On the other hand, suppose this group, supported by the U.S. and launched from our territory, does succeed in ousting Calderon. Other Latin American countries could get indignant about such blatant involvement in toppling Pranagua's government."

"Unless," I hazarded, "they made it less blatant—by bringing in a fall guy to stir up Pranagua so badly everybody could see Calderon wasn't capable of handling it?"

"A couple fall guys," Rambert said. "DelMundo—and Tri-Arms. But now we are only guessing."

Victoria nodded. "Yes, but we know enough, between us, for it to be fairly *informed* guesswork. I can do my best to find out more. But in the meantime, let's pool our guesses and see what we arrive at."

We did so, late into that night. What we arrived at, finally, was this:

Richmond would give us the money to supply DelMundo's guerrillas with arms. Not enough for DelMundo to succeed—but enough for him to launch an attack that would scare the hell out of Pranagua City's defense forces. DelMundo was sure to make that attack if he believed Richmond's promise to have the commander of the army out of the country at the time—and his other promise, to leave Pranagua City vulnerable by diverting the bulk of its defenders.

Since Richmond would remain privy to DelMundo's plans, through me, he'd be all set inside Pranagua City when the time came. And he'd be able to tip off the section of the army defending it about the direction from which the attack would come. The *correct* direction.

By then he'd probably also have some of his own rebels from Puerto Rico hidden inside the city, waiting. With most of Pranagua City's defense troops locked in battle with Del-Mundo's guerrillas outside the city, the rebels inside it would come out in the open to stir up its citizenry. Since most Pranaguans would be anxious to support any group that offered real hope of kicking Calderon out, this task would be fairly simple. The whole city would explode into an orgy of wild rioting and bloody street fighting.

And the world would have the spectacle of a Pranagua bereft of coherent leadership, with both its capital and its countryside convulsed in civil war.

By that time the bulk of the rebel group from Puerto Rico would be on ships not far from Pranagua's coast, waiting for a signal from Richmond. When he sent the signal they would strike directly into Pranagua City—not to topple the government in a coup, but to restore law and order for a government that was obviously unable to do so for itself.

That, Richmond's superiors hoped, would take the onus off the U.S. for what followed. The group from Puerto Rico would move swiftly—from establishing law and order to taking over control of the government. They would banish Calderon and his hated henchmen. And they would quietly erase any of DelMundo's guerrillas who had survived their battle with the army.

That was the picture we finally put together between us that night in Victoria's house. It was still guesswork. A lot of guesswork. Even so, it turned out to be not far off the mark.

As Victoria had said, it was a trap for fools.

If we walked into it blindly.

"Jesus," Christian concluded tiredly, "why don't we just take our commission off the top and go through the motions. Supply DelMundo as best we can, and jump out of Pranagua before he gets the chop. And forget about the other three hundred thousand we'll never see anyway."

I shook my head in a stubborn negative. "I want more out of this than a fast ten percent and goodbye," I said vehemently. "I want the same thing Alexandre wants—those millions that are there to be made, every damn year, by whoever wins control of supplying Pranagua's future military requirements. And I want the clout it would give us, in the States and with every other government. DelMundo could be that step we've been hunting for, up into the big leagues."

"Remember what Victoria said," Rambert told me. "Everybody she has spoken to is quite sure DelMundo has no chance." He wasn't contradicting me, just probing.

"Everybody *could* be wrong." I said, "But I think it's about time we start having faith in Tri-Arms' future. I want to go down there and meet this DelMundo and decide for myself."

Instinctively, I looked to Victoria for confirmation.

Her eyes met mine. "It wouldn't hurt," she agreed quietly, "to get some firsthand information. To find out, for example, how many men DelMundo actually has and how determined they are. Also," she added after a slight pause, "what they would *really* need to have a chance."

I grinned at her. It was as I'd figured: we were thinking on the same wavelength. I said, "While I'm gone, you be sure to keep your friendship with Clark Alwin warm."

"I intend to," Victoria said, just a bit stiffly. "Has anyone ever told you, Gar? You have the makings of a dedicated pimp."

* * *

I phoned Arthur Richmond at the State Department early in the morning and told him Tri-Arms would take his deal.

It didn't surprise him. The deal sounded like a good one, if you didn't know what was inside it. He warned me he'd call it off if I neglected to keep him informed every step of the way. Then he gave me the current address of DelMundo's aide, Miguel Gomez.

It was a small motel in the Spanish heart of Miami. I sat down in the only chair in his room and Gomez sat on the edge of the single bed, facing me. The room was so small our knees were only four inches apart. The smell of garbage and cooking came up the airshaft outside the window. The lightbulbs were low wattage, shining yellow on the cracked plaster of the walls.

Gomez looked like a man who had once been used to better than this. He also looked like a man who didn't mind going without better as long as necessary. About fifty, he had a thickset body and a hard face with small, fierce eyes. The former colonel in him showed in the way he held his back perfectly straight and his shoulders squared, even sitting on a mattress that sagged deeply under his weight.

"I made a couple calls after you phoned me for this appointment," he told me directly. "Nobody seems to have heard of your company, Mr. Bishop."

"Tri-Arms is based in Europe," I said. "It's a small firm, but building. We represent Hiroshi Yukada and we've represented Ahmed al-Zadar. I imagine you know of them."

"Of course. Al-Zadar I have met. Some months ago when I was in Europe to raise arms. I was a weekend guest at his home in Monte Carlo."

"Enjoy yourself?"

Gomez smiled faintly. "It was most pleasant. Al-Zadar is a gracious host. But ..." He let it dangle.

"But he couldn't help you."

"Since we don't have much money, and he doesn't have faith in General DelMundo's cause, no."

I made a note that he still referred to DelMundo by his former military rank. "*I* can help you," I said.

"Mr. Bishop," he said politely, "if you've come here to sell me some weapons you have wasted your time. As I've made clear, we are extremely short of funds."

"I'm not here to sell you anything. I'm talking about *giving* you some of the arms and ammo DelMundo needs."

Gomez frowned at me. "Why?"

"Because I'm being paid to."

"By whom?"

"Certain influential Americans who would like to see General Calderon ousted."

His frown deepened. "The American government has never been friendly toward General DelMundo."

"I didn't say the government. I said certain Americans— who are prepared to help your cause, if I report back that it has a chance."

"You will have to be more specific about who these Americans are."

"I will be, when I talk to DelMundo himself."

Gomez became silent, studying me anew. "That is very hard to arrange."

I shrugged. "If you can't arrange it then I *am* wasting my time here. And yours. Unless I talk with DelMundo personally, the offer is withdrawn." I paused and then let him have it: "I'm talking about an offer of over two and a half million dollars worth of weaponry, Colonel."

He stared at me. More than excited—overwhelmed. It took him time to recover his voice, and it came out strained: "That—is a very large amount."

"It is. Now, about getting me together with DelMundo . . ."

"Your offer could be a trick," Gomez said slowly, studying me uncertainly, "to learn how I enter and leave Pranagua.

To discover where General DelMundo's base is hidden, and betray him after your return."

An officer who serves the same commander for as many years as Gomez had DelMundo sometimes becomes like that: a combination of awed kid brother and overprotective mother. He was worried about the safety of his chief, in spite of his excitement over my offer. I couldn't blame him for that.

"Just figure a way for me to get into Pranagua without you," I said. "That way I won't know your route. Pick a place to meet me. Take me the rest of the way blindfolded if you want. As for my giving away DelMundo's base, there must be more than one place to hide in those mountains. If he decides I'm a phony, after he's talked with me, he can shift his base to someplace else."

Gomez nodded impassively. "Or he can have you killed."

"Or that," I agreed, and grinned at him.

He did not smile back.

* * *

A lot of Latin Americans referred to 1976 at the "Year of the Generals." In Argentina, a junta of generals kicked former nightclub dancer Isabelita Peron out of her presidential office and took over the government. In Chile, General Pinochet intensified the repressive measures of his regime. In Paraguay, General Stroessner marked his twenty-second year of absolute rule. In Peru, General Bermudez celebrated the first anniversary of his takeover, by *coup d'etat*, from General Velasco. In Brazil, a junta of generals running the nation quelled efforts to unseat them.

That was the year I went into Pranagua to find out if it was possible to oust General Calderon and replace him with former General DelMundo.

I flew down to the island of Jamaica first. There I met with a smuggler Gomez had told me about. Two nights later, the fast boat that had carried me across the Caribbean dropped me off at an isolated, jungle-hemmed strip of beach on the southernmost stretch of Pranaguan coast. It was an hour before dawn when the boat sped off to the east and vanished over the cloud-obscured horizon, leaving me alone. I began walking back and forth along the short length of beach, just above the surf line where the sand was hardest, while I waited.

Shortly after the first light of dawn, Miguel Gomez emerged out of what looked like a solid wall of jungle. He was flanked by a couple stocky, dark-faced men wearing patched peasant clothes. Gomez had a pre-war Swiss Luger stuck in his belt, and his flankers carried sharp, heavy machetes. The old, scarred AR15 automatic rifle Gomez carried was the most modern weapon in sight. The other two men had submachine guns of World War II vintage slung over their shoulders: a Mark-2 Sten and a Schmeisser MP.

If that represented the best DelMundo's guerrillas had, I figured almost anything I could get them would be an improvement.

"Come," Gomez said.

He turned and went back into the jungle. I followed close behind him. The other two men brought up the rear until we were about half a mile in along the path they'd cleared to reach the beach. Then they moved into the lead, using their machetes to hack through dense underbrush and hanging vines as we diverged into a different route.

They didn't blindfold me. That would have made the trek even harder, for all of us. It took two days to reach the hidden base camp of DelMundo's guerrillas, inside the mountains that straddled Pranagua's southern frontier.

* * *

The explosions of rockets blasting apart a section of mountainside carried across the distance to where I stood watching with former General Augustin DelMundo. It was an hour before sunset. The mountain behind us cast dark shadows that provided concealment from the A-37 Dragonfly jet making wide, lazy circles in the sky above. We were on a high ledge, with a direct view between two mountain slopes of the third one that was being blasted. The Dragonfly had strafed it first. Now a pair of Cobra helicopter gunships were using their rockets on it.

"That's where my base was until two weeks ago," DelMundo told me matter-of-factly. "Then I learned that one of the new men who had joined us was a spy for Calderon's secret police. Fortunately I learned it in time to move before they began these strikes."

"How did you find out he was a spy?" I asked him.

"Calderon is not the only one who has his secret informants."

"Yours must be fairly high up in Calderon's government or military to have gotten you that kind of information in time."

DelMundo didn't answer the implied question. Instead he said, "The fact that they continue to strike at the wrong area is comforting. It means we have no other spies among us."

"What did you do with the one you had?"

"We had to execute him. There was nothing else to do." DelMundo said it with genuine regret. He had a human warmth that differentiated him from the two other generals he resembled in so many other ways: DeGaulle and MacArthur. The first semblance was the height. DelMundo stood a head taller than me, and towered over everybody else I'd seen him with. Then there was the unusually prominent nose, and the same unshakable dignity with a good deal of practical intelligence behind it.

I nodded toward the needle-nosed helicopter gunships. They had finished off their missiles and were giving the distant slope a final spraying with their machine guns. "Shame you don't have some one-man rocket launchers over there right now. The way those choppers are hovering, that close to the ground, they'd make easy targets."

"We do have several launchers," DelMundo told me. "Taken from an army convoy we ambushed. What we lack is any more rockets for them. We used the last of them to destroy some tanks trying to work their way into these mountains. Of course," he added, "they wouldn't have gotten close enough to become a threat anyway. The only passable road for trucks or tanks ends in the foothills."

The two gunships suddenly veered away from their abandoned target and headed east. The Dragonfly jet stopped its circling and flew off in the same direction, flitting past Calderon's U.S.-supplied helicopters.

"They're going back to the Andreas Valley," DelMundo said. "Calderon's engineers recently finished building a military airfield there. Now that his planes can be based so close, the danger from them has increased. Before that we were relatively safe from his air force. Since his tanks and armored personnel carriers can't get in here, all we had to deal with was his infantry."

He led me off the high ledge. As we made our way down a narrow, cliffside path, he added, "We held the Andreas valley until three months ago. Then Calderon's army launched a full-scale campaign to take the area. We almost managed to break their attack. But then we ran out of ammunition and were forced to retreat and let them have the valley."

Gomez was waiting for us at the bottom of the path. He

followed us at a discreet distance. Gomez felt most comfortable when he had his commander in sight, where he could make sure he was okay and shoo away guerrillas who wanted to chat idly or ask too many questions.

We passed groups of his guerrillas as we entered the big, densely-wooded ravine where DelMundo had established his new base. Some of them had an assortment of old weapons they'd brought with them when they'd joined DelMundo, or that had been purchased with what little funds his movement had raised. Others were armed with up-to-date weaponry looted from Calderon troops they'd ambushed. A lot had no arms at all.

I'd asked DelMundo how many guerrillas he had in all, and hadn't gotten an answer. He didn't trust me that much yet. I guessed there were several thousand. But he could have more, hidden at other bases.

DelMundo's headquarters was a big cave with a small entrance. Near it we came upon three prisoners sitting on the ground with their ankles tied together and a guerrilla with an M16 standing guard over them. They were Calderon soldiers, captured by guerrillas who'd ambushed their scouting patrol. They'd surrendered after the rest of their patrol was killed. DelMundo had just finished questioning them before we'd gone up to watch the air strike at his former base.

They looked up at him, when we passed, with scared, forced smiles.

"What happens to those three now?" I asked him, thinking about the spy he'd caught.

"Some of my men will take them back to where they were captured, and let them go."

"That's pretty humane of you, considering."

He shrugged. "They were brought here blindfolded, and they will be taken off the same way. They didn't learn anything here." DelMundo shook his head at me: "Don't overrate me, Mr. Bishop. It is not only out of humanity that I usually set prisoners free. It is also good advertising. They go back and tell other soldiers. The next time the others are involved in a battle with us, they will be more inclined to surrender than to fight us to the death."

I had no illusions about former General Augustin DelMundo. In Latin America, an idealistic rebel who succeeds in overthrowing a tyrant and taking over the government almost invariably develops into the country's next tyrant. I didn't expect any different from DelMundo if he succeeded. But I couldn't help liking him.

There was a roughly made wooden bench outside his cave headquarters reserved particularly for those occasions when he chose to sit down with someone for a private talk. DelMundo motioned for me to sit first, then sat down beside me. I gestured toward a group of young peasants being taught how to strip, clean and reassemble a brand-new, recently captured M-79 grenade launcher.

"New recruits?"

DelMundo nodded, a bit sadly. "They keep joining us, more all the time. I have no shortage of men. But how can I make any practical use of them? We don't have the weapons for them, first of all. Then there is the problem that most of them *know nothing* about weapons. And what you see those recruits being taught, over there, is *all* we can teach them. We can't teach them how to shoot because that alone would use up more ammunition than we have."

He gave me a wry smile. "The ammunition problem again. It keeps cropping up."

"That would be one of the first things I'd take care of," I told him, "with our starting shipment. Your basic requirements. A lot of rifle ammunition, all the same standard caliber. And a big supply of good automatic rifles that all take that caliber. Along with one-man rocket launchers and the missiles for them."

DelMundo was regarding me thoughtfully. "And of course I will be more than grateful for it," he said slowly. "I certainly need everything you can get me, as you see. And the three million dollars that your Mr. Richmond of the State Department is offering . . ." He corrected himself: "Somewhat less than three million, after your company's commission. But still a great deal of money—which will buy a great many arms."

"Especially if we spread it by buying good surplus."

"Yes. But I can't help wondering—"

He stopped as we heard a sound that made us both look up. A C-47 transport plane was flying over us, high enough to avoid the mountaintops but beginning to descend as it continued to the east.

"Heading for that new airfield in the Andreas Valley," I hazarded.

"Probably."

I looked at DelMundo and said: "You were wondering . . ."

"The offer this man Richmond has made *is* a generous one. And his willingness to help in other ways when I attack Pranagua City—that is encouraging. But I find myself comparing his offer of less than three million with what other expenditures, in military aid to Calderon, have cost those whom Mr. Richmond represents.

"That military transport plane which just passed, for example. That one plane alone cost more than I'm being offered to buy arms. Take the campaign Calderon launched to wrest the Andreas Valley away from us. That single assault cost *three times* as much as Mr. Richmond is prepared to spend for me. All paid for by your government's aid to Calderon."

He didn't blink: just waited.

"I think," I told him, "that they plan to sucker you into

making your move—and then double-cross you when you do."

Then *I* waited, looking at the guerrillas scattered around us and Gomez standing nearby.

DelMundo got off the bench, rising to his impressive height. "Let us take another walk."

Motioning Gomez to stay put where he was, DelMundo led me deeper into the wooded ravine and partway up the other side. When we were out of the sight of the others, where no one could possibly overhear us, he stopped and turned to face me.

"Now, you have something to say."

I told him all of it. How Richmond had approached me with the offer. Everything he'd told me his people hoped to achieve from it, and the cooperation they were prepared to give in order to get what they wanted. And exactly what I and my partners figured was going on behind their offer.

DelMundo was a good listener. He didn't interrupt me once. When I was finished, he didn't say anything for a long time. He stood with his hands locked together behind him and his head tilted, looking at the darkening sky, thinking through all I'd said.

Finally, he looked at me again: "I believe the commission you would earn through obtaining these arms for me is important to you."

"Three hundred thousand dollars is important money in my world," I admitted.

"Then why are you jeopardizing your chance of getting it by revealing all this to me?"

I grinned at him. "Because I want to supply Pranagua's military needs after you're in charge of the country."

DelMundo shook his head. "There is little hope of that if Mr. Richmond won't deliver more for arms than his present offer. And if he also won't deliver the diversion in Pranagua City which he promises."

"Then somebody else will have to deliver them," I said—and told him what I had in mind.

Chapter Twenty-three

Garson

Victoria listened eagerly. Nobody else knew I was back from Pranagua yet, not even Richmond. I'd come directly from Dulles International to her house in Alexandria immediately after my plane landed. It was 11:30 at night. She'd been getting ready to go to sleep, but she came wide awake when she saw it was me on her doorstep.

I began telling her about my stay with DelMundo while she made us coffee in her kitchen. I continued it in the conference end of her study. Before long I had her sitting forward with her arms on her knees, focusing on me excitedly while she took it all in.

I'd spent four days and nights with DelMundo. He had more guerrillas ready to rally to him than I'd thought. "The ones I met are as tough and dedicated a bunch as I've ever seen. They're utterly loyal to DelMundo and they hate Calderon with their guts. On the minus side, most of them need training in handling weapons. Rambert and I can help with that. I figure on taking him with me when I go back in there with the first shipment."

Victoria listened with absolute concentration to the plan for overthrowing Calderon, worked out between me and DelMundo. Her brain dealt with each detail as I told it, and she didn't need any of it repeated. I'd brought back something else that was essential for formulating the final details of the coup: detailed maps of Pranagua City, along with precise information about the size and disposition of its defenses. These had been slipped to DelMundo by the same man who'd tipped him off about the Calderon spy.

"We've got an unexpected plus there," I told Victoria. "He's a colonel in Calderon's air force, secretly committed to Del-Mundo. He stands ready to do everything he can to help when DelMundo makes the do-or-die attempt. And he's in a perfect position for it: in charge of running Calderon's main military airport just outside Pranagua City.

Victoria was grinning. "That's beautiful."

"It is," I agreed, grinning back. I gave her the last details of the plot DelMundo and I had worked out. Then I looked at Victoria for a long moment. "You can see how much the final stage of it depends on *you*. And two men. It won't work unless you can persuade Yukada to cooperate—and make sure you have Clark Alwin in hand when the coup breaks."

She nodded. "I'll do my best. With both."

There was no doubt about that. I hadn't seen her display so much excitement since long ago, in what seemed now another life—back in the days when she used to take me on tours of the work she was doing to restore the château in Perigord. The big ashtray beside her had become filled with unsmoked cigarettes she had lit and forgotten about while I told her about Pranagua.

"*I* turned up an unexpected plus for us, too," Victoria told me. The American ambassador in Pranagua, Joel Becker, *loathes* Arthur Richmond. Becker was an assistant to the ambassador to Syria when Richmond went in to plot his coup there. Richmond didn't bother to consult the embassy— that's his way, and it's made him a lot of enemies. Becker fired off a cautionary letter to the Secretary of State, warning that the coup would fail. It did, and Becker and Richmond have been enemies ever since. Whenever Richmond goes to Pranagua he deals directly with Calderon, ignoring the embassy. Sometimes Becker doesn't even know Richmond's been there until after he's left. You can imagine how he feels about that."

I nodded happily. "Ambassador Becker could be a *big* help in the final stage. Nice going."

"I have more for you," Victoria said briskly. "Plus number two: Ben Mallory, the man who manages the mining interests for Clark Alwin's company in Pranagua, has become close friends with Ambassador Becker. They play chess together."

"Better and better . . ."

Victoria's smile was tranquil. "Isn't it? Everything begins to come together so very neatly."

We spent almost three more hours working out exactly how Ambassador Becker and Alwin's Pranagua manager could best be tied in with the planned coup. Victoria also came up with some suggestions about the original plan. It didn't surprise me that each point she made helped its chances that much more.

It was almost five in the morning when I went to bed in her guest room. That, too, reminded me of old times in Perigord: me in the guest room and Victoria close by in her master bedroom. It was tempting—but I was just too worn out by then, and there were only four hours left to nine a.m. I didn't want to call Richmond much later than that because I didn't want to risk his discovering I was back and perhaps becoming suspicious about my delay in contacting him.

I got my four hours sleep. At nine I found Victoria in her kitchen, making us breakfast. It took two cups of strong black coffee to clear my groggy head.

But Victoria seemed immune to fatigue, and she'd had less than four hours sleep. She'd already reserved her seat on a late morning flight to Tokyo and her bag was packed. I could almost see the adrenalin flowing in her veins. Her skin had a fresh glow and her big, dark eyes had an alert shine to them.

I made my call to Richmond while she scrambled me a second batch of eggs and bacon. A few minutes after ten I was in his office at the State Department.

* * *

Arthur Richmond was exceedingly pleased with me. Everything I told him was calculated to please—and none of it gave him an inkling of what DelMundo and Tri-Arms really intended to do.

DelMundo, I assured him, was both excited and grateful for the offer of arms. He would prefer more, but I was certain he would launch the attack on Pranagua City with whatever he could get—relying on Richmond's promise of secret help in diverting the defense forces. DelMundo had some two thousand guerrillas, eager men but not very knowledgeable about weapons. I intended to take my partner Rambert back with me to train them as the weapons arrived. While we were gone, Richmond could deal with our other Tri-Arms partner, Christian Frosch, in Rome.

Richmond was insistent, once again, about the necessity of keeping him current about DelMundo's preparations. Every step of the way, as he was fond of repeating. Once I vanished back inside Pranagua, we'd communicate by shortwave radio. When I informed him that DelMundo was ready to make his move, Richmond would take up residence inside

Pranagua City. From that point on I was to brief him daily, right up to the moment of the coup attempt.

The beach I'd used to enter and leave Pranagua could be used for receiving the shipments of arms. Richmond left it to me to make the arrangements for those. But he specified that I was to do it through a Venezuelan firm that had several big, speedy fishing trawlers capable of handling the job. I gathered that the company had CIA connections. That would give Richmond one way to keep tabs on what I was doing.

Before I left the State Department, Richmond set the wheels in motion for Tri-Arms to receive payment for the first shipment. Six hundred thousand dollars. It would be paid into our Rome bank account by a dummy company established in Luxembourg for such purposes.

I informed Richmond that I intended to get as much weaponry and ammunition for his money as I could by buying surplus. "The biggest dealers in surplus," I told him, "are Sam Cummings and Solomon Alexandre. I think I'll try Cummings first."

I watched Richmond start to say something, and then stop himself. He didn't want me to start wondering why he would prefer that I get the surplus from Alexandre. I knew why. It would enable him to keep track of exactly what I was ordering and when DelMundo had enough to make his move.

After leaving Richmond I caught the next plane to Rome. By then, Victoria was already on her flight to Japan. In Rome I met with Rambert and Christian. I filled them in on my time with DelMundo, my meeting with Victoria, my arrangements with Richmond—and what Tri-Arms was really going to do about the Pranagua situation.

They went off to begin preparing their parts of our double-double-cross. I made a few phone calls and took a plane to Switzerland.

A couple hours after my appointment there, I made another series of calls—and finally got Stuart Peel on the phone.

* * *

Sir Solomon Alexandre placed his watch on the ebony desk top between us, next to his intercom.

"I can spare you ten minutes, Bishop. So be brief and to the point."

He had aged. He'd gotten skinnier, his strong face was wrinkled and his hair had gone totally white. But his voice was still that of an absolute monarch, and his piercing eyes still studied me as though I were an object to be opened or broken.

I acted a little hurt. "When Peel talked to me in Munich, he gave the impression you'd like to see me."

"That was a long time ago. The reason no longer exists."

We both knew that. The Japanese government had finally announced its decision three months ago. The APCs it had chosen were home-grown ones, made by Hiroshi Yukada. Tri-Arms was already attempting to sell some of them in the West.

"Unless," Alexandre added, "you have *other* information that would be valuable for me, about Yukada. Or about your friend al-Zadar."

He knew I wasn't there for anything like that. I was quite sure he'd known the reason even before I'd phoned Peel to ask if he could get me this appointment with him.

I said, "I thought al-Zadar was *your* friend, too."

Alexandre pointed a lean forefinger at the watch on his desk. "You now have nine minutes."

Behind him, the wall of glass framed a spectacular scarlet and gold sunset splashing out of the dense chemical smog across the river in New Jersey. We were in his private office high up inside Manhattan's newly erected Olympic Tower. Alexandre wasn't the only arms dealer who had decided to move his New York headquarters into the heavily guarded condominium office building. Adnan Khashoggi had bought a duplex a couple floors below him. It was tenants like Khashoggi and Alexandre—and former President Nixon—who'd caused journalists to dub the building the "Tower of Power."

I said: "I'm here to buy arms and ammunition. Two million, seven hundred dollars' worth."

"Who is the buyer?"

Since he already knew, and would expect me to be keeping it a secret, I avoided the question. "I can tell you this," I said. "If this order serves its purpose, I'll be in a position to buy *a lot* more, every year to come, for the country involved."

"Which you would purchase from me," Alexandre said tonelessly, "out of gratitude."

"Sure, if you give me a fair deal now. Look, I want this money to buy as many as possible. That means buying surplus. You and Cummings have the biggest supplies. I'm coming to you with it first."

Alexandre rapped a fingertip on his desk, impatiently. "You've already been to Cummings. He turned you down."

That had been my appointment in Switzerland. Cummings had turned me down because I couldn't convince him that the end-user certificate would be legitimate.

I fashioned an embarrassed grin. "You've got a sharp man in your Stuart Peel."

Alexandre showed no response at all to that. It *could* have been Peel, working very fast—though I knew it was Richmond who'd told him.

He asked me coldly: "And if I turn you down—for the same reason—what will you do?"

"There are other people with surplus to sell."

"If I turn you down, that will make *two* refusals. Whoever does sell to you will know that you must be getting desperate. Your desperation would be added into the selling price."

That was true enough. But I counted on his taking the deal. Not because of the money he'd get out of me. For Alexandre, what I was offering was a pittance. Orders that small were handled by the underlings who ran his branch offices. Ordinarily, he'd have had me thrown out after learning I'd come to talk to *him* about that kind of money. But this wasn't ordinarily. He was going to get a modest kick out of helping Tri-Arms and DelMundo walk into the booby trap that was supposed to insure his own continuing grip on Pranagua.

"I would need to see an end-user certificate," Alexandre said, "for a nation that would be acceptable to France in order to get my license to export the surplus to you."

"I can get one for Thailand," I told him.

"From Hiroshi Yukada, I imagine. And once you have the goods aboard a ship outside French territorial waters you can divert it to its actual destination." Alexandre didn't expect me to comment on either statement of fact. "Very well," he continued without expression, "I will notify Christopher Boyd to make the arrangements with you. He is the man now in charge of my surplus operation. In Perigord, as I believe you know."

That was as close as he came to acknowledging that we'd ever met before.

He picked up the watch and strapped it back on his wrist.

"Goodbye, Bishop."

* * *

"How does he look?" Victoria asked. Her curiosity was natural. It was some thirteen years since she'd last seen her former husband.

"Older," I said. "Otherwise the same. Tough, smart and mean."

"In good health?"

"From what I could see, yeah."

Victoria had a moody, far-off expression that was rare for her these days. "According to my information," she said, "he had some heart trouble a few months ago. It apparently cleared up."

Her tone was just a tinge regretful—whether about Alexandre's illness or his recovery I couldn't tell. But at the moment I was too impatient to probe her about it. We had vital information to exchange and we didn't have much time. She'd taken a flight from Japan to England so that we could meet in person, but in just three hours she had to take another flight to the States. I'd picked her up at Heathrow in a rented car for an aimless drive around the countryside near the airport while we talked.

"Will Yukada supply what we want?" I demanded.

"Yes, but his terms are stiff."

Stiff was the word. Yukada wanted us to pay him thirty percent interest on his investment. Plus a guarantee of a minimum of twenty percent of Pranagua's future arms business if we pulled it off.

"From his point of view," Victoria said, "that's fair. He would be gambling. It's a big investment. He could lose all of it if DelMundo fails. So he wants a gambler's return if it works."

"We're gambling the entire future of Tri-Arms on it."

"He understands that. It's because we believe in it that much that he's willing to gamble with us."

I turned my head to give her a dry smile. "Because *you* believe in it that much."

"You too, Gar. He's gotten a healthy respect for your judgment. You've never let him down in anything you handled for him."

I shrugged. "Yukada knows we have to accept his terms. None of it'll work without his help."

Victoria nodded. "I've already told him it's a deal."

"We have to check with Christian and Rambert, first," I reminded her. "They *are* our partners."

"They'll go along with it. They have to, or forget about Pranagua entirely."

I drove slowly along a winding, empty country road while Victoria told me about the method Yukada suggested for delivering his end of the bargain. Then I filled her in on my visit to Alexandre's surplus plant in Perigord.

"Boyd, the new man in charge there, is already starting the job of filling our order. I've had a talk with Christian and Rambert about that first shipment. They've agreed we'll only take a third of our commission off it to get DelMundo as much as possible for a starter. Do you go along with that?"

"Of course. How sure can we be that what he sends will be good quality?"

"First, this Boyd is a topnotch man with used arms. Second, we'll be checking everything he ships."

"The people Solomon hires are always topnotch," Victoria said. "As for checking, you and Rambert will be away when later shipments are sent."

"But we'll check the goods when they arrive in Pranagua. Thoroughly. If any of it's less than the best, I'll get on the radio and complain to Richmond. And threaten to call the whole thing off."

Victoria nodded approval. "That should take care of that. He'll have committed himself too deeply by then to risk the project going sour."

"Also," I told her, "I had a long walk and talk with Boyd. I let him know what happened to Paul Rambert and my father. And Boyd gave me some information. The man who had the job before him got fired because he couldn't get a big order in shape as fast as Alexandre wanted. Boyd knows the same could happen to him. I told him if it does, he can come to work for us. I think we can count on him to send our goods out in prime condition."

Victoria smiled at me. One of the old smiles. "You're getting better at this all the time." She reached out and her fingers caressed my cheek where her knife had scarred it long ago. "I was right when I decided you were the one I should team up with."

I pulled off the road, took her in my arms, and kissed her.

She kissed me back with a sexual abandon that took me by surprise. It also took me back to the other time she'd surprised me in that way, beside the pool in Perigord. But this time she suddenly pulled away and looked at her watch.

"We have to start back now or I'll miss my plane." Her voice was a little shaky.

I was more than a little shaky. It took me time to get it under control before I started the drive back to the airport.

Victoria lit a cigarette and took a long drag at it before she spoke again. "Gar, while you were down there in Perigord, did you by any chance have a look at the château?"

"From the road. I stopped for a minute on my way to the plant. Did you know Alexandre sold it?"

"Yes."

"It's up for sale again. Nobody's lived in it for years."

"Leaving it to deteriorate again." Victoria grimaced and shook her head. "All that work I put into it. All for nothing."

"If Pranagua works out for us," I told her, "you'll have enough money to buy it for yourself and fix it up again."

"I'll *never* go back there." She said it more fervently than she might have intended.

"I guess not. That was a different life."

"No," she said darkly, "that's the trouble. It's part of *this* life. The same one I'm still living."

She was silent the rest of the way into Heathrow. When I saw her off on her flight to Washington she kissed me again. But not the way she had in the car.

* * *

Six weeks later Rambert and I went into Pranagua with the first shipment Richmond had paid for. I only got to see Mei-lin once in the time between coming out of Pranagua and returning there. I was too busy. In those six weeks, I'd flown around the world three times: to Tokyo to finalize the methods and timing of Yukada's deliveries to us; then on to Washington to work out the last details Victoria was going to play in our coup; then back to Europe to conclude the arrangements being made there by Rambert and Christian.

As promised, I reported to Richmond, every step of the way, our progress with Boyd in preparing the shipments of Solomon Alexandre's surplus for DelMundo. It was essential that Richmond stay confident that we were ignorant of his plans for us.

I didn't inform him of my flights to Tokyo and Washington.

Nor that a Yukada freighter delivering government-ordered electrical appliances to the harbor of Pranagua City would be carrying a load of modern weaponry in one of its cargo holds—including eight of his APCs and the first batch of LB-75 rockets and launchers turned out by his factory.

Nor about the tanker, which, after unloading its Venezuelan oil in Japan, would be chartered by Yukada on its return voyage to Latin America.

Nor about the four big troop-transport helicopters it would be carrying on its main deck under camouflage.

Nor about the mercenary chopper pilots who would be on board the tanker—recruited by Rambert and paid by Yukada—ready to fly them off the vessel and into action when the time came.

* * *

After Rambert and I settled inside the Pranaguan mountains to help train DelMundo's guerrillas, I kept in touch with Richmond by coded radio messages. I used another wavelength of the powerful shortwave radio to communicate with Victoria—via DelMundo's smuggler-sympathizers in Jamaica, and from there to Christian Frosch, who passed on the coded messages to her by telephone.

Once the final shipment of surplus arms from Alexandre had arrived, Richmond began pressing me, with increasing urgency, to push DelMundo into making his move before the year's end. Ford had lost the election to Carter in November. Richmond's faction in the State Department wanted its Pranaguan coup to be a *fait accompli* before the next administration took over in January of 1977.

With the old administration packing up and the new one not yet in, Richmond's people figured the confused interperiod was perfect for getting away with it, no matter what either president thought of it afterwards.

DelMundo was as ready as he'd ever be by the first week of December. I notified Richmond. He immediately flew down to wait in Pranagua City. Since he didn't trust anybody at the American embassy there, he established his base in a rented apartment. There I could contact him by phone as well as radio.

At the same time I notified Christian Frosch. He flew in to Jamaica to offer a more direct and quicker communications link between me and Victoria. His first message from her was that Richmond had persuaded a TV crew and two newspaper journalists to come to Pranagua a few days after him, on his promise of an unspecified scoop. That suited DelMundo's objective—and that of Tri-Arms—just fine. Victoria had established a rapport with another popular news commentator—and one of the journalists coming in was Mei-lin.

On the night before DelMundo's guerrillas launched their attack, I slipped into Pranagua City with Rambert, to make certain Richmond would carry out *his* part in the scam—according to our scenario, rather than his own.

Chapter Twenty-four

Victoria

Victoria surprised herself by finally giving Clark Alwin, Chairman of Alwin Minerals and confidant of presidents, an unequivocal no.

The widower had just asked her to marry him.

Alwin didn't take her refusal too hard—nor too seriously. "I'll tell you something, Victoria. Mrs. Alwin's boy didn't get where I am today by caving in when I hit opposition. A girl as beautiful as you are, *and* smart as a whip—who can cook a meal like this one—I'll keep pressing you, kid. You got a tiger by the tail, you'll see."

Victoria laughed softly. "Give a girl a break, Clark. Don't you steamroller me."

He grinned at her. "That's not how I go after something I want. My way's more subtle, but just as effective in the long run."

They were in Victoria's dining room, just finishing the first course of a late Sunday lunch. There were two more leisurely courses to come after the *hòrs d'oeuvres.* Victoria had planned for the meal to be late and long, to insure that Alwin would still be there with her when the news broke. Since it was Sunday, her job was easier. Alwin was less likely to have any late appointments he couldn't break for her if the waiting drew on longer than she anticipated.

Outside her windows a cold winter rain was falling on her enclosed garden. But down in Pranagua it was summer. Victoria prayed that there it would be dry as well as hot. That would help DelMundo's assault.

She was acutely—almost painfully—aware of each stage of what was happening down there this day. She no longer needed a glance at the kitchen clock or her watch to keep track. Her nervous system had developed an inner clock of its own, ticking off each minute that brought it closer to triumph or defeat.

Some hours had passed since Gar Bishop would have told Richmond that DelMundo intended to make his attack. "Tomorrow morning," Gar would have said. Richmond would have notified the general who'd been left in command of Calderon's armed forces. On that point Richmond hadn't lied: Pranagua's commander-in-chief was in Washington for an urgent military talk with Richmond's faction. This maneuver was supposed to make a takeover easier for the rebel group from Puerto Rico.

By now the bulk of Pranagua City's defense forces would be far outside the city, advancing to cut off DelMundo's line of approach.

By now, also, Gar and Rambert would have Richmond firmly in hand, seeing to it that he couldn't communicate with anyone else for the next day or two.

The attack, which much of the army stationed in Pranagua City had gone off to block, was being made by a token force of DelMundo guerrillas, who would fade away as soon as they'd accomplished their purpose as a lure.

The real attack was coming from an utterly unexpected direction. From inside the capital itself. Not tomorrow morning. Today.

Soon.

Her phone rang. Victoria's heart was pounding when she got up to answer. The woman at the other end was Alwin's secretary. Wherever he went, Alwin always left the number with her.

Victoria turned to him. "It's for you, Clark. Your secretary. Why don't you take it in my study?"

"Thanks, Victoria." Alwin heaved himself out of his chair and trudged off.

Victoria waited, holding the phone to her ear, the mouthpiece turned away so it wouldn't pick up her stilled breathing. When Alwin took up the extension, she jiggled the phone, as Christian Frosch had showed her, to create a sound as if she were hanging up. In fact, Christian had rigged the extensions in her house so that if she did pick up or put down any of her three phones, it would make no sound at all for someone listening on another.

"I'm sorry to disturb you, Mr. Alwin," his secretary said, "but there's a long-distance call from Ben Mallory in Pranagua that seems urgent. Shall I connect him with you?"

"Do that, Mary, thank you."

There was the sound of the connection being made, and the secretary hanging up once Mallory was on the line to Alwin.

"Something's going on down here, Mr. Alwin." Mallory's voice came through clearly. Pranagua's long-distance communications system was the best that American technology could devise. "I don't think it means real trouble for us, but I thought I'd better let you know."

"That's your job, Ben. So tell me." Alwin spoke calmly. He already knew what it would be. He was one of the small number of men who were in on Richmond's plan. Naturally. Alwin Chemicals and Minerals, Inc. was the biggest industry in Pranagua and in large measure accounted for the importance of the American presence there. The company's agreement with Calderon's government insured a hefty annual profit. Richmond's people knew of Alwin's influence with both the outgoing President of the United States and the incoming one. They had assured him, ahead of time, that the agreement would continue to be honored after their group from Puerto Rico took over Pranagua's government.

"About four hours ago," Mallory told him, "more than half the army stationed here left Pranagua City heading southwest. Truckloads of troops, along with tanks, armored cars, cannons, the works. Then a rumor started circulating around the city that Augustin DelMundo was coming down out of the mountains. That his guerrillas slipped past the army units stationed out there and are gonna join together for a dawn attack on the capital."

"Have you seen Calderon?"

"Just came from him, Mr. Alwin. He says the rumor's true. Only he knows where DelMundo's guerrillas will be assembling tonight. He says his army will trap and hold them there. And come first light tomorrow morning his planes will go out to strafe and bomb them. I've got to say, Mr. Alwin, Calderon looks pretty confident."

"As he should be, Ben. DelMundo doesn't have the men, equipment or arms to break through Calderon's armored forces—let alone stand up under concentrated air attacks."

"That's true," Mallory said hesitantly. "And that's what bothers me. Why would DelMundo make such a dumb try? Unless he's got some reason to think it'll work. I've heard some bad things about him, but not that he's stupid."

"Perhaps merely misinformed."

"You know, Mr. Alwin, most of the citizens here would join DelMundo's guerrillas if they did break in."

"They won't. Take my word."

"I hope not. Our agreement with Calderon—"

"Will continue," Alwin said with assurance. Under the new government, he meant.

Mallory was silent for a moment. Then he said, cautiously: "I guess you know more about what's going on here than I do."

Alwin chuckled. "I guess maybe I do. Look, Ben, just relax and keep me in touch with developments. But don't go out in the streets more than necessary. Could get hairy for a couple days. After that, it should be all over."

In the kitchen, Victoria hung up the phone when Alwin did. She was warming up the second course of their lunch when he returned from her study, looking satisfied with himself.

"Sorry about that interruption, Victoria. A little disturbance down in Pranagua. Nothing serious."

"As long as it hasn't spoiled your appetite."

"Not a chance," Alwin assured her, and resumed his seat at the dining table.

Victoria checked her inner clock against her wristwatch. She was right on the minute. Sometime within the next quarter hour, down in Pranagua City, the attempt to overthrow Calderon would begin.

It would start on a radio signal from Gar Bishop, inside the city, when he judged that the defense troops sent out were far enough away. Some of DelMundo's guerrillas had infiltrated Pranagua City singly, over the past few nights. On the signal they would emerge from their hideouts to stir the populace into joining their fight against the dictatorship.

But DelMundo himself, and the majority of his fighters, were aboard the Japanese cargo ship that had docked in the harbor in the heart of the city that morning. They were heavily armed with the surplus from Solomon Alexandre and the newer weaponry from Yukada. With them they had the vehicles Yukada had also supplied: trucks, jeeps and eight strongly armed personnel carriers.

On the signal—at any minute now—the ship's cargo bay doors would open and DelMundo's forces would pour out onto the docks, some on foot, the rest in the APCs leading the way and the jeeps and trucks following.

On the same signal, Colonel Francesco Varda, the officer in charge at the main military airfield outside the city, would be seizing control there, with the help of certain junior officers who'd had enough of Calderon. They would take over the armory at the base, lock up personnel whose political convictions were uncertain, start readying two of Calderon's bombers ...

Victoria found herself staring at the kitchen clock. The attack was starting. Now. She could *feel* it.

She served the second course and took her seat across the table from Alwin. Her voice remained absolutely steady as she chatted with him during the remainder of their meal.

It was an hour and a half later when they finished dessert. Victoria began preparing coffee. She looked at the kitchen clock again.

At this moment the coup was very close to being an accomplished fact—or a disastrous failure.

With a harsh effort Victoria pulled her mind back to her own role in the coup. "Let's have this in the living room," she told Alwin as she poured the coffee into a silver serving pot.

He knew the way. Victoria followed moments later with the coffee tray. Alwin had settled down on the sofa. She sat in her favorite armchair, facing him, and set the tray on the low table between them. She poured their coffees, adding just the right amount of skim milk to Alwin's. She left her own black, but dropped in two sugars. Stirring, she began making casual conversation. When she raised her cup, she looked at it and was pleased with her control. Not the faintest tremble.

Her nerves were on fire.

DelMundo's attack forces had spread through the city almost two hours ago, separating into different units, each speeding toward its own assigned objective.

Each objective was a vital one: if all of them could be seized, and held, the coup had a good chance of success. One, the military air base on the city's outskirts, should already be in Colonel Varda's hands. Now the rest had to be taken, swiftly, almost simultaneously.

The first objective, in order of timing, had to be Pranagua's communications centers: radio, phone, telegraph. With those taken, the capital would be cut off from the rest of the country and the outside world. Most important, it would become virtually impossible for government officials and military leaders of the Calderon regime to communicate with each other and find out what was happening—except when DelMundo's guerrillas chose to let calls go through.

Immediately after that: the storming of the main police headquarters—and the capture of the general in charge of the nation's police forces. It was DelMundo's opinion that the police general didn't have the mettle to prefer death to treason. With a gun to his head, he would be forced to make calls to his subordinate officers, and to the military chiefs remaining in the capital. He would summon each to an immediate secret conference, concerned with the defense of the city from terrorists. Each officer would be seized upon showing up. Pranagua City's defense forces would be left almost leaderless.

Almost. Enough subordinate officers would be left, at the city's main army barracks, to react when they became aware of the insurrection. They would rush troop carriers, armored cars and tanks to the defense, first, of Calderon's presidential palace. The barracks were too strong for DelMundo's forces to take them quickly enough. They would have to ward off the danger by seizing and blockading the approach roads near the palace.

Victoria was most concerned about the tanks. Gar and Rambert were sure their little one-man LB-75 launchers, with their improved armor-piercing rockets, could deal with the tanks. She could only hope they were right.

Clark Alwin, finished with his coffee, suggested that they go out for drinks at a cocktail lounge he liked.

Victoria made a face. "Sunday evening out in Washington is so dull, Clark. Why don't we have those drinks right here? Besides," she smiled at him, "one of your favorite television programs will be coming on soon."

Alwin looked at her wryly. "You say you don't want to be my wife, but you certainly act like one sometimes. Sure you won't change your mind and marry me?"

She made herself relent a little: "Not today, anyway."

He laughed. "Okay, we stay here. My pleasure."

"Cognac?"

"Fine."

Victoria got up and went for their drinks.

The most crucial position that DelMundo needed to take was the presidential palace itself—along with its most important resident: General Calderon. Everything else happening in Pranagua now became wasted and doomed if they couldn't accomplish that.

By now four big Chinook transport helicopters had lifted off from the main deck of the giant oil tanker cruising slowly past Pranagua's coastline. Each of them piloted by a hired mercenary. Each carrying forty of DelMundo's most seasoned fighters. One of them carrying DelMundo himself.

By now, also, a pair of Calderon's bombers had taken off from the main military airfield. One of them was piloted by Colonel Varda and the other by a pilot who shared his convictions, and guts. Both had a minimum crew of trusted men.

The bombers would strike at the presidential palace first, flying in low and placing the bombs they dropped to create maximum confusion among the sizeable force of police and troops that guarded the grounds, residence and administrative building. Coming in immediately after the bombing would be the four Chinooks. They would land inside the palace grounds to disgorge DelMundo and a hundred and sixty heavily armed guerrillas. The guerrillas would then shoot their way into the bombed buildings, find Calderon, and place him under arrest.

But all of it had to be accomplished swiftly, and in coordination, or it wouldn't work. . . .

Alwin's TV program came to an end. It had become early night outside. Victoria had turned on the living room lamps. Several times she'd been unable to stop herself from looking towards the phone. It should have rung by now.

Alwin stood up and turned off the television set. "Well, it's getting a little late. Guess it's time for me to be on my way."

"I'm hungry again," Victoria told him. "Suppose I fix us a little snack before you go."

He looked at her uncertainly, and a bit hopefully. "At least you're not anxious to get shucked of my company. I guess that's a good sign. . . ."

Victoria started for the kitchen.

The living room phone rang.

Her legs felt weak as she went to pick it up. She listened, and turned to Alwin, her expression controlled. "It's for you again, Clark."

When he took the phone from her, she left the room, closing the door behind her. She strode into her study and picked up the phone there with a swift, smooth movement, the way Christian Frosch had taught her.

". . . and all hell's broke loose out there," Ben Mallory was telling Alwin. "I tried to get to you earlier, but they've got control of the telephone exchange and they wouldn't let the call go through until now."

"They? Who're you talking about, Ben?"

"DelMundo's guerrillas. They're taking over the city. They've already taken the presidential palace. That's where I am right now. Along with Ambassador Becker. Courtesy of an American who seems to be some kind of advisor to Del-Mundo. Maybe I better start calling him *President* DelMundo. Because that's what he is, as of this moment."

"What's happened to Calderon?" Alwin's voice was steady enough. He was a man who knew how to take a punch as well as give one.

"They've got him, too. He just finished making an announcement to the nation, over the radio. I saw it all: he had a machine gun jammed in his spine. He abdicated as ruler of Pranagua and formally turned the country's leadership over to DelMundo. I reckon that's the deal. Calderon resigns, accepting DelMundo as the new president. In exchange, Del-Mundo lets him go off into exile alive. Instant new government."

"How the hell could it happen that fast?" Alwin demanded.

But it was an expression of exasperation rather than a question. He *knew* how. It had happened that fast in Libya, in Chile, in Uganda—in so many other cases and places. That was why it was called a *coup*. Not a protracted civil war, as in Lebanon. An abrupt *cut*.

"All I can tell you at this point, Mr. Alwin, is that it did happen. DelMundo made a radio speech saying he'll only stay in charge long enough to eradicate what he calls fascist elements. Then he'll hold free, democratic elections and the people can choose the president they want. Since they're sure to vote for him, that won't change a thing. I'd say it's all over but a bit more shooting."

"What about the army?"

"There's still fighting in the streets. And I guess the troops that were sent out on that wild goose chase in the provinces are on their way back. But who've they got left to fight for? By now they know Calderon's quit, and named DelMundo the new president. And in his radio speech, DelMundo offered amnesty to all government forces that surrender to him immediately. It's my guess that most of the troops will accept his offer. Including a lot of top officers."

There was a brief silence as Clark Alwin thought it out. Victoria was certain he was thinking about the rebel group from Puerto Rico, poised at this moment for their own invasion of Pranagua.

"You said you're in the palace," Alwin said speculatively. "Have you talked with DelMundo?"

"Yeah. DelMundo's not such a bad guy as I figured. Ambassador Becker's just been on the phone to Washington, telling the President the same thing. DelMundo comes on surprisingly friendly, considering some of the things he's said about the U.S. in the past. Maybe that's the influence of this American I mentioned. Name's Bishop. Hold on, Mr. Alwin—he wants to talk to you."

A moment later Victoria heard Gar Bishop's voice come through: "Mr. Alwin, this is Garson Bishop—"

Alwin cut in: "Exactly what is your relationship with DelMundo?"

322

"Friend . . . advisor." Gar didn't expand on that. "The point is, there are some American television and newspaper people down here. Their coverage of the change in government will show everyone that President DelMundo is in full control, will hold democratic elections shortly, and wants no further bloodshed. Under those assurances, the situation here is calming down. We'd like your help in keeping it calm."

"You'll have to explain what sort of help you're asking me for," Alwin told him.

"I told Ambassador Becker about the group from Puerto Rico that's waiting in ships off the coast for a signal to invade."

"I don't know what you're talking about."

Gar didn't argue the point. "The ambassador mentioned it when he was on the phone to the President, in Washington. The President seemed surprised to hear about it. Ambassador Becker strongly advised him to have that group turned back. I'm giving you the same advice."

"I still don't understand what you're talking about."

"Think it over. While you're thinking, President DelMundo is waiting in another room for a private word with you. Shall I put you through to him?"

"Okay. . . ." Alwin was beginning to sound just a bit off balance. The unexpected changes were coming too fast, one on top of another.

The connection was made. The voice that came through was strong, its English hardly accented: "This is President DelMundo, Mr. Alwin. I am pleased to finally make your acquaintance, even if only over a telephone."

"Likewise . . ."

"Mr. Alwin, your manager here in Pranagua, Mr. Mallory, seems to be worried about the status of your company under my new government. I want to reassure you. Alwin Chemicals and Minerals is a major source of income for my country and its people. I have no intention of doing anything that might jeopardize that income."

"Such as nationalizing my company's Pranaguan subsidiary?" Alwin suggested.

"I have become convinced that doing that would result in our getting no income at all out of our mineral resources for some years to come. No, Mr. Alwin, you can feel safe on that score."

"That," Alwin said slowly, "is good to hear."

"I hope we will soon have an opportunity to discuss it further, in person. I assure you, you would be treated as an honored guest in my country."

"I just might take you up on that."

"Good. And now, if you will wait a few moments, Mr. Bishop has something further to say to you."

Alwin was waiting to be reconnected when the living room door opened and Victoria came back in. He looked up at her in surprise. It wasn't like her to walk in on a private conversation like this. She sat down in her armchair, facing him with a placid, unrevealing expression.

His own expression changed as he listened to the voice coming over the phone. His face hardened, his eyes narrowing on Victoria. He lowered the phone and told her, stiffly: "A man named Bishop wants to talk to you."

Victoria reached across the coffee table and took the phone from him. "Hello, Gar. Sounds like we made it."

"There's a lot of dead and dying out there in the streets who helped. But yeah, we made it. So far. Now if we can just *hold on* to it. . . . Everything under control at your end?"

Victoria looked at Alwin. He was still regarding her with a narrow-eyed scowl. "I think so. Call me again in the morning. By then I'll be able to give you a definite answer."

When she hung up the phone, Alwin asked her quietly:

"How do you know this Bishop fellow?"

"We're business partners," Victoria told him, "in a company called Tri-Arms International. You may have heard of it from Arthur Richmond."

The Pranaguan coup, she had decided, made now the time to start coming out of the closet—to launch the American branch of Tri-Arms and to announce herself as its director.

"I see," Alwin said, with more resignation than anger. "All this time I thought you had some affection for me, you were just using me. Pumping me."

"I do have affection for you, Clark. I also have a business to protect."

"You are also," he told her without raising his voice, "a scheming bitch."

Victoria smiled at him. "And you are a sweet man—but a scheming bastard, where business is concerned."

Alwin forced a disillusioned smile. "I did say we'd make a good pair. Didn't know how right I was."

She leaned toward him and spoke decisively: "So let's take care of both our businesses. Right now. Add your advice to what Ambassador Becker told the President. Make *certain* that rebel group from Puerto Rico gets called back."

"That would be good for *your* business, of course."

"And yours. At this point DelMundo is in control down there. He won't nationalize your Pranaguan interests. If the country stays peaceful under him, your mines will continue to be productive. But if that other group attacks, there'll be a full-scale civil war in Pranagua. No way your group could achieve a quick coup now—not with DelMundo's forces knowing about the danger and preparing to fend it off. Civil war could keep your mines from operating for months to come. It could also weaken the country enough for the communists to take over. They *would* nationalize your Pranaguan interests."

"You've figured it all out pretty carefully, Alwin acknowledged, with a certain grudging admiration.

"That's the business side of the situation," Victoria went on. "You want Pranagua peaceful and productive. Let's deal with the political side. If that force from Puerto Rico attacks, the world will be treated to the spectacle of the Del-Mundo democratic party, now the government of Pranagua, fighting a patriotic defensive war. Against invaders that *I* can prove come from the United States."

Alwin whistled softly. "You play very hard ball."

"I mean every word."

"I know you do." Alwin considered it for a bit. Then he picked up the phone and dialed his secretary. "Mary, I want an appointment with Bill Caldwell, immediately." Caldwell was leader of Richmond's faction in the State Department. "Then with the President—as soon as possible. Say I consider it a matter of the utmost urgency."

Ten minutes later Clark Alwin drove away to explain the facts of life to Richmond's group—and to add his own advice to what the Pranaguan ambassador had already told the President.

* * *

Two hours later Victoria landed at New York's Laguardia Airport on the jet shuttle from Washington. Before leaving the airport she phoned Alwin to check on the results of his two appointments. She was smiling when she took the taxi into Manhattan.

Her appointment there was with Teresa Cotten, one of the best television news analysts on any network. Following that, Victoria spent several hours with Teresa's chief re-

searcher, going over the TV footage coming in from Pranagua.

She got back to her house in Alexandria the next morning
just in time to watch the results. The exclusive inside facts
she'd given made Teresa Cotten's coverage of the Pranaguan
coup the most informed of any news broadcast. Because of
that, her network gave more time to it than the others. It
was clearly a scoop.

Teresa always paid her debts. Her broadcast was highly
favorable to Tri-Arms. There were shots of dozens of de-
stroyed Calderon tanks choking approach roads to the presidential palace. Then the camera zoomed in on a guerrilla
carrying one of the weapons that had done the damage: an
LB-75.

The camera pulled back to cover a big tank advancing on
the guerrilla. He aimed the launcher and fired. The tank
came to a shuddering, smoking halt with a huge, jagged hole
torn through its armor. Teresa's voice-over commentary revealed that the weapon that had done that was something
new: presently made only in Japan, but soon to be manufactured in the U.S. as well.

Teresa did *not* explain that the rocket, in addition to its
armor-penetrating warhead, carried a fragmentation charge
which exploded once it was inside the tank, insuring that its
crewmen were ripped to shreds. Victoria couldn't blame her
for that omission. Even Lenin, in speaking of the price in
human lives that had to be paid for carrying out a revolution, hadn't had the guts to speak frankly. He'd said you had
to break eggs to make an omelet. He'd meant people, but
he'd said eggs.

The Pranagua coverage ended with President DelMundo,
smiling paternally as he announced that free elections
would be held as soon as Calderon's fascist supporters were
all under control. On one side of him stood Miguel Gomez,

who had just been named Vice-president. On the other was Colonel Varda, now a general and the new commander-in-chief of Pranagua's armed forces.

Victoria caught sight of Gar Bishop, standing in the background behind them, watching with a thoughtful smile.

Victoria switched off her TV set and got down to reading the accounts of the Pranaguan coup in newspapers she'd picked up at the airport. It didn't surprise her that the most informative bore Mei-lin Shaw's byline. The girl had Gar down there to give her the inside story.

She was finishing Mei-lin Shaw's article when Gar phoned her from Pranagua.

"Good or bad?" he demanded without preamble.

"Good," Victoria told him. "That group we were worried about is on its way back to Puerto Rico. And the President will announce later this morning that the United States is officially recognizing DelMundo's new government."

"DelMundo will be glad to hear it."

Victoria told him the other piece of good news: "Teresa Cotten gave our LB-75 a big plug on her news broadcast. With film of it in use."

"Nice. Gonna make it that much easier to get a good deal out of an American manufacturer."

"Gar, she hear herself asking, "how much longer will you have to stay down there?"

"I can't leave until I'm sure the danger from Calderon elements is past, DelMundo is really solid here, and he and I can talk out our future business agreements."

"Well don't let it drag on too long. I want you back to help start our new branch here. And the sooner we do that, now, the better."

"I'll be there as soon as I can get away," he promised.

"Do that," Victoria said, and hung up her phone. She sat for a long moment, thinking of Gar and Mei-lin Shaw together down there. Then she cursed herself silently, jumped up, and went into the kitchen to brew some coffee.

She'd gone all night without sleep, but she still didn't feel the need for any. Her nervous system was on hyper-drive, charged with self-renewing energy that seemed to have a motivating force all its own. She didn't want to take a pill that would stop that and knock her out. There was so much still to do, and a full day ahead in which to do it.

Carrying her coffee into the study, Victoria sat behind her desk and began formulating the announcement that the American branch of Tri-Arms International was about to open for business, with herself as director.

She was still a long way from what she was after.

But she was that much closer.

Part III

In revenge and love, a woman is more barbarous than a man.

—Nietzsche

Chapter Twenty-five

Garson

After telling President DelMundo the good news I'd gotten from Victoria, I left the palace and headed across the city to Arthur Richmond's apartment.

At DelMundo's insistence, I travelled in an armored car. It had belonged to Calderon's secret police. Now it flew the brown-and-gold colors of the victorious party, along with Pranagua's flag. I was accompanied by a pair of well-armed freedom fighters, formerly called guerrillas, and soon to be upped to protectors of democratic government. Whatever you cared to call them, they were with me because Del-Mundo was concerned for my safety.

There were still pockets of fighting and hidden snipers scattered around the city. Die-hard resisters: most of them men who'd handled people so brutally that they knew the populace wouldn't allow them to be included in the amnesty if they surrendered.

There was also the sound of heavy firing from the city's outskirts. But not as much as on the previous night. Die-hard Calderon commanders had tried to keep news of the amnesty offer from their troops. But early this morning Colonel Varda—now General Varda—had sent planes to drop leaflets over them bearing DelMundo's announcement. Since then troops had been deserting in droves, coming over to join our side.

A couple more former guerrillas were on guard outside Richmond's building. They grinned and shook my hand gleefully before letting me go inside. The apartment door was unlocked. Richmond lay on a couch with his fingers laced under his head, gazing with a bored expression at the ceiling. Rambert sat in a comfortable chair across the room from him, resting a Smith and Wesson .38 revolver on his thigh.

"You can put the gun away," I told Rambert. To Richmond I said, "And you can make your call to Washington now. They'll let it go through."

He swung his legs off the couch, stood up and looked at me sourly. "I don't imagine I'll learn anything I'm likely to enjoy?"

"I don't expect so."

Richmond shrugged philosophically, walked to the phone, and placed his call. I had to hand it to him. In addition to being an old-school gentleman, he could also take a blow without crumbling. It took five minutes for his connection to the State Department to be made. He asked for Bill Caldwell, his boss. After he got him, he spent the next couple minutes listening. Then he put down the phone and turned to us with a crooked smile.

"They want me to come back immediately. To explain my failure."

He looked depressed by it, but not desolated. According to Victoria, he'd had other failures. And survived them. He would probably come through this one, too. Experienced specialists in his line were hard to come by. Government, unlike business, accepts the human fact that nobody can be perfect.

Rambert and the two guards outside escorted Richmond to the airport and saw him off on a flight to Washington. I headed off to the Hilton, where I'd been given one of the best suites. I was weary and sweaty, in need of a shower and a change of clothes, if not a nap.

I had installed Mei-lin in my suite during the night. But I wasn't expecting to find her there at that time of day. There was too much for her to photograph out in the city streets. So it was a surprise to come upon her in the big square in front of the hotel. She was taking pictures of something that hadn't been there when I'd left.

Six men were hanging from the square's lampposts by wires deeply embedded in their necks. Big cards fastened to their chests said they'd been members of Calderon's dreaded secret police. I doubted that they'd died by hanging. From the condition of their faces, and what could be seen of their bodies through their shredded clothing, I gathered that they'd been unpleasantly killed before being strung up.

When Mei-lin finished her roll of film, she turned and saw me. She came over and walked into the Hilton with me. We went up in the elevator without a word between us. Inside my suite I poured us drinks, got ice cubes from the refrigerator and dumped them in, and handed Mei-lin her glass. I took a big swallow from my glass and went into the bathroom for my shower.

When I came out she was standing by one of the windows, gazing down at the hanging bodies in the square.

"Looking at them won't bring them back to life," I told her.

"I know." Mei-lin took a sip from her glass, not turning from the window.

"And you can stop feeling sorry for them," I added. "Each of those men down there tortured people to death. And probably enjoyed it."

"I know that, too." Mei-lin took a bigger drink before she turned to look at me.

I was expecting a replay of one of our old fights. But it didn't come. Instead she said gently, "You know what would be the best thing for you, Gar?"

"Tell me."

"You ought to marry me," she said it in the same tone, without a smile. "And let me make an honest man of you."

"I guess that means making me get out of the arms trade."

"For one thing."

I shook my head. "Then I must decline your offer. Regretfully." The arms business was only one of my reasons for turning her down. Victoria was still too much under my skin. But I did regret it.

"Maybe I'll be reminding you of the offer, though," I said, "one of these days."

"By then I might no longer be available," Mei-lin told me quietly, and shrugged. "Too bad."

"I'm sorry, Mei-lin."

"Me too."

The next day she flew out of Pranagua.

Even if I hadn't been so attached to Victoria, I would have turned down her proposal with the condition she had attached to it. I wasn't about to quit the business just when it was starting to pay off. I had arms sales to Pranagua in my pocket. A monopoly on sales to a small country—that was in essence how Sam Cummings, the biggest American dealer abroad, had made his own stunning leap from petty operator to tycoon—and Latin America had been his springboard, too. Now Tri-Arms was making the same leap.

On my way to Washington three days later I began calculating what Tri-Arms would have going for it when we opened in the States.

We had Yukada's distribution in Europe and the Americas: that was going to amount to something now that he was ready to compete with the big dealers of the West. We'd almost certainly wind up handling most of al-Zadar's American sales and purchases. With my lock on Pranagua and the publicity our LB-75 had just gotten, other business would gravitate to Tri-Arms. The big leagues.

As I saw it, that had to translate into enough political clout to spring my father.

I knew it would take a little more time to get a grip on all the necessary levers of power. And I expected to have to trample over some opposition in operating those levers. What I didn't anticipate was that the first opponent I'd have to trample would be Victoria.

Chapter Twenty-six

Garson

I sprang it on Victoria, Rambert and Christian over a celebration dinner we were treating ourselves to at the Lion d'Or, a favorite of Washington gourmets with unlimited expense accounts.

The U.S. Army had just chosen our LB-75, over stiff competition from rival rocket-launching systems, to become its new shoulder-mounted infantry assault weapon. The Pentagon was preparing to license Ward & Hubb, the biggest manufacturer of small arms in the United States, to produce the first American version under a cushy royalty agreement with Tri-Arms.

We were in a triumphal mood. To my three partners that win meant a massive surge of income and status for our company. To me it meant we had the final levers needed to pry the inventor of our LB-75 out of prison. With the Army's decision that his invention was what it needed to outclass the Soviet RPG-7, and the powerful Ward & Hubb hungering for the contract, I figured the time had come.

Victoria vehemently disagreed.

It was eleven months after DelMundo had taken power in Pranagua and Tri-Arms had opened for business in the States. Eleven months in which all four of us had worked like demons, and seen Tri-Arms International skyrocket.

Victoria, I had to admit, deserved much of the credit for that swift rise. Especially for her work in the first month. That was when Solomon Alexandre, furious over his loss of Pranagua's arms business to us, mounted a campaign to persuade the U.S. government to help him destabilize the new DelMundo government.

Alexandre waged his campaign through his topmost people in Washington. He had Richmond's faction in the State Department. He had two Pentagon generals. He had Jesse Reed of the Senate Foreign Relations Committee. And he had a national security advisor to the new President. All of them he used with implacable pressure, and the skill of his decades at the game.

Victoria fought back with a fury and cunning that matched her ex-husband's—and she had one important advantage over him in the struggle. Alexandre was applying his pressure from a distance. The destabilization of Pranagua was one of many big operations he had to direct. Victoria poured all of herself into countering his attempt. And she was in Washington—and *of* it. Some of her connections went back to her girlhood there: young men who'd since risen to positions of prominence. Others she had cultivated in the years after her return from Europe.

She had discovered long ago one of the benefits of doing business with a large, loosely structured government. There were so *many* departments and power groups. If you couldn't get some on your side, there were always others. She applied her pressure, daily, on those she had: the Assistant Secretary of Defense for International Security Affairs. Her Pentagon admiral. Shan Huxley of the House Armed Services Committee and Defense Appropriations Subcommittee. And Clark Alwin, as close to the new President as he'd been to the former one.

Victoria beat Solomon Alexandre's destabilization campaign into the ground.

He retaliated by provoking one of the countries bordering Pranagua to reassert a century-old claim to some of the mineral-rich mountain area just inside the Pranaguan frontier. Victoria fought that threat with Alwin alone. The prospect of having his company mines shut down by warfare in those mountains sent Alwin rushing to another private talk with the President. Two days later the Defense Department's Military Assistance Program began releasing some of the really heavy stuff to Pranagua, through Tri-Arms. I found myself delivering the latest jet fighters and bombers, heavy tanks and antiaircraft batteries to DelMundo. Pranagua's neighbor took a look at that kind of defense capability and pulled back.

By then it wasn't only U.S. weaponry I was selling to Pranagua. As soon as European arms makers realized I had an exclusive there, they were asking me to sell for them as well. I did, in exchange for licenses to peddle their goods in other Latin American countries and Africa. In the same way, I was able to pressure American firms that wanted Pranaguan sales into letting Tri-Arms sell for them elsewhere. Tri-Arms began banking some serious money.

Ahmed al-Zadar provided another source of early income. The number of American arms manufacturing companies he controlled was on the increase. He gave Tri-Arms the rights to act as broker for a couple of them on foreign sales to non-Arab nations—depending on Victoria to come up with the necessary export licenses. She seldom failed him, or Tri-Arms. Before long we were acting as sales agent for all his U.S.-made weaponry.

Then there was Hiroshi Yukada. His APC was hot in Asia

but not moving well in the West. The United States didn't like to buy foreign products, and many other countries had a preference for American-made goods. So he began building an APC plant on the land Victoria had purchased for him from Rear Admiral Carrighar. Once the new plant opened for production, Tri-Arms would have another big source of income. And we were already seeing steady profits from a different Yukada operation. He was now producing Rambert's PR-100 automatic rifle as well as our LB-75. The Tri-Arms royalty on Asian sales of each individual weapon was tiny, but he sold a lot of them. It added up.

The upward mobility of Tri-Arms became so demanding, it was all I could do to keep a handle on all its ramifications. I was so totally centered on business that when I heard Mei-lin had gotten married to a newspaper editor in Germany, my emotional response was dim and fleeting. It reminded me of what Victoria had told me about the effect of taking heavy drugs. Mei-lin's marriage—Mei-lin herself—didn't seem quite real to me at that point.

I managed the proper tone of sadness in the congratulatory note I dictated to my secretary. But I wasn't sure I genuinely felt it. If I had a suspicion, somewhere inside, that I had lost someone I needed, it didn't surface strongly enough to hurt.

I was just too busy taking care of business. That was the period when we'd found out the U.S. Army had instituted a search program for a new type of one-man rocket-launcher system. It wanted to find something that could at least match the rugged reliability and hard-hitting accuracy of the inexpensive Soviet RPG-7. Rambert and I were spending all our time extolling and demonstrating the virtues of our LB-75 to Army engineering and procurement officers. At the same time, Victoria kept applying her own kind of pressure and persuasion in the Defense Department's corridors of power.

The combination worked. The Army included the LB-75 in the trials it was carrying out on one of its proving grounds. Our weapon was tested out in competition with the rival systems that the Pentagon had under consideration for American production: The STRIM rocket-launcher system from France. Sweden's M-2 Miniman. The German ARM-BRUSTER.

Paul Rambert had upgraded both of our prototypes since Lebanon. One big improvement for the LB-75, as well as the PR-100, was in the sights. He'd added a new laser range-finder that increased long distance and night accuracy considerably. Another improvement, for the LB-75, was a more devastating anti-bunker round.

The primary purpose of an infantryman rocket-launcher, of course, is killing tanks. The Army's testing teams had placed a lot of old tanks around the proving ground, at graduated distances, for the competitors to smash away at. But they also wanted something that could knock out an enemy bunker or bust through other fortification obstructions. So they'd constructed a number of thickly armored bunkers. Inside each they'd put a number of plaster dummies dressed as Russian soldiers.

None of our three competitors could come near matching what the LB-75's anti-bunker round did. After the rocket's penetration warhead punched a big hole through fifteen inches of steel and reinforced concrete, its follow-through fragmentation charge left nothing of the dummies but a lot of plaster dust. If the dummies had been live troops, the interior of the bunker would have been knee-deep in blood, bones and flesh.

One or another of the rival rocket-launchers outpointed the LB-75 in certain tests. But in the overall testing our weapon scored higher than any one of them. The STRIM was a shade more accurate than ours when fired at target tanks positioned at the longest range, but didn't have as much penetration speed left when it got that far. The Mini-man field-stripped and reassembled faster, but had an annoying backblast which our enclosed round eliminated. The German weapon was a better tank smasher at short distances, but its rocket strayed off course on longer flights.

The final trials were against the RPG-7. The Russian weapon was cheaper to make than our LB-75 or its three competitors. But the LB-75 was more accurate, delivered better penetration, and stood up better under rough punishment.

When the trials had finished, we had won hands down.

Having our product selected by the Army was one source of joy for Tri-Arms. Getting a high prestige company like Ward & Hubb as its U.S. manufacturer was the other. Christian Frosch flew over from our Rome office to join Victoria, Paul Rambert and me in celebrating.

So there we were, eleven months after Tri-Arms had opened for business in the States, congratulating ourselves over dinner at the Lion d'Or—when I dropped the bomb that ended the festive mood.

* * *

"I made a promise to myself before I went into this business," I began. "In fact, it's the most important of my various reasons for going into it. I want to get my father released."

"We all want to see that happen," Paul Rambert assured me.

Victoria nodded. "And we will."

Christian Frosch raised his champagne glass as though

about to propose a toast: "I'm with you there, kid. One hundred percent."

"Good," I said, "because now we've got a situation that makes it possible. Now that the Army knows what a beauty our LB-75 is, it's eager to get it into the hands of the troops as fast as possible. Ward & Hubb's panting for the contract. And not only for that one. The Army's seal of approval will make a lot of other countries greedy for our weapon. Ward & Hubb stands to make a bloody fortune off it."

Christian grinned at me. "Bloody is the word for it. A lot of people are gonna kill a lot of other people with that baby."

I ignored his interruption, though less than two years later I'd have reason to remember what he'd said.

"So that gives us the Army and Ward & Hubb," I resumed. I looked at Victoria. "Put that together with the friends you and your cousin Lee have in the Justice Department. Not to mention your connections elsewhere. We have all we need to push it through."

Rambert was frowning. "I have had too much to drink, perhaps. Please explain. Simply."

"Tri-Arms owns the LB-75. We refuse to let Ward & Hubb have it unless its chairman and director cooperate. They petition to have Lou Bishop, inventor of the LB-75, released. They need him as a technical advisor, urgently, in order to tool up quickly to produce his invention—cheaply enough to meet their budget from the Defense Department. The Pentagon formally confirms both the need and the urgency. The government reduces his sentence and releases him now —to serve the interests of national security and defense. It's that simple."

"It can be done," Victoria agreed cautiously. "But not so simply. And not now."

I stared at her. "*Now* we have the leverage."

"We'll have more in a year or two. Listen to me, Gar," she added quickly, to forestall my angry retort. "Tri-Arms is just beginning to get established. Wait until we're more solidly entrenched. Then we can get Lou freed without having to give away more than we can afford for it."

I was shocked and mad. I had never expected this kind of betrayal from Victoria. It took an effort to keep my voice under control. Even so, a lot of the anger came through: "It's my father who'd have to do the hard waiting. A year or two? Do you know what that kind of time means to him?"

"Yes, I do," she answered firmly. "Tell me, Gar, am I right in thinking you intend to give Lou back his share in the LB-75 after he's released?"

That seemed so different a subject to me that the question merely irritated me. "Yeah. So?"

"So he could find himself a millionaire by then—if we don't do anything, now, that slows the progress of Tri-Arms. Look, right now we *are* in a position to ask some favors of the Defense Department. But if they give us this big one, we'll have lost that position—with Defense, and with the other agencies involved. That would be a setback for Tri-Arms. But it's the smallest negative factor in what you're suggesting."

Victoria's expression was troubled, but her eyes met my accusing ones steadily. "In a couple days Lee and I will be sitting down with the Ward & Hubb people to negotiate our royalty contract. We're in a position to demand, and get, very healthy royalties. You're right, they're hungry to sell our LB-75 to the Army and abroad. They'll make a fortune —but we will too, unless we ask this favor of them.

"Of course they'll do it. But for something in exchange: we'd have to accept lower royalties. That would lose us—

each of us individually, as well as Tri-Arms—millions of dollars over the next ten years or so."

I gave her a sardonic look. "That'll still leave us enough millions to buy a few more dinners like this one."

She kept her tone calm and reasonable: "The royalties we'd have to give away are funding we need to increase our company's growth rate. If we take less, that growth will be much slower."

"So let it be slower. I'm not in that much of a hurry."

"I am. You have more years ahead of you. For me, time is getting short."

I thought she was referring to *her* age. I was wrong, but that's what I thought, so I dumped some sarcasm on her: "You ought to play a violin with that tune, Victoria. Then we can all cry." I shook my head disgustedly: "It's my father's time that's getting short. I want him *out*."

"I'm not saying *no*, Gar. I'm saying *not yet*. We will get him out. In another year—two at the most. If you want, I'll go see Lou and explain why it's necessary. I think he'll understand. Knowing he *will* get released—and be a rich man by then—will give him the patience to wait it out."

"I want you to think back, Victoria. Back when you were a prisoner in that sanatorium. Suppose you'd had a chance to get out, immediately. And then somebody asked you to wait a couple more years. How would you have felt about it?"

I watched her give that serious thought. I'm sure she believed the answer she gave me: "If I'd known that the waiting would serve a good purpose—for myself and others who cared about me—yes, I would have been patient."

"Well *I* won't be," I snapped. "I want him out of there. *Now*."

Victoria shook her head. "No. It would cost too much at this point."

"You're only one partner," I reminded her. "There are four votes at this table."

She looked at Christian Frosch. He'd slumped in his chair as he'd followed our argument. Now he met Victoria's gaze with an uncomfortable expression. She continued to look at him.

Finally he shrugged. "What you say makes sense," he told her, his voice low. "So . . . okay, I vote with you. I'm sorry, Gar, but she's right."

He was too embarrassed to meet my eyes. He continued to look at Victoria, although she was watching me again.

I should have expected it. I'd known how Christian felt about her: the way she could wind him around her finger. She had anticipated my demand, and talked it over with him beforehand. I didn't blame Christian too much. He couldn't help his susceptibility to her. I did, however, blame Victoria.

I looked to Paul Rambert, who was sitting very erect, his face like stone. "Paul?"

He looked surprised that I had to ask. "Lou Bishop is my good friend," he said stiffly. "Naturally I agree with you. He should be freed now, since it is possible."

The set of Victoria's mouth betrayed her own rising anger, but not her voice: "Paul, think about what we'd be throwing away. Millions of dollars in royalties, and the power that goes with them. It means slowing the growth of our company just when it's begun to—"

"Victoria," Rambert interrupted her, "we speak from two different worlds. You are what is called these days a gamesman. I am just an old-fashioned craftsman. My needs are small. I only need enough to pursue my craft as I wish. And to pay for my little pleasures—which are somewhat wicked but not that expensive."

"It's not the *money* I'm interested in," she growled at him, and her anger was out in the open now.

"I know that. You are interested in the *game*. In playing to *win*. And then playing again, for higher stakes, and winning again. That is not my world."

"And it's not a game to me! Don't you realize the potential of Tri-Arms? I want us to belong to a company that means something in this world."

"I belonged to the French Army," Rambert told her. "It proved disappointing, in the end. Since then I have considered myself an individual. As an individual, I could not look at myself in the mirror if I allowed my friend Lou Bishop to remain in prison any longer, if I had the ability to set him free."

Victoria stared at him, and saw what I saw. He'd made his decision and would stick with it. Rambert had a great respect for her. But she couldn't get inside him, the way she had with Christian. Rambert's obsession with kids precluded that.

She turned back to me. "Then we're deadlocked," she said slowly. "Two against two."

"That's right. And a deadlock means Tri-Arms can't make a move, in either direction. We can't trade some of our royalties for my father's release if you two vote against it. And you can't make *any* kind of deal for the LB-75 if Rambert and I vote against it."

Victoria studied me with disbelief. "You'd throw the whole deal away like that? Everything we've worked for?"

"It's not me who'd be doing it, Victoria. The decision is up to you."

"You're bluffing."

I didn't know, myself, if that was true. But I did know that I intended to carry it as far as I could: to find out which of the four of us chickened out first.

I looked at Christian. "It's not a bluff," I told him emphatically. "It's an ultimatum. You and Victoria don't want to give up some of our royalties and clout for the man responsible for the invention that can bring them in. But if you go on playing it stubborn, we lose *all* of it. And maybe the company, too."

Chapter Twenty-seven

Garson

I paid the check and we went to my suite at the Sheraton-Carlton and continued fighting for three more hours. When we called it quits for the night, out of sheer exhaustion, it was still a standoff: two against two.

We went at it again the next day, in Victoria's house. The contract meeting with Ward & Hubb was scheduled for the morning after that—drawing closer with every hour we argued. Victoria wouldn't budge. I wouldn't budge. Rambert remained silent through most of it, just sitting there and watching the two of us fight. He'd given his decision. Christian didn't say much, either. But he began pacing a lot. I watched the panic building in his eyes.

It was a few minutes past three in the morning, with the Ward & Hubb conference only six hours away, when Christian caved in. He didn't like giving away the millions in royalties Victoria had talked about. But he couldn't stand the increasing probability of throwing *everything* away. Finally he agreed to accept the fewer millions in royalties we'd be getting if we did it my way.

That made our vote three to one, and Victoria was left with no choice but to accept the decision. She'd been right about what it would cost us: Tri-Arms had to trade away almost half its future income from the LB-75 in exchange for Ward & Hubb's help in springing my father.

The personal relationship between Victoria and myself, after that, became one of cool, polite reserve. And it didn't change until over a year and a half later. When it did, my life changed with it.

* * *

My father came out of prison less than six weeks after his rocket launcher was chosen by the U.S. Army. He only worked as technical advisor to Ward & Hubb's engineers for a couple months—just long enough to prove everybody had been sincere in requesting his release "in the interests of national security and defense." Then he quit, "for reasons of health."

He had no interest in getting back into any aspect of the arms business. Offhandedly, he tried to explain some of the reasons to me: "Guns . . . I guess life just got to feel too precious to me in there. Mine and everybody else's." He gave me an embarrassed grin. "Anyway, I want to spend as much of my time *outside* as I can, from now on, doing whatever I want to do."

He moved up to Vermont and took an old house with some good ground around it, in the countryside near Rutland. The money he used to buy the place came out of an advance I gave him against his share of our future earnings from the LB-75. When I visited a few months after he'd moved up there, I found he'd taken a job driving the local school bus. He seemed to enjoy snapping gruff orders at the kids to quiet down and board the bus in an orderly fashion, and they looked up to "Major Bishop," but it didn't take up much of his day. The rest of it he was devoting to repainting the outside of the house and creating a sizeable vegetable garden on part of his property.

It seemed a dull life to me. But he was obviously content with it, and it had certainly done him good physically. He'd come out of prison looking like a dying man. Five months later, in Vermont, he looked twenty years younger. I couldn't apply the word "content" to my own life at that period. I was handling too great a diversity of business pressures for that. It was hectic; but also damned exhilarating.

Victoria and I didn't allow the personal coolness between us to interfere with our professional dealings. And of those, we had a leapfrogging amount. The loss of half the royalties we could have gotten from Ward & Hubb, and concessions Tri-Arms had made to various government agencies to obtain my father's release, did slow our growth as Victoria had predicted. But not for as long as she'd feared. Over the next year and a half we more than made up for it.

One big source of income was our commissions on sales of helicopter gunships for a Texas company now controlled by Ahmed al-Zadar. Another was our sales abroad of Yukada's American-made APCs. Still another was Ward & Hubb. Our royalties on the LB-75, though halved, mounted up. Ward & Hubb had also gone into production with Rambert's PR-100, encouraged to do so by the U.S. Marine Corps, which was considering adopting it as a new assault rifle. As it turned out, the Marines didn't buy it. But a lot of other countries did. And the royalties and commissions Victoria negotiated on the PR-100 were extremely lucrative for Tri-Arms.

One reason for our rapid expansion was Pranagua. It was not only what we sold *to* that country. More important was the way that we were able to use Pranagua to sell our wares to other countries—especially in Latin America and Africa.

Arms manufacturers had to come to Tri-Arms to make sales in Pranagua. We were able to use our lock on sales there to pressure those manufacturers into letting us handle their sales elsewhere. And then we stimulated those sales by the oldest trick in the arms trade. A country would purchase in large quantity from us because our selling price was cheap. Then we'd let its neighbors know the quantity and quality it had. That would scare them into making equally big purchases from us—expensively.

The second way we used Pranagua was not as simple, but even more lucrative. Europe and the United States always have changing lists of countries to which they will not sell arms for one reason or another. They demand end-user certificates from *approved* countries and stipulate that those countries must not resell without approval. The U.S. Defense Department, for example, attaches to any arms shipment abroad its Form 1513, Condition 7: "The purchaser shall not transfer title to or possession of the items furnished under this sales agreement to any person or organization or other government, unless the consent of the government of the United States has first been obtained...."

To police this, the ATF bureau (Alcohol, Tobacco and Firearms) of the U.S. Treasury Department stations agents abroad who check the validity of end-user certificates and whether the arms exports actually go to the approved countries designated in them.

My special relationship with President DelMundo insured that Pranaguan authorities would confirm to the ATF that my end-user certificates were valid. ATF agents could also see for themselves that the arms shipped to Pranagua did arrive there. However, they had no way to keep track of what happened to the shipments after that. If all the weaponry Tri-Arms shipped to Pranagua had stayed there, the country would have cracked under its weight. But most of it we soon transshipped out of Pranagua to non-approved countries.

The beauty of selling American weaponry to foreign countries is that the U.S. manufacturers—and through them dealers like us—know they'll be paid. A number of government agencies are involved in controlling procurement contracts between a foreign nation and an American arms company. The State Department has to okay foreign sales of U.S. small arms. With big stuff like planes, tanks and ships, the Defense Department's approval is needed. Sometimes the Commerce Department takes part, too. But once such a contract is okayed, the government guarantees the shipment abroad will be paid for. If the country receiving the arms later neglects to deliver the money for it, the U.S. government has to come up with it. And so we were often reimbursed for our sales of U.S. arms abroad from the pockets of every American taxpayer.

* * *

With Tri-Arms expanding at that rate over the next year and a half, Victoria, Christian and I had to shoulder increasing workloads. Not Paul Rambert: he spent most of his time in his workshop outside Paris, tinkering with a new submachine gun he expected to outclass the Israeli Uzi and British Sterling. Only the most vital conferences could induce him to leave his work. Rambert was quite satisfied with the income he was already getting.

Victoria and Christian weren't. Neither was I. It wasn't more money we were after. It was the excitement of the ever-higher goals within reach—a lot like the thrill you feel in mountain climbing. You choose a peak and fight your way up to it. When you make it, your next climb has to be higher. If you start wondering why, you shouldn't be doing it. You should be sitting around a pool in Florida, sipping a cold drink in the hot sun and eyeing the bikinis out of vague habit, like the other dying and half-dead. That, anyway, was how I saw it at that point in my life.

In directing our U.S. operations, Victoria became in some respects the most important partner. The United States sold more weaponry abroad than any other Western nation. It also bought more—and preferred to buy products made in the States, to stimulate the economy. Working at the hub of all that activity, in Washington, made Victoria responsible for an increasing percentage of Tri-Arms' prosperity. Her position became even stronger after she maneuvered herself onto the Defense-Industry Advisory Council, which acted as a liaison between the government and the arms business.

Christian Frosch took over complete charge of all our European operations, out of our expanding headquarters in Rome. I acted as the firm's rover, going wherever I was most needed. I lost count of the number of times I circled the globe in those one and a half years, negotiating deals, making round-the-clock sales pitches, scrambling for new and old weaponry, and engaging in no-holds-barred battles with competitors.

By the middle part of that period I was also conducting a lot of our weaponry demonstrations in Nevada. We bought a big chunk of desert property there, as a place to show our small arms, APCs, helicopters and other tools of the warfare trade to prospective buyers.

It was close enough to Las Vegas that they could also be given a lot of entertainment along with the sales demonstrations. We called the place the Ranch. Six former Army and Marine sergeants handled it and the weaponry. But I was the one who had to be there when there was a session, to supervise both the business and the partying. Victoria sensibly never attended any of these Nevada bashes. They were strictly what she called boy-games.

Usually I'd have the potential customers flown in for a weekend: military attachés from Washington embassies and purchasing agents from foreign governments. They were given Vegas hotel suites stocked with the best liquor and girls, stacks of chips to gamble with, free meals, dinner shows and nightclubbing. There were chauffeured, air conditioned limousines to ferry them between Vegas and the Ranch. Out there we put on a good show for them, and usually let them join in when they got into the mood of our miniature mock battles.

The display they always got the biggest kick out of was held at night, at the end of the other weaponry demonstrations. We set up cans of petrol and started shooting them up with our assault rifles set for four-round bursts. The weapons were loaded with tracers, which created a display of their own in the darkness. And when a tracer burst hit a petrol can, the flaming explosion was spectacular. A few minutes of that and you couldn't have stopped our fascinated guests from grabbing the tracer-loaded rifles and trying it themselves. They all had girls waiting back in their hotels. But feminine attraction couldn't compete as long as the fireworks lasted. Those middle-aged officers could shoot the cans into bursting flames again and again without stopping—which was more than most of them could do with the girls.

In between the shooting, the drinking, the weaponry displays, the gambling and the wenching, I slipped in the sales talks. It almost always paid off, with at least one subsequent sale out of each weekend's bunch of guests.

* * *

By the middle of 1979, Tri-Arms International was a multi-million dollar company, and growing bigger by the month. By then, too, the pace was beginning to tell on me. I was in my thirties now. Constant jet-lag, too much drinking and un-relenting deal-making, and not enough sleep made for morn-ings when I had trouble pulling myself together. It was still exciting, but sometimes I felt older than I was.

Victoria was forty-six, going on forty-seven, and she looked fabulous. Since the United States was both the big-gest buyer and the biggest seller of weaponry, her workload was often the heaviest that any of us four partners had to carry. And she devoted herself to it—to the entrenchment and expansion of Tri-Arms—with a totality that verged on obsession. The incredible amount she accomplished in any given day *should* have taken its toll on her. But I couldn't see any sign of it happening. She thrived on it.

But if Victoria possessed her own secret source of self-re-newing energy, it could not stretch the number of hours available in each day and week. Time imposed its limits on her as well as the rest of us. Attention had to be divided be-tween the many projects being handled in the same period. Inevitably, there were details we neglected to take care of on time in the midst of the juggling. That, as much as una-voidable bad luck or wrong timing, resulted in a number of nasty setbacks for Tri-Arms during its climb.

The worst came in July of 1979, from Solomon Alexandre.

* * *

"This is your fault," Hiroshi Yukada told Victoria point-blank. "I hold you entirely responsible for this loss."

The loss was bad enough to have brought him to Washington to find out what had gone wrong. He was furious about it, and we couldn't blame him.

"You're right," Victoria told him without flinching. "It is my fault. I was looking the wrong way. I should have anticipated it."

"And prevented it," Yukada added coldly.

"Yes," she admitted with an anger of her own. The anger was directed, not at Yukada, but herself.

The Marine Corps wanted a new armored personnel carrier. Victoria and I worked as a team to swing the contract for the APCs made at Yukada's American plant. Solomon Alexandre was pushing to get it for a California company he controlled. We gave top priority to beating him in that struggle. Finally Rear Admiral Carrighar slipped us word that the Pentagon was going to decide in our favor.

Victoria relaxed enough to shift attention to another high priority: persuading officials of the Departments of State and Defense to okay the sales of two hundred million dollars worth of Phantom fighter-bombers to one of al-Zadar's Persian Gulf clients. At the same time I flew down to Argentina for yet another priority: to help Christian Frosch nail down the sale of French Exocet antiship missiles to that country at six million dollars per missile.

It proved the wrong time for any shift of vigilance away from the APC priority. We made the mistake partly because of Rear Admiral Carrighar's assurance that we had that deal cinched. The other reason was that we didn't think Alexandre was capable of his usual roughshod drive that summer. Tri-Arms always retained investigators in different parts of the world to keep tabs on Victoria's ex-husband. Their latest reports indicated he was having serious health problems. He was making fewer plane trips, and when he did, his personal physician travelled with him. The prescriptions the doctor obtained for Alexandre were to combat an overactive thyroid and serious high blood pressure.

But if the Old Wolf of the arms business wasn't quite up to his normal fighting strength that summer, he still had very sharp teeth. He also had Stuart Peel. Two days before the Defense Department was to announce the awarding of the APC contract to Yukada's company, Peel pulled the plug.

The news media jumped on the scandal he served up. Point one: Yukada's APC plant was built on land bought from Rear Admiral Carrighar. Point two: Yukada could have purchased similar land near it for very much less. Final point: Rear Admiral Carrighar was the Pentagon officer most responsible for swinging the contract to Yukada's APC. Peel furnished iron-clad evidence for each point. Everyone drew the natural conclusion: the high price Yukada had paid Carrighar bought more from the admiral than his land.

Asked to resign, Carrighar went home, burned his admiral's uniform in the fireplace, sat down naked in his bathtub, and blew his head apart with a shotgun.

The Defense Department reconsidered the APC contract and awarded it to Solomon Alexandre's company.

I flew back to Washington to help Victoria handle the shock of Carrighar's suicide and face Yukada's wrath. But whatever guilt she was experiencing over Carrighar she kept hidden inside herself. Yukada's fury, however, was not hidden: he was close to making a decision to take all his business away from Tri-Arms.

I couldn't do much at that meeting between the three of us but lend Victoria some support and put in a reasonable word now and then to cool Yukada's anger. With the strong relationship between them, if she couldn't make him forgive our failure, nobody could.

"I made two bad mistakes," she told him honestly. "I should have buried the financial details of that land sale much deeper so that Stuart Peel couldn't dig them up. I didn't because I wanted to be able to use them to apply pressure on the admiral if I had to. Also, I should never have used him to push this particular deal through. We probably could have mustered enough Pentagon support without him. But I wanted to be absolutely sure. So I did use him, and I was wrong."

"That is an unusually frank admission," Yukada said. "But your frankness does not bring back the millions of dollars I have lost because of your mistakes."

"We'll make up for it," I told him. "We'll get you other contracts, as big or bigger. Just like we've done before."

He turned an expressionless stare on me. "Getting me other contracts is a normal part of what I expect of an agent. They won't cancel out the loss of this one."

"Nobody can win *every* fight. You have to accept losing one now and then."

"I do," Yukada told me stonily, "when it is unavoidable. This loss was avoidable."

Victoria spoke to him again, her voice quiet and steady: "Hiroshi, I want you to take something into consideration. Have we *ever* failed you in this way before?"

He looked at her. After a moment he said, "No. But that does not—"

She interrupted him firmly: "I had breakfast this morning, shortly before you arrived, with two of my friends in the Defense Department's Security Assistance Agency. I think I'm going to be able to get approval of that Hercules order you've been after."

Yukada's eyes got a little smaller. Lockheed sold its Hercules C-130 military transport plane for over five million dollars. The Philippine government wanted twenty of them. That came to more than a hundred million dollars. Yukada's go-between fees and rake-offs would come to a nice percentage of that sum—and so would our cut. The U.S. government, however, had so far been withholding permission for the sale.

"You *think* you can get it?" he demanded of Victoria. "Or are you sure you can?"

"Is Tri-Arms still your agent?" she asked blandly.

Yukada was silent for several moments. Then he smiled faintly. "Yes."

She returned his smile: "In that case you can be sure I'll get it."

And that seemed to be that. Our failure with his APCs was, if not forgotten, at least forgiven. I left them shortly after that to tend to other business. The next morning, after Victoria had seen Yukada off on his flight back to Tokyo, I dropped into her office to ask if his anger had been completely dispelled.

"Toward us, yes," Victoria told me. "But not toward Solomon. He's added it to a number of past injuries—all of which he intends to repay in kind when the time is ripe."

I had much the same feeling toward Solomon Alexandre. But personal sentiments didn't prevent either of us from sitting down at the same conference table with him, a month later, to join in a conspiracy that would be to our mutual advantage.

The purpose of the conference I was invited to that August was to organize one of those games that big arms dealers sometimes play with other nations. The other players present besides Yukada, Alexandre and me, were Ahmed al-Zadar and a new member of the trade's Golden Circle, Otto Scheiber, the chairman of a German-French arms consortium called NEMEZ. The fact that I was being asked to join their game indicated how close Tri-Arms was to becoming part of the Golden Circle itself.

Chapter Twenty-eight

Garson

I dropped in on Paul Rambert before going to that Golden Circle meeting. He was going off, too, the next day, to be a guest of honor at the annual celebration of DelMundo's election as President of Pranagua. We'd both been invited, but since it coincided with the Golden Circle meeting, I could not attend, and at least one of us was obliged.

I tried out his new submachine gun on the range behind the workshop. It was a beauty to handle and shoot. But I found a couple faults in comparing it with the best weapons it would have to compete against. When field-stripped, it couldn't be put back together as speedily as the Sterling submachine gun. And while it was as light and rugged as the Uzi, it wouldn't be nearly as cheap to manufacture.

Rambert agreed with my criticisms. "Those are two of the problems I will have to work on more when I come back from Pranagua."

We sat down at a tree-shaded table between the workshop and his house, and he opened a bottle of red for us. He gave me an odd, squinty look as we touched our glasses together and drank.

"You won't guess who is going to Pranagua with me, Garson." He wiped his mouth with the back of his hand and told me: "Mei-lin Shaw."

I put down my glass. There'd been a small lurch in my guts, something I hadn't felt in awhile. "How did that happen?"

"I ran into her in Paris last week. She asked if I would take her along with me and make sure she got a chance to have a private talk with DelMundo. She wants to do an article about what has happened to the country since he took over."

I could understand why Mei-lin wanted to do that. Del-Mundo had held the free and democratic elections he'd promised. As expected, almost everyone in the country voted for him and for his choice of vice-president: his devoted, long time aide, Miguel Gomez. Firmly established as President, DelMundo had set about putting the country "in order." The cleanup naturally included hunting down and arresting a lot of supporters of the former dictator. Then he shut down newspapers that objected to any of his policies, on the grounds that they hampered his reform programs.

It didn't surprise many people when he outlawed the communists. But then he banned two other opposition parties. That didn't leave any genuine political party to run against him when the next election rolled around. If it ever did. President DelMundo was beginning to act very much like your typical Latin American dictator. More benevolent than most of the breed, perhaps, but still not a ruler who accepted arguments as well-intended.

The number of arrests grew, and began to include people who didn't support the communists and had never been sympathetic to the former dictatorship. DelMundo even hired back some of Calderon's former secret police—with the explanation that they, after all, had the most experience in ferreting out "trouble makers." Varda, the air force colonel who'd aided DelMundo's coup and been upped to commander of the armed forces, objected to this ruling too strongly. He was placed under house arrest and stripped of his command.

Naturally, a lot of people who'd had high hopes were becoming disillusioned. So Mei-lin wanted to find out if it was as bad as it was beginning to look.

I wasn't disillusioned because I hadn't had many illusions to begin with about the type of leader DelMundo would probably make. But I wouldn't have minded being proved wrong, in this particular case.

"How is she?" I asked Rambert. "Happily married?"

"Mei-lin? I wouldn't say so." He gave me another odd look. "As a matter of fact, she told me she is getting a divorce."

"What happened?"

Rambert shrugged. "She didn't tell me why, so I didn't ask. I do have a certain delicacy, you know."

I took my time emptying my glass. He poured more wine in it. I said, casually, "Well, tell her—tell her I'd like to see her again."

"Tell her yourself. She still has the same studio in Rome. She never gave that up."

I sipped at the wine. "Paul, what would you think I if I decided to quit the business?"

"Do you want to?"

I laughed. "Probably not. Hell, we're going to be the biggest, the way Tri-Arms is growing." I had some more wine. "It's just that sometimes I feel my enthusiasm slipping. Not often. Just when I run out of steam. Then I get a good night's sleep and the feeling goes away."

He studied me thoughtfully. "Well, you already have what you wanted out of the business. Lou is a free man. You are rich. My accountant tells me each of us four partners is now worth over ten million American dollars, and that's just what each of us could walk away with in cash. So it is natural if you sometimes wonder what there is left to strive for."

"The fun of it, Paul. It is damned exciting."

Rambert shrugged.

"Would you quit?" I asked him.

"Why should I? I continue to do what I want to do most. Tinkering with weapons, solving technical problems, trying to come up with something better. But that is myself. What do *you* want, Garson?"

I didn't say anything for awhile. I knew the answer to his question. What I wanted was to become part of the Golden Circle. To prove I could beat those boys at any game they cared to play. To . . .

"Just tell Mei-lin," I said finally, "I'd really like to see her."

* * *

One of the world's biggest concentrations of vacation estates for the ultra-wealthy is the stretch of Spain's Costa del Sol, between Puerto Banus and Marbella, known as Billionaire's Row. That concentration had been intensified over the past decade by holiday palaces build by petrodollar princes from the Middle East. Some older European and American tycoons there objected to the architectural tastes of the Arab infiltration of their enclave. One Syrian's home away from home was a copy of the Alhambra, but twice as big, with such additional touches as heliport, yacht dock, private zoo and parking garage for forty cars. When U.S. Secretary of State Haig was the weekend guest of Saudi Arabia's Prince Fahd, he was startled to find himself put up in a triple-sized replica of the White House.

But not all the new billionaires there were Arabs. The

meeting place for the arms game I joined, two days after seeing Rambert, belonged to the head of NEMEZ, Otto Scheiber. He had bought it from an Italian auto magnate as an occasional weekend retreat. It was a modest twenty bedroom mansion, with an amusement park in the back yard for the entertainment of the children of his fourth marriage and their young guests.

Our conference was held in a separate building at the other end of the estate, far removed from the noise of the kids. The pieces in the game our German host had invited us to play were the countries of Iran and Iraq: neighbors and long time enemies. Between them they had all of the immensely lucrative oil producing area at the top of the Persian Gulf. Their squabbles over which country most of it should belong to frequently included threats of war. At the moment, however, their enmity was quiescent.

"But I am certain," Otto Scheiber said, "that if we all put our best efforts together, we can heat it up. To the profit of each of us."

Nobody contradicted him. It was apparently not the first time some of them had discussed it.

"The situation and timing," Solomon Alexandre added decisively, "could not be better for it."

Al-Zadar smiled and Yukada nodded. As the newcomer, I kept my mouth shut and my expression blank. Alexandre had looked at me once, balefully, and ignored my presence since. I was there because the others thought I should be, not him. For my part I spent much of the early phase of the meeting studying Alexandre. I was looking for signs of illness, but I couldn't spot any. His hands were skeletal and there were dark pouches under his eyes, but these could have merely been indications of his age. He was still sharp of mind and cold of eye, and his imperial self-assurance was as strong as ever. For Solomon Alexandre, *everybody* was a newcomer.

He was the one who outlined the basic situation—the "opportunity," as he put it.

The Soviet bloc countries made billions out of keeping Iraq's military arsenals full to overflowing. The United States and its NATO partners had made more from arming Iran. But the latter situation had altered drastically in the first month of that year. The Shah had fled and Khomeini's distaste for the evils of Western civilization led him to institute such reforms as outlawing college education for women. It also led him into a nasty confrontation with the United States. Since then, the NATO nations had banned further sales of weaponry to Iran.

When Khomeini assumed power, the amount of orders Iran had placed for future arms deliveries from the United States alone came to almost thirteen billion dollars. Those orders would no longer be delivered.

So far the arms embargoes against it had not bothered Iran too much. Its military stockpiles, like those of Iraq, were already enormous.

"But should war occur between Iran and Iraq," Alexandre pointed out, "the stockpiles of both would get used up rapidly. That would place Iran in considerable difficulty. It would need more spare parts, replacements and ammunition for all its NATO weaponry. It could no longer obtain what it required from the NATO suppliers—not directly."

"This means," Otto Scheiber said complacently, "that Iran would have to get it from *us*. That in turn would place us in a position to set the prices for filling its requirements."

Yukada said quietly, "Under the Shah, Iran spent an average of one hundred and forty million dollars per month on military goods."

"And that," al-Zadar added cheerfully, "was *without* a war."

"Precisely," Otto Scheiber said.

The question before us dealers, then, was how to provoke such a war. The simplest way would be to incite Iraq to attack Iran and seize the oil wells it wanted. There were two persuasive arguments that could be used to induce it to do so:

One: Now, if ever, was the time for it. As long as NATO nations were refusing to supply Iran with arms, Iraq had the significant advantage. If Iran's military capability ran out, Iraq would easily win. Iraq had to be reassured that NATO would not lift its embargo if Iran was attacked—at the present time.

The second persuader would be a warning: Relations between Iran and NATO were not likely to continue like this forever. Important American political figures were looking forward to a future time, perhaps after the aged Khomeini died, when the U.S. and Iran could patch up their differences. Iran was already planning for that time. Once the NATO arms embargo was lifted, Iran intended to attack Iraq—and steal *its* oil wells.

The reassurance on the first point, and the warning of the second, could be dropped into the ears of Iraqi government leaders, gradually and cumulatively, until they took effect. This would be accomplished by members of foreign embassies stationed there. Each of the Golden Circle dealers had influence with enough diplomats to achieve that.

Similarly, it could be insured that Iraq's ambassadors abroad heard the same rumors in foreign capitals. Victoria could be especially helpful in spreading the word among members of the Iraqi delegation at the U.N.

None of the diplomats passing these rumors to the Iraqis would be consciously telling any lies. They would simply be misinformed—by us.

The part Victoria could play was one reason I had been asked to attend this meeting. More important was my special relationship with Pranagua's President DelMundo. When that subject came up, Solomon Alexandre became oddly silent, gazing neutrally at some point on the wall behind me. I assumed, at first, that he was simply continuing to be a sorehead about losing Pranagua to Tri-Arms.

The Pranaguan ambassador to Iraq could be one more voice adding assurances of Iran's present vulnerability and future hostile intentions. But that was a minor part of Pranagua's usefulness to the game plan. The major one was that Tri-Arms had turned that country, by mid-1979, into one of the easiest conduits for big shipments of weaponry from the United States.

The discussion continued for some time. The game plan arrived at, as everyone knows, worked just fine. The following year Iraq did attack Iran. By the end of 1984 half a million Iranians and Iraqis had died in the war that ensued between them. And a lot of private arms dealers got fat on the killing.

I was not one of them, as it turned out—because at one point in the meeting, the phone rang in Otto Scheiber's conference room.

Scheiber picked it up promptly. His staff was under orders to break in on the meeting only for news of the utmost importance. As he listened, he gave me a startled look, and then frowned thoughtfully in Alexandre's direction. Alexandre was once more gazing disinterestedly at the wall behind me.

Scheiber hung up the phone gently. "Gentlemen, I'm afraid there may be some complications regarding Pranagua's part in what we have been discussing. President DelMundo was assassinated two hours ago, while being driven to the presidential palace."

I got very slowly to my feet. The way Scheiber was looking at me said it before his words hit me:

"Mr. Bishop, I am very sorry to tell you that your partner, Paul Rambert, was also killed in the attack on the car, along with the driver and a female journalist."

* * *

I got to Pranagua a few hours before the funeral. It was to be a state affair, with the public sorrow presided over by DelMundo's former Vice-president, Miguel Gomez. He was now the President of Pranagua.

Gomez received me courteously. He even had me accompany him, in the new presidential limousine, to the funeral. On the way President Gomez explained what his police investigators had already discovered.

The assassination had been committed by a young man who was a known member of an Italian terrorist group with communist affiliations.

"Obviously," Gomez told me, "he was sent by the Reds to commit this crime. As a favor to Cuba and the communist insurgents who still plague this country."

"Is that what the assassin says?" I asked him.

"Unfortunately, it was not possible to question him. He was killed by a colonel of our police while trying to escape after the attack."

I studied Gomez. It didn't surprise me, later, when I learned the colonel was subsequently upped to general.

"That *is* unfortunate," I said coldly. "Also damned convenient."

"Please explain what you mean."

"You know what I mean, Miguel. It's just too neat, too fast. Culprit killed, crime solved, no more questions about who was really behind it or why."

Gomez looked at me stonily. "I will take into consideration that you are upset. But I don't think you are acting in a manner appropriate between friends."

"*Are* we still friends?"

"Of course."

But of course we weren't.

Gomez had finally gotten tired of always being DelMundo's sidekick, and the growing feeling of disillusion in the country had made the time ripe. So he'd been approached. It had been explained to him that he could become the new President without lifting a finger to accomplish it. Others would do it for him. All he had to do afterwards was sweep it under the carpet.

No, he was no longer my friend.

He was Solomon Alexandre's friend now.

* * *

I didn't really care about that, on my one and final day in Pranagua. I was too involved in trying to cope with the way Mei-lin and Rambert had died, along with DelMundo and his driver. The funeral made it worse. It wasn't four bodies I saw buried that day—but four coffins containing plastic bags of assorted flesh and bone.

They'd been disintegrated by a fragmentation warhead from an LB-75 rocket launcher.

Chapter Twenty-nine

Garson

The acrid odor of cigarette smoke woke me. Not right away. I was in no condition to respond to anything without giving it some time and effort. It happened gradually: the smoke intruding, luring me up out of the dark depths bit by bit. But not all the way out. The pills I had taken were too strong for me to manage that.

I'd flown to Rome after the funeral, and used a key Mei-lin had given me long ago to get into her studio. It was the most painful place I could find to hole up. My mood was so savage that I wanted to suffer for awhile. Three days and two nights. Mei-lin's presence was too strong there for me to take more of it.

I moved back into my Rome apartment over in Parioli. I disconnected the phones, didn't open telegrams that were stuffed into my mailbox, didn't answer the couple times somebody knocked at my door. Sometimes, very late at night, I went out and walked for hours. Now and then I ate, when it occurred to me. Sleep was hard to come by. Liquor could knock me out for a couple hours. Then I'd be wide awake again.

Finally I went to a doctor and told him part of my problem. He looked in my eyes, checked my pulse, blood pressure and heartbeat, took my money, and gave me a prescription. After that I slept most of the time. If I was awake late at night, I took walks. If it was day, I sat on the little garden terrace outside my living room and stared at the roofs of Rome. When I had enough of that I went back inside and took a couple more of the pills.

The cigarette smoke had a familiar odor.

I got my eyes partly open, squinting at her. She was sitting comfortably in the wing chair, regarding me, the cigarette stuck in the corner of her mouth. Her legs were stretched out with her feet resting on my bed, ankles crossed. The rust-colored jeans and green silk blouse were calculated to advertise her lithe figure. A warm breeze coming through the opened french doors stirred her hair.

I looked at the pale daylight outside. "Is it morning or evening?" I asked thickly. It took work to articulate each word properly.

"Evening."

It had been mid-afternoon when I'd fallen asleep. The pills had some hours yet to go before they finished with me. I started to push myself up to a sitting position, but settled for propping myself a bit higher on the pillows. My head was very fuzzy.

"How'd you get in?"

"Christian gave me some passkeys." Victoria stubbed her cigarette out in a dessert dish she'd gotten from my kitchen. "I decided nineteen days was enough of this masochistic performance." She wasn't scolding, merely giving me a casual, matter-of-fact opinion.

"I wasn't keeping track," I told her.

"I guess you weren't." She'd picked up the pill bottle and was reading the label. "This is a hell of a way to be in mourning."

"I'm not in mourning. Victoria, I'm thinking of quitting."

"I doubt if you can think too straight, with these. Take them much longer and you'll be an addict. Take enough, and you'll be dead. I suppose it *is* a gentler way to commit suicide than shooting yourself."

I managed a lopsided smile. "I'm not planning to kill myself."

"Good news." Victoria got up from the chair and bent over me briefly, kissed me softly. "Go back to sleep, Gar." She started toward the living room, taking the pills with her.

"Where're you going?"

"There's hardly any food in your kitchen. I'll do some shopping—while you finish sleeping it off."

It wasn't hard to do. I just let the pills take over again, and they dragged me back down into that deep darkness.

The next time I woke it was night. It was like awakening into a dream of warm, fleshy delight. She was in bed with me, her naked body pressed against mine, our arms around each other, our hands moving, seeking, demanding. My body had begun responding to hers while I was still asleep. I was fully roused when I opened my eyes.

Her face was exquisite in the moonlight. I kissed her and the softness of her lips opened, her tongue entering my mouth and finding mine.

* * *

She stayed with me for two days and nights. We took each other impatiently in the beginning of that time, the initial sexual hunger demanding urgent, frenzied release. It was as though a dam burst and years of lust held in abeyance were surging through and engulfing us. But later, when we had sated that domineering hunger, we became more leisurely with our love play, prolonging and delaying gratification while we explored and savored, exulting in a new world we were discovering.

Often, we would find ourselves lazily smiling into each other's eyes. Or suddenly laughing out loud with the pure joy of it.

When we ate, it was always with ravenous appetites. Sometimes we left the apartment and strolled aimlessly, holding hands like kids. Sometimes we sat together on the terrace, sipping drinks and watching the moving sun change the colors of the city, or the movement of the moon altering its shapes. But the bed was our true home, and when we were together there I knew the woman in my arms was infinitely precious to me, indispensable.

We didn't talk much, in those two days and nights, of anything unconnected with our pleasure in each other.

* * *

And then, on the third morning, we began discussing it.

We were finishing breakfast out on the terrace, under a clouded, sultry sky. Over a second coffee I told her, "I meant what I said about quitting. I'm thinking of wrapping it up and getting out."

"Seriously?"

"I'm not sure if the thought's a passing one or here to stay," I said honestly. "But it's there."

Victoria lit her first cigarette of the day. "Why?" she asked me.

"I've grown sick of it. Arms dealing, double-dealing, triple-dealing . . . with people dying from every move I make."

"You're not responsible for the deaths of Paul Rambert and Mei-lin Shaw, you know. Solomon Alexandre is the one responsible for that. I imagine you know that, too."

"I guessed it was him."

"No guess. It was. I did a great deal of digging while you were holed up here. Stuart Peel was in Pranagua before the assassination. He probably arrived on the same plane as the assassin. He was still there when Solomon arrived—the day after you left—for a talk with the new President. Solomon's gotten back his exclusive in handling Pranagua's arms business, and Tri-Arms is out. You won't be welcome there again."

"I figured."

"He killed them, Gar. Wouldn't you like a chance for revenge?"

"I thought about killing him," I told her. "But I know I'm not going to. It wouldn't bring Mei-lin or Paul back to life."

Victoria looked at her cigarette for a moment, as though seeking something in the way its smoke curled. "Don't quit on me," she said slowly. "Not now, not yet. There's something happening I need your help for. After that, get out if you want to. But help with this first."

"What is it?"

She crushed out the cigarette and leaned back in her chair, a special excitement creeping into her expression.

"I had a talk with Hiroshi Yukada. Two weeks from now Japan is going to start looking for a new Mach-2 long range fighter-bomber. The one made by the California firm Solomon controls is already the leading contender for the contract. General Tashiro told him the buy was coming before anyone else knew about it. Even Yukada."

"How big a buy?"

Victoria answered almost reverently: "More than one and a half billion dollars worth, over the next eight years."

I *was* impressed. Thinking about it, I said: "And that's only a starter. Next year the U.S. Air Force begins its own search program for a new fighter-bomber. If Japan chooses Alexandre's, that will help persuade the Pentagon it's the best."

Victoria nodded. "And if the Pentagon takes it, as well as Japan, that will influence Europe's NATO nations to do the same. Meaning many more billions of dollars. Solomon intends to go to Tokyo next week, and stay there as long as it takes him to sew it up."

I found myself getting interested, out of habit. "Al-Zadar's plant in Georgia turns out as good a fighter-bomber as Alexandre's. Does Yukada know if it's in the running?"

"It's one of the three planes Japan is considering. Al-Zadar has just asked Yukada to represent him in negotiating with the Japanese government. Since Yukada doesn't make planes himself, there's no reason he shouldn't try to swing the contract for somebody else—for a healthy commission."

"You said there are three contenders."

"The fighter-bomber made by the NEMEZ combine is the third. Otto Scheiber has also asked Yukada to act for him."

"Scheiber's never done business with Tri-Arms," I said. "Al-Zadar has, and will again. If you can get Yukada to go with al-Zadar, Tri-Arms will wind up with a nice piece of the action."

"I think I can." Victoria said it in the way that meant she was sure of it.

"In that case, Scheiber's NEMEZ will be left looking for somebody else to represent its interests. Whoever he gets, he won't stand much of a chance. There's nobody else in Japan with the kind of connections Yukada and Tashiro have."

"Which will make it a fight between Solomon and al-Zadar." Victoria's voice acquired a cold, implacable intensity I had never heard from her before: "Solomon wants that contract. He wants it badly. And I want him to lose it, just as badly. I have my own score to settle with him. . . ."

She leaned closer and seized one of my hands in both of

hers. "I need your help for that, Gar. Tri-Arms can earn itself a percentage on every one of those fighter-bombers sold to Japan. But one of us has to be there, in Tokyo, to act as liaison between al-Zadar and Yukada, and help win this one. There are too many things that have to be kept going in Washington for me to be away more than a few days at a time. We need somebody there in Tokyo through this whole operation. All the time. Or we'll lose it to Solomon. You're the only one who can handle that."

I shook my head. "Beating your ex-husband out of some dollars—even billions of them—wouldn't make up for what he did to Mei-lin and Paul Rambert."

"Nor for what he did to me. But it's the best revenge I can manage. And I *want* it. Now—before he dies and it's too late."

"He doesn't look like a dying man to me."

"He's a sick man. I know it. I can *feel* it."

"Don't turn mystic on me, Victoria. We've got some evidence he's got high blood pressure and a couple other physical problems. And that's all."

"I want him hurt! As much as possible. Now."

"You always said you put the past behind you," I reminded her.

"I lied."

And then, abruptly, Victoria let go of my hand and leaned back in her chair, laughing. But the laugh was forced. "My God . . ." she said shakily, ". . . I did get worked up. Sorry. But I do, so very much, want to take this multi-billion dollar deal away from him. And I do need your help to do that."

"Have you discussed it with Christian?" I asked her.

"And with the woman who inherits Rambert's share of Tri-Arms. Janine Lacoste. She's his cousin, and only living relative."

"What's she like?"

"A brilliant woman, in her field. Not too knowledgeable outside it, and aware of that. She's a professor of classical languages in Paris. We got along well. She's given me the right to make all company decisions for her."

That would, in effect, give Victoria two of the four Tri-Arms partnership votes. "And of course," I said, "you didn't have much trouble getting Christian to agree with your decision to go for the Japanese fighter-bomber contract."

She shrugged, and smiled a little. "He's already in Tokyo, working with a Japanese electronics team that Yukada uses for his surveillance and anti-surveillance work—in preparation for your coming there. *Will* you?"

I was still not certain whether I intended to carry out my threat to quit. Even if I did, the prospect of making my exit by kicking the multi-billion dollar fighter-bomber deal out from under Solomon Alexandre was tempting.

"Okay," I told her.

Victoria took a deep breath, and let it out slowly. "Thank you, Gar."

It began to drizzle at that point. We carried the breakfast service into the kitchen. As we finished stacking them, I took her in my arms and kissed her. She put her arms around my waist, tightly, and rested her head against my shoulder.

"Victoria," I said, "let's get married—or at least start living together if making it legal scares you."

I felt her tense a bit. She didn't raise her head from my shoulder. "Gar . . . I'll be an elderly lady before you know it. So far I've managed to keep it from showing too much. But that will become more difficult with the years—and then impossible. And—"

I interrupted her firmly. "Also you smoke too much and I

377

don't like the smell of cigarettes, especially in the bedroom. Also, you're dedicated to becoming the king of the mountain and I'm losing interest. Also, you've got a better educational and social background than me. Et cetera. Age is the least of a hundred things that may or may not go wrong between any couple. Why don't I just move in with you, in Alexandria, and we'll see how it works out."

"Not now. We can talk about it after Japan."

"You're stalling me again."

"No." She raised her head and looked me in the eyes. "If you still want to, after Japan, we will."

Chapter Thirty

Garson

It wasn't until it was all over that I finally caught on to what had really been happening during my six weeks in Japan.

That was also true of most of the Occidental principals in the battle for the fighter-bomber contract. But the failure to understand was crucial in my own case. The conning of others pivoted on my ignorance.

Non-Japanese can easily become baffled when attempting to operate there. Part of the reason is an acute shyness many Japanese experience in dealing with foreigners. Not only with Occidentals. They also have trouble understanding, and being understood by, other Asians. The Japanese call foreigners "*hennagaijin*"—which translates as "weird outsiders."

The Japanese aversion for speaking frankly or negotiating directly with weird outsiders causes them to avoid the need whenever they can. That was why neither Solomon Alexandre nor Ahmed al-Zadar could handle the high-level manipulations themselves in this case, as they would have been able to in their own parts of the world. This meant that they—and I—comprehended only as much of what was going on behind the scenes as our go-betweens told us. Al-Zadar and I became totally dependent on Hiroshi Yukada for our information. Alexandre was just as dependent on General Tashiro, Yukada's strongest foe through two decades of political power struggles.

There was also, it transpired later, an Occidental hidden in this particular Oriental woodpile, adroitly orchestrating the befuddlement of the rest of us.

* * *

I flew to Japan accompanied by the sales manager of al-Zadar's Georgia aircraft plant and its chief of engineering, Joe Jordan and Frank Carlotti. Between them those two could answer any questions the Japanese had about the performance and construction of their fighter-bombers, along with production and delivery schedules. They were down-to-earth men, their efficiency leavened with humor, and we got along fine. Al-Zadar was entrusting the opening stages of his fight for the big contract to us and Yukada. He had too many balls in the air elsewhere to come himself, until negotiations were close to being finalized—or the infighting reached a crisis requiring his presence.

Solomon Alexandre also had deals percolating in other parts of the world. None of them, however had the enormous potential of this one. While that was true of al-Zadar's other deals, as well, Alexandre didn't have anybody he trusted to carry this ball for him, the way I was going to for al-Zadar. Alexandre figured that the nailing down of a contract of this monstrous size called for his personal attention from start to finish. He had already settled into Tokyo four days ago. When I'd heard about that, via a phone call from Yukada, I'd hastened my own departure with Jordan and

Carlotti.

It was late afternoon when our 747 glided in low over the oily waters of Tokyo Bay. We were met at Haneda Airport by Satsuo Murata, a Yukada employee who'd been assigned to look after me on my previous visits to Japan. He served as a combination interpreter, guide and liaison man. A thin, cheerful man of forty, Murata had gone to college in Illinois and worked for several years in Detroit before returning to his native country. He was one of a new breed of Japanese who had no problem whatsoever in handling weird outsiders.

He led us out of the terminal to a waiting limousine. "I've booked you three adjoining suites at the Okura Hotel," he told us as we were driven to central Tokyo, "with a fourth you can use for your offices, complete with a scrambler unit for the phone. All four suites will be vetted daily, to make sure the opposition doesn't plant any acoustic bugs in any of the rooms."

Christian had worked with Yukada's electronic surveillance experts during his earlier visit to Tokyo, and reported that they were topnotch. The scrambler was for long-distance calls to al-Zadar and Victoria, to make sure what the opposition heard was garbled. For local calls without the scrambler, we would just have to be careful about what we said. It was impossible, even for somebody as good as Christian Frosch, to guarantee the safety of any phone conversation completely. Telephone lines could be tapped too far away for detection.

It was after five p.m. when our limousine entered central Tokyo. The streets were jammed with people going home from work, slowing the limousine to a crawl as it worked its way towards the Okura Hotel.

Solomon Alexandre, Murata told me, was staying at the other Tokyo hotel with a "superior luxury" rating: the Imperial. "He took over an entire floor for him and his entourage."

"Who has he got with him?" I asked Murata.

He reeled off the list from memory. Among the staff were Golz, Alexandre's chief business manager, and the head of his legal department, Tom Haggard—along with the doctor who'd been travelling with Alexandre for the last year.

"We've got surveillance teams keeping check on the doctor as you suggested," Murata said. "And you were right. The prescriptions he's had filled for Mr. Alexandre are for high blood pressure and an overactive thyroid gland—a dangerous combination for a man his age. Especially for one who continues to work under so much constant tension."

"Alexandre didn't bring Stuart Peel with him?"

"No, but he sent for him after settling in. Mr. Peel arrived two days ago. Of course, General Tashiro is working for Mr. Alexandre and has his own informants. But Mr. Peel has also hired some of his own investigators from a business security firm. We think they were recommended by an old FBI friend of his that is stationed here."

"You're well-informed."

Murata grinned at me. "The people Mr. Peel hired are not as good as Mr. Yukada's, believe me. Nor General Tashiro's for that matter."

The Okura Hotel was finally in sight ahead of us. I told Murata, "I want to get together with Yukada as soon as possible."

"He is waiting for you at his office. As soon as you've checked in—"

"You check me in—and let me have the car."

"Okay. I'll have your things in your suite and Mr. Carlotti and Mr. Jordan settled in comfortably before you get back."

Jordan draped an arm around Murata's narrow shoulders.

"If you've got young blondes with big tits in this country, that's my notion of comfort."

Murata laughed. "Coming up, Mr. Jordan." He looked questioningly at Carlotti.

"Frankly," Carlotti told him, "I'm too tired from the flight for any nonsense like that. And feeling too old right now. All I want's a bottle of bourbon and a big soft bed—all to myself. Tonight, anyway."

The limousine pulled up to the hotel. Murata jumped out first and barked orders to the uniformed hotel employees who scurried over to get our luggage. As soon as Jordan and Carlotti climbed out beside him, he told the driver to take me to the new Yukada Tower building.

* * *

By the time I got there, through a succession of traffic jams, the sun was lowering into the Hakone Mountains and the city's streets blazed with thousands of multicolored neon signs trying to out-dazzle each other in the approaching dusk.

The street where Yukada's steel and glass office building had been erected bore a centuries-old name: *Kabuto-cho*— "War Helmet Quarter," so named because this was where the best makers of swords, armor and other medieval weaponry had once been concentrated.

I'd once asked Yukada, jokingly, if that was why he'd picked that site for his building.

He'd taken the question seriously: "No, I built here because the space became available. And because the Stock Exchange is so close, just down the street. Your thought never occurred to me before, to be honest."

His no-frills private office was on the next-to-the-top floor.

The floor above was his apartment. The home where he lived with his wife was out in the country, miles from Tokyo, but he often had to stay overnight in the city. That was especially necessary whenever Yukada had business to transact by telephone or telex to the West. It was not until midnight in Japan that New York and Washington began their workdays. When I was ushered into his office that evening, America was still asleep.

"The date for the preliminary trials of the three fighter-bombers," Yukada told me as I sat down across the desk from him, "was set this afternoon. For six days from now. The planes in competition for the contract—al-Zadar's, Alexandre's and Scheiber's—are already being moved to the testing field."

"Six days," I said. "That's closer than you told me it would be."

Yukada nodded solemnly. "That is General Tashiro's influence." Tashiro had retired from the Army some years back to open an office as a business consultant. With his combination of military, government and family connections, he was the only man in Japan who had as much clout as Yukada. "Through him," Yukada continued, "Alexandre has made his opening moves more swiftly than I expected. General Tashiro has already disbursed over two million dollars from Alexandre."

In Japan, that amount of bribe money—just for openers—was not extraordinary. Not where a contract of one and a half billion was at stake, with more billions likely for whoever won it. Less than eight years earlier, Lockheed had paid out almost twelve million to Japanese middlemen to secure another big contract.

"General Tashiro has distributed this money," Yukada informed me, "among men who will judge the performance of the three planes and aeronautic engineers who will take them apart after the trials and write their appraisals of durability and maintenance factors.

"Alexandre's only been here four days," I said, not liking it.

"He's not wasting much time."

"He wants to nail the contract down and get back to other vital business. This contract is Alexandre's first priority. But he is on the phone constantly to other parts of the world, trying very hard to keep other deals alive until he finishes here."

Yukada told me exactly how much of Alexandre's money had been given to each of the trial judges and post-trial experts. "We must offer them at least as much. More would be better. In cash, not checks. And before the trials—or their judgments will go so heavily against al-Zadar's plane that we will have lost the contest before we have even begun it."

"What about Otto Scheiber's fighter-bomber?"

"Scheiber is due to arrive in two days with several technical specialists from his NEMEZ aircraft plant. He has already retained a Japanese consultant. Masaaki Shishime. Who has undoubtedly advised Scheiber that surviving the trials requires money. Shishime is a good man at these lower levels, but without sufficient influence at higher levels. After the trials, I think we can forget the NEMEZ fighter-bomber. The final decision will narrow down to Alexandre's and al-Zadar's.

"*If*," he added, "al-Zadar supplies the funding I need in order to act for him. The time for that is growing very short. Four hours ago General Tashiro met with Alexandre and assured him they have the contract won."

"That's damned detailed inside information," I said, "considering you got it so fast. Tashiro's security must be pretty ragged."

"Not General Tashiro's—Alexandre's. General Tashiro speaks only Japanese. So Alexandre has had to hire a man to interpret between them. The interpreter passes on everything they say to my people."

"Careless of Alexandre."

"General Tashiro assured him that this interpreter is trustworthy," Yukada explained blandly. "He was—until certain gentlemen I know had a talk with him. About an easy way to supplement his income—and about the future safety of the family he loves, I believe."

The gentlemen he referred to were, of course, gangsters from the part of Yukada's world we never mentioned: the underworld. From what I'd heard of Japanese mobsters, a threat from them would suffice to turn a saint away from his faith.

Yukada took me out to dinner, accompanied by two of his bodyguards: burly men with nightmare faces, who remained utterly silent and totally vigilant the whole time. We dined in one of the quieter restaurants in the Akasaka quarter. Its prices made me blink—and by that year I'd dined in a lot of the more expensive restaurants of the world. We took our time over the meal, while Yukada explained in detail which power figures he could get to, which ones Tashiro was likely to go after, and how much more bribe money would probably be needed to do the job properly.

After dinner it was late enough to wake up Ahmed al-Zadar. According to the schedule he'd given me, he would be spending a couple days in Copenhagen at that point. I used the phone in Yukada's office. Once I got through to al-Zadar, we hooked in Yukada's scrambler and al-Zadar attached the portable one he travelled with. Then I told him what was going on. I said it looked like Yukada could get solid control of developments if he got the working capital he was asking for.

I explained how much was needed immediately, and how much more Yukada would need to grease things after the trial competitions of the planes. Al-Zadar didn't squawk at the final figure. It was a small sum considering how much he stood to earn—if he won the contract.

Almost exactly nineteen hours later, one of al-Zadar's assistants paid a quick visit to Japan to hand me a suitcase. What was inside it was four million dollars, in cash, half for the men who would be judging the three planes, the rest for the upper level struggle that would follow the competition trials.

Seven days later I attended the trials with Joe Jordan and Frank Carlotti. Solomon Alexandre was there with his own experts, and Otto Scheiber was there with his. The bribes each of the three contenders had slipped the judges simply insured that one plane wouldn't receive too much of an edge. On performance, the three planes were judged fairly even.

After that the Japanese aeronautics engineers took the planes apart and began testing their components for strength, endurance and ease of maintenance. That went on endlessly. Since they'd been taken care of by all three contenders, their comparative findings would be truthful. And the truth was that all of the three planes would be equal assets to Japan's fighting capabilities.

The real competition was going on elsewhere. I kept al-Zadar and Victoria briefed on that one every day.

Yukada was exerting his influence, and applying al-Zadar's contributions, within a growing circle of government decision makers, starting with those with whom he had the longest close connections. Tashiro was leaning on his own top-drawer decision makers. Both were trying to steal key figures from each other.

As Yukada predicted, Scheiber's lobbyist was having trouble finding any important people left over for *him* to influence. Bribery on an issue that big, in an elected democratic government, isn't as easy as you might think. What follows, between the asterisks, is a brief exploration of how complicated it can get, in some countries. You can skip it if you don't ever expect to have enough money to try it yourself.

* * *

The Japanese government had been run by the same party ever since 1952. It was a conservative party that called itself Liberal Democratic. Yukada and General Tashiro both belonged to it. Their enmity had grown, not out of differing political viewpoints, but out of competing for power within the party's hierarchy.

In spite of this one-party control of Japan's administration and House of Representatives, choosing the right people to apply pressure through, and enough of them, was extremely delicate. In addition to such power rivals as Yukada and Tashiro, the Liberal Democrats encompassed a number of other separate factions which seldom saw eye to eye. Any one of these factions could plant a booby trap in the path of a plan—just out of pique, if it felt that it hadn't been greased with its fair share of the financial contributions being passed out.

Also, though the Liberal Democrats dominated the House of Representatives, there *were* other parties seated in it. The Socialists had over a hundred seats. Three other parties—the Communists, the Democratic Socialists and the Buddhist oriented Komeito (Clean Government) party—had much less. These four out-parties detested each other even more than they did the government. But each could make problems for any program the government wanted to push through. And if the four combined, they could muster almost as many votes as the Liberal Democrats. So each of them, too, had to be soothed with donations.

On top of all this, there was the Prime Minister. Plus certain of his cabinet and military appointees who were involved in any decision relating to defense: the ministers of Finance, of Foreign Affairs, of International Trade and Industry. The leader of the Defense Agency and the chairman of the Public Safety Commission. The directors of the Cabinet Secretariat and the Science and Technology Agency. The superintendent of the Defense Academy and the secretary-general of the National Defense Council.

These men frequently disagreed about projects. As regards the fighter-bomber purchase, for example, the chief of the Defense Council was automatically in favor of any measure to expand Japan's air combat ability, while the head of the Defense Academy was predisposed against such measures.

Any of these defense figures—as well as any of the above-mentioned out-parties and in-party factions—could create trouble. If enough of them got mad enough, they could always bring up Article Nine of the Japanese constitution. That article states that Japan shall have *no* armed forces of any size. Everybody usually just ignores it, of course. But every time people shout about it loudly enough, it slows down the government's de-facto rearmament policy for awhile.

So, who would wind up with the fighter-bomber contract hung on whether Yukada or Tashiro could get most of those political factions, government departments and military figures on the side of *his* client. Swinging the contest to either Solomon Alexandre or Ahmed al-Zadar, as you can see, required a lot of inside know-how and contacts. It also required spreading around more cash than most readers are likely to get a peek at in a lifetime of honest toil.

* * *

The contest began to seesaw back and forth as the weeks piled up, and the sums handed out mounted.

Three weeks after my arrival in Tokyo, I made one of my daily calls to Victoria in Washington, to keep her abreast of the situation—and just to hear her voice and get some of the rapidly mounting nervous tension out of my system.

It was early Friday morning, her time. She wasn't at home. I tried her office a little later. Her secretary told me that Victoria had been feeling tired, and had gone off for a long weekend of rest. No, she hadn't left word where she was going. Yes, she had left a message for me: don't worry.

I didn't like it. Not at all. It wasn't something I expected of Victoria: to disappear that way, even over a weekend, in the middle of something as important as the fighter-bomber negotiations.

Late Sunday night (my time) she phoned me.

"I was just worn out," she explained. "So I flew down to Jamaica for some swimming and sunning myself on the beach. Did the trick. I feel great now."

"I wouldn't have minded going with you," I said, still not liking it. "I'm pretty worn out myself."

"What's happening?"

"The most important happening is that your ex-husband has increased the amount of dough he's spreading around—to eight million bucks."

"Sounds to me as if he's getting desperate."

"That's not the word I'd use. I'd say determined. Very. We're going to have to at least match his offers or we'll be out of the running. NEMEZ is already out. Yukada was right. Otto Scheiber's lobbyist lost his way in those upper corridors of power. Scheiber wrapped up his campaign and went back to Germany. He's got other fish to fry.

"So does Solomon," Victoria pointed out. "If *he* doesn't get out of there soon, other deals are bound to unravel on him."

"He's on planes half the time," I told her. "Flies out to keep those deals alive. Flies back, sometimes less than forty-eight hours later, to keep his grip on this one."

"Not too good for a man his age."

"That's for sure. The doctor travelling with him is feeding him heavy sedatives to make him get some sleep during the flights. According to his interpreter, Alexandre's suffering from constant jet-lag and time confusion. And he's so worked up all the time he's got his doctor scared. During an argument with Tashiro the other day, he got so mad about the time it's taken to settle the contract that he had a dizzy spell and fell down."

"Good," Victoria said. She said it quietly, but with relish.

"I'm not feeling too great myself," I told her. "Rest is hard to come by. It's all these frustrating ups and downs. Every time I think we're about to win, I find out it's up for grabs again. Mostly because Alexandre keeps upping the ante. Yesterday I had to tell al-Zadar he's got to come up with another four million or forget it."

"He'll give it," Victoria said assuredly. "It's still a small sum compared with what he stands to gain."

"No question. But he's getting edgy. It'll bring what he's paid out so far up to more than eight million dollars. That's an amount even al-Zadar notices. This four million he's bringing himself. Flying in tomorrow. He wants to see for himself if he still has a real chance at that contract. Can't blame him."

"He's not likely to find out anything more than Yukada has already told him, through you."

"Not likely," I agreed.

We were both right. Al-Zadar landed the next day, in one of his big jets, bringing the money and his usual travelling entourage: his barber, his masseur, an old chum going back to his boyhood days, three British bodyguards and two male secretaries. No girls this trip.

Yukada and I had fixed up appointments for him with a number of high officials who were on our side in the contract struggle. I and Murata, my chief interpreter, accompanied him to these appointments. Each of the officials expressed great enthusiasm for al-Zadar's chances of winning the contract. Each answered every question he asked fully and politely, without telling him anything new.

Al-Zadar even had a long lunch with Japan's Prime Minister—who told him he'd heard excellent reports on his fighter-bomber. The Prime Minister felt duty-bound to add that he had also heard good reports on the other two planes under consideration. And so—the final decision must be expected to take time, with a great deal of thought and inter-governmental discussion. Al-Zadar left the lunch knowing exactly as much as he'd known when he'd arrived.

After three days he gave Yukada the additional four million and flew off in frustration to attend to other business.

* * *

It was just as hard on the opposition. *Five* weeks after my arrival in Japan, Solomon Alexandre paid another furious visit to General Tashiro, accompanied by his interpreter (and our spy).

Golz and Haggard also went with him. So did his worried doctor. But not Stuart Peel. Alexandre had sent him out of Japan, after deciding Peel was next to useless in that country. Tashiro's informants clearly outclassed Peel's hired investigators in finding out what was going on.

Tashiro's business offices were in one of the high-rise buildings that had been shooting up lately on the west side of Tokyo's Shinjuku district. He wasn't in his office when Alexandre and his entourage got there. His secretary apologized for the delay: General Tashiro was up on the roof of the building, flying kites with a childhood friend.

It was, his secretary explained, a way General Tashiro had of relaxing his tensions, in times of stress. He and his friend were from Hamamatsu, where kite building and flying were part of a revered tradition. Our informant snickered as he described the scene that followed:

Alexandre, who had never himself found any such effective method of relaxing tension, was steaming by the time Tashiro entered his office. Standing, the veteran arms dealer towered over the diminutive former general. "You promised we'd have the decision by this morning!" Alexandre shouted at him. "What happened *this* time."

The interpreter translated that, and Tashiro's regretful reply:

"Unfortunately, during this morning's government meeting to render the contract decision—in your favor—the Trade Ministry people raised a new point. They asked if awarding the contract to Ahmed al-Zadar, instead of you, might not result in more favorable reactions among the Arab nations which al-Zadar serves. Nations which supply Japan with much of its fuel, as well as provide excellent markets for our industrial exports. The members of the Finance Ministry at the meeting agreed that this was a point that should be taken into consideration."

"You told me we had the Finance Ministry on our side almost from the beginning," Alexandre snarled. "And you bought most of the Trade Ministry people for me last week. You said they were the *last* obstacle to my getting the contract."

"They were bought, that is true. But yesterday Hiroshi Yukada got to key men of both ministries, distributing almost two million dollars among them. And changed their minds, for the moment at least."

"The Prime Minister could have stopped them! He's supposed to be one of your best friends."

"He is also dependent on Yukada to handle much of his personal finances. Also, the Prime Minister doesn't like to countermand the decisions of too many of his cabinet members at the same time. Some would complain to the press. The Liberal Democratic Party cannot afford dissension this year."

Tashiro went behind his desk and sat down with a sigh. "This morning's meeting adjourned with a decision to postpone the contract award for another week or so, while they all take time to consider and discuss it further."

Alexandre remained standing, glaring down at him. "Something like this has happened *every* time you've sworn you had that contract for me."

Tashiro nodded. "Al-Zadar and his people here are being exceedingly stubborn. And unexpectedly generous."

"And now you want more money from *me*."

Alexandre had forced his voice lower. "The effort made veins bulge in his forehead," our informant said. He never took as many of the sedatives as his doctor thought he required. He needed his mind razor sharp for this unending struggle, not dulled by drugs. In place of the drugs, Alexandre tried to control his nerves with a reassertion of sheer willpower, not always successfully.

The doctor, alarmed by the way he looked now, tried to place a restraining hand on his arm. Alexandre shoved him away without looking at him.

General Tashiro appeared not to notice the incident. "That depends entirely on what you want, Sir Solomon. If you wished to stop now, I would understand."

"I'm not going to accept losing that contract *and* everything I've already paid out. You know that."

"The choice is yours. If you wish to contribute more to these officials—"

"And how much of it goes into your own pockets?" Alexandre demanded sarcastically.

General Tashiro looked up at him coldly for a long moment. "No greater percentage than *you* have been accustomed to taking whenever you have functioned in the same capacity as I am now."

In the end, our spy related, Solomon Alexandre agreed to come up with another three million. He left Tashiro's office looking shockingly old and tired.

* * *

Four hours later I phoned al-Zadar with the bad news I'd just gotten from Yukada. It didn't look like we had the contract won yet, after all.

"You *told* me we had it in the bag at last!"

"The bag's developed a few holes that have to be sewed up." I explained that the officials we'd bought away from Tashiro had just been bought back.

Al-Zadar took it without a trace of his former jovial self. But, like Alexandre, he was in too deep at that point to be ready to call it quits.

* * *

Six weeks after my arrival in Japan, al-Zadar's bribes were up to eleven million dollars and Solomon Alexandre's to thirteen million.

And there they both dug in their heels, refusing to donate another penny.

I phoned Washington to give Victoria the news. It had been a couple days since I'd last been in touch with her. They'd been the most nerve-twisting days of all, leaving me too exhausted at night to make late calls, especially since I knew I'd have to wait up for two or three hours until she got back from some appointment and returned them.

She wasn't in when I called this time, either. Her secretary told me Victoria had left Washington two days ago—for Japan.

That puzzled me, naturally. If she'd flown directly to Japan two days ago, she would have been in Tokyo for more than a day. Surely she'd have contacted me by now. I phoned Christian Frosch in Rome. But he told me Victoria hadn't stopped off there. No, he didn't know where she might be.

I didn't have too much time to worry about Victoria's whereabouts, though, because at that point the bubble exploded. The Japanese government announced the awarding of the fighter-bomber contract: to Otto Scheiber's NEMEZ product.

The contract wasn't a simple one. There were unexpected ramifications which could only have been worked out over a considerable period of negotiation:

The reason for the choice, the government explained, was that NEMEZ had agreed to manufacture a new version of its plane *in* Japan. This would provide employment for many of its people and a source of revenue for the country.

NEMEZ would contribute half the financing needed to build the Japanese plant and tool up to produce its fighter-bomber there.

Industrialist Hiroshi Yukada would provide the other half of the financing, and share equally with NEMEZ in the profits.

Retired General Tashiro would become the managing director of the new Yukada-NEMEZ company.

I was with Joe Jordan and Frank Carlotti when the news came out.

"Don't look now," Carlotti said, "but I think we've been had."

Chapter Thirty-one

Victoria

When Solomon Alexandre got the news, he stormed over to Tashiro's office, with Tom Haggard and his doctor in tow.

General Tashiro's secretary said he wasn't in: "He has gone home to Hamamatsu for a short holiday."

Alexandre didn't believe it. He barged past and slammed open the door to Tashiro's office. He took two steps inside and stopped dead. The secretary had told him the truth. General Tashiro wasn't there.

It was Victoria sitting behind his desk.

She smiled at him. "Hello, Solomon. It's been a very long time, hasn't it?"

He stared at her unbelievingly. "You . . . I don't. . . ." His lips seemed to have difficulty forming the words.

"Don't get it? Poor Solomon, you used to be quicker than that. You've been *had*, my dear. Stung. Conned. By me." She smiled at him again. "With some help from Yukada and Tashiro."

"But . . . they hate each other," Alexandre said thickly.

"They did, yes. Until I brought them together. For their mutual benefit, as you were always fond of putting it."

Victoria looked at the distended veins pulsing in his forehead, at the way his lips began to twitch uncontrollably.

"Everyone will be laughing at you when this gets around," she told him complacently. "And it will. I'll see to that." She drove the point in deeper, deliberately taunting his rage:

"You gave away thirteen million dollars. *Gave* it away. And probably lost much more than that on other deals you fumbled while you were stuck here reaching for this one. All for nothing, Solomon. For less than nothing. For a contract that was already in someone else's pocket."

A spasm of fury seized him. He took a lurching step closer, raising a fist to strike her. Then he gasped and the spasm clutched the muscles of one side of his face, twisting it hideously. His raised fist sprang partly open and then seemed to become frozen, clawlike.

He turned away from Victoria, very slowly. Bumping into his attorney, he lost his balance and toppled over, falling stiffly, his arms making no effort to shield his head as he thudded to the floor.

The doctor crouched over him. "Oh God, he's had a stroke!"

Tom Haggard stared down in horror at his stricken employer. Then he wrenched himself around to face Victoria again. "See what you've done? Quickly, get an ambulance!"

Victoria rose to her feet. "Get it yourself," she told him evenly. "I have more important things to do."

She strolled over to gaze down at Solomon Alexandre. The arm he had raised to strike her was still bent stiffly, the hand half open. On the paralyzed side of his face, the eyelid had drooped almost shut. His other eye was opened wide, looking up at her helplessly.

She said, "Goodbye, Solomon."

Stepping over his frozen figure, she walked out of the office.

Chapter Thirty-two

Garson

By the time I found out Victoria had been in Tokyo, she was gone. I spent the next couple days finding out exactly what had hit me, and avoiding al-Zadar when he flew in to find out the same thing. When I finally understood all of it, I went to face al-Zadar's anger. It wasn't easy. The genial Arab had turned into a block of ice. There was no way I could convince him that I hadn't been in on the sham contract battle from the start, helping Yukada and Tashiro milk twenty-four million dollars from him and Alexandre.

I flew to Washington. It was early night when the plane landed at Dulles International. I took a taxi to Victoria's house in Alexandria.

She opened the door seconds after I knocked, and stood there looking at me for a moment—like someone just awakening from an odd dream. Then she turned and walked away through the entry hall. I followed her, slamming the door shut behind me.

In the living room, she turned to face me.

"Well," I said bitterly, "your ex-husband's turned into a paralyzed vegetable, I hear. Can't walk or talk, his brain damaged beyond repair. Satisfied now?"

"Not enough," she said flatly, "but it will have to do."

I looked at the way she was standing there, head up and feet braced apart, meeting my bitterness without flinching. Lamplight reflected in her dark eyes and gleamed in the auburn cascade of her hair. Seeing the beauty of her and knowing the perfidy inside made keeping control of my anger hard work.

"You used me for a fool," I said as steadily as I could. "You suckered me into thinking I was jockeying a genuine operation."

Victoria stayed dead calm before my anger: "It was necessary. I had to make you believe it from start to finish to make absolutely sure al-Zadar would, too."

"And *he* had to be kept convinced he was grabbing for one of the biggest deals of his life so Alexandre would have to keep fighting him for it all the way. So you could get your revenge."

"Yes."

"Well you've done it very neatly. You got even, Yukada and Tashiro got richer—and I got the shaft."

"I got more than that out of it. And so did you. Yukada is depositing two million into the Tri-Arms Swiss account for our share in it. Tashiro is putting in the same amount. That makes your share in Tri-Arms, and mine, worth that much more."

"Swell." I said it sarcastically, but sarcastic wasn't how I felt. I felt mean. "Also very nice, the way you used everything you've got—and everything I felt for you—to bring me into it. Including that clincher about us moving in together, *after* I finished doing my job for you.

"I wasn't lying to you," she said quietly. "I told you I would live with you if you still wanted that, after Japan. I meant it. Well, *do* you still want it?"

I was in no mood to take that question seriously. So I ignored it: "Al-Zadar thinks *I* engineered the swindle with Yukada and his new pal Tashiro. He's not the kind of man who likes being conned—especially if the word gets around."

Victoria suddenly looked tired. "Did you tell him *I* was the one to be angry at?"

I hadn't. I wasn't sure why. I told her, "What would be the point? He's not the only one who thinks it. I can't run all over the world telling people I was a dumb, innocent dupe. Nobody would believe me. And nobody will ever trust me to broker a deal for them again."

"You intended to quit the arms business anyway," Victoria reminded me coolly. "You'll walk away a fairly rich man, whether you decided to sell your share of Tri-Arms or keep it and continue drawing earnings on it."

The anger began boiling up in me: "I get out of the partnership if and when *I* want to. Not because I'm pushed."

Victoria shrugged. "What would you get out of staying in it now? As you said, no one will trust you to negotiate for them anymore. And we won't let you try because it would hurt Tri-Arms."

"We?" I demanded coldly.

"You know I can usually persuade Christian to vote as I wish. And I've already been given Rambert's vote. That makes three votes to your one. You won't be able to do a thing."

I slapped her then, with uncontrolled force. The sound of my open hand striking her face was shocking in that tasteful room. It spun her off her feet. She fell against an armchair, overturning it as she tumbled to the floor.

Victoria shook her head and propped herself up on one elbow. The side of her face was turning an angry red and there was a trickle of blood at the corner of her mouth. She didn't try to get up for a time, just stayed there on the floor, looking at me without any expression at all on her face.

Without another word between us, I turned and left.

* * *

Victoria must have gotten back on her feet and gone to the front windows. She must have watched me turn away from her house and start off along the pavement in the direction of the nearest taxi stand four blocks away. Because then she saw something else: a car with its lights out, pulling away from the opposite curb and angling across the street after me. When it glided under a streetlamp she saw a glint of metal in its opened rear window.

Her warning scream brought me twisting around in time to see the danger before it came up alongside me. Instant body response from the years in Vietnam hurled me down toward the cover of a parked car just as a submachine gun let go a long burst. The abrupt dive saved me from most of it. But two of the slugs burned their way deep inside my midsection before I hit the pavement.

I heard the murder car speed away, its tires squealing as it turned into the next cross street. I rolled over in a spreading pool of blood, feeling little pain but not much ambition to get up, either.

Then I saw Victoria bending over me. I tried to tell her it was al-Zadar's retaliation, for his humiliation as much as for his financial loss, but I wasn't up to speaking, either. She ran back toward her house. I just lay there, trying to hold my guts in with both hands while I slowly passed out.

* * *

According to medical reports I read somewhat later, blood

loss and shock to vital organs had me fairly close to checking out by the time Victoria climbed into the ambulance with me for a ride to the hospital.

Five hours later I was out of surgery, the bullets removed, my internal injuries patched up, the bleeding stopped and several quarts of new blood pumped into me. It was the next day when I came to, briefly and vaguely. I was in an intensive care unit, with tubes plugged into both arms and Victoria sitting close beside me.

I knew visitors weren't usually allowed into intensive care. But I also knew Victoria could get pretty much anything she wanted. She saw my eyes open, and smiled at me: "You're going to pull through, Gar."

I tried to tell her I'd had worse, in 'Nam, but while I was dredging up the words I slipped away again. The next time I surfaced she was stroking that scar on my cheek, the one I'd received as a teenage boy, stopping a maddened woman who was trying to commit suicide with a little knife. I cracked my eyes open a little. She didn't notice this time.

Suddenly I saw the tears that were streaming down her face. I wondered if she was crying for me, or for the boy I'd been when she'd first known me. Or for herself, and what she had become. Or for both of us. Probably she wasn't sure, herself.

I saw her sit back in the bedside chair, get out a handkerchief, and wipe the tears from her beautiful face. I've got a feeling, now, that they were the last tears she would ever shed for anyone. Including herself.

The day after that I was moved into a normal private room. And Victoria was on her way to Dulles, booked onto the next direct flight to France.

* * *

She came back two days later. I was propped against the pillows of my hospital bed, weak and drugged, but on my way to recovery. Victoria stood beside me, studying me so intently I smiled a little.

"I'll be okay," I told her. And then: "Victoria, I'm sorry I hit you that hard."

She continued to study me for a bit. Then she sat down on the edge of my bed and took one of my hands in hers. "I deserved more than that slap. I almost got you killed. Only luck saved you."

I almost managed a laugh. "I hope my luck's better than *this* the next time al-Zadar's killers come after me."

"There won't be a next time," Victoria said. "I've been to see him."

"I hope you didn't tell him it was you instead of me who suckered him. He wouldn't believe I wasn't in on it. You'd just give his boys *two* targets."

"I told you, Gar. Neither of us will be targets, not again. I told him that any further attempt against you would result in my throwing all my weight against him. Any time he entered a competitive situation, I'd automatically side with his competition—even in situations where it would normally be of mutual advantage for me to cooperate with him."

"Could cost him a lot," I said. "Especially in the United States, with your Washington pull."

Victoria nodded. "Al-Zadar is a man whose mind is always in full control of his emotions. He is still angry, but he is not about to prolong it to the point where it may cut into future profits or complicate future dealings. He and I came to an agreement. His desire for retaliation has been satisfied by what has already happened to you—and by the assurance that you have decided to quit the arms business. He can always tell people he got his revenge by forcing you out."

"You're sure I will decide to get out."

"I strongly advise you to," Victoria told me seriously, "for the sake of both Tri-Arms and yourself. I know you want to, so what's to stop you? You're rich enough, young enough to launch yourself in any other field you wish. Free to start over with a different kind of life."

I knew she was right. I didn't want to get shot at again, and I did want out anyway. Studying Victoria, I said: "But *you're* not getting out."

She smiled crookedly. "I've already started over. In *this* business. For me, it is getting too late to change again."

"And you still want to prove to yourself that you can be as big as Solomon Alexandre in it."

"No," she told me. "Bigger."

Victoria bent down to give me a brief farewell kiss on the lips. As she straightened, I gripped her arms and pulled her back to me—and returned her kiss with considerably more warmth. For a few seconds, I felt her respond. Then she pulled away, her face pale, and rose from the bed.

I smiled up at her. After a bit, Victoria smiled too, faintly. Both of us remembering back—over the years. Both remembering summer days in France.

Then she turned and went out of the door. She strode off to lead Tri-Arms International into future battles and games, into the game of arming the world against itself, the first woman to become part of the Golden Circle: Victoria Nicolson, arms dealer.

Ordering Information

If the following books are not available at your bookstore, you can order copies by sending a check or money order payable to National Press, Inc., 7508 Wisconsin Avenue, Bethesda, MD 20814. Add $1.25 per book for postage and handling. Maryland residents add five percent for sales tax. Mastercard and Visa credit cards are accepted when you order by telephone, toll-free (800) NA-BOOKS.

Title	Code	Price
Under the Streets of Nice by Ken Follett and R. Maurice	25-X	$5.95
Katharine the Great: Katharine Graham and the Washington Post by Deborah Davis	43-8	$17.95
Black Mondays: Worst Decisions of the Supreme Court by Joel D. Joseph	44-6	$15.95
Edward Bennett Williams for the Defense by Robert Pack	47-0	$9.95
Persistence of Memory: A Personal Biography of Salvador Dali by Amanda Lear	40-3	$8.95
On My Own: A Single Mother by Choice by Marla Weisenberg	45-4	$6.95

Ordering Information

If the following books are not available at your bookstore, you can order copies by sending a check or money order payable to National Press, Inc., 7508 Wisconsin Avenue, Bethesda, MD 20814. Add $1.25 per book for postage and handling. Maryland residents add five percent for sales tax. Mastercard and Visa credit cards are accepted when you order by telephone, toll-free (800) NA-BOOKS.

Title	Code	Price
Under the Streets of Nice by Ken Follett and R. Maurice	25-X	$5.95
Katharine the Great: Katharine Graham and the Washington Post by Deborah Davis	43-8	$17.95
Black Mondays: Worst Decisions of the Supreme Court by Joel D. Joseph	44-6	$15.95
Edward Bennett Williams for the Defense by Robert Pack	47-0	$9.95
Persistence of Memory: A Personal Biography of Salvador Dali by Amanda Lear	40-3	$8.95
On My Own: A Single Mother by Choice by Marla Weisenberg	45-4	$6.95